Repo Girl Homecoming

By Jane Fenton

This is a work of fiction. References to real people, events, establishments, organizations or locales are intended only to provide a sense of authenticity and are used fictitiously. All other characters, incidents, and dialogue are drawn from the author's imagination and are not to be construed as real.

 For information address Blue Morpho Books, P.O. Box 191, Ferrum, VA 24088.

ISBN: 978-1-7321165-9-7
Paperback Edition

For my mom who always encouraged me to follow my heart. Love you bunches!

Books by Jane Fenton

Repo Girl Series
Repo Girl
A Repo Girl Christmas
Repo Girl Homecoming

Mystique Books Collection
Crazy For You

Chapter One

The red florescent light glowed *HOT NOW* in the early, icy, January morning. It was a sign—literally. How could she possibly resist?

Andrea Sloan pulled into the Krispy Kreme drive-through and ordered a half dozen Original Glazed doughnuts and a bottled water. She wanted the hot chocolate, but she was trying to be healthy.

After she paid for her breakfast, she chose a parking space that gave her the best view of Brooks Funeral Home and turned off the engine of her Jeep Wrangler. She could see both the front and back parking lots of the funeral home from here. Raising the green and white cardboard box to her face, she lifted the lid, closed her eyes, and inhaled the aroma of fried dough bathed in a sugar glaze. *Heaven.* She set the box on the front passenger seat, reached inside, and picked up a doughnut. It was still warm and soft. She took a bite.

Oh. My. God. The tasty sugar confection practically melted in her mouth. It was so light that it only took her a few minutes to devour two of the doughnuts. She carefully licked each of her fingertips to capture any remaining sugar and then reached for a napkin to dry her hand.

Okay. Now she could focus on work. Reaching into her oversized black purse, she pulled out a manila folder and her Gram's heavy black binoculars. She placed the strap of the binoculars over her head so that her hands were free and then opened the folder and scanned the file. The sun was beginning to rise, so there was enough light to read the contents of the file without having to turn on her interior light. She'd been repossessing cars for less than a year, and this was her first hearse. Wrinkling her nose, she considered how creepy it would be to drive a car that had hauled countless dead bodies to their final resting place. Well, at least there wouldn't be an actual dead body in this one. She'd already driven a car with a naked dead guy as her passenger, and that was an experience she'd prefer never to repeat. She shook her head to clear those mental images. *Best not to think about it. It's just a car*, she thought to herself. Heck, she would simply pretend she was collecting a custom SUV.

Looking back down at her paperwork, she read that the owner of Brooks Funeral Home, Travis Moulder, had taken out a loan for the black Cadillac XTS Heritage Hearse two years ago and was now three months behind on his payments. Andi studied the exterior of the funeral home. The front parking lot was empty, and she saw an old brown Ford Bronco parked near the back entrance of the building. She set the manila folder on top of the Krispy Kreme box and lifted the binoculars to her eyes. No one appeared to be in the Bronco. She scanned the building for movement.

Wow. The building has seen better days, for sure. The exterior was brick that had been painted white a long time ago from the looks of the flaking paint. Black shutters framed most of the windows, and a few shutters were missing. Funerals were depressing enough without saying farewell to a loved one in a rundown building. Business must be slow, which was probably why Travis was behind on his car payments.

Where in the heck could her repo be this morning? It was too early for a funeral which is why she'd come for it now rather than at a more reasonable time of day. She didn't want to accidently drive off with a body and casket. She shivered at the thought. It was doubtful that Travis would keep it parked at his house when he wasn't using it. *I'm sure his neighbors would love that.*

Andi released the binoculars and pulled out her cellphone. She did a quick scan on his social media pages. *Hm.*

Nothing too unusual there. Reaching over, she lifted the lid to the cardboard box and grabbed another doughnut. So what if she hadn't found it yet? Research always made her hungry. She took a bite of the doughnut as she scrolled through photos of Travis with friends out on a boat at the lake. There were none of him with the hearse.

Lights caught her attention. Looking up from her phone, she saw the funeral vehicle pulling into the back-parking lot next to the Bronco. *Bingo.* She set her phone on the seat and raised the binoculars in time to see the driver with a neatly trimmed mustache. He had to be Travis. The other passenger, a guy about the same size as Travis, maybe a little younger, was carrying a white fast-food bag and a drink tray with two cups. They both walked into the building.

This was her chance. Andi tossed her phone in her purse, grabbed the file folder and the key to the Cadillac and hopped out of her Jeep. She slung the big purse over her shoulder, locked her car. Odds were in her favor that they would be there for a while—at least until they could finish their breakfast. Andi wasn't taking any chances, so she ran full speed to the Funeral parking lot.

She stopped in front of the driver's door, bending over, and placing her hands on her thighs to catch her breath. *Jeez—I'm out of shape.* After a few seconds, she stood, placed the key to the Cadillac into the lock, and opened the door. No alarm sounded—*thank goodness.* It was going to be a good day after all—hot doughnuts and an easy repo all before 8 a.m. Who could ask for more than that?

She got in and quietly closed the door. Putting the key into the ignition, she started the engine. Andi sent up a silent thank you for the almost soundless hum of the engine and automatically glanced in the rear-view mirror to back out of the parking space. The mirror reflected blackness. *Oh yeah.* She'd almost forgotten she was driving a hearse–*ew*! She turned her head and was relieved to see there was glass separating her from the empty "body area." Besides, it was too dark to see anything in the back. Facing forward, her gaze traveled down from the rearview mirror to the dash. That's where she saw the screen with a backup camera. She quietly pulled out of the parking space and turned on the headlights as she merged onto Orange Avenue. She glanced out the side view mirror.

No one was chasing after her by car or on foot. *That's a relief.* She blew out a breath. "Okay, it's a short drive to the repo lot. I've got this." The sound of her voice startled her in the quiet of the cab. Andi inhaled slowly through her nose and exhaled through her mouth. Mags had taught her this slow breathing method to relax her when she was feeling stressed. She reached over to turn on the radio. Music would help distract her.

The song *If I Die Young* was playing. *Not helping.* She switched stations only to hear the chorus to *Another One Bites The Dust.* Andi changed stations until she found a pop song with an upbeat tempo. *Better.* She merged onto I-581 and had only been on the highway for about two miles when an eighteen-wheeler next to her began to come over to her lane.

Holy Mary Mother of God.

She checked the sideview mirror but there was a car racing up in the left lane leaving no place to escape. Andi slammed on the brakes so as not to be flattened by the back of the huge truck. By some miracle, the truck missed hitting her by mere inches—*Thank God.* She jerked back, constrained by the seatbelt and then was jarred as something banged into her from behind. *Oh no!* She must have been rear-ended. Looking in the rearview mirror and seeing nothing, she did a quick check in both side mirrors. Still nothing, but she wasn't about to open her door in the middle of the highway to look. Getting off the road was a top priority. Heck, she'd probably bring whoever was attached to her bumper with her. Andi gently pressed the gas pedal and slowly moved forward, continuing to look in her sideview mirrors. No one was there? Did they hit her and just quickly drive off?

Andi shrugged. Nothing she could do about it now. Jerry was going to be really mad if there was a lot of damage to the Cadillac. At least it was drivable. She'd just have to wait until she got back to the lot to look at the damage.

Fifteen minutes later, Andi was singing loudly and off-key to the song *Girls Just Want to Have Fun* as she pulled into the parking lot of The Repo Doctor. She lowered her driver's side window, punched in the keycode and then waited just a moment as the gate opened. She pulled in and parked her repo in one of the empty spaces. There weren't that many. Business had been booming and their lot was almost to capacity. They were so busy, in fact, Jerry had even begun advertising for another repo agent.

She yawned and stretched her arms. Mornings were not really her peak time of day. She could use another shot of sugar in the form of a doughnut but that would have to wait until she got back to her Jeep. Andi grabbed an empty plastic bag from her purse and looked around the front seat. She didn't see any trash or personal items. Reaching over, she popped open the door of the glove box and only saw the car manual and registration. She closed it and then grabbed her purse and got out of the Cadillac.

Andi walked around to the back to see the damage from the collision. The sun was up, and it was light enough to take a good look at the bumper. *Wow—not a scratch.* There was no way a car even tapped into the bumper. She bit her lower lip. That loud bump must have come from inside. *Oh God. Maybe they stored funeral supplies or something in the back?* It was the "or something" that had her worried. She made the sign of the cross with her right hand, touching her forehead, her heart, and then her left and right shoulders, sending up a silent prayer that there wouldn't be a coffin in the back. Andi counted to three and opened the door. The interior lights illuminated the cargo area.

Sweet Baby Jesus.

There was no coffin. No, instead there was some sort of gurney and a guy in a grey bathrobe on the floor next to the bed on wheels. Dead and apparently not wearing anything but the robe.

She slammed the door closed and took a few steps back. Reaching into her purse, Andi grabbed her phone with a shaky hand and called her boss, Jerry. He wouldn't be happy, but he'd handle this. He always handled the stuff left in the car. The phone rang four times and then, when it should have rolled over to his voicemail, she heard that annoying message, "This user's mailbox is full."

Jerry. She disconnected and began to pace. Jerry was terrible about answering his cellphone, so he probably wouldn't even notice that he had a missed call from her. *Why was this happening to her?* Andi weighed her options. She couldn't wait around for Jerry to show up. That could be at least two hours because he was even less of a morning person than she was. *But I just can't leave the dead guy here. Ew.* She definitely wasn't going to drive him back to the funeral home because there was no way that she was getting back into that corpse carrier.

Oh. My. God. He'd been in the back of the car the whole time. She placed a hand over her stomach. She wasn't feeling very well—s*tupid doughnuts.* Plus, she couldn't return the dead guy to the funeral home. Skips were always angry when their vehicles were repossessed. She couldn't imagine how Travis would feel once he realized she'd taken his hearse AND the body.

Andi stopped pacing. *Wait. What if the body in the back is not just a regular "customer" of the funeral home? Maybe this was foul play.* This wasn't the first dead body she'd discovered in a repo car. She knew what she had to do. This was almost as bad as the thought of getting back in the death wagon. Andi bit her lower lip, trying to think of an alternative as she stared down at her phone. There was one person she could call, but he wasn't going to be happy to hear from her. *Too bad. It's not like I'm happy about it either.* She exhaled and dialed the number.

Chapter Two

Detective Kendricks stopped in front of the captain's open office door. "You wanted to see me, sir?"

The man sitting behind the desk reading a report looked up, leaned back in his chair, and said "Yeah, close the door and have a seat."

Following the order, Kendricks took a seat in one of the chairs across from the captain. Carlson had been his immediate supervisor ever since Kendricks had transferred to Roanoke from Washington D.C. almost six years ago. He appreciated his direct, no bull-shit management style.

"I'm reassigning Dixon. Starting this morning, he'll be working with Detective Johnson."

Kendricks raised his brows. This was a surprise. He hadn't been particularly close with Dixon, but after the mess with his previous partner, he figured it was perfectly reasonable to be a little cautious.

"Was it something I said?" Kendricks asked.

"Hardly. Dixon said that you are very reserved and private, but he still found you to be more than competent. This switch has nothing to do with you. I'll talk with Johnson and Dixon about their new partnership after we finish here."

Carlson studied Kendricks for a moment before speaking, "How are you doing, detective? Not still blaming yourself about Richardson, are you?"

Hell yes. His former partner had been the head of the largest drug distributor in the city, responsible for ordering the hit for several of the homicides that they'd investigated, and he hadn't a clue until the end. He of all people should have been the person to uncover that fact. Instead, he hadn't realized it until she'd tried to kill him.

Although Kendricks' face remained unchanged, he unconsciously rolled the shoulder where he'd been shot. Because he had no desire to resume those uncomfortable sessions with the department shrink to discuss his feelings, he answered Carlson's question with a simple lie and change of subject.

"Of course not. Does this mean I get to work solo?" Now that would be a scenario he could handle. The only downside would be that he'd have to do all the paperwork.

The captain almost smiled. "You remind me of me when I was a detective." He slid the file he'd been reading to Kendricks. "I do miss those simpler days when I didn't have to deal with all the political crap." Carlson nodded toward the file. "Like your new partner." The captain raised his dark hand and said, "Before you ask, there's nothing I can do about it."

Kendricks looked at the file. *Ryan Hughes.* "He doesn't even look old enough to apply to the academy." He scanned the file. *No wonder.* Hughes was barely twenty-two years old, graduated high school at eighteen, Radford University with a Criminal Justice degree four years later, and the academy six months ago.

Kendricks looked up at Carlson. "This kid has only had six months in the field. No way is he ready to be a detective."

Carlson sighed. "Technically, his degree in Criminal Justice can be used to replace experience in the field."

Well that was just bullshit, and they both knew it. He glared at his captain. It was dangerous to put someone this inexperienced in the field as a detective. He shook his head. Carlson had said he didn't like to deal with political crap, and this reeked of it. "Who is he?"

Carlson leaned back in his chair, placing both hands behind his head and sighed. "He's the Police Chief's grandson."

"So? The best thing you could do for this kid's career is to assign him as a patrol officer. Let him work a few years on the streets to get some real experience, and then I'll be happy to teach him all that I know about being a detective."

Kendricks saw that hint of a smile flash across the captain's face and then it was gone. "I'm afraid that's not an option."

Kendricks leaned forward. "The kid is going to get himself or someone else killed if he starts this job without any experience. You know this. You think the Chief will be unhappy if you don't assign him as a detective. Wait until his grandson ends up killed in the line of duty."

Carlson sat forward in his seat, mirroring Kendricks. "That's why I've assigned him to you. It's your job to train him, keep him out of trouble, and most importantly, keep him alive and uninjured."

Kendricks' mouth dropped open to say something, some sort of counter argument. Surely the captain saw all the reasons this was a bad idea. Before he could say anything, Carlson raised his hand to silence him.

"Save it, detective. I've made my decision. You're dismissed. Hughes will report to you first thing tomorrow morning." The captain raised his brows. "Look on the bright side. You've got your wish - a full twenty-four hours working without a partner. Enjoy yourself."

Damn. Kendricks stood up. *Why is this happening to me?* He shouldn't be saddled with this kid. How the hell was he was supposed to train a new detective and teach him how to tell when suspects were lying when he hadn't been able to tell that his own partner was corrupt? At one time he'd been arrogant enough to think he was a damn good detective. Now he wasn't so sure.

Kendricks turned and walked to the door. As he opened it to leave, Carlson said, "Cheer up detective." Kendricks turned to look at him. "Who knows? This new assignment might be good for both of you." Then a big smile crossed Carlson's face and the bastard even chuckled as Kendricks left his office.

Stalking back to his desk, Kendricks sat down and took a drink from his cup of coffee. It was cold, *dammit.*

"I'm back from Richmond and brought boxes of fresh doughnuts. Help yourselves. They're in the conference room."

Kendricks looked up to see Detective Sanchez smiling and greeting officers, detectives, and administrative staff as more than half of the people in their large office area surged towards the conference room. *What the hell?* Kendricks had almost never seen the detective smile. Last time he saw a grin like that on Sanchez's face, Kendricks had been on a stretcher with a gunshot wound, headed to the hospital. *Bastard.*

Sanchez had been away from the office for the last couple weeks attending some sort of training. Frankly, Kendricks didn't care to know the details. He had been enjoying the narcotics detective's absence. Their cases usually overlapped since drug deals often accompanied homicides. He couldn't pinpoint it exactly, but there was something about Sanchez that always annoyed the hell out of him. The damn narc had been even more impossible to work with since he'd basically saved Kendricks' life last summer.

Opening the bottom drawer on the right side of his desk, Kendrick's pulled out a file folder for one of his current cases. He opened the manilla folder and looked over the list of people he needed to call, making a note next to the name of one of the witnesses he was going to see this afternoon.

Sanchez dropped into the chair on the other side of his desk and asked, "Miss me?"

Terrific. Kendricks didn't look up from his folder when he replied, "Why? Did you go somewhere?"

Sanchez laughed and leaned forward. "Who pissed in your cornflakes?"

Kendricks looked up. "Shouldn't you be arresting some drug dealer rather than harassing me?" *Why the hell was Sanchez so goddamn cheerful?* Frankly, he much preferred the quietly angry side of Sanchez. That, at least, he could relate to.

Sanchez smiled again as he leaned back in the chair getting comfortable. *Great.* Just because the bastard had saved his life didn't mean they had to be friends now, did it?

"Ah, this is about your new partner, isn't it? Chief Bogan's grandson, Ryan Hughes." Sanchez had the nerve to look a bit sympathetic.

How the hell did he know already? Kendricks just found out about it a few minutes ago. His face must have communicated his thoughts, because Sanchez said, "Hey, if you bring in some doughnuts once and awhile, you can get great intel from the admin staff."

Kendricks raised a brow, studying Sanchez when a brilliant idea occurred to him. "You don't currently have a partner. How'd you like to take mine?"

Sanchez held up both of his hands in refusal. "No thanks. Anyway, I've been assigned a new partner too, only I got lucky. She's transferring from a unit in Richmond. We attended a special narcotics team training together and let me tell you, she's got some damn amazing skills." He leaned forward. "It is like she's got these superpowers. She's trained in narcotics, explosives, and homicides. I can't wait to see her in action out in the field." He pointed a finger at Kendricks. "She can run circles around you, detective. Just wait until you meet her." He stood up and looked down at Kendricks. "And you better stay on her good side. I've seen her take down a man twice your size. Speaking of staying on her good side, I've got to go get her a jelly doughnut before they're all gone. They're her favorite." He turned and walked out the door.

Terrific. A serious and irritable Sanchez was bad enough. This new happy narc was even worse. A minute later, Kendricks' cellphone rang. Pulling it out of his pocket, he glanced down at the name. *Andrea Sloan.*

An image of her from the last time he'd seen her flashed through his mind. It was Christmas Eve, and she'd been standing in her living room in shock, eyes wide, her shaking hands pointing a Colt 1911 at the man who'd minutes earlier threatened to use the same gun to end her life. He'd felt an unwelcome urge to wrap her safely in his arms and kiss her until that haunted look on her face vanished, despite the presence of her boyfriend and several uniformed police officers. Instead, he had appealed to her stubborn nature and managed to talk her into giving him the weapon before anyone was shot. He was an idiot, and his reaction to her still really pissed him off.

"Kendricks," he answered the phone, irritation clear in his tone.

"Detective, this is Andrea Sloan. I'm sorry to call you, but I sort of have a situation, and I didn't know what to do. You sound," she paused and then said, "busy. I'm sorry. I shouldn't have bothered you with this. Don't worry about it. I'll figure it out on my own. Sorry."

Figure it out on her own? Kendricks rolled his eyes. That sounded like trouble.

"Wait, don't hang up before you tell me what kind of situation you're dealing with." Knowing Andi, she was probably calling from a bank during a robbery. The woman was a magnet for trouble. He lightened his tone and teased, "Don't tell me you've found another dead body?"

There was silence on the other end.

Jesus. "Don't touch anything. Where are you?" he asked. He grabbed a pen and notepad from his desk.

"I'm at the repo lot."

"Why didn't you call the police?" He tucked the pen and notepad in his jacket pocket, stood up and began walking towards the door.

"I did. *You* are the police," she said.

"I'm going to send the closest patrol car to you. I'll be there in about five minutes."

"Please don't. I'm not sure it's a crime. That's why I called you first."

"Is there a dead body at the repo lot?" he asked as he walked towards his black SUV. He realized she'd never actually answered his question the first time. He clicked the FOB to unlock the car, opened the door, and got in.

"Yes. He's in the hearse I just repoed."

Kendricks closed his eyes a moment while he pinched the bridge of his nose. He could feel the beginning of a headache. *Coffee.* He started the engine. He needed a large, black, hot coffee. Now.

"You repoed a hearse during a funeral?" He put her on speaker, set the phone in the holder, and pulled out of the parking lot.

"No, of course not. Give me some credit, detective. I repoed it first thing this morning specifically to avoid the whole casket-dead body situation."

"But you managed to take a casket and body anyway. You really need to start looking inside the vehicles before you take them." He turned on his emergency lights without the siren and sped down the highway. The sooner he got this over with, the sooner he could get his hands on the blessed coffee.

She muttered something he couldn't quite understand. He almost smiled as he imagined the expression of annoyance on her face right now. "There's no casket. Just an old, naked, dead guy in a bathrobe."

Why were they always naked?

"Hey, I'll be there in three minutes. Meet me at the gate so you can let me in."

***

Andi hugged herself as she paced in front of the gate waiting for Detective Kendricks to arrive. It was so cold outside even wearing a winter coat and fleece gloves. She wouldn't be surprised if the vapor from her breath began forming ice crystals. There was no way she was going back inside the vehicle to warm up with the dead guy in the back, and Detective Kendricks had asked her to meet him at the gate.

Detective Kendricks. For as annoyed as he'd seemed on the phone, he'd still dropped everything to come over immediately—probably assuming Andi was in over her head again. Andi shrugged. She did seem to get tangled up with his investigations a lot—not that it was her fault.

She spotted his dark SUV with the grill lights flashing as he approached the gate. Andi punched in the code opening the gate, and he drove through and parked in front of the hearse. By the time she walked back over, Kendricks was stepping out of his car. *Like Thor, if the superhero wore a black parka and a tie.*

Detective Kendricks always made her feel a little nervous, so she began talking to him immediately just to distract herself. "I really appreciate you coming over. I was surprised to find the body in the back. He must have fallen off the gurney when I was cut-off by the tractor trailer this morning. I had to slam on my brakes, and then I heard a loud thud. Originally, I thought someone had rear-ended me." She made a face like she'd just sucked on a lemon. "I hope I didn't injure him."

Kendricks raised a brow.

She widened her eyes. "Well, obviously he's dead already. I hope I didn't damage the body." *Oh my God, I'm rambling. Get a grip.* Well, dead bodies sort of freaked her out. She bit her lower lip and bunched her brows before turning abruptly and heading towards the back of the hearse.

"He's back here," she said as she opened the back door.

The dead guy was still there alright. Just where she'd left him – robe gaping open showing everything. She stepped aside so Kendricks could see him. The detective still wasn't saying anything, so Andi began talking again.

"See. No casket. Just the gurney and a dead guy."

Kendricks pulled out his phone and took a few pictures, and then he tucked it away and withdrew a small notepad and pen. Without looking up at her, he said, "Start from the beginning. What time did you pick up the vehicle?"

She glanced at her watch. "About thirty minutes ago? My plan was to get there early this morning, grab it and be back before the funeral home opened for business. I parked in the Krispy Kreme lot next door. It gave me the best view of the back-parking area of the funeral home. Unfortunately, the hearse wasn't there. A little while later, my skip, Travis Moulder, drove up in the hearse and got out with some other guy. They both walked inside the funeral home carrying what looked like a fast-food breakfast. That's when I ran over and grabbed the hearse. I drove back here, and as I was checking for personal items, I found the body."

He made a couple notes and then lifted that laser blue gaze on her. Kendricks had this way of looking at her like he could read her mind if he concentrated hard enough. Her eyes instinctively widened. She remembered the first time she'd met him when he'd interrogated her about another dead body in a car she'd repoed. More recently, it was those eyes and his condescending attitude that had pulled her out of the terror after she'd almost been killed at gunpoint. A cold chill raced down her spine. She still had nightmares about that night.

"I couldn't reach Jerry to let him know about the body in the car. I didn't want to just leave the guy like that," she said as she pointed in the direction of the body without looking at it. *Ew.* "I was trying to figure out a way I could return the body to the funeral home, but this doesn't seem quite right. I mean, I don't know much about the whole funeral process but why would they leave this guy in the hearse? Wouldn't they need to take him inside to embalm him or something? Wouldn't they have strapped him in or for God's sake covered him up?"

Kendricks nodded. "It's definitely unprofessional, but I don't believe they've done anything illegal. I could call in the medical examiner, but I suspect this is a case of carelessness rather than foul play. Did you see any paperwork in the front seat like a death certificate?"

Andi shook her head. "No. The front was clean. The only thing left behind was the body in the back."

"Do you have a phone number for Travis?" he asked.

Andi nodded, looked in her purse, and pulled out her repo file for the hearse. She opened the folder and scanned down the form. Here it is," she said, pointing at a cellphone number in the report for Kendricks to see.

He nodded and made the call. "Mr. Moulder? This is Detective Kendricks with the Roanoke City Police Department. Did you transport a body this morning in your hearse?"

Kendricks listened for a few minutes and then said, "Yes. I've got him here. Your vehicle wasn't stolen," he glanced at Andi.

She narrowed her eyes. Oh, it irritated her when people accused her of stealing. Her job was completely legitimate.

"I'll need you to bring the appropriate identification, including Mr. Snead's death certificate over to The Repo Doctor repossession company immediately. If everything is in order, you may transport the body back to your funeral home. You'll need to bring another vehicle for transport. Your hearse has been repossessed."

Kendricks disconnected and tucked his phone, notepad, and pen away and closed the door to the hearse. "I should have stopped on the way to get a cup of coffee." He sighed and then glanced at her with a hint of a smile. "But with you, I never know what kind of situation I'm about to walk into."

He was teasing her. Andi pretended outrage by placing her hands on her hips. "What's that supposed to mean, detective?"

Kendricks simply raised a brow. "Last time I was called to your location, you were pointing a gun at a guy tied up in Christmas lights." He rolled his eyes and his lips curved into a half smile.

Everything faded away except for the image of Peter, but he wasn't tied up in Christmas lights. Instead, he was standing in front of her, pointing the gun at her chest saying that it wasn't personal. That he'd make it quick. Someone said her name. *No, no, no.* She began taking quick shallow breaths. He was going to kill her. She had to do something. *Anything.*

"Andi!"

Coffee. She needed to splash hot coffee on his face. That had worked last time. Andi glanced down at her hands, but she was holding a folder—not coffee. *No, no, no.* A sob escaped from her. She was going to die this time. His eyes were so hard, serious, and she knew he would kill her. *Oh Cooper. I'm sorry we didn't have more time.* He was going to be so sad. Peter grabbed her by the shoulders and shook her.

"Please don't shoot me," she pleaded. "I don't want to die."

"Andi, look at me. It's Kendricks. Peter can't hurt you. He's locked away in prison for a very long time. You are safe."

Peter's cold hard eyes were gone and replaced with those familiar fierce blue eyes. *Oh, thank God.* She knew that concerned face—an expression he wore most of the time.

"Thor?" she whispered and reached out, wrapping her arms around his strong body and buried her face into his neck.

***

"Jesus Andi," Kendricks said. She was trembling. "You're safe. It's okay." He held her tight until she stopped shaking. He knew the moment she'd fully recovered from the flashback because she released him and stepped back.

She was embarrassed. He could tell by the way she was looking down at the ground. "I'm so sorry. Wow. That's never happened before."

"Do you have nightmares?"

Andi bit her bottom lip, "Yes, but they aren't as frequent as when it first happened." She looked just past his shoulder, not making eye contact. "Now I only have them maybe three nights a week."

"Are you talking to someone about it?"

She met his gaze then and gave a small smile. "Yes. Dodger is a great listener."

He raised a brow. "Not your dog. I meant a professional like a psychiatrist or counselor. Sometimes talking through the trauma helps you deal with it. When you try to ignore it or push it out, it tends to sneak up on you in other ways."

She shook her head. "I thought I was doing better. It must have been the dead body that set it off."

"I could have triggered the flashback too. You haven't seen me since that night, and then I joked about it. I'm sorry. I should have realized." He reached up and rubbed the back of his neck. *Damn.* He'd just been remembering that night and her haunted expression. He should have known it was likely she'd be having issues, despite the sassy, independent demeanor she presented to the world.

She studied him a moment and asked, "How do you handle it? Your partner tried to kill you, and you were shot. That's way more traumatic than anything I went through."

"I was put on mandatory administrative leave and forced to talk about it with the department shrink. Good times," he said with a forced smile. "Let's just say I'm getting by okay. I still occasionally have those nightmares you're talking about."

She couldn't help but smile back and shake her head. "You've obviously recovered well. You're working with a new partner now. Detective Dixon, right?"

"I just found out this morning that Dixon's been reassigned. I really hate change. I'm getting a new partner tomorrow that I get to train—practically fresh out of the academy."

"You don't sound excited."

Kendricks shook his head. "It's a babysitting assignment. He's the Police Chief's grandson. I don't care what his grades were in college, he needs more time on patrol to gain experience." Why was he even talking to her about any of this?

Just then, a Ford Bronco pulled up to the gate. "Looks like Travis is here." He studied her a minute. "I can handle this on my own if you still need a little more time." He glanced at The Repo Doctor office. "Why don't you wait inside?"

She smiled at him. "I'll be okay, but thanks for the offer."

He was still studying her. Reliving a traumatic event like she'd just done—he shook his head to shake off his own memories—was unpleasant. Well, she appeared to be alright, and he'd be there if something triggered her again.

"Come on, Sloan. Let's get this over with so I can get that cup of coffee."

After Travis had transferred the body to his Ford Bronco and left the lot, Kendricks insisted on giving Andi a lift to her car. He'd said that he was headed to Krispy Kreme for coffee anyway, but he really wanted to make sure she was still okay after having a PTSD episode at the repo lot. Okay, and if he was being honest with himself, maybe he wasn't ready to say goodbye to her just yet. *Idiot.* He shook his head, annoyed with himself.

He glanced over at her sitting in his passenger seat. She was nervous, and he knew that because she was doing that thing again where she talked without really taking a breath. *How the hell did she manage that?* She'd done it earlier when he'd first arrived back at the parking lot. Kendricks tried to focus on what she was saying rather than remember how she'd felt when she'd clung to him trembling or how her warm breath felt against his neck because that sure as hell wouldn't be very professional. He pulled up next to her Jeep, and Andi stepped out and turned to face him. "Thanks for the help with the dead body."

Kendricks just nodded. Be professional and just get the damn coffee.

She paused and glanced down at the ground before saying, "And helping me through that other thing, too."

His expression softened at her words. She was still feeling embarrassed about her PTSD moment back there. "Of course," he said in a gentle tone. She looked up at him with large, vulnerable eyes. *Shit.* He swallowed and felt an uncomfortable ache in his chest. He didn't want to care about this crazy woman, at least no more than he cared for any other citizen he was sworn to protect and serve. *Damn.* He took a deep breath and gave her his best serious, no-nonsense expression. "Just make sure you talk with a *human* professional. Soon."

She smiled at him, obviously relieved to be back to their normal exchange. Andi saluted him and closed the door and turned to her Jeep to unlock the door.

He lowered the passenger window and said, "Hey Sloan." When she turned back towards his car he asked, "So you really think I look like Thor?"

Her eyes widened, and he smiled at the look of mortification on her face before pulling away to get that coffee.

Chapter Three

Andi ate another doughnut as she was driving—*stress eating*—and found a free one-hour parking spot near the City Market Building. It was still early, so the lunch crowd hadn't taken all the free spots yet. She grabbed the green and white doughnut box and walked across the street into the old brick building, making a beeline to her best friend's smoothie kiosk. She stopped at Simon's Hot Dog Heaven booth that was next to Maggy's and set the box of doughnuts on his counter.

"Simon, please save me. I'm afraid that I can't be trusted with these last two doughnuts."

Simon grinned and opened the box. "Always happy to help one of my favorite customers. No sacrifice is too great for you, Andi."

"What's wrong?" Maggy asked as Andi approached her booth. "It can't be that bad. It's not like you found another dead body."

"Bingo," Andi replied.

"What?! I was only kidding!" Maggy said as she reached under the counter for a vegan chocolate peanut butter cup. "Here, eat this and tell me what happened." Maggy pushed the candy towards Andi.

Andi lifted it off the counter and popped it in her mouth, made a face, and then spit it out into her hand. *Oops.* She began to unwrap the wet gold foil.

Maggy's eyes widened. "You've got to unwrap it first." She reached under the counter, unwrapped a candy for herself, and took a bite.

"The short version? I repoed a hearse that had a naked dead guy covered only in a bathrobe which didn't conceal the essentials." She gave Mags a look. "Jerry was MIA, so I called Detective Kendricks. He determined it wasn't foul play, I had a PTSD breakdown in front of him—hugged him as in latched onto him like a bear hugging a tree—and then accidentally called him Thor, and he *heard* me. I've eaten four Krispy Kreme doughnuts, and I almost ate a candy with the wrapper on." Andi shook her head. "Mags, I think I'm finally losing it."

Simon was eating the doughnut, watching with complete fascination. "Hey Andi, you handled the dead guy, survived the breakdown, and trust me, nobody minds being called Thor. You both can call me Thor, and I won't even bat an eye. Go ahead." Simon took another bite of the doughnut, chewed a few seconds, swallowed and said, "Really. Go ahead and call me Thor. Watch my reaction."

Mags glared at him, and he shrugged. "I'm just saying..." and turned away to fix himself a Dr. Pepper to go with the second doughnut.

"How do you know he heard you?" Mags asked.

Andi shook her head. "Before he left, he asked me if I thought he really looked like Thor." She covered her face with her hand. "This is so humiliating."

Mags shrugged. "I hate to agree with Simon," she looked over to make sure he wasn't listening, "but he's right. You just stroked his ego. No harm done." She reached out and squeezed her hand. "Now, tell me about the PTSD thing. What happened?"

Andi waved her hand. "It was just weird. Kendricks was teasing me about last time he saw me, you know, on Christmas Eve, and I sort of freaked out. Everything disappeared except the scene from that horrible moment, but it kind of blended with the present too." Andi shook her head. "God, Mags, do you think I'm crazy?"

She squeezed Andi's hand and nodded. "Well of course, but not in the way you mean. Maybe you should talk to someone about it."

"I am," Andi said.

"No, like a professional."

"That's what Thor said." Andi rolled her eyes. "Okay, I've got to stop calling him that."

"You've been through a lot. Talking to a counselor is worth a shot if it makes you feel better." Mags shook her head. "I can't believe you found another dead guy. Repoing a hearse? That's a first, isn't it?"

"First and last, thank you very much. Jerry can have all the funeral vehicles from now on." Andi blew out a breath. "So, let's not talk about me anymore. Have you figured out what you're going to do while the City Market Building is closed for repairs?"

Mags frowned. "No," she said and lifted her thumb to her mouth, starting to bite her nail. She quickly realized what she was doing and dropped her hand, walked over to the sink and washed her hands. "I'm biting my nails again. Do you know how many times I've caught myself today and had to rewash my hands?" She frowned.

Andi tilted her head while studying her best friend. "Maybe you can just take a vacation while they do construction. Goodness knows you deserve one. You put in such long hours. I can't even remember the last time you took a day off."

Maggy puffed her cheeks and exhaled. "I can't afford to lose three weeks of sales. That's almost an entire month."

"Hm. I'm sure you're not the only one in this situation. I wonder what the other merchants are doing?" Andi turned to Simon and asked, "Simon, what are you doing during the market renovations?"

Simon grinned and leaned against his counter. "I've been cleaning up my dad's old food truck – The Bull Dog. He used to sell hot dogs from it back in the day. Not to brag or anything, but The Bull Dog's looking good. I'll be selling my hot dogs just down the street from the market, so I'm hoping I won't lose any business. My regular customers wouldn't be able to survive three weeks without my dogs."

"Your customers have one foot in the grave already with the fat grams in your hot dogs. By shutting down for the next month, you could save a life."

Simon grinned. "Don't be bitter Mary Margaret. Just because I've had more customers this week than you is no reason to get defensive."

"Your girlfriend from Tasty Scoops who comes by every day this week to flirt with you doesn't count as a customer since she doesn't ever buy anything."

Simon's face flushed a bit as he said, "She just stops by here on her breaks because she's bored. She's not my girlfriend or anything."

"Yeah right. She wants to be your girlfriend," Mags said and rolled her eyes.

Andi turned to Maggy, "Maybe you can rent a food truck to sell your smoothies."

"I've already checked. There aren't any available. Plus, they're way out of my budget." Maggy began to lift her hand towards her mouth again but stopped at the last second and clasped her hands together at her waist.

Simon raised his brows. "You could share the truck with me. I mean, it might be a little cramped with the two of us working in the small space together." His face began to flush. "But it's just for three weeks and you don't need the fryer. The truck's got plenty of freezer space for your ice and lots of counterspace for your blenders."

Simon is too adorable and sweet. Andi looked over at Maggy. She could see by the expression on her face that Mags was about to turn down his generous offer.

Andi beamed and said, "Simon, you're a godsend. Mags says yes, and she just can't thank you enough for your generous offer." Andi turned so she was standing in front of Maggy and blocking Simon's view of her dear, stubborn friend. She placed a hand on each of Maggy's shoulders and in a quiet voice, Andi said, "You're going to swallow the refusal you were about to give Simon, put a smile on that gorgeous face of yours, and tell the man thank you. He's offering you a lifeline and you're going to reach out and take it."

Maggy opened her mouth to object, but Andi simply cocked her head and gave her a stern look. "You know I'm right

Mags. Swallow that stubborn pride of yours and make the smart business decision. What are you so worried about anyway? It's not like you don't work next to the guy every day."

"Oh, I don't know, working that close to him, I might finally give in to my urge to kill him. Three weeks in a small space with the hot dog guy is an eternity. His body might be the next dead one you come across."

"Uh huh. You know what I think?" Andi asked. "I think you're afraid to be that close to him. Face it, Mags, Simon's funny, sweet, and cute and just maybe you're afraid of falling for someone like him."

Maggy rolled her eyes dramatically. "Right. It's all a moot point because I have a perfectly sexy, wonderful boyfriend."

"That you rarely see," Andi pointed out.

"We're both busy," Mags said.

"Mm hm." Andi glanced down at her watch. "Speaking of busy, I've got to get back to work."

"Don't you want a smoothie or something to calm down your nerves. You were so stressed about the dead body and Thor."

Andi chuckled. "You've worked your magic again, Mags. I already feel better. I can't wait to stop by the truck tomorrow and check things out." Andi winked dramatically and turned to leave. "See you tomorrow, Simon," she said and waved goodbye as she walked out the door.

***

Andi pulled into the front parking space at The Repo Doctor. She'd pop in, inform Jerry she was no longer handling any vehicles associated with funeral businesses, grab a couple new repo files, and get back to work so she could make some money. She gathered the paperwork and keys for the hearse, her purse, and picked up her phone off the seat. Glancing down at her phone, she saw the text from Cooper.

Missed waking up next to u Margarita.

She was replying to his text message as she walked into the office. Without looking up, she said, "Jer, I need a pay raise. I tried to call you this morning, but like usual, you didn't answer your cellphone. I had to handle the mostly naked dead guy that was left in the hearse. *You're* supposed to take care of that aspect of the business." Andi dropped in the chair in front of Jerry's desk, finished the text, and pressed send.

A woman's voice asked, "Whoa, what do you mean mostly naked dead guy?"

Andi looked up from her phone. "You're not Jerry."

A woman with shoulder-length straight blond hair and heavy makeup was staring at her in alarm. "Jerry said I'd just have to do light filing and answer phones. He never mentioned anything about dealing with the dead." The woman sitting at his desk made the sign of the cross with her right hand.

"Where's Jerry?"

"He's down in North Carolina tracking down a car. He's been complaining about being shorthanded. Apparently, it's just him and some guy named Andy handling all the jobs that come in." She shrugged, "We've only been going out a little over two weeks, but he's adorable, so I offered to help. I've done some work as a receptionist at the salon, so I figured how hard can this be?" She looked Andi over. "You know, I can probably get you a discount on a cut and color." The blonde woman ran her hand through her straight hair that fell softly at her shoulders.

Rude—there was no need to flaunt her gorgeous hair.

"They might even be able to straighten that," she waved her hand to indicate Andi's hair, "crazy mess for you." She smiled again. "I'm Madison. Who are you?"

"I'm Andi, you know, the guy that handles repos with Jerry."

Madison mouth gaped.

Andi shrugged. "Don't worry about it—happens all the time. Andi's short for Andrea."

Madison pursed her lips and frowned. "I had no idea he worked with a woman." She studied her much closer this time, as if eyeing up possible competition.

Yeah, he's all yours. Jerry was more like an aggravating older brother. Well, she'd had enough female bonding time. Andi walked over to the completed basket and deposited her file folder and key. She reached into the other basket and picked up two more repo folders.

"They're all set. Those just came in this morning, so I filled out the paperwork and included the key with each file."

The office phone rang, and Madison answered, "Hello, you've reached The Repo Doctor." She paused and then giggled. "Why thank you. I'm the new receptionist. How can I help you?"

Oh lord. Madison sounded all breathy and flirty on the phone, no doubt thrilling some bored male lending agent. Andi shook her head. Somehow, she didn't think this was one of the nice girls Jerry's grandma, her neighbor Mrs. Harper, had in mind for him. Slipping the folders in her purse, she headed out the door.

***

Andi drove over to Mill Mountain Coffee & Tea on Starkey Road, ordered a hot sweet peach tea and sat at a table by the window, soaking up some of the sunlight shining through the glass window. Roanoke weather was so weird for January. Yesterday, it had been mild and about fifty degrees Fahrenheit. Today, it was cold and barely above freezing. She sipped her tea, careful not to burn her mouth, and then pulled out the file folders and studied her targets.

The first repo folder identified Victoria (Vickie) Ledford, owner of a two-year-old Obsidian Blue-Pearl Honda Odyssey mini-van. She was thirty-two and employed as a dental hygienist at Phelps Family Dental on Hershberger Road.

Hm. It is Friday, so there is a pretty good chance that the dental office is closed. Best case, they'll close by noon.

Andi looked at her phone and pulled up the website.

Closed. Figures. Vickie could be anywhere on her day off, so she'll be more difficult to track down.

The next file listed a Lunar Silver Metallic CRV owner, Gabriel (Gabe) Berg, twenty-nine, working as a receiver/stocker employed at Premier Corporation on Nicholas Avenue NE. Maybe she'd be able to snatch this car from the plant parking lot. It would be an easy grab as long as he was working the day shift.

Now that her tea had warmed her from the inside out, Andi typed in the address for Premier Corporation into her cellphone, slid her folders back into her purse and headed out the door. Twenty minutes later, she pulled into the unsecured lot at Premier Corporation, driving up and down the aisles looking for Gabe's silver CRV.

Nothing. Huh. Maybe he doesn't work dayshift.

Those kinds of details were never in the paperwork. If she was lucky, he was either home sick or sleeping. She scanned the folder for his home address, entered it into her phone—Homestead Apartments over on Plantation Rd.

Thirteen minutes later, Andi was pulling into the parking lot in front of her skip's building. She spotted his CRV immediately. Maybe her luck was changing for the better. She pulled into an empty space, just five cars down from her target. Andi unclipped the key FOB from the folder, grabbed her purse, and stepped out of the Jeep, locking it behind her. She casually walked over to the vehicle, checked the license plate to make sure she had the right car, and used the key FOB to open the driver side door. As soon as she tried to open the door, a loud car alarm began blasting a warning through the quiet parking lot.

What?! This doesn't make any sense!

She pushed the button on the key FOB again. Unfortunately, the alarm didn't stop. Why wasn't it working? She couldn't unluck the darn car!

An angry deep voice yelled from above her, "What the hell?! Get away from my car, bitch!"

Andi looked up to a second-floor balcony where a twenty-something, bearded-guy with dark hair wearing blue plaid sleep pants and a white t-shirt yelled, "I'm calling the police!"

Yikes. "It's okay, I'm just repossessing your car. It's all completely legal."

Andi heard him swear. She spared a glance back up to the patio and saw him pointing at her. "Don't touch my fucking car. I'm coming down." A moment later she heard the sound of a door slamming.

Why isn't this stupid key unlocking the car?

She heard someone running down the stairs.

Oh no!

Andi ran to her Jeep, unlocked it with a quick click, hopped in the driver's seat, slammed her door closed and started the engine. Gabe was running towards her car. He reached out and banged on the hood of her Jeep and in the next second he was reaching for her door handle.

Jesus, Mary, and Joseph.

She put the Jeep in reverse and pressed the gas pedal. He lost his grip on the door as soon as the car zoomed backwards. Andi turned the wheel, threw the gear into drive, and sped out onto the street. Once she pulled out onto the main street, she let out the breath she hadn't realized she had been holding.

Chocolate. I need chocolate. Glancing down at her gas gauge she realized her Jeep could use fuel too. There was a Shell Station just up on the right, so she pulled in, filled up her Jeep with unleaded gas, and bought a bag of M&Ms. Before starting her car, she popped a handful of M&Ms in her mouth while she figured out her next move. She closed her eyes a moment, enjoying the crunchy candy mixed with the creamy chocolate. Her phone rang bringing her back to the present. She glanced at the screen and answered it.

"Hey Ben. What's up?"

"You need you to come home right now."

"Why, what's wrong? Is it Dodger?"

He sounded stressed, but her roommate could be a bit dramatic sometimes. Correction—he was usually dramatic.

"No. I need you here so I can do your final fitting. This is the only chance that I'll have to finish your gown because I'm working this evening and then headed over to Daniel's for the night. You either come home now so I can complete this masterpiece, or you'll be wearing an unhemmed gown to the

Police Charity Ball tomorrow night." When she didn't respond right away, he said, "By the way, that's not really an option. You'll be wearing a Benjamin Palmer original, and I have a reputation to uphold."

She glanced at the clock on her dashboard. *Might as well head home.*

"On my way. See ya soon," Andi said and disconnected.

Gabe was going to be on guard now that he knew she was trying to repossess his car. He'd probably hide it someplace—that's what they usually did. It was going to take her some time to stalk his social media presence and identify possible friends and family that would let him hide his car at their place. Plus, she'd need to do some research for the mini-van or just wait until tonight to get the van from her skip's home address. That was a risk because if Vickie had a garage and parked her car there, Andi wouldn't be able to retrieve it.

Why had the key FOB failed on the CRV? She'd never had that problem before. The lenders always gave reliable keys and she'd taken this directly from the file folder, so it wasn't like she'd mixed them up. Jerry was so meticulous with the paperwork. Andi sighed.

But Jerry wasn't the one who put the paperwork together. *Madison.*

Both jobs were Hondas, so it was possible that Jerry's girlfriend had attached the keys to the wrong folders.

Andi pulled out of the gas station and headed home.

Chapter Four

Twenty minutes later, Andi pulled into her driveway and walked up the porch steps. She still lived in her childhood home where her grandparents had raised her. The neighborhood had been nice about fifty years ago, but now she lived only two streets away from a rougher part of town. As she unlocked the front door, she could hear Dodger barking. Who needed an alarm system with this pup around?

"Hey buddy. Have you been keeping the house safe?" she asked as she stepped into the living room and crouched down to give him love. She laughed as he licked her on her face and then began sniffing her purse. "Okay, I know what you really want." Andi stood up and reached in her purse. Dodger sat—sort of—in front of her waiting for his treat. His tail was wagging so hard that he kind of slid around the floor as he stared up at her waiting for the reward. She lifted out a large open bag of cheese curls, reached in and pulled one out. "Who's my best boy?" she asked. When he barked in answer to her question, she tossed him the cheese curl. He swallowed it whole.

She gave him two more before returning the bag of curls to her purse and placing it on the table by the door. After hanging her coat in the closet, Andi walked upstairs with Dodger trailing behind her. She stood in the doorway of her childhood bedroom, which was now her roommate's sewing studio. Ben was standing in the center of the room behind a dress form with his latest creation, hand stitching the back of her gown.

The navy-blue full-length gown had a lace, high, halter neckline, a sleeveless, darted bodice, and a sexy open back. A matching navy-colored georgette cascaded below a fitted waist into an elegant maxi skirt.

"Wow, Ben. This is gorgeous!"

He grinned at her compliment and looked up at her after he'd finished the stitch. "I know, right?" He shrugged. "I'm a genius, what can I say? Go ahead and get undressed. We can slide this on you and see if I need to make any adjustments before I hem it."

Ben studied her a moment, and his eyes widened in alarm when he noticed Dodger licking Andi's fingers. "Wait! Don't touch anything. Have you been feeding Dodger cheese curls again?" Before she could answer he was pushing her out of the room.

"Go wash your hands before you ruin the dress with that orange powder!" He glared at Dodger and pointed at him. "And don't let that beast anywhere near my creation. He chewed through my Versace belt in under five minutes this morning!"

Dodger whined and ran back down the stairs. "Sorry about the belt, Ben."

Ben sighed, "I'll get over it eventually. Probably. Thank God, I thrifted it rather than paid full price. He's just a dog, but you should know better than to come into my design studio with cheese dust, young lady."

She laughed. "You sound just like my grandmother."

"Of course. She was obviously a very wise woman."

***

An hour later, Andi and Ben were downstairs in the kitchen enjoying a lunch consisting of ham and cheese sandwiches on white bread, a pickle spear, and potato chips.

Andi took a sip of Coke out of the can. "The gown is beautiful, Ben. I bet you'll get a lot of new requests after I wear it tomorrow night."

"I'm banking on it, babe. Oh, that reminds me," Ben said as he reached into his back pocket. He placed a pile of small white cards on the table and slid them to Andi. "I had new business cards made. What do you think?" Ben took a bite of his sandwich.

The cards were white with Benjamin Palmer Fashion Designer printed in a bold, elegant black font. Below his name was a phone number and email address. To the right was a beautiful fashion sketch of the blue gown she'd worn last year to Cooper's brother's wedding.

"I love these! Who designed them for you?"

Ben shrugged, "Oh, I just put them together. I thought the other ones were kind of boring. Do you really like them?" He glanced down at the cards and looked back up at her.

"Yes, I do," she said with a smile and shook her head. "You are ridiculously talented."

A genuine smile spread across his face. "Thanks, Love." He put his elbow on the table and rested his chin in his hand. "I can't wait for the day that I can do this full time. I need a stage bigger than a few local weddings and a charity ball in Roanoke to highlight my gowns. I would kill for the chance to design for Fashion Week in New York City, or I'd even settle for an LA Oscar's red carpet."

Andi lifted the piece of white bread from her sandwich, layered potato chips on the ham and returned the bread. She pressed the bread firmly until the chips made a crunching sound like knuckles cracking. Then, she lifted the sandwich to her mouth. Before taking a bite, she said, "I have no doubt you'll make it to The Big Apple someday, Benny. You're too talented not to."

Ben frowned. "Thank you for the compliment, but don't ever do that again."

Andi frowned back at him. "What are you talking about?"

He pointed to her sandwich and made a face. "Potato chips should *never* be part of a sandwich. That's just disgusting."

Dodger ran to the front door and barked ferociously. Then they heard the doorbell.

"Are you expecting anybody?" Andi asked.

Ben shook his head, got up from the kitchen table, walked over to the front door, and peeked out the window. He turned back to Andi and asked, "What did you do now? All three Golden Girls are here."

Oh lord.

Ben opened the door wide and said, "How are my favorite ladies?"

Mrs. Barzetti walked in first, patted Ben on the cheek, and said, "Hello Benjamin. I brought some homemade brownies for you both."

Andi stood up and walked to the living room, "Did someone say brownies? Would anyone like a cup of tea or some milk to go with them."

Mrs. Harper and Mrs. Davis stepped into the living room, and Ben closed the door.

"Oh no dear, we can't stay," said Mrs. Harper. She clasped her hands together in front of her and beamed.

Uh oh. They are definitely up to something.

Andi glanced at Ben who just shrugged.

Mrs. Davis handed a piece of paper to Andi. "We came to talk to you about this. It's absolutely perfect, and we've already registered you."

Oh God.

Andi looked at the flyer. "Women's Self Defense Class – Turn Your Fear Into Power."

She looked up at the women that had taken the role of grandparents after hers had been killed in a car accident. "I'm sorry, I don't have time to take a class."

Mrs. Davis said, "Don't be silly, of course you have time. We paid for the class, so it won't cost you a cent."

Mrs. Harper said, "You always seem to be getting yourself into dangerous situations, dear. We thought this would help you be prepared for your next adventure."

Mrs. Barzetti chimed in. "I told them I just needed to teach you how to shoot a rifle and you'd be fine, but they're so excited about this." She shrugged. "It can't hurt to check it out."

Andi looked over to Ben for help.

"Honestly, I think it's a great idea. Our girl here needs all the help she can get." Ben winked at her and said, "Come on Andi. They've already paid for your class. You have to go."

She glared at Ben. "Thanks for chiming in Ben. I owe you." Then she turned back to her well-meaning neighbors. They looked so excited, and their intentions were kind. "Oh, okay," she finally said, and they beamed and hugged her.

Mrs. Barzetti looked about as excited as Andi felt. Still, she smiled at Andi. "Well, now that that's settled, we're on our way to the senior center to play pinochle."

"Have fun," Andi said as the Golden Girls stepped out on her porch.

Mrs. Davis turned to her and said, "We'll pick you up and all go to the first class together. Oh, it's going to be such fun!"

Mrs. Harper added, "It's just to ensure that you don't skip out on us, dear. You'll learn so much that nobody's going to even think about messing with you. We'll all go for an ice cream afterwards."

Just great.

"Looking forward to it!''" she said as she watched the ladies pile into Mrs. Davis' Subaru Forrester. She heard Ben laughing behind her.

"Benjamin Palmer," Andi said as she turned around and started walking towards him. "We'll see who's laughing when I practice those self-defense moves on you." She playfully jabbed at his stomach, and he jumped back just out of her reach.

This only made him laugh harder. "Aw, but did you see how excited they were?" He shook his head. "What I wouldn't give to watch the four of you in class."

Andi put her hands on her hips and smiled. "I'm happy to give you my spot. Then you'd get to see firsthand."

"Nice try, but no thanks. I already know how to throw a knockout punch. You, on the other hand, need to work on your timing and speed." He took a brownie from the plate and set the dish on the kitchen table. Then, he headed up the stairs.

"Now I'm off to finish that hem before I head to work. Later, Love."

"There's nothing wrong with my timing and speed!" she hollered up to him. *Well, not much anyway.*

***

It was almost six pm when Andi turned right onto Willingham Drive. Her skip, Victoria Ledford, lived in a quiet community just outside the city. Andi was looking for the Obsidian Blue Honda Odyssey. *Who came up with the names for the car colors anyway?*

She brought both sets of keys this time–the one she'd used unsuccessfully this morning on the CRV and the key that was attached to Victoria's folder. She was certain that Madison had mixed up the Honda keys when she'd put the files together. Andi would be prepared this time by having both keys.

Parking across the street a few doors down from Victoria's home, Andi glanced at her folder to double check the address. *Darn.* The two-story home had an attached garage, and the door was closed. *Figures.* Chances were good that the blue van she needed was parked safely inside the garage.

I'm just not getting any breaks today. What to do?

Andi pulled out her smartphone and looked on social media to see if she could locate Victoria. She was a "mini-van mom" after all. There was a pretty good chance she'd post photos of her adorable family, and if Andi was lucky, she might find out what Victoria's family was doing this evening.

"Gotcha!" Andi said as she scrolled across a photo of two young identical looking dark-haired girls, each with a matching gold crown pinned to a bun on the top of her head. One little girl wore a pink dress with a tutu, the other wore a purple dress. Each girl wore white tights and pink ballet slippers. Oh my goodness, they were adorable. The photo had just been posted five minutes ago.

Aww.

Andi glanced down below the photo. Maybe she was about to get a break after all. The post indicated that Victoria had just checked in to Dancer's Dreams on Electric Avenue. If she was lucky, mom would still be watching her girls dance, and Andi could grab the van.

By the time Andi reached the shopping center parking lot, she spotted a light blue van. She verified the license plate belonged to her skip. *Bingo.* She quickly parked the Jeep in the first empty spot she found, grabbed both sets of Honda keys and her purse, and scanned the parking lot for anyone that might be coming towards the Odyssey. The coast was clear, so she used the same key FOB she had for the CRV this morning and clicked the unlock symbol. She heard the sound of a click. *Yes!* Climbing into the van quickly, Andi started the ignition, pulled out of the parking space and made a right onto Electric Road, merging with the evening traffic. She stopped at the traffic light and checked her rearview mirror.

Oh no.

There were two car seats in the back seat. This was a problem. How was Victoria going to be able to safely transport those sweet little girls back home without her car seats? Andi pressed her forehead against the steering wheel for a moment and then sat up straight. When the light turned green, she merged into the left lane heading back to Dancer's Dreams.

As she pulled into the parking lot, she saw Victoria holding each girl's hand. She was frowning and looking around the parking lot. Victoria looked even more confused when she saw Andi pull up next to her and park the van. Andi lowered the window.

"Victoria Ledford?" she asked. "I've been hired from your lender to repossess your vehicle. I returned as soon as I noticed the car seats in the back. I wanted to make sure you had them when you called someone to give you a ride home."

"Oh fu," she paused, glanced down at her girls and said, "fudgesicles." She looked back at Andi. "Is there any way I could hold onto my van for another week? My ex-husband is behind on his child support. He's scheduled to go before the judge next week. Once the court orders payment, I should be able to catch up with the bank."

Andi shook her head. "I'm sorry. I'm going to have to take the van. Look, why don't I at least give you a ride home? Once I drop your van at the lot, I'll check with my boss. He can talk with your lender and see if they can get you some kind of extension. It's been my experience that when you're 3 months late, they pretty much always take the car."

"How am I possibly going to make it without a car? I've kept the girls in dance because they love it. The girls ride the school bus to school. I can maybe ask my co-worker Michele for a ride to work, but how can I get them to dance twice a week?" Victoria frowned. "I guess they'll just have to miss it for a week or so."

The girl in the purple dress tugged on Victoria's hand. "Mommy, no! Ms. Trish said that if we miss a class, we won't be able to dance in the show." Her lower lip extended out into a pout.

"We can't miss any more classes, Mommy. You promised." The little girl in the pink dress gave Victoria a matching pout.

Andi felt her heart squeeze inside her chest.

"I'll take them," Andi blurted.

What? Holy Mary Mother of God. The words were out of Andi's mouth before she realized what she was saying. Andi watched as all three of them stared at her –Victoria with an expression of shock and her girls were looking at her like she'd just offered them ice cream.

Andi could feel her lips curve up just the slightest. How hard could taking two girls to dance class be anyway? Vickie would get the money from her ex and catch up on her car payments.

She glanced at Victoria who was shaking her head. "That's too much to ask of you."

"I don't mind, really. Look, I understand what it's like when you're in a tight situation financially." Andi shrugged. "We're just talking about a week, right?"

Vickie nodded, eyes wide. "You'd do that?"

Andi shrugged. "Why not? Hop in, and I'll give you all a ride home."

***

By the time Andi pulled into the parking lot of Star City Bar & Grill, she was exhausted and hungry. She had dropped the Odyssey off at the lot and placed the paperwork and the correct key in the completed box. The office had been dark, locked, and empty, but evidence of Madison's earlier presence lingered in the air. The woman must be nose-blind to the floral scent she wore. *For the love of God, please let Jerry be back in the office in the morning.* Andi had left him a text about the key debacle, and asked him about giving Victoria an extra week with her van, although she was betting the answer to that was going to be no.

She pushed the heavy wooden double doors that had the Roanoke Star carved into them open and walked straight to the bar, sitting in one of the few empty stools. Star City Bar & Grill usually brought in a decent crowd on the weekends, but whenever Cooper's band, Riot Act, performed, they were packed.

Ben spotted her and gave her a nod. He was busy taking a customer's order, so she turned around to watch the band perform. All three members were good looking, but she was partial to the lead singer. The man oozed sex-appeal, standing on the stage singing to the crowd. He wore simple jeans and the black t-shirt she'd gotten him that read "Rockstar" in white letters on the front. His hands moved over the strings of his electric guitar effortlessly while he sang the lyrics to a song on the pop charts. As the band sang the chorus, Cooper spotted her at the bar, and his smile widened.

She felt her lips automatically return his smile. He winked at her as the song ended and then turned to say something to his bandmates. He switched to his acoustic guitar, spent a moment tuning it, and then addressed the crowd.

"Here's a little something I wrote for a special woman out in the audience."

He looked at each table like he was going to sing the song just to them and then his gaze landed on Andi sitting at the bar. She noticed a few people in the audience turn to follow Cooper's gaze. He held his attention on her as he began to strum the guitar. "We're going a little country with this song. This is a new song that I wrote just for you, Margarita."

Cooper nodded to Zach who played bass, and then he turned towards Danny, the drummer, and counted, "One, two, three, four."

Cooper spun around dramatically, and with a sheepish expression, sang into the microphone.

"I'm embarrassed to confess
One taste and I'm a mess
This simple fact can't be denied
Friend, I can drink any ole whiskey
That kind of liquor has no effect on me.

But I get drunk on Margarita's
Sassy smile when she's incognita
The sexy blond wig cannot disguise
The desire in her blue-green eyes

Her kisses make me intoxicated
Just holding her close I'm inebriated
And there's one more thing I must confide
The woman hardly even blinks an eye
When she stumbles across a naked dead guy

Everybody – sing along

That's why I get drunk on Margarita's
Sassy smile when she's incognita
The sexy blond wig cannot disguise
The desire in her blue-green eyes

One more time

That's why I get drunk on Margarita's
Sassy smile when she's incognita
The sexy blond wig cannot disguise
The desire in her blue-green eyes

Cooper paused and looked around at the crowd with a serious expression and then strummed his guitar and slowly sang.

You know, I can't help but wonder why
She's still with this lucky guy
Heaven help me, I get drunk on my Margarita.

The crowd went wild as Cooper strummed the last chord on his guitar. A woman in a low-cut red sweater hollered, "I'll be your Margarita, darlin'!"

Andi smiled as she watched Cooper place his hand on his heart and wink at the woman. Andi sighed and turned back to the bar. She wasn't jealous—well, not really. Cooper was an entertainer and knew how to get the biggest reaction from the crowd. He was cute, charming, and had a beautiful voice. What woman wouldn't fall for him? She certainly had, despite her best efforts to resist him. The crazy thing was that he was madly in love with her too. She didn't quite understand why, but she was smart enough not to question it.

Ben set a plate of fish tacos in front of her and a large margarita next to it.

"What's this? You put an order in for me?! How did you know I was starving?" Andi asked.

Ben raised a brow. "Please. You're always hungry."

"Oh Benny, you know me so well!"

Andi picked up the soft-shell taco stuffed with chunks of fried fish, crisp lettuce, shredded white cheese, topped with a spicy, red salsa and took a bite. *Heaven.* She closed her eyes as she chewed and moaned.

Ben leaned in and laughed. "Good lord, woman. The tacos here aren't *that* good."

She took a sip of her margarita. When she set her glass down, she wiped her mouth with the napkin and shrugged. "They're delicious. Besides, you know that repo work makes me hungry."

In the next moment, she felt arms wrap her in a gentle hug from behind.

"Miss me, Margarita?" the soft, sexy voice whispered in her ear.

Cooper. She turned around so that she was facing him. Up close, the man was delicious and right now he was looking at her in that way that made her want to melt into a puddle of desire. Instead, she tilted her head, pretending indifference while she looked into those yummy, chocolate-brown eyes.

"I'm sorry, have we met?" she teased, her lips curving up just the tiniest bit.

He broke into a huge grin.

"You're too cute," he said and leaned in to kiss her fully on the lips. After a minute, he broke off the kiss and stepped back to look at her.

He wasn't smiling now but was a little breathless looking at her like she was a snickerdoodle—his favorite cookie.

Before she could collect her wits to think of something clever to say, Zach stepped up to them, grabbed Cooper in a playful chokehold with his left arm and pointed his finger at Andi. "Woman, what have you done to this man? We used to be a cool band. Now he's got us singing songs like "I Get Drunk On Margarita's?' What the hell? He's making us look like wusses." Zach glanced around and then leaned in close to whisper, "Frankly, it's getting embarrassing."

Cooper elbowed Zach in the ribs. "Whatever. You can't deny that the crowd *loved* the song."

The blond who'd been sitting next to Andi stood up and approached them. She looked at Cooper and then Andi. With a frown she said, "You must be his Margarita. That's too bad." She turned her attention to Zach and said, "But you look like you might enjoy a drink or two after that performance." She stood so close to Zach that she was practically brushing him with her body. "Why don't you let me and my friend buy you a round of margaritas?" She reached over to run her fingertips over Zach's bare, brown arm. "Mm...these poor muscles have got to be achy from playing the guitar all evening."

Andi rolled her eyes. The way some of the women threw themselves at the band members was nauseating, though Zach didn't seem to mind.

He gave the woman his easy-going smile and asked, "You wouldn't be trying to get me drunk, would you?"

A woman with pink streaked hair stood next to her friend and said, "Maybe. We promise not to take advantage of you. Too much."

Zach laughed and released Cooper and draped an arm over each of his new drinking buddies. "Okay ladies let's go find a table. You know, I prefer beer and it makes me a little tipsy if I drink more than five. That would give us plenty of time to get to know one another."

He looked back at Andi and Cooper and gave them a wink.

Andi laughed. "I don't think he's too upset about the song anymore."

Cooper slid onto the bar stool next to Andi and reached over to her plate, picked up a fish taco and took a bite.

"Hey," she said and playfully smacked at his hand. "That's my dinner."

He smiled and swallowed. "Oh, this is delicious. I don't know what it is about playing music that makes me so hungry. I'll order another plate for us to share," he said before popping the rest of the taco in his mouth.

The drummer of the band, Danny, sat on the empty stool on the other side of Andi. Ben popped the cap from Daniel's favorite, local, craft beer and placed it in front of him.

Daniel grinned and leaned over the bar and gave Ben a chaste kiss on the lips. "Thanks, Benji."

Ben fought a grin and lost. "Mm. That was nice, but I expect a bigger tip tonight when we get back to your place after my shift," Ben said and gave Daniel a pointed look and then a wink.

Danny leaned forward and whispered something in Ben's ear and then sat back on the stool. Ben chuckled and then his expression softened. He looked at Danny with such love, like he was an Oscar De La Renta gown in mulberry silk.

A customer a few bar stools down from Andi hollered, "Hey, can we get some service here?"

Ben sighed and said to Daniel, "Hold that thought. I'll be right back." Then he tossed the bar towel over his shoulder and walked to the other end of the bar.

Danny turned on the stool to face Cooper and Andi. "Okay guys, later tonight, I'm planning to ask Benji to move in with me," Danny said rubbing his right hand up and down his pants leg.

Andi's mouth dropped wide open, and she heard Cooper say, "Damn man. That's a big step."

Danny smiled at Cooper over Andi's shoulder and said, "I know, but I'm ready to take it." Then he turned his attention back to Andi. "Andi, before I ask him to move in with me, I want to make sure you'll be okay financially without his share of the rent. If he says yes, I can maybe cover it for another month until you find someone."

Andi just stared at Danny. Ben was going to freak out, he'd be so excited. She was so happy for them both. Danny was such a nice guy, and she'd never seen Ben happier. Oh, but she was going to miss him. The house would be quiet without Ben's big personality filling every square inch of her place.

"If you need time to advertise for a new roommate, I can wait to ask Ben."

Wait to ask Ben?

"What?" Andi realized she'd never responded to Danny. "No, don't wait. I'm fine, and I'm sure I can find another roommate pretty quickly, although I won't ever find one like Benjamin Palmer." She reached out to touch Danny's arm.

"Anyway, these days he spends more nights at your place than he does at home. Ben's going to be ecstatic!"

Just at that moment, Ben walked back up to them and looked at Andi, brows raised. "What am I going to be ecstatic about?" He glanced at Daniel and then back at Andi.

"Um," Andi widened her eyes at Danny and then turned to face Ben. "It's a surprise?"

Ben's face lit up. "I love surprises! What is it?"

Danny said, "I'm sure Andi will tell you all about it tomorrow."

"Yes, I promise to tell you tomorrow," Andi said, *because you'll already know by then.*

"Andi, I think we should tell him now," Cooper said with a grin.

"What?! Cooper knows too?" Ben asked. "You've got to tell me. Right now!" He crossed his arms across his chest and stood in place.

Andi glanced at Danny who looked furious and was shaking his head no, and then back at Cooper who was chuckling as he looked between Andi and Danny. "Okay. If they won't say anything, I'll tell you Ben."

Andi and Danny both yelled "No!" at the same time.

Cooper laughed and said, "Ben, the surprise is that Danny got you both tickets to the Police Charity Ball that my mom's organizing. It's for a good cause, there will be amazing food, and you'll be able to mingle with potential new customers at the country club. I can't wait to see the amazing new gown you made for Andi. Danny asked me to pick up the tickets for him because he wanted to help your fashion business."

Ben gaped at Cooper and then walked over to Danny and gave him a quick kiss on the lips. "I can't believe you bought us tickets! Isn't it five-hundred dollars a plate?"

Danny choked on his beer, and Andi patted him on the back.

"What am I going to wear? I've got less than 24 hours to put together an outfit!" Ben saw someone down the bar waving to get his attention. "I can't believe we're going tomorrow night.

You're amazing Daniel. Be back in a minute," he said as he walked down to the other end of the bar to fill an order.

Danny glared at Cooper. "I appreciate the save Coop, but damn, couldn't you have picked something a little less expensive. One-thousand dollars? Seriously?"

Cooper laughed. "Hey man, don't worry. I've got a pair of extra tickets that our company purchased for clients. You'll get in for free."

"But I'm not a client," Danny objected.

"Hey, I give you advice all the time. Occasionally it's about money."

Daniel laughed. "You mean like when we were in college and you told me not to buy the cheap sushi, but I did anyway and got food poisoning?"

"Exactly," Cooper said, grinning.

"Thanks man. I owe you one," Danny said.

"Nonsense. Think of it as a housewarming gift," Cooper said with a grin before taking another bite of a taco.

Chapter Five

The next morning Cooper was standing in Andi's kitchen frying strips of bacon in an ancient iron skillet. Using tongs, he carefully picked up the individual strips and turned each over until they reached the perfect crispness. Reaching into the upper cabinet, Cooper pulled down a platter and placed it on the counter. He smiled to himself. He was as familiar with Andi's kitchen as he was his own.

He'd been spending a lot of nights at Andi's place lately. Sure, his place had better views of downtown and the mountains, faster internet, a nicer television with surround sound, a kitchen with new appliances, and a bigger bed. He'd prefer to be making her breakfast in his kitchen this morning and probably would be if not for Dodger. The drooling, furry guy was sitting at his feet waiting for Cooper to drop a piece of bacon.

The problem was that his condo had a no pets policy, and whenever Ben stayed at Danny's, Andi had to stay home to make sure Dodger wasn't alone. *Face it, you want to be wherever Andi is.* He glanced down at the adorable, odd-looking mutt. He even loved her damned, ugly dog.

The lace ruffle from the old-fashioned, faded yellow floral apron that he was wearing was itching his neck again. Cooper wore it because it was the only apron in the house, and he didn't want a big grease stain on his sleep pants or t-shirt. Good thing he and Andi were alone in the house. He grimaced. If either of the guys from the band saw him dressed like this, he'd never hear the end of it.

He looked over at the kitchen table where Andi sat concentrating on the screen of her laptop. She had a sexy mess of brown curls piled on top of her head and was wearing her oversized green sleepshirt that read "You Had Me At Donuts." He swallowed back his desire, determined to feed them. But damn, he was so tempted to walk over there right now and enjoy convincing her to put off breakfast for another hour or so.

His fantasy was disrupted when her cellphone began playing the song "Fashion" by Lady Gaga. Her gaze met his.

"It's Ben! Finally," Andi said. She grabbed her phone and answered it. "Hey, I've got you on speaker with Cooper. What's up?" *Like she didn't know.* She winked at him.

Instead of a greeting, he began with, "Are you absolutely sure my living with Daniel won't put you in financial ruin?"

She laughed. "Oh please, my financial ruin was so last month."

"I'm serious."

"You're sweet Benny, but I'm okay. Plus, I can easily replace you with two roommates and make some real income. I'll just make sure I don't rent to another guy that needs an entire second room for his design studio."

Another guy for her roommate? Cooper's gut twisted. He really didn't like that idea. Honestly, last night when Danny said he was asking Ben to take their relationship to the next level, Cooper had been too surprised by the idea of his friend's relationship development to give serious consideration to Andi's roommate situation.

Maybe she wouldn't have to get a new roommate. *Right.* She was finally experiencing moderate financial stability but something like an unexpected major home repair could send her back to the edge of foreclosure, and with this old house, that was a real possibility. She might be able to go a month or two, but she counted on the extra money that Ben contributed, so she'd definitely be getting a roommate, maybe two.

Why can't things stay just like they are now? It was nice. Comfortable. Well, for the most part. He rubbed the itch on his neck.

"Please. You know I am irreplaceable. How will you manage without me? Who is going to make sure your diet doesn't solely consist of artificially orange-colored foods? Who is going to make sure you don't dress like a homeless person when you head out the door?" Ben laughed. "Actually, I've seen some homeless folks more stylish than you, sweetheart."

"Hey, I resent that. Anyway, just because you are moving out, doesn't mean you get out of your vital best friend responsibilities. I'll need special BFF time with you since I won't get to see you around the house every day." Andi glanced over at Dodger who was faithfully sitting like a good-boy next to Cooper's legs, silently begging for a bacon-handout. "And Dodger is still going to want time with you, too."

"Well of course. We have joint custody of that sweet, ugly beast. He's my top dog model anyway. He'll need to come over for regular fittings," Ben said.

In a whispered voice Ben asked, "You don't think this is too soon, do you? It feels so right, but I just don't want to screw things up by rushing it, you know?"

Cooper was screaming inside his head, Hell yes you're rushing it Ben. This will change everything.

"Are you kidding? I've never seen you so happy, and Danny is just as crazy about you." Andi looked over at Cooper. "Right Rockstar?"

He was frowning when Andi said, "Tell him, Cooper."

What? Andi was waiting for him to say something. "Oh, right. Congrats Ben. I'm happy for you guys."

Ben took a deep breath. "Okay. I guess it's happening!" Cooper could tell Ben was smiling when he said, "I can't believe this! Oh my God! Danny said I should use the second bedroom for my studio. It's huge! I'll come by this afternoon to do some packing and then get ready for the Police Charity Ball tonight. There's so much to do. Hey, I'll check at work to see if anyone is looking for a place to stay. Thanks guys! Gotta go tell Daniel the good news. Bye."

The smoke detector started to go off and Dodger began barking.

Shit. Cooper turned back to the frying pan. His beautiful bacon looked like slabs of burnt charcoal. He turned off the burner and opened the kitchen window to help get rid of the smoke. "Damn."

Andi got up and stood behind him, her soft body pressed against his back while she wrapped her arms around his waist. Before he took his next breath, her warm hands found the edge of his t-shirt and began inching up. He swallowed.

She whispered in his ear. "Hey, forget the bacon. What do you say we take a nice long, hot shower? We can always go out for breakfast much, much later"

He turned in her arms until he was facing her and looked into her hazel eyes. *So damn sexy.* Her eyes were dark green this morning, picking up the color in her sleep shirt. *Yes. I want things to stay just as they are.* "That's funny, I was thinking the same thing a few minutes ago," he said and leaned in to kiss her.

***

Andi was still smiling thinking about the steamy morning spent with her Rockstar as she drove on 460 East. Ever since she and Cooper had said I love you to each other last month on Christmas, everything between them had become even more intense. It was like they couldn't get enough of each other. She knew she had it bad when she found him irresistible standing in her kitchen wearing Gram's apron this morning. Well, it could have been the bacon. She laughed.

Lately there was an urgency to their relationship, and she suspected she knew why. Things felt so perfect just the way they were, and this kind of euphoria never lasted. Did Cooper feel it too? He'd been sleeping over most nights, and when he wasn't at her place, she'd packed an overnight bag and stayed at his condo. This thing between them was almost too good to be true. Honestly, she couldn't remember when she'd felt this happy.

Making a left onto Ruritan Road, she thought about tonight's event at the Police Charity Ball. *Ugh.* It would be the first-time seeing Mrs. Barnett since the disastrous Christmas Eve party. His mother couldn't stand Andi and made that perfectly clear in every interaction they'd shared. Andi couldn't avoid his parents forever, could she? At least this time, she'd have Ben with her. He hadn't had the pleasure of meeting Mrs. Barnett yet.

Almost there. Andi made a right turn onto Denise Circle NE and began looking for the house address that belonged to Gabe's parents. She was on the hunt for his Honda CRV and was taking a chance that he'd tucked it away in their driveway. Skips often resorted to storing their vehicles with family or friends when they knew they were being repossessed. If it wasn't here, she'd just have to try to collect it from the parking lot at his job. She suspected he was going to bum a ride from a friend during the next week, since he knew she was looking for his car. She slowed as she approached his parents' address. *Hm.* The CRV wasn't on the street or in their driveway. *Darn it.*

Andi turned around to make another pass by their house. She parked the Jeep on the other side of the street, a couple houses before his parent's place. Pulling out her binoculars, she scanned the yard. She could see most of the backyard from this angle. It looked like his folks kept their yard well-manicured. The only unusual thing that she saw was the pile of tree branches and vines on the side of the house. *It's an awfully large pile for this size yard. Wait a minute. Could it be the CRV?* It was about the same size as a small car. There was a good chance there was a Honda under there. She'd have to get a closer look to be sure.

Andi scanned the house. Judging by the lack of cars in the yard, it didn't look like anyone was home. She glanced around at the other houses on the street. It was quiet for a Sunday. Chances were good that most the residents were at church. She'd just go over and take a quick look.

Tucking her binoculars back in her purse, Andi slung her purse over her shoulder, locked her Jeep, and casually walked over to Gabe's parent's house. She took another quick look around her surroundings before stepping in their yard and walking to the pile of yard debris. Once she got close enough, she could see there was just a light layer of branches and vines draped over a brown tarp. Andi lifted the tarp and bingo! There was her CRV. She walked around to what had to be the front of the car and lifted the tarp to verify the license plate.

YES! This was the car.

She grabbed a hold of the vines and branches and pulled them off the tarp, dragging them into piles on each side of the car. Then she pulled the tarp off and tossed it to the side. She'd kicked up a lot of dust, which made her eyes itch and caused her to sneeze. She brushed her hands on her jeans before rubbing her eyes to clear them. Opening the door to the car, she slid in the driver's seat and began rummaging in her purse. She finally found the car key at the bottom. Andi started up the engine and drove through the grass over the curb and onto the street. She glanced in her rearview mirror. No one was running after her for a change, but she caught a glimpse of her reflection and frowned. Her face was covered in dirt. She felt something crawling on her neck.

"Ahhhh!" she screamed and brushed it away. Probably just an ant or something. She shook her head in case she'd picked up any other little bugs and wiped her face again. Turning on the radio, Andi drove to the repo lot.

***

Andi was running late if the clock on her dashboard was correct. *Maybe the Golden Girls will go to the Self-Defense class without me.* As soon as she pulled into her driveway and stepped out of her Jeep, Andi heard the horn.

Nope, that was just wishful thinking.

She glanced out on the street in front of her yard and there was Mrs. Davis behind the wheel of a garnet red 1995 Buick LeSabre. Mrs. Barzetti was riding shotgun with Mrs. Harper in the backseat. Mrs. Barzetti's window lowered, and she said, "You might as well get in, Andrea. Once these girls get their minds set on an idea, there's no talking them out of it. Let's go ahead and get this over with. I can show you how to shoot my rifle later." Mrs. Barzetti winked at her.

Great. Andi locked her Jeep and opened the back door of Mrs. Davis' car. As soon as she sat down and fastened her seatbelt, Mrs. Harper smiled at her as she leaned over and pulled a twig out of Andi's hair.

"What on earth have you been doing?" Mrs. Harper asked and then opened her purse and pulled out a wet wipe and wiped Andi's left cheek. "You've also got a little smudge of dirt right here."

Sometimes she still felt like she was five years old when she was around these women she loved so much. "Thanks. I got a little dirty when I tracked down a car that was hidden under a pile of brush."

"Did anyone come after you?" Mrs. Davis asked, looking at Andi through the rearview mirror.

"Not this time, thankfully."

"Oh," Mrs. Davis said, sounding a little disappointed.

The neighbors tended to glamorize the challenges she faced as a repo agent. They had always been involved in her life, but even more so after her grandparents had died more than a year ago in the fatal car accident. Sometimes, it seemed they were a little too involved – like dragging her to this self-defense class.

Mrs. Barzetti swatted Mrs. Davis on the arm. "Eyes on the road, Gladys."

"Oh, for Pete's sake, Hazel. I know how to drive. I've been driving longer than you have."

"Here we go," Mrs. Barzetti said rolling her eyes. "You're less than a month older than me. I don't think those twenty-three days made that much of a difference in your driving experience."

Mrs. Harper said, "Well, I don't know why you two never let me drive. I'm the safest driver out of all of us."

Both women in the front seat groaned.

"I am," insisted Mrs. Harper. She looked at Andi and patted her on the knee. "You know, I taught Jerry how to drive. His parents didn't have the nerves to handle that young boy. That's why I'm so calm sitting in the back seat while Gladys swerves all over the road."

In the next moment, everyone in the car jerked to the left when Mrs. Davis made a last-minute decision to switch lanes, and then they were thrust forward when she hit the brakes at the stop light.

A moment after the car came to a stop, Andi heard a loud bang that sounded like a gun shot and felt the car shake.

"Get down!" Andi yelled as she dropped her head to her knees, instinctively covering her head with her hands to protect herself from shattered glass in case the bullet hit the windshield. Heaven only knew who was shooting at her now.

"Don't worry dear," said Mrs. Davis from the front seat. "Lola just had a little hiccup."

Andi sat up and placed her hand on her chest and resumed breathing. "Little hiccup? Who's Lola?"

Mrs. Barzetti sighed from the front seat. "She trying to tell you that her car backfired. Lola is her ridiculous name for this old car." She turned to look at Mrs. Davis. "You really should get a new car, Gladys."

Mrs. Davis' mouth dropped open. "Shh, she'll hear you and comments like that hurt her feelings." Mrs. Davis took her left hand off the steering wheel and gently rubbed the dash. "Don't you mind her, Lola. I'm not trading you in sweetheart. I'll never get another car. Til death do us part."

Mrs. Harper leaned over to Andi and whispered, "Til death do us part is right. The way Gladys drives, she and Lola are both leaving this world together in a flame of glory." She reached into her purse and pulled out a small butterscotch candy wrapped in a golden cellophane wrapper. She held it up to Andi and asked, "Butterscotch?"

"No thank you," Andi said as Mrs. Davis whipped the car into a space at the parking lot of the senior center.

"Looks like a full house today," Mrs. Barzetti said.

"Duh. Everyone here is hoping to get body pressed by the hot instructor," Mrs. Harper said.

"That's so ridiculous," said Mrs. Barzetti.

"Admit it Hazel, you used to think he was hot before you hooked up with your very own Santa Claus," said Mrs. Harper, with the candy clicking against her teeth.

"Ethel!" Mrs. Barzetti said as she whipped her head back to glare at Mrs. Harper. She looked at Andi and said, "Stanley Coleman and I are in a respectable, romantic relationship as you very well know." She glared at Mrs. Harper before turning back around in her seat. "I suppose some people might find the self-defense instructor attractive. Single men are a rare find at our age, but he's a player."

"I wouldn't mind if he played me," Mrs. Harper said as she winked at Andi.

They all got out of the LeSabre and headed into the building. The large structure had several smaller classrooms. Andi followed The Golden Girls as they entered the room with the large cardboard "Self-Defense" sign taped to the door. There were about a dozen women already in the room crowding around a white-haired man who had to be in his early eighties. Douglas Kinser was probably a very attractive man back in the day and was obviously used to handling all this female attention by the look of things.

Andi leaned over to Mrs. Barzetti and said, "Do they have an age limit for these classes? I think I might be too young to participate."

Mrs. Barzetti patted her arm. "Nonsense. You're with us, you'll be fine."

Great.

Douglas asked everyone to sit down in the folding chairs lined up at the back of the room. "Alright let's get started. I think I know just about everybody here except you, young lady." He looked at Andi with his brows raised.

Mrs. Harper said, "This is Andrea Sloan. She's family and works as a repo agent for my grandson at The Repo Doctor. She's run into some sticky situations so we thought it would be good if she could learn a few self-defense techniques."

"Well good. I'm glad you're here. The earlier you learn the basics the better. Everyone deserves to feel secure. Now for the rest of us that are a bit older than this young lady, as our bodies age, we get slower and weaker which makes us more vulnerable to attacks from criminals. These physical limitations don't have to keep you from defending yourself. Today, we're going to go over defense basics. One of the most important things you can do is be aware of your surroundings. If someone asks you to give them your purse or your wallet, do it. Your life isn't worth the price of whatever material things you're carrying."

"If anyone approaches you in a threatening way, stand tall, make eye contact, and use a loud voice when you're talking to them. Your loud voice will draw attention to you. Criminals are looking for an easy target. If you act strong and tough, they're more likely to pass you by for someone who won't put up a fight."

"If they do come after you anyway, you can also use things that you are carrying with you as a weapon." He walked over to a woman wearing a hot pink t-shirt that read "Queen of the Machine in Vegas."

Douglas said, "Stella's got this beautiful cane which can be used as a powerful weapon. May I borrow it a minute?"

Stella blushed and handed her purple metal cane to Douglas. He held it in his right hand pretending to use it to steady himself. Then he said, "Imagine someone approaches me to ask for my purse."

All the women laughed, and he smiled and winked at the group. *The man was definitely trying to charm the ladies.*

"I can do this to block a strike from the side," he said as he lifted the cane to his side. "I can use it to push my attacker away by striking him with the bottom of my cane in the chest." He turned to face the women, "And of course, you can always bring your cane in an upward thrust and strike him in the groin." He made a dramatic face with a pained expression and said, "Ouch. That hurts just thinking about it."

Mrs. Davis leaned over to Andi and whispered, "I like this cane maneuver. I've got one tucked in my umbrella stand. I'll have to start using it again."

Douglas returned the purple cane to Stella and then turned to the group. "You can use just about anything you're carrying as a weapon–especially a purse or even items in your purse. If you've got pepper spray, you can spray your attacker's eyes. Take a look in your purse and tell me what you've got."

Mrs. Davis reached in her purse and pulled out a peacock printed scarf. "What about this?" she asked.

Douglas approached her and said, "What a beautiful scarf. May I borrow it?"

"Sure, it's a good color on you," Mrs. Davis said and winked at him.

He chuckled and said, "You're a funny gal," and took the scarf.

"You can wrap each end around your hands and drape it around your attacker's neck and choke him like this," he said, demonstrating the move on the imaginary assailant in front of him.

He returned the scarf and said, "Thank you. Anyone else?"

A woman at the other end of the row yelled out, "Oh, I have spray deodorant! In the eyes, right?"

Douglas beamed. "Yes! Anyone else? What about car keys? Any ideas?"

A woman with bright red hair said, "Yes, hold them in your hand with your index finger over the largest key and you can aim for the eyes, right?"

"Yes! Good! You can also aim for the cheek. Remember a heavy purse swung at your attacker's head also works well." Douglas clapped his hands together once and said, "Okay. Next, I'd like you to pair up, and we'll practice some simple moves that you can use on your attacker no matter his size."

Once everyone had a partner he said, "I need a volunteer. How about you Ethel?"

Mrs. Harper had a big smile on her face as she stood inches in front of him and put her hands around the back of his neck like she was ready to pull him in for a kiss.

"Um, that's a little too close for this demonstration. I do offer private lessons for anyone interested," he said and waggled his eyebrows which caused several women in the class to begin giggling. "Why don't you stay right there while I take a few steps back." He gently removed her hands from his neck. He pointed his finger to his chest. "This time, I'll pretend to be the attacker. I'm going to grab you from behind, like this," he said as he leaned in with his right hand to demonstrate the move. "To break out of my grip, you're going to put your hand over my knuckles like this." Douglas reached over to Ethel's hand and put it in the proper position. "Then you're going to swing your arm and grab my wrist. Once you're in this position, push down. Your attacker will drop to the ground. Even if he tries to stand up, he won't be able to from this position. The goal is to disengage from the attack and escape."

"I've had several suitors drop to their knees to propose back in the day, Douglas," Mrs. Harper said with a laugh, "but never quite like this. I feel so powerful."

"Exactly. Once you get your attacker in this position, you want to leave the area and get to safety." Mrs. Harper released her grip and Douglas stood up. "Okay," he said as he brushed the dust off his knees. "I want you to try it with your partner. Be gentle. You don't need to take anyone all the way down to the floor."

The students practiced the move with their partners as the instructor walked around the room and made corrections in their positions and hand grips. After everyone had plenty of time to practice, he showed them how to survive a knife attack. He asked Mrs. Barzetti to come up and help him demonstrate.

"What would you do if I came at you like this with my knife?" he asked her while he waved a toy rubber knife in front of her.

Mrs. Barzetti reached into her purse and pulled out her handgun and pointed at the floor. "Well, I would just pull out my 357 Magnum and suggest that you put that knife away and instead of spending your time threatening sweet, harmless old ladies, you should go take confession with Father Mark."

Douglas' mouth dropped open and the entire class gasped.

It took just a moment for the instructor to regain his wits. "That's certainly one way to approach the situation, but you don't want to shoot your attacker, just disarm him."

Mrs. Barzetti mumbled, "Speak for yourself."

"Hazel, please secure your gun in your purse, and I'll show you how to disarm a knife attack without a gun."

Mrs. Barzetti rolled her eyes. "Seems like a lot of extra work, if you ask me, but okay. Show me what you've got."

Douglas grinned at his feisty student and then walked through each step with the class. Then he passed out practice rubber knives and had the students practice. After he walked around the room observing everyone, he asked, "Okay, does anyone have any specific questions?" Douglas brushed the palms of his hands together ready to wrap up the class.

Mrs. Davis raised her hand and asked, "Can you show us what to do if we're held at gunpoint?"

Douglas gave a charming smile. "Well Gladys, that's for a more advanced class. We won't be covering it today."

Mrs. Davis was not impressed and placed her hands on her hips. "That's exactly what our Andrea needs help with. She always runs into hoodlums who are pointing guns at her. As a matter of fact, she was held at gunpoint just last month."

Douglas frowned and studied Andi. "What exactly do you do for a living?"

"I'm a Repo Agent," Andi said.

"Oh, I see," Douglas said, and nodded.

Mrs. Harper offered her two cents. "There's nothing to see, Douglas. She works for my grandson at The Repo Doctor. It's a perfectly respectable business."

Thanks, Mrs. Harper.

"It's her personal life that is dangerous," Mrs. Harper continued. "She was attacked in her living room by a gangster. You know, the guy responsible for killing Santa at the mall?"

Douglas studied her. "I thought you looked familiar. You're the elf, right? Aren't you kind of tall for an elf?"

Andi sighed. *Not the elf thing again. What did people have against a tall elf, anyway?*

Mrs. Barzetti stepped forward and glared at Mrs. Davis. "I told you this Self Defense class was a waste of time. Let's go and take Andi to the shooting range where I'll teach her how to properly defend herself with my Magnum."

"Now just hold your horses, Hazel." Douglas glanced at his watch and looked back up at her. "I can show the girl what to do." He reached over to his supply bag and pulled out a neon orange pistol. "Step up here, Andrea, and I'll show you how to safely disarm a gun."

Oh terrific.

Andi stood about three feet from the instructor. He placed the rubber pistol in Andi's hand and asked her to point it at him.

"I want to emphasize that the best thing to do is just give your attacker what they want. The only reason to attempt to disarm the attacker is if you believe that they are going to kill you."

The instructor walked the students through the steps to remove the pistol. It seemed very easy as he talked through each step, and the pressure he placed on Andi's hand caused her to release the rubber gun.

"Okay, now it's your turn," he said as he stepped back and pointed the prop at her.

"Look lady, hand over your purse, or I'm going to kill you," Doug said in a deep, firm voice.

Andi just stared at the gun, unable to move or speak. It didn't look like a real gun—not like the gun Peter had pointed at her. She knew it wasn't real because she had just held it in her own hand. For the love of all that was holy, why wasn't she able to make herself move or even speak. She couldn't even look away from the ridiculous orange object. She heard Mrs. Barzetti calling her name, but it sounded strange and distant, like her neighbor was talking to her from another room. That's when the trembling began. It started in her hands and quickly spread to her entire body.

"Oh, for heaven's sake, sweet child, you're shaking worse than my washing machine when it's overloaded," Mrs. Barzetti said as she stepped in front of Andi and wrapped her in a comforting hug. "It's alright. You're safe. Everything is going to be okay."

Douglas nodded and said, "I've seen this with a few of my Army buddies that saw some action overseas. Poor, kid. She needs to talk someone." He turned his attention to the rest of the class. "Well, looks like that will be all for today. Go home and practice the moves we went over in class. Stay safe and alert out there, ladies."

The trembling finally stopped leaving Andi feeling like a wet noodle. "Thanks, Mrs. Barzetti," Andi said as she stepped out of Mrs. Barzetti's embrace feeling awkward and embarrassed. "I'm good now."

"I had no idea you were having issues, young lady. You should have told me," Mrs. Barzetti said, frowning.

Andi shrugged. "I just don't like guns, I guess."

Mrs. Barzetti said, "Well, I suppose you don't when they're pointed at you. I think Douglas is right. You might need some counseling."

"What the girl needs is some ice cream. That makes just about everything a little better. Let's go to the shop next door," Mrs. Davis said. "My treat."

Chapter Six

Two hours later, Andi stepped out of the shower and dried off. She slid on her fleece bathrobe, tied the matching belt around her waist, and wrapped her hair in a towel on top of her head. Cooper was picking her up in an hour, so she had plenty of time to get ready for the Police Charity Ball. Using her hand towel, she wiped the sink mirror to clear away the steam.

She let out a scream when she looked at her face in the mirror.

Sweet baby Jesus. What were the red blotches all over her face? Had her shower been too hot? Andi gingerly touched the red rash that was present on her forehead, cheeks, nose, and chin.

Or worse, could this be caused by her nerves? Were those hives? Yesterday, she'd had the awful flashback with Detective Kendricks, and this afternoon she'd frozen and got all shaky when the instructor pointed that ridiculous fake gun at her.

She leaned in closer to the mirror to examine the red rash on her cheeks. This wasn't some instant acne breakout, was it?

"Ben!" she hollered. His bathroom was directly above hers on the second floor. She'd heard the water running from the upstairs sink, so she knew he would hear her.

Three minutes later, Ben burst into her room wearing nothing but a pair of classic navy-blue dress slacks with the same-colored satin stripe down the outseam of each leg. He stood in front of her bathroom; the left side of his face covered with a foamy beard of shaving cream.

"What's wrong? Where's the dress? What did you do to it?" he asked in an accusing tone holding a razor in his right hand.

He stared at her bathrobe for a moment in confusion and then his eyes widened as he looked at her face. "Holy hell! What happened to your face?"

"I don't know!" she reached up to her cheek and rubbed it. "It itches so I don't think it's some kind of freaky spontaneous acne breakout."

His mouth dropped open and he grabbed her hand and pulled it away from her cheek. "Don't scratch the rash! Look, it's on the back of both of your hands too." He studied her hands. "This looks like poison ivy. I had it once when I was a kid. Nasty stuff." He raised his brows. "Have you been playing in the woods? That's how I got it."

"No, of course not." Andi blew out a breath. "There must have been poison ivy in the brush I removed from my repo this morning." She stared in horror at the back of her hand that she'd just used to rub her face before turning back to the sink to wash them with soap and water. "Is it contagious? I've never had it before."

"You should be fine after your shower. You must have gotten some of the oil from those branches on your face and hands." He leaned in to look closer. "Maybe a lot of oil." He stepped back and shook his head and let out a breath. "You're going to want to put gloves on and drop the clothes you were wearing directly into the washing machine."

Andi dried her hands and stared at her reflection in the mirror. "I can't go tonight looking like this."

Ben's eyes widened. "Sorry, but you don't have a choice. I've spent too many days working on that gorgeous creation hanging on your closet door for you to decide you're not going."

Andi gaped at him. "Hello! No one will be looking at your dress because they'll be gawking at my face." She lifted her hand to rub the itch on her nose and stopped herself when her fingertips were a few inches from her chin. "Plus, it's so itchy. How am I going to stop from rubbing my face all night?"

He pointed to her and said, "Don't move. I'll be right back." He turned and abruptly left her room.

She looked back in the mirror over the sink and leaned in closer, searching for blisters. There was no way she was showing up looking like this. She knew Ben would be disappointed, but what other choice did she have?

Ben came racing back to her bathroom doorway and handed her a glass of water and two small pink pills. "Here. Take these Benadryl. They should help with the itching."

Andi swallowed the pills and chased them down with a couple gulps of water.

"Thanks Ben, but this doesn't solve my problem," Andi said as she pointed a finger to her face.

"Oh, that's nothing that a little foundation can't fix."

Andi frowned in the mirror at her reflection. "I don't think so."

"I've got some fantastic concealer upstairs that will cover that rash, and no one at the country club will have clue that you wrestled poison ivy and lost. You'll see. Have I ever steered you wrong?" Ben asked.

Andi rolled her eyes.

Ben smiled. "Stop worrying. There's no way Cinderella is going to miss the ball tonight."

"I've gotta tell you that I don't feel much like Cinderella," Andi said, trying not to scratch her face and hands.

Ben laughed. "Not you, silly." He placed his hand on his bare chest over his heart, "I mean me. Everyone there is going to fall in love with my gown that you'll be wearing, and I'll be overwhelmed with new clients." He began swaying. "Plus, I'll dance the night away with my gorgeous man. Oh, and I get to order drinks for a change rather than serve them. Tonight," he said as he spread his arms wide, "I'm going to be the toast of the ball." He lifted his chin and grinned.

He looked ridiculous with half of a white foamy beard, but Andi couldn't help but smile at the look of joy on his face. She sure hoped the Benadryl and concealer made a huge improvement because she didn't want to do anything to ruin this evening for him.

"Fine," she said. "Bring me your concealer."

***

Two hours later, Ben was sitting in the large ballroom at the country club at a round table that was draped with a gold lamé tablecloth. In his opinion, the lamé was a bit much. He would have gone with something a little more subtle—maybe a cobalt sateen. The blue would have accented the color in the gorgeous five-piece china place setting in front of him. He discreetly lifted his empty coffee cup and glanced at the pattern description printed on the bottom—Wedgewood Renaissance. *Nice.* Oh, to be able to afford to have an elegant china setting like this for when he and Daniel entertained at their place.

Their place. He still couldn't quite believe he was moving in with the sexy, kind, fun-loving man next to him. He glanced over at his love who was laughing at something Cooper was saying. Daniel looked positively splendid in his snug charcoal grey suit with the navy/white Churchill dot tie. Of course, Ben had picked it out for him so that they would coordinate this evening. They make such a handsome couple. They really needed to go to more formal events like this one just to have an excuse to get dressed up.

Daniel draped his arm on the back of Ben's chair so that it casually brushed against his back and leaned in to ask, "By that smile on your face, I'm guessing you're having fun already. They haven't even brought out the food yet."

Ben grinned and gave him a brief kiss on the lips. "Maybe just a little. I've always wanted to come here."

Daniel's smile widened like it always did whenever Ben showed him affection in public. "I'm glad, Benji. Just so you know, it's my intention to seduce you with food, alcohol, and dancing before I take you back to our place where we can properly celebrate you moving in."

Ben leaned toward Daniel so that he was inches from his lips and whispered, "You had me at our place, but I am a sucker for romantic gestures. Bring your best, Drummer-boy."

He leaned back and watched as Daniel's face shifted from fun flirtation to hot sexual tension in an instant. Ben resisted the urge to climb on top of Daniel's lap and devour him with kisses. That would have to wait until they got home. The image evaporated instantly when he felt a sharp pain on his right leg.

"Ouch," he said and turned and glared at Andi. "What the," was all he managed to say before Cooper said, "Hey Jess, you remember my friend Danny. This is his boyfriend, Ben Palmer."

Jess? Ah. Cooper's ex. Ben looked over at the attractive blond standing in front of the seat next to Cooper, her arm linked with a Mr. Tall Dark, and Handsome like he was an accessory. Jessica Rainier was classically beautiful with long, professionally styled hair, a flawless face, and a fabulous designer gown that accentuated all her perfect features. *Damn.* Now he was beginning to appreciate Andi's insecurity about Cooper's past relationship with the woman. Jessica was not only beautiful, but she also had excellent fashion sense. Every heterosexual man here was probably fantasizing about removing her exquisite gown. Hell, he was even imagining disrobing her, but only so that he could get a better look at the fabric and the gown construction. He was almost certain she was wearing Tom Ford. Maybe someday his label would be that big.

"Hi Danny. It's great to see you again," Jessica said gracefully shifting her long silky hair over her right shoulder before turning her attention to Ben. He couldn't help but notice that she moved in a choreographed way so that she was positioned in the most flattering posture. It was so subtle that only a fashion designer like himself or maybe a professional photographer would notice it. He wondered if she had ever done any modeling.

"Ben, it's nice to finally meet the designer that so many of my friends have been raving about. Maybe you could create a unique gown for me sometime. It seems like I'm always needing something formal to wear with all the charities I'm involved in. I don't ever wear a gown more than once." She ran her hand down the exquisite black sequin gown and said, "Even one as beautiful as this Tom Ford."

I knew it was a Tom Ford.

Never one to miss an opportunity for business, Ben put on his most charming smile—the one he used while tending bar that yielded the biggest tips–and winked at Jessica. He reached into his pocket, retrieved a business card, and handed it to her. "Give me a call love when you're ready to stop wearing clothing off the rack. I'll be happy to create a one-of-a-kind gown for you."

Was this a ridiculously bold statement considering the gown she was wearing probably cost close to ten thousand dollars? *Hell yes.* But designers had to exude complete confidence in their work in order to sell it to their clients, and he was absolutely self-assured in the quality of his innovative designs and gorgeous, detailed sewing skills.

"Andi is wearing one of my unique creations this evening." He turned to Andi and asked if she would mind standing up so Jessica could see it. She gave him one of her subtle looks of annoyance before flashing her waitress smile to the rest of the table. After she stood, she slowly turned so everyone could see all the fabulous detail of the gown. He had to admit that the gown fit her beautifully. She was stunning.

"See how the gown flatters her tall frame. The halter bodice accents her elegant, slender shoulders. The lace overlay is seductive in a classy way. I'm especially pleased at the design of the open back. Sexy, yes?"

"Definitely," Cooper said, and Ben grinned down at him.

"Exactly! Finally, the georgette layer in the maxi skirt gives her the illusion of floating across the ballroom floor when she dances." Ben let out a breath and clapped his hands together in front of him. He loved this dress like he loved each garment he designed.

He turned his attention to Jessica in time to see her eyes narrow in a flash of anger, no doubt because everyone's attention was on someone other than herself. He knew her type. Her irritated expression was quickly replaced with a forced, fake smile. "How nice," she said before her eyes widened and she stared at Andi. "Wow! What happened to your face?" Jessica tried to disguise the laugh that burst from her as a cough. "Excuse me," she said after clearing her throat.

Rude.

Ben looked over at Andi.

Uh oh.

The concealer was covering the redness of the rash, but her neck was now blotchy and flushed. That always happened whenever she was embarrassed or angry—two emotions that usually occurred simultaneously with her. The bumps from the poison ivy were still visible through her makeup, but only if you studied her face looking for flaws.

Back at the house, he'd assured her she looked fine, and she really did. His exquisite gown was certain to be the focus of everyone's attention. Cooper had promised her that a little poison ivy couldn't detract from her loveliness. The guy was a true romantic, and Ben adored him for it. Leave it to Jessica to make a socially awkward remark and take pleasure in it. *Really, just because you had money wasn't a guarantee you had class.*

Jessica turned to her handsome date who was frowning at her, his expression clearly a reaction to her faux pas. Oblivious to any of it, Jessica said, "Noah, maybe you could refer Andi to a dermatologist to help with her adult acne." She glanced at the table and said, "Everyone, this is Doctor Noah Burke." She looked at Cooper and said, "He's one of the top doctors in the emergency department at Roanoke Memorial Hospital."

Oh girl, you are so obviously trying to make Cooper jealous. Ben glanced at Cooper to see if her words had the desired effect on him, but the darling wasn't even looking at Jessica. He was on his feet standing next to Andi in solidarity. He'd placed a hand on her bare back and was cupping her fisted hand in his other hand no doubt trying to keep her from reaching over and slugging Jessica. *Smart man.*

Dr. Hottie left Jessica's side and walked over to Andi to get a closer look at his newly assigned patient. Ben guessed ER doctors were never really off-duty. When he stood in front of her, Andi lifted her chin in her usual defensive way and said, "It's not acne, just a little poison ivy that I picked up when I was repossessing a car this morning." She shot Ben an accusing look as if this was his fault. *Please.*

The good doctor had been studying the bumps on her chin but looked up into her eyes.

"Wait, are you the Repo Girl?" he asked. "The one who's always finding dead bodies?" He grinned as he studied her face. "Yes. The tall mall elf. Of course." He smiled wider and looked her up and down. "I have to say, those newspaper photos of you don't do you justice. You're much prettier in person."

"I have to agree with you, doc," Cooper said and leaned in and kissed her temple.

Jessica cleared her throat. "Noah, honey, be careful. You might catch it."

Noah smiled and looked over at Jessica like he might reassure a young child in the ER. "The rash itself isn't contagious, just the oil from the plant." He turned back to Andi and said, "I suspect you've showered all that off before you put on this pretty dress. Would you mind if I take a look at your hands?" he asked.

Andi held out her free hand when Cooper didn't release the one he was holding. Ben noticed that their roles were reversed and now Andi was holding Cooper's clenched fist. Picking up on the tension, Noah glanced at Cooper cautiously before holding Andi's hand and examining the rash. "You must be really sensitive to poison ivy. This is a classic textbook case. Wish my interns were here, so I could show them."

"Noah!" Jessica said in an urgent tone.

Dr. Hottie looked up at her while still holding Andi's hand.

She pouted and said, "Come sit with me. I think they're about to start."

"Be right there," he said to Jessica before turning back to Andi. "Wait until I tell the guys back at work that I ran into you this evening! Maybe later you can share some stories about your job." Grinning, he shook his head and said, "Repo Girl." He gave her hand a gentle squeeze and said, "Let me know if this doesn't clear up in a day or so. I can prescribe some cream to help with the itching." He glanced at his annoyed date and quickly walked back to his seat sitting next to a frowning Jessica.

Just as everyone was seated, another couple joined them, filling the last two seats at their table. The man had to be Cooper's brother, Phil. The two men resembled each other, although Philip's hair was much shorter. His blond companion must be Brittany, Phil's wife and sister to Jessica. Ben studied them both as Cooper made the introductions. The sisters shared the same hair and eye coloring, both women were exceptionally beautiful, but Brittany's smile seemed more genuine and in Ben's opinion, that somehow made her the more attractive of the two. Clearly the newlyweds were very much in love. Ben glanced at Daniel. He knew exactly how they felt.

Phil turned to Cooper, "We just made it. Mom asked us to stop by the house and bring her notes. She left them home this morning and was frantic when she realized she didn't have them."

Just then, the lights dimmed and a striking older woman standing behind a podium spoke into a microphone. She introduced herself as Mrs. Barnett of the Barnett Foundation. *Cooper's mom.* Ben had never met the woman that was pushing for a Cooper-Jess relationship, but he'd heard enough about her from Andi to get a pretty clear picture. He'd asked Daniel about Cooper's mom since he'd met her once. Sweet Daniel never had a negative thing to say about anyone, so it was no surprise that he'd only said that she wasn't a fan of the band. Understatement based on what Andi had shared with him. *Andi.* Ben glanced over at his best friend to catch her frowning as she watched the stage. Ben shook his head and sighed. Relationships were tricky enough without having to deal with a disapproving family. Daniel reached under the table and took Ben's hand in his, giving it a gentle squeeze.

Ben looked at his love and smiled to reassure him. Daniel was so in touch with Ben's moods and always seemed to know just what he needed. Daniel's lips lifted on one side and his eyes crinkled as he lifted Ben's hand and gave it a gentle kiss. Daniel had the kindest eyes—Ben could stare into them for hours.

Thank God their relationship didn't have to undergo the kind of family censure that Andi and Cooper dealt with from his family. He and Daniel hadn't done the meet the parents thing yet. It helped that their families lived a thousand miles apart.

"We are proud to support our local police department in the Roanoke Region through this event as well as other fundraisers that we hold throughout the year. Thank you so much for coming this evening. I hope you enjoy the food and dancing. Several of the officers and detectives are here, so you'll have the opportunity to talk to them and learn firsthand why we have the best police force in the country. I'd like to introduce Police Chief Kevin Bogen and Captain Robert Carlson."

Mrs. Barnett stepped aside, and the police chief spoke for several minutes describing their plans for the upcoming year and several initiatives they had begun within the community. He asked the other detectives and officers to line up on the stage. Men and women filled the small stage area. Ben immediately recognized the king of the Norse gods, Detective Kendricks. He looked quite unhappy to be on stage.

Mrs. Barnett took the podium again and requested a standing ovation for the police officers before dismissing them from the stage. Then, she invited everyone to enjoy the evening four-course meal. With the wave of her hand, servers paraded into the room with large trays of food.

Oh, how Ben wished this night would last forever.

***

Oh, how Andi wished this night would end already.

At least Ben finally got to see the dreadful Jessica in her passive aggressive performance. She couldn't wait to talk to him about it. *If he makes her a custom gown, I hope it makes her hips look huge.* They'd finally finished the four-course meal. Thank goodness Phil and Brittany were at their table, too. Jessica had just dragged the good doctor away to show him off to someone she knew, and Ben and Daniel got up to dance. They were so adorable. Andi felt an itch on the tip of her nose. As she reached her hand up to scratch it, Cooper intercepted her hand in his. She watched as he pressed a kiss to her palm—one of the few spots on her hand that didn't itch.

"I shouldn't have come tonight. The Benadryl has helped some, but my face still itches."

Looking into her eyes as he continued to hold her hand in his, Cooper grinned as he said, "Here, let me distract you. Dance with me." He stood up and pulled gently until she was standing up pressed against him. Still standing next to their table, Cooper held her close and began swaying to the music.

He sighed. "I finally get to hold you in my arms. Is this better?" he asked as he wrapped his arms around her waist. "Ben's a genius. You in this dress, Andi." He began gently moving one hand up and down her bare back. "So damned sexy."

Oh God. This was definitely better. She closed her eyes for a brief moment, inhaling his delicious cologne. She reached her arms over his shoulders to pull him even closer. "Mm-hmm," was all she could manage in response. When he held her like this, she was lost. Ben had said earlier that his gown would make her appear like she was floating on the dance floor. She felt like she was as she danced with Cooper.

He continued to hold her close, swaying to the music, leading her to the left away from the center of the room.

When Andi opened her eyes, she realized that Cooper had maneuvered them between the last two tables near the exit. "What are you doing? We're not even on the dance floor, Rockstar."

"I know. Look, we couldn't leave without a dance, right? So, I'm slowly dancing you over to the exit. We made an appearance. Hell, I don't even know how we made it through dinner. I should get some sort of award for being able to keep my hands off you this long. I've been thinking about getting you out of this dress ever since I saw you in it when I came to pick you up." He nuzzled her neck for just a moment and then whispered in her ear. "Let's sneak out while no one is looking. I want to take you back to your place and get your mind off all that itching. What do you say Margarita?"

She looked at him with a smile. "How can I refuse such an offer?"

"Cooper, what on earth are you doing?"

Oh lord. She'd recognize Mrs. Barnett's voice anywhere.

Andi heard Cooper sigh, and then twirled Andi into a dramatic spin which had her laughing before he pulled her close to him again.

"Just dancing with my girl," he said smiling at Andi and then gave her a wink. He looked at his mother while he continued to hold Andi close to him. They swayed gently as he said, "You almost missed us. We were just heading out."

Mrs. Barnett rolled her eyes and sighed. "You can't leave yet. I need you to go on stage to announce tonight's raffle winners."

Cooper sighed and released his embrace on Andi, but still held onto one of her hands, linking his fingers in hers so that she wouldn't escape. *Mind reader.* That's exactly what she was considering.

"I'm sure Phil will do it if you ask him. I'm taking Andi home because she's not feeling well."

Mrs. Barnett stared at their linked hands with a frown before returning her gaze to her youngest son. "Oh, I'm sure Andrea won't mind waiting a few minutes longer so you can do this one thing for me. After all I've sacrificed for you, why do you always insist on making me feel like such a horrid person when I ask for your help? Really Cooper, it's such a little thing that will only take a few minutes."

Mrs. Barnett returned her attention to Andi with a critical eye before turning back to Cooper. "Honestly Cooper, you fuss over her too much. Andrea really doesn't look any worse than usual."

Gee, thanks. Andi could feel her waitress smile slide into place. She was getting lots of practice tonight. Cooper tensed beside her.

"Mother, don't be rude." He took a slow deep breath and released Andi's hand only to wrap it around her waist and pull her to his side. "You're quite right. Even when Andi is under the weather, she still manages to look beautiful. I'm sorry, but I can't help you this time. I'm taking her home."

Based on Mrs. Barnett's expression of shock, Andi guessed Cooper rarely said no to his mother. Mrs. Barnett placed her hand over her heart, and when she spoke, her voice pitch was higher and faster. "Well, I see. You've left me in quite a bad spot Cooper. I'm not sure what I am going to do." She looked around a bit frantically. "I don't know where Phillip has run off to. I have to make the announcement now, but there's no one left."

Cooper's hand squeezed Andi's as his entire body seemed to tense while he held her close to his side.

"Why don't you just announce the drawing?" Cooper asked with a sigh.

"Me?" Mrs. Barnett shook her head. "Oh no. It wouldn't be appropriate. I'm the Mistress of Ceremonies. The raffle is sponsored by Barnett Investments. This needs to be done by one of the executives."

"So ask dad to do it."

"Oh please. You know your father barely tolerates these events. He'd never agree to it." Mrs. Barnett nervously clasped her hands together in front of her while she looked tenderly at her youngest son. "Please help me with this dear." She glanced at Andi and said, "He'll only be a few minutes, Andrea. I promise to deliver him back to you immediately." Mrs. Barnett gave her a small shy smile, before returning her attention full blast to her son. "Can you find it in your heart to help me out this one time?"

Cooper stood stiffly next to Andi. *Poor guy.* He cleared his throat and said, "I'm really sorry mother. I am taking Andi home now."

The look on his mother's face was one of disbelief. Normally, this moment would be rather satisfying, but when Andi glanced over at Cooper, he looked completely miserable. Andi kissed him on the cheek and said, "A few more minutes won't make that much difference. Why don't you go help your mom out? I'll wait here, and we can leave as soon as you're finished."

He turned to face her. "Are you sure? I'm certain they can manage just fine without me." He glanced over at his mom with a flash of irritation on his face.

Poor guy. He'd no doubt been dealing with that all his life. Cooper turned back toward Andi. Looking into her eyes, he said, "I love you. We don't have to stay if you want to go home."

Oh my. It still amazed her how much she loved this man. Andi leaned forward and gave him a gentle, soft kiss on his beautiful lips.

"I love you too," she said in a whisper. Then, she gave him a playful shove on the chest and said, "Now, go announce a raffle winner, so you can take me home."

He just shook his head ever so slightly, a look of wonder on his face. Then he leaned in and gave her a fierce, searing kiss that sent heat racing from her lips all the way to her toes. He stepped back, a little breathless and pointed to her. "I'll be right back for you." Grinning, he looked over at his frowning mother. "Okay mother. Let's get this over with."

As Cooper and his mother headed towards the stage, a server with a tray with champagne filled flutes walked by and offered one to Andi. She gratefully accepted it and took a sip.

Mrs. Barnett clearly hates me. She sipped some more of the champagne.

Is it me specifically she has a problem with or is it because she still had hopes of Cooper and Jessica ending up together? Andi took a larger swallow of the bubbly liquid.

On paper, Jessica and Cooper should be a perfect match. They were childhood friends, their fathers are business partners, both are ridiculously beautiful, run in the same social circles, and now that Phil and Brit are married, they are in-laws. Jessica will forever be a part of Cooper's life. Ugh, now that's a depressing thought. Andi frowned as she took another drink from the crystal flute.

Except that Cooper and Jessica had tried several times to make things work romantically and it never stuck. Andi took a gulp of the champagne and sighed.

Because despite everything, Cooper loves me. A lot. Her lips curved up just a little with that thought. And thank heavens he did because her Rockstar had pushed his way into her life and gone and stolen her heart. Andi emptied the remaining liquid into her mouth and swallowed.

Whoa. Her head suddenly felt so light, like the bubbles had all floated up from her stomach and were collecting at the top of her head, trying to escape. Her scalp felt tingly and suddenly the room was spinning. Was she drunk? From one little glass of champagne? That was ridiculous. But there was no denying that the room was spinning faster, and as Andi tried to maintain her balance, the floor began shifting below her feet.

There was an empty table just a few steps ahead. If she could make it there, she could sit down until whatever was happening to her passed. She took a couple steps forward, but the movement only made things feel more unsteady. *Oh no.* She was going to fall. Reaching out desperate to grab on to something, anything, Andi's arms flailed wildly at her side as she only found air. It was no use. Just as she was tumbling backwards, she hit a solid, warm wall. *What? That doesn't make sense.* The wall was too far away from where she had been standing. She glanced down in front of her and saw large arms wrapped around her waist. *Huh.*

"Easy there Sloan. Are you drunk?" asked a deep, familiar male voice in her ear.

"Thor?" she asked. *What is he doing here?*

He chuckled and then said, "Yeah, well I guess that's a yes. Do you think you can make it to that chair? It's only a few steps in front of you. I can either hold onto you as you step forward or I can carry you. What's it going to be?"

Mm. Carried off by Thor sounds nice—like a fantasy come true. But this wasn't a fantasy. She shook her head to try to clear it, but that movement only made her feel dizzier. Closing her eyes to stop the spinning, Andi ordered herself to snap out of this fog now. *Concentrate.* She opened her eyes and looked around. Music was playing, people were dancing, there was a large police presence. She was at the Police Charity Ball and not starring in some Marvel Avenger movie. She glanced down and noticed someone was holding onto her waist and pressing her back against his solid body.

"Hey," he gave her a gentle shake. "Are you still with me?" he asked. His voice serious with a hint of concern.

Holy Mary Mother of God. That definitely isn't Thor, but Detective Kendricks using his interrogation tone. Had she called him Thor? Again? She could feel the heat rush to her face as mortification crept in. Well, that helped pop some of those annoying bubbles that were making her feel light-headed.

She cleared her throat. "Um, yes Detective. I seem to be having trouble walking. I'd appreciate your help to the chair."

How pathetic. Who needs help to reach a chair a few steps away? She was going to have a hard enough time looking him in the eye after this. Of course, if he had to carry her, she'd never be able to face him. Oh, she hoped her legs would cooperate. She took a careful step forward. It was so much easier this time, with someone holding her upright. Andi continued taking careful steps until they reached the chair. Then, he held her with one arm and pulled the chair out for her, helping her into it.

Kendricks sat down in the chair next to her and repositioned it so that she was facing him. He studied her eyes and then looked at her face. Frowning, he picked up her hands turning them over and looked up each of her bare arms. Then he placed an index and middle finger on the inside of her wrist at the base of her thumb and looked at his watch. He released her wrist and placed his elbows on his knees and looked up at her.

"Are you having trouble breathing?" he asked, studying her face.

"No," Andi said. Why would he ask her that? She had trouble standing not breathing.

"Want to tell me what's happened? You act like you're drunk, but based on your skin, it looks like you're having some sort of allergic reaction.

"No, and I can't be drunk. I only had," Andi paused and looked down at her hand. She slowly lifted her right hand up and raised her index finger. She concentrated on her index finger for a minute before looking into Kendricks' concerned blue eyes. His eyes were such a beautiful color of blue. She was sure he must have like a zillion girlfriends. She looked back at her finger. What was she saying? Oh yeah. "One glass of champagne and then whoosh, the room started spinning."

Andi moved her finger in circles and then began swaying in the chair. "Oh my."

Kendricks reached out and grabbed her by the shoulders to steady her in the chair. Then he gently leaned her back.

"I see. What about the rash on your face and hands? Are you allergic to seafood or something?"

Her eyes were wide, and she leaned forward. "No." Andi looked down at her hands and then back at Kendricks. "It's poison ivy, but don't worry. It's not contagious anymore," she said in a loud whisper, slurring her speech. She frowned. "And it's not adult acne like Jessica said." Andi scowled. "Cooper's ex-girlfriend is not the nice person she pretends to be. Don't be fooled by her, Kendricks." She shook her head. "I got the poison ivy during a repo this morning."

"Of course you did," Kendricks said.

"It was so itchy, and my face was really red and blotchy earlier. I wasn't going to come tonight," Andi said as she looked out on the dance floor and smiled. "But Benny made me this gorgeous dress." She looked down at it and touched the fabric of the bodice with her fingertips. "Isn't it beautiful?" Leaning forward, she said, "He worked so hard on it. Did you know he wants to work as a full-time designer someday?" Andi spread her arms wide and said, "A world famous designer!" She began to tip to the right.

Kendricks quickly reached for her and straightened her again before she fell out of the chair.

"Ben and Danny are so cute together, don't you think?" Andi pointed to them dancing in the center of the room. "Danny just asked Ben to move in with him." Andi frowned. "I'm going to miss Ben." She looked up at Kendricks. "He's not just a roommate. He's one of my best friends." She could feel her eyes fill with tears. She bit her lower lip. She didn't want to feel sad right now or cry in front of the detective. Andi looked away and brushed away a tear that had escaped her left eye.

"Andi, look at me," Kendricks voice had that no-nonsense tone.

She looked back at Detective Blue Eyes. A laugh escaped from her lips. *Detective Blue Eyes—Ha, I didn't think of him as Thor!* Andi tilted her head and tried to focus on him. She couldn't call him Detective Blue Eyes either. That would be very embarrassing.

"Your eyes are sooooo blue, Detective. I've never asked you if you have a girlfriend. Do you?"

"Andi, that one glass of champagne was all the alcohol you've had tonight?"

"Yes, Detective…" *Blue Eyes* she said in her head and placed a hand over her lips as she began to laugh.

His frown deepened. "Did you take any medication for the poison ivy?"

"Ah, no fair Detective. I answered one of your questions. Now, it's your turn to answer my question," she said, her words came out thick and slow.

He sighed in frustration. "What question?"

"Do you have a girlfriend?"

"No," he answered in a clipped tone. "Your turn."

Andi laughed and tilted her head. "Aw, Detective, you know I have a boyfriend. His name is Cooper Barnett, and he's up there." She pointed to the stage at Cooper and then leaned in and whispered, "but his mom doesn't like me very much. In fact, I'm pretty sure she hates me. She doesn't think I'm good enough for her son."

Andi sat up straighter and lifted her chin. "But I am good enough." The people that were important to her loved her just the way she was, and she loved them back with her whole heart. *That's all that really matters.*

A wave of sadness swept through her, and she looked into Detective Kendricks' blue eyes. "But I wasn't good enough to keep my mom around. Did you know that my grandparents raised me? I was only a few weeks old when my mom left, so I don't remember anything about her. She never contacted us after all these years. My sweet grandparents worried about her until the day they died." Andi felt the pain again in her heart. *Why after all these years did it still hurt so much?* She frowned and looked down at her hands. *It's my fault she left. Maybe, if I'd never been born…*

Kendrick let out an explicative and said, "Sloan!" in his tough, frustrated tone. He lifted her chin with his finger so that she was looking at him. "This is important. I need to know if you took any medication to treat the poison ivy."

Andi thought a minute, scrunching her face in concentration and tilted her head. *Medication?* She raised her brows and said, "Yes. Benny gave me two pink Benefiber pills."

"Benefiber?" he asked. "Do you mean Benadryl?"

Andi frowned. "Yes, that's what I said."

Kendricks nodded. He waved a server over to the table and ordered a bottle water and a coffee. When the server left, Andi leaned in and said, "I don't like coffee, but maybe I'll have another glass of that yummy champagne." She raised her hand and yelled, "Champagne please?" Andi began looking for the lovely server that gave her the flute earlier.

Kendricks reached for her raised hand and placed it on her lap. "I think you've had enough champagne. You need to hydrate."

"Fine," Andi grumbled and then she looked at him. "So, why no girlfriend detective?"

He raised a brow. "That's a rather personal question, Sloan."

"Pft, after everything we've been through together? We're good friends, aren't we?" she asked looking up at him with a smile. "It's not like I'm involved in one of your homicide cases. We're just a couple of friends having a conversation. You know, you don't always have to be so serious and professional." She tried to raise her eyebrow like he always did but couldn't quite manage it.

"What are you doing with your face?" he asked. "Are you having a seizure?"

Seizure? She burst out laughing. "No, never mind."

Kendricks reached behind his neck and rubbed it.

The server returned with their drinks. Kendricks opened the bottle of water and handed it to her. "Drink," he commanded.

"Did anyone ever tell you that you are kind of bossy, Detective?" Andi lifted the bottle to her lips and took a couple swallows of the water. It tasted pretty good even if it wasn't champagne.

Kendricks sipped his coffee.

She studied him. "Sooooo, have you ever been in a serious relationship, Detective?"

He raised his eyebrow again and sighed. "You're not going to let this go, are you?"

Andi grinned and said, "Nope."

He looked over at her and said, "Fine. I was engaged six years ago. Jenny decided she didn't want to be married to a cop, so she ran off to Vegas and married my former best friend. I hear they're still together and have a couple of kids."

Andi's eyes widened. "I'm so sorry."

Kendricks shrugged. "It's for the best. Some people are just not cut out for a relationship."

Andi took a drink of her water and said, "It was her mistake and has nothing to do with you. Jenny is obviously a fool to walk away from a great guy like you."

Kendricks frowned and said, "Yeah, I'm sure that's it."

Andi put her hand on his shoulder and Kendricks looked up at her. "I'm serious, Kendricks," she said with a slur. She waved her hand at him, "I mean, for goodness sake, you look like Thor. You're smart, honest, kind, brave, patient, and responsible." She stared into his eyes. "You're an all-around amazing guy and a good friend." Andi leaned forward a little unsteady and put her index finger to his chest. Very slowly she said, "And one day some woman is going to come around and knock your feet right out from under you." Andi leaned back with a satisfied smile and laughed. "And you won't even know what hit you." She took another drink of water. "I can't wait to see that."

Kendricks couldn't help but laugh back. He shook his head and took a sip of his coffee. "I have no doubt you'll be there, Sloan. You always seem to show up unexpectedly in my life."

Then he turned to her. "You know, you should take your own advice."

Andi laughed. "What, some woman is going to knock my feet right out from under me?" Still smiling, Andi pointed her empty water bottle at him. "You know, that already happened to me with Detective Richardson."

"Don't remind me." Kendricks was back to his no nonsense, seriousness. "No, I'm talking about when you mentioned that you didn't think you were good enough for your mom. You need to take your own advice."

Andi hated talking about her mom. She didn't even remember mentioning her to him. She rolled her eyes and then held onto the table so she wouldn't tumble out of the chair. "What wisdom is that, Detective?"

"That leaving you was *her* mistake and has nothing to do with you. She obviously didn't know that she was missing out on having a relationship with an amazing daughter when she walked away from you."

Andi stared at Detective Blue Eyes for a moment. He was serious. *Oh my God, that is the nicest thing anybody has ever said to me.* Her eyes filled up with tears and she lunged forward, wrapping him in a big hug and holding on tight. "Thank you," she said and began to sob into his chest.

***

Kendricks was surprised—*understatement*—when Andi flung herself into his arms. He instinctively wrapped his arms around her to keep her from sliding off his lap and falling onto the floor.

That was a big mistake.

Okay, not the part about keeping her off the floor, but damn, her dress had no fabric in the back. For the second time tonight, he was holding her close to his body and unlike yesterday morning at the repo lot when they'd both had layers of insulated coats between them, this time his hands were on the bare skin of her open-backed, sexy as hell dress. His palms were pressed against her back and that brought all kinds of unwanted images—most involving them tangled together naked.

What the hell am I thinking? She's in love with her boyfriend and she sure as hell wouldn't be in my arms like this if she weren't impaired by the dangerous combination of Benadryl and champagne. If she remembers any of this conversation in the morning, she'll undoubtedly regret it.

But Andi had somehow managed to breakthrough his protective shield—the one he'd built around his heart after Jenny broke it. He'd even fortified the protective barrier after he'd been burned last year when his former partner betrayed him and the badge with her criminal activity. He genuinely cared about Andrea Sloan, and he hadn't felt that way about another woman since Jenny. *Shit.* Still, he couldn't help but enjoy this beautiful, strong, determined, caring, sexy woman in his arms, even though he knew full well that she was in love with another guy. He sighed.

Speak of the devil, that guy was on his way over here now, and from the look on his face, he wasn't too happy about seeing Andi in Kendrick's lap, not that he blamed him.

"Kendricks, what the hell are you doing?" Cooper asked, his expression held a combination of confusion, rage, and hurt all at once.

"Calm down Barnett. This is not how it looks," Kendricks said. He couldn't do more than talk reason with the guy, what with Andi on his lap, crying into his shirt.

At the sound of Cooper's voice, Andi lifted her face from Kendricks' suit and wiped her eyes with the palm of her hand. "Oh hey. You're back."

"Jesus, what the hell happened? I've been gone less than twenty minutes." Cooper said. He squatted in front of Andi and gently cupped her face. Now he just looked worried.

Andi and Kendricks both replied, "Champagne."

"What?" Cooper asked, clearly confused.

Andi leaned back onto Kendricks' chest and closed her eyes. "I'm just going to rest my eyes a minute before we go home, 'kay?" In the next instant, she was sleeping soundly.

Cooper narrowed his eyes at Kendricks, disgust and accusation in his tone. "Did you drug her or something?"

Kendricks shook his head. "No. Apparently, she took some Benadryl earlier this evening and then drank a glass of champagne. I saw her wobbling and caught her before she fell. I sat here with her to make sure she was okay until you got back. She drank a bottle of water, so that should help some. I think she just needs to sleep this off, and she should be fine by morning."

"Why the hell was she crying? Did you threaten to arrest her again?" Cooper asked. "You know, she really hates when you do that."

Kendricks sighed and said, "Of course not. You can ask her about it in the morning, although I wouldn't be surprised if she didn't remember any of this." Kendricks said, looking down at the woman sleeping in his lap. She was out cold, but her breathing seemed regular, so he didn't think she needed a trip to the ER. He looked back at Cooper. "Listen, I know you're upset. Why don't you get her coat and things, and I'll help you carry her out to your car."

He watched Cooper's emotions morph from defiance as he glared at Kendricks, to concern when he looked at Andi, and finally to acceptance. "Fine. I'll just be a minute."

Fifteen minutes later, Andi was buckled in Cooper's car. Kendricks said, "Well, I'd better head back in and make the rounds, or I'll get grief from my Captain."

Cooper looked over at him and said, "Thanks for looking out for Andi. I knew she wasn't feeling great, and I should have just taken her home. I appreciate you making sure she was safe."

"Of course." Kendricks said and began walking back towards the building. He turned back to Cooper and said, "Listen, I know you really care about her."

"Damn right. I love her," Cooper replied a bit defensively.

"I can see that. Maybe you can talk her into speaking with a professional about what happened at Christmas. She's definitely still suffering from post-traumatic stress from it. She might start sleeping better if she can talk with an expert."

Cooper nodded. "I will. Thanks."

Chapter Seven

"Hey sleeping beauty," Cooper whispered.

Andi felt a kiss on her forehead and smelled the intoxicating combination of minty mouthwash and Cooper's cologne.

"Mmm," Andi said. "Not so loud. My head hurts." It was currently throbbing to the rhythm of Uptown Funk.

"No doubt," Cooper said. She could hear the smile in his voice. "I brought you some ibuprofen and water that will help with that. Then you can go back to sleep."

Her mouth was dry, and she'd do anything to get rid of the pounding. She opened her eyes, squinting up at her Rockstar. He was dressed in a suit and tie, looking gorgeous as usual. She slowly sat up and swallowed the two pills he gave her with a couple of big gulps of water.

"Besides the headache, how are you feeling?" he asked as he sat next to her on the bed.

She downed the rest of her water, set her empty glass on the nightstand, and leaned back against her headboard. "Okay." Andi glanced down at her hands and made a face. Her rash was still there, but at least it wasn't itchy. She would be skipping the Benadryl today.

Oh God—the Benadryl and champagne. Spotty images of last night came flashing through her mind like a handful of puzzle pieces tossed on the table—not enough to get a complete picture of the evening, but enough to see some of the details of her alcohol induced state. She closed her eyes and shook her head. When she opened them, Cooper was looking at her with compassion in his eyes.

"Oh Cooper. I'm so sorry I ruined our evening. After you left with your mom, I drank the flute of champagne completely forgetting about the Benadryl I took earlier in the evening."

Cooper's lips lifted on one side. "My mother has that effect on people. You wouldn't be the first to turn to alcohol after a conversation with her."

Andi leaned forward and put her hand on his arm. "The alcohol hit me hard. Please tell me I didn't throw up in your car again," she paused and said, "or ruin Ben's dress!"

Cooper looked at her and said, "I'm happy to report that last night was a vomit-free evening, and both my car and your dress came away unscathed."

Andi leaned against the headboard and released a breath she didn't realize she'd been holding. "Thank God," she murmured.

"But I was kind of surprised to find you on Kendricks' lap crying into his suit." His tone was a mix of hurt and confusion.

Andi stared at Cooper, trying to make sense of that last sentence. In the next instant, more bits from last night were freed from the locked passages of her mind. *No, no, no.* Andi covered her face with both hands. She'd called Detective Kendricks Thor again. Her stomach turned when she remembered telling him his eyes were blue and had even asked him if he had a girlfriend. *Sweet Baby Jesus*—this was too embarrassing. Andi frantically searched her memories about sitting on his lap. Her mind was blank. *Oh lord.* If she was lucky, maybe she'd never see the detective again. *Ha, I'm not that lucky.*

Cooper reached out and gently moved her hands away from her face and held on to them in a comforting gesture. "Do you remember why you were crying Andi? What did he say that upset you?"

She didn't remember much beyond talking to him about his love life. *Oh my God.* She was pretty sure she'd given him advice. Everything after that was pretty much a blur.

"I don't remember. Are you sure I was on his lap?" Andi asked, hoping she'd misunderstood him.

"Oh yeah," Cooper said with a serious tone. "Trust me, I'm not likely to forget that image anytime soon."

Andi reached out and touched the side of his face, caressing his cheek with her thumb. "I'm so sorry that I hurt you. I honestly don't remember much after drinking the champagne," *except for some awkward and embarrassing comments that I might have said about his blue eyes and relationship advice.* Andi closed her eyes and scrunched her face trying to remember. This wasn't helping the pounding in her head. She opened her eyes and looked at Cooper. "Can we talk about this later? It's hard to think with the pounding in my head."

"Sure," he said and smiled tenderly at her. "Of course." He reached over and took one of her hands in his. "I know you weren't yourself last night. It's just that I happen to be madly in love with you, so seeing you in the arms of another guy makes me a little crazy. I love you Margarita," he said before leaning forward to kiss her lightly on the lips.

"Love you too, Rockstar," Andi said as she wrapped her arms around him in a warm hug. "So much."

He held on to her for a moment before leaning back to glance at his watch. "Shit, I've got to head to work so I'm not late for a meeting." He stood up and walked to the bedroom door and turned to look at her. "Drink plenty of water and try to get some rest. Do you still feel up to meeting me for our lunch date today at 2pm?"

"Wouldn't miss it. Farmburguesa at the Grandin, right?"

"Yes. I'll see you there," Cooper said and then he was gone.

She heard him close the front door and start his car engine. Closing her eyes for a moment, Andi blew out a breath. *Well, there's no sense trying to go back to sleep now.* She got out of bed, took a shower, dressed, and continued drinking water. The ibuprofen was already working because her headache had transitioned from pounding to a light buzzing background pain. She studied her face in her bathroom mirror. Applying Ben's concealer helped disguise the poison ivy rash, but her eyes were bloodshot, watery, and sensitive to the light over her mirror.

Walking out to the kitchen, Andi opened the back door to let Dodger inside. Cooper usually fed and let Dodger outside in the mornings when he slept over, which was more often than not lately. You could tell a lot about a person by the way they treated your dog. That was one of the many things she loved about the guy. Dodger sat, mostly, wiggling his entire body because he was excited to see her and even more happy to receive the treat she had in her hand.

"How's my best boy?" she asked him before she gave him a treat. The little snack disappeared in his mouth, and he wiped away any remaining crumbs with his large tongue. Dodger danced around her as she fixed a cup of tea and cut a slice of Mrs. Barzetti's pumpkin bread. When her tea was ready, she took her cup and the slice of pumpkin bread over to her kitchen table and opened her laptop.

Please let this be an easy repo. She didn't have the luxury of taking a sick day, not with Ben moving out. If she found a replacement roommate in the next two months, she'd be fine. God how she hated the thought of having to find another human that she could actually tolerate well enough to share her home. Dogs were easy, she thought as she absently scratched Dodger behind the ears. And she'd lucked out with Ben. He was hilarious and they'd become friends while working at Star City Bar & Grill. When her grandparents died in that car accident and she was struggling to pay the bills, Ben had offered to rent her old room upstairs. Oh, how she was going to miss him.

Andi opened a manila folder that had the paperwork for a White Hyundai Tucson belonging to thirty-four-year-old Bradley Foster. She unclipped the car key from the folder and tucked it in her front pocket. At the time of the loan, Bradley was an assistant manager at Bingley Furniture Company on Electric Road, and he was three months late. *Aren't they all?* She looked at her kitchen clock. It was Monday and the furniture store wouldn't open until 10am. It was way too early to try to retrieve the Hyundai.

While she opened the folder for the next job, Andi heard someone knock on her front door. Dodger immediately ran to the living room, ferociously barking. He was far better than any high-end alarm system.

Who would possibly come by the house this early? It was not even eight o'clock. Maybe Ben forgot his key? He was supposed to move the rest of his things this morning.

Looking through the door window, Andi saw the back of woman with long, straight dark hair capped with a fuzzy knit hat. She was facing the street, looking at Mrs. Barzetti's place. Maybe she was selling something, and Mrs. Barzetti had scared her off with her rifle. That thought made Andi smile. Well, she looked harmless enough. Plus, Andi had Dodger for protection, although he was more likely to kiss the woman to death if she gave Andi any trouble. Andi unlocked the door and opened it.

At the sound of the door, the woman turned to face Andi and gasped, covering her mouth with her gloved hand. Most of her face was covered, the upper half by a pair of expensive-looking large, framed sunglasses that concealed her eyes, and the gloved hand that covered the lower half of her face.

"Can I help you?" Andi asked. The question came out automatically, old habits from her waitress days.

The woman lowered her hand, which Andi could see was shaking, and asked, "Are your grandparents home? I need to speak with them. It's urgent."

My grandparents? "I'm sorry, do I know you?" Andi asked.

The woman glanced nervously behind her towards the street as if she was expecting someone to show up. "Do you mind if I come in a minute? I can explain everything inside."

"Sorry, but I don't let strangers inside my house."

The woman bit her lower lip and considered Andi for a few seconds. "You don't know me, but I'd know you anywhere Andrea Sloan." She gingerly took her glasses off, and the first thing Andi noticed was that this woman had a huge shiner on her left eye. Andi could tell she'd tried to cover it up with makeup, but she didn't have Ben's special concealer to cover the dark purple bruised swollen skin that surrounded an eye that was barely visible. It was when Andi took in the rest of the features of the woman's face that her heart nearly stopped.

Holy Mary Mother of God. It was almost like looking in the mirror, well, except for the black eye, and if you added seventeen years to the reflection.

"I know I have no right to ask, but can I come inside. Please?"

Breathe, she reminded herself. Andi opened the door and stepped to the side to allow her only living relative inside. How many times had she imagined her mom coming home? Andi used to dream of opening the front door and her mom would run inside, tell her how much she'd missed her, pick her up, and swing her around. She would say that she loved her so much, that she'd made a terrible mistake when she left her, but she was back home to stay, and they would make up for all the lost time together. Grams and Pop would be so happy to have their daughter back home, safe and sound, and together, they'd all live happily ever after.

Andi had given up on that dream ten years ago on her fifteenth birthday. Most of her life, all she ever really wanted was her mom to come home. Once, she'd prayed to God every night for an entire month, and just to make sure her prayers were answered, she prayed a special Novena to St. Anthony—the saint of lost souls—to return her mother to her family where she belonged. *Nothing.* And now her grandparents were gone, so there would be no sweet reunion for them.

Andi felt a surge of unbearable sorrow and regret build up in her chest, but she shoved it down. She would not cry in front of the woman who had broken all their hearts. Taking a deep breath, Andi closed the front door and locked it. Dodger was dancing around her mother and attempting to sit for attention. The woman laughed and bent to pet him. "Oh, aren't you a big sweetheart? I always wanted a dog when I was growing up, but Daddy was allergic." She stood up suddenly, her smile fading as she looked at Andi. "Oh no, Daddy doesn't live here anymore? Is he in assisted living?" she asked.

What? Andi felt numb and sort of disoriented. None of this felt real. Her mother was here, in Andi's living room, petting her dog and talking to her like they were acquaintances or something. *Maybe I'm dreaming? It felt more like a nightmare.* Andi absently walked past her to the kitchen and said, "Let me get you something for your eye."

Her mother followed her to the refrigerator. Andi pulled a bag of frozen sweet baby peas out of the freezer. Then she reached down to the second drawer by the sink and automatically picked out a dishtowel. Wrapping the towel around the peas, she handed it to her mom. On autopilot, Andi said, "Here, put this on your eye. Why don't you sit at the table, and I'll get you something to drink. Would you like a cup of hot tea?" She checked the countertop. Good, Ben hadn't taken his coffee maker yet. "Or I can make coffee?"

"Tea would be great, thank you."

Andi switched the kettle on and turned to see her mother standing next to the kitchen table, holding the towel wrapped bag of peas on her left eye as she studied at all the framed pictures hanging on the wall. About one-third of them were of Andi's grandparents with Kitty—her mom. The remaining photos were of Andi with her grandparents, several included the Golden Girls with Andi, and a half-dozen with Mags and Ben. Her latest additions were the photo with everyone around her table last month for Christmas dinner and her favorite selfie with Cooper. When she saw Kitty wipe a tear from her eye, Andi quickly turned around and busied herself preparing the tea. She felt a burst of rage fill her chest. How dare Kitty cry, pretending that she cared about any of them. After all, she's the one who left them. She could have stayed here. Heck, she could have even come back after a decade or so, and still have been welcomed home with open arms. That welcome expired after her grandparents died.

Andi had just finished making the tea for them both and set the cups on the table when she heard the front door open. Ben yelled, "Lucy, I'm home!" in his best Ricky Ricardo voice.

Oh thank God Ben was here. "Um, I'll be right back," Andi said to her mom and ran after Dodger to greet Ben in the living room.

Carrying a large stack of flattened moving boxes with a roll of packing tape balanced on top, Ben pushed the front door closed with his foot. Dodger was greeting Ben with his usual vigor when Andi ran up to him and whispered, "Help me."

Color drained from his face, and he whispered, "Is someone in the house? Now?"

Andi nodded and Ben dropped the boxes and pulled a box cutter from his back pocket, holding it with both hands in front of him. He motioned to the floor and whispered, "You grab the packing tape in case we need to tie him up."

She shook her head. "No, not a burglar. It's much worse. My mom is here."

Ben closed his eyes, put a hand on his chest and let out a long breath. As he carefully put his box cutter back in his pocket, he pointed a finger at her. In a quiet tone, he said, "Don't you ever scare me like that again."

She put her trembling hand in his, whispering, "Feel my hand. I'm a mess. The woman walked out on me when I was only an infant and shows up on my porch this morning with a nasty black eye. She's sitting in my kitchen, and I'm a freaking out. You've got to help me, Benny."

He rolled his eyes. "Would you relax? Take some deep breaths and let me handle this. I'm a natural charmer of mothers. You see how I am with our Golden Girls. Watch and learn."

Ben walked into the kitchen with Andi close behind him. He sat at the table next to Kitty and said, "Well isn't this just a wonderful surprise. You must be Andi's mom." He looked at Andi and then back at her mom. "You two could be sisters, the resemblance is uncanny. I'm Benjamin Palmer, Andi's dearest friend and former roommate. My friends call me Ben. What can I call you?" he asked as he extended his hand for a handshake.

Her mother's lips curved just the slightest as she shook Ben's hand. "It's nice to meet you, Ben. My name is Katrina, but everyone calls me Kitty. You used to be roommates with Andrea?"

"Yes. Please, call her Andi. We just adore her. I came by today to finish packing up my rooms. I'm moving in with my boyfriend, Daniel." Ben lifted his eyes upward, "He's absolutely divine. I can't wait for you meet him. I had the two rooms upstairs, one for my bedroom and the other for my design studio. Did I mention that I'm a fashion designer?" He leaned towards Kitty. "In fact, Andi just dazzled everyone at the Country Club last night in one of my gowns. She looked absolutely stunning." He turned toward at Andi. "I gave out more than a dozen cards last night. We were a hit!" he said and winked at her.

Kitty looked a little confused. "If you had the two bedrooms upstairs, where do you sleep Andi?"

Yep, I knew we'd circle back to this. "In the first-floor bedroom."

"Are mom and dad in a nursing home or something?" Kitty asked quietly.

Or something.

Ben shot Andi a look that said *This one is all yours, babe.*

"They were both killed in a car accident just over a year ago."

"Oh God," Kitty said as she stood, pushing the chair back. "I'm sorry. I didn't know. I should have known, but I didn't." She pressed her lips together. "Is it okay if I use your bathroom?"

"Sure," Andi said and watched Kitty walk quickly out of the kitchen.

Andi put her hands over her face. "Oh my God, Ben. I can't breathe." She stood up and began pacing the kitchen. She pressed her hand to her chest, "My heart is racing like it's going to gallop out of my chest." She turned to him and whispered, "Why is she back after 25 years? She's obviously in some kind of trouble, but I can't deal with it, you know? I have too many conflicting feelings. One minute, I want to roll into a ball on the floor and sob and the next minute I want to grab her by the shoulders and scream at her for abandoning us."

She turned to him. "I have to get out of here. I don't trust myself around her just yet. I need maybe an hour or two?" She walked over to him and grabbed his hand like a lifeline. "Can you just give me a little time to figure out what I'm going to say to her? Please Benny?"

"Of course. Breathe. Go. Get out of here. Just remember you do have to eventually come back." He gave her his charming smile. "In the meantime, I'll see what information I can get from her and text you."

"Oh Ben. I love you," she pulled him into a hug. "Thank you. I promise I won't be too long. I just need to get my head on straight." She wiped at a few stray tears that snuck from her eyes.

"We don't have *that* long."

She smiled, grabbed her purse and keys, gave him a quick kiss on the cheek, and ran out the front door.

Chapter Eight

Minutes later, Andi was in her Jeep headed for the City Market downtown. While taking slow breaths to calm her nerves, she called Cooper. Unfortunately, he was still in that meeting he mentioned this morning, so she asked his administrative assistant to have him call her when he had the chance.

She pulled into a free parking space on the street. It was still early, so she had no problem finding a spot to park. Locking her car, Andi walked two blocks to Simon and Maggy's new temporary location across the street from the Farmer's Market. Like Simon, several other food vendors had opted to house their businesses in food trucks during the City Market Building's renovations.

WOW! Simon's truck was impossible to miss. The boxed truck was a bold fire-engine red. An image of a cute cartoon Bull Dog with his tongue hanging out had been painted near the serving window, and there was a large—it had to be at least fourteen feet long—hot dog in a bun on the roof. Andi smiled genuinely for the first time since her mom showed up this morning.

Mags has got to be loving this situation—not. She could always count on her friend to distract her from her own problems. She walked up to the truck. The serving door was open, although clearly they weren't serving lunch yet. Her two friends stood facing each other, Simon with his hands on his hips, and Maggy moving her arms wildly in the air talking about her menu and the fact that there wasn't a good place to put it, or something like that.

"Excuse me, can I get a burger?" Andi asked in a loud voice.

Simon closed his eyes and pinched his nose and spoke in a tone like he'd already explained this a million times before. "We don't serve hamburgers. We only sell hot dogs."

Maggy hit him lightly on the arm, "And smoothies and juices. You have to remember we're in this together."

Simon rolled his eyes and rubbed his arm. "It's a little hard to forget with you hitting my arm constantly, Mary Margaret."

Simon turned towards Andi. "Oh hey, Andi."

"Love the truck, Simon. You guys have a great location too. How's the new setup?"

Simon leaned his elbows on the counter and said, "Great except Mary Margaret can't keep her hands off me. I don't know how I'm supposed to set up for lunch." He winked at Andi.

Maggy shoved him playfully. "Don't you have friers to heat up or something."

"See what I mean?" Simon grinned, thoroughly enjoying himself. "I guess I'll get started. You can see which one of us is pulling all the weight around here," he said and placed his thumb on his chest before standing up and moving to the back of the truck.

"Oh my, Andi. It will be a miracle if I don't kill him before the day is over." Maggy shook her head. "He's in my space every time I turn around."

Andi laughed. "Well, yeah, you're practically on top of each other in that truck. You don't have those convenient vendor stall counters to keep all that unbridled passion safely contained." She grinned at Maggy.

Maggy rolled her eyes. "Don't even start with that again. Simon and I are just friends—barely."

"Mmhmm. You just keep telling yourself that, girlfriend." Andi smiled.

Changing the subject, Mags asked, "Oh, how was the Police Charity Ball last night? Did you have a good time?"

Andi closed her eyes and shook her head. *God, that whole debacle seems like a lifetime ago.* She opened her eyes and grabbed hold of Maggy's hand. "I'll tell you about that later. I came over first thing this morning because I'm totally freaking out. My mother showed up this morning on my front porch."

Maggy's face showed the appropriate shocked expression. They'd been friends since kindergarten, so her best friend knew how much she'd missed having a mom and that she would have done just about anything to have her in her life.

Maggy's expression morphed from shock into the brightest, happiest, 'I've just won the lottery' kind of look. "That's amazing Andi! After all this time, your wish to have your mom in your life finally came true." Mags squeezed her hand as her eyes began to fill with tears.

"Um, no?" Andi said, frowning. How could Mags of all people be missing the point? "I'm freaking out because when she didn't show up by my fifteenth birthday, I let go of that wish. Heck, for all I knew she was dead. I'm sure my grandparents went to their grave hoping that Kitty would come home, but I'd long since given up that dream."

"But she's here now. Maybe at least you'll get some closure. Find out why she left and stayed away all this time. Get to really know her. Maybe even become friends."

Andi already knew why her mom left. She didn't love Andi, and frankly, Andi didn't need that thrown in her face right now. She shook her head. "It's too late Mags. I really don't care what her reasons were. It doesn't change the fact that she not only left but stayed away all this time."

Mags squeezed her hand and said, "Wait right there. I'm coming down." She released Andi's hand and walked to the back of the truck, hopped off the bottom step and ran around to Andi and wrapped her in big hug. "I'm so sorry."

Andi felt the tears begin to flow and she didn't even try to stop them this time. She couldn't have even if she wanted. After crying for a few minutes, Andi stepped back and began wiping her eyes. Mags reached up to the truck's counter and grabbed napkins for them both. "Here," she said as she handed a pile to Andi before wiping her own eyes and blowing her nose.

Andi took a deep breath. "Thanks Mags. I've been holding that in since Kitty showed up this morning with a black eye."

"A black eye? Oh my God. Do you think she's running from someone?"

Andi shrugged. "Honestly, I've been in shock, so I haven't thought much about anything."

"Where is she now?"

"At the house. Ben is staying with her while I figure out what to say to her."

Maggy shook her head. "I can't even imagine what you must be going through."

"Honestly, I never expected to see her. I mean, after all this time, why would she bother to show up now?"

"Maybe she had nowhere else to go, so she came home."

"She didn't even know about my grandparents. I had to tell her."

"Oh Andi, that's awful. Please tell me what I can do to help."

Andi bit her lip and felt her eyes fill up with tears. She smiled and hugged her sweet friend. "You're already doing it," she said squeezing her tight. "Love you, Mags." Andi pulled back and wiped her eyes with another napkin. She puffed out her cheeks and exhaled. "Thank you. I guess I'd better go back home and find out why she came back."

"Love you. Call me later, okay?" Mags asked. "I'm here for you. Say the word if you need anything. I mean it."

Andi smiled. "I will and I know." She began walking back to her car when her phone buzzed. She pulled it out of her coat pocket. It was a text from Ben.

> *OMG. She's been in NYC all this time. She's a dancer! Ex gave her the shiner, but she won't say more than that. Her coat is Burberry and sunglasses are Michael Kors. I am so good I could work for the FBI. I wonder if they have a fashion division?*

Another text came in from Ben.

I love her already. Can we keep her?
R U Okay?

Andi shoved her phone in her pocket. She had planned to head home and face Kitty, but after reading Ben's text, she knew that she wasn't ready. Unlocking her car, she opened the door, sat inside, and turned on the engine. She was so cold that she was shivering. Or maybe that was just her nerves. She turned the heater on full blast anyway.

What had she expected? Of course her mother had created a life for herself over the last twenty-five years. Andi had always liked to imagine that wherever her mom was, she was sad, regretting leaving her parents and baby behind in Roanoke.

Stupid reality. It's just that over the years, Andi had been able to tuck the pain of her mom leaving into a little box and bury it deep enough that she rarely thought about it. That had been working pretty well until today.

Now it looked like her mom left her to live out her dream of dancing in New York City. She couldn't very well do that with a baby. Did she marry and have other kids? Did Andi have a half-brother or sister somewhere in the world. Had Kitty been a loving mom to another child?

STOP! This line of thinking was only going to make her crazy. Her mom's arrival had knocked her out of kilter. She needed to do something normal to regain her footing. Then she could go back and deal with her mom.

Andi pulled out her phone. It was almost ten o'clock. She could drive over to Bingley's Furniture and see if her skip's car was in the lot. Her paperwork was still on the kitchen table, but—she reached into her front jean's pocket— she had the key for the Hyundai. If the car was there, she'd drop it off at the Repo Lot, get Jerry's advice on her mom situation, pick up her Jeep, and then go home whether she was ready or not. Realizing she'd never replied to Ben's question if she was okay, she typed out a quick reply.

> *Not really.*
> *I'm going to pick up a car for a repo job and then I'll be home.*
> *I owe you BIG for this. Love you.*

***

Andi set her phone back in her coat pocket and headed to Bingley's Furniture. When she arrived, she noticed there were four cars parked near the front entrance and about a dozen cars parked on the side of the building—most likely the employee parking. *Bingo.* That's where the white Hyundai Tucson was parked. Andi drove over to the next lot, a busy CVS pharmacy, and parked her Jeep. She walked over to the White Hyundai Tucson and did a quick scan of the area before inserting the key into the door. Andi didn't see anyone in the area, so she tried the lock, sighing in relief when it turned without an alarm sounding. She slid into the front driver's seat, started the car and began backing out of the parking spot. She was driving on Electric Road in less than a minute.

Okay, that was surprisingly uneventful. The tightness in her chest eased immediately. There was nothing like a clean and easy repo to lift a girl's spirits. Reaching over to the console, Andi turned on the radio and began playing some music.

She made a right onto Colonial Avenue and then took several back roads, taking the most direct route to The Repo Doctor lot. As she drove, she thought about what she would say to her mother when she saw her again. Just considering it, made her hands begin to tremble.

What she needed was to a good old-fashioned pep talk to build up the courage to face her mom.

"I can totally do this," she said aloud in the empty car. "I'll just deal with my mother the way I deal with every other challenge in my life. I'll face it head-on with the help of my friends and move through it as quickly as possible. What am I afraid of anyway? It's not like she can do anything that will hurt me more than she already has, right?" Andi nodded her head as she glanced at her reflection in the rearview mirror and said, "Right."

THUMP…THUMP…THUMP…THUMP

Oh no. Recognizing the unmistakable sound of a flat tire, Andi pulled way off the road onto a small section of grass that ended in the woods. At least she was on a back road and not a busy highway. Getting out of the car, Andi walked around the Hyundai, carefully checking each of the tires. By the time she walked to the rear passenger-side of the car, she'd found the problem. The tire was completely flat.

Just great. Well, this wasn't her first flat. She bent down and examined the tire and immediately found the culprit—a large nail in the tire wall. She opened the trunk and found the jack, jack handle, and wheel lug nut wrench stored in the luggage compartment under the luggage box cover with the donut tire. She pulled everything out of the trunk and began to change the tire.

Her grandfather had made sure she knew how to change a tire before she got her driver's license. She loosened the wheel lug nuts and jacked up the car. Once the flat tire was lifted off the ground, Andi removed the loose lug nuts with her fingers. Then, using both hands, she pulled the wheel from the studs and the hubcap fell off and rolled into the bushes. *Great.* Andi set the flat tire on the ground and retrieved the donut spare and installed it on the studs of the hub. After tightening the lug nuts with her fingers, she lowered the car by turning the jack handle. Finally, she tightened the lug nuts with the wrench and loaded the tools and flat tire back into the trunk. Before closing the trunk, she remembered the hubcap that had rolled away.

Andi walked over to the bushes and bent down to retrieve the hubcap. As she reached down to pick it up, she noticed a flash of light on the ground to her left.

Jesus, Mary, and Joseph! The sun was reflecting off a gold signet ring on the pinky of a man's hand. An unspoken scream lodged in her throat as she took several steps back, tripped on a rock and landed in the grass on her butt. Her breathing was shaky and rapid as she scrambled back to her feet. She kept her eyes on the bushes for movement. Nothing.

Okay, calm down, she told herself even as she was running to the driver's side of the car ready to flee the scene and call the police from somewhere safe.

But if she left, would she be able to find this exact spot to direct the police to the body?

What if the guy wasn't dead but only injured, and she was wasting precious time when she could be saving his life?

Or maybe she'd only imagined the hand in the dirt? It was entirely possible she was having some sort of psychotic breakdown. She'd been under enough stress what with the flashbacks from her own near-death experience last month, the combination of Benadryl and champagne last night and the only partially remembered conversation with Detective Kendricks. Add to that a long-lost mother showing up at her door this morning, and hallucination was a very real possibility.

She shook her head to clear it. *Think.*

First, she'd make sure she hadn't imagined the hand. If someone was still in the woods, they would have come after her by now. *Probably.* Just in case, she really should get a weapon. Andi walked to the opened trunk of the car and retrieved the lug wrench, gripping it with both hands. *Okay, you've got this. Probably imagined it anyway,* she told herself as she walked back to the bushes, careful to avoid the rock this time.

Nope. The hand was definitely there with the gold signet ring that had originally caught her attention. It looked like there was some sort of symbol on it with Marino written underneath. Andi took a deep breath. Now that she wasn't totally freaking out, she could see that the hand was attached to an arm. *That's a good thing, right?* She used the lug wrench to move one of the branches and she could see what looked like the rest of the guy's body.

She cleared her throat, "Excuse me sir, are you alright?" *Of course, he's not alright, idiot. He's lying in the dirt.*

She couldn't see any injuries but there was too much brush to get a good view of anything. Using her lug wrench, she lifted the branches that were covering his face.

Oh God. Not again. Now that she could see his face, she knew there was no need to call the paramedics. A chill ran down her spine, and she quickly turned away from the body. Andi closed her eyes and sighed; the man's startled, unblinking eyes were already etched in her mind. *Great.* Another dead gaze to haunt her dreams. *Well, this helps put things in perspective.* No matter how bad her day was going, it was infinitely better than his. She opened her eyes, squared her shoulders, pulled out her cellphone, and called 911.

As soon as she hung up with the 911 operator, her next call was to Ben.

"Hey Benny. I need a favor."

"Another one, already?" he asked. "I'm still in the middle of your last favor."

"I know. I'm sorry. I wouldn't ask, but it's sort of an emergency. Is there any way that you can bring the folders that are on the kitchen table to me right away? I want to have them before the police show up."

"Police? Are you alright? Were you in a car accident or something?"

"More like something. My repo had a flat tire and while I was changing it, I found a dead body in the bushes. I want to have the repo paperwork, so there's no question about what I'm doing with this vehicle. The lender should have already reported their intent to repossess the car, but I don't want there to be any confusion about why I was driving it."

"Holy hell, woman! You need to stop finding dead guys."

Andi blew out a breath. "It's not like I'm purposely looking for them. Can you bring me the files?"

"Of course. I've already located you on my phone app. I'll be right there."

A Roanoke City police car pulled up with lights flashing. "Hey, the police are here. I've got to go. Thanks! I owe you."

"Oh sweetie, don't worry about it. I'm keeping a log." Ben was laughing as he disconnected the call, but Andi wouldn't be surprised if he was serious.

The next ten minutes went by in a flash. Andi showed the officers where the body was and how she found him. They asked her to wait by her car while they secured the scene with tape.

She was leaning against the white Tucson when Ben pulled up in his used yellow Fiat 500. Kitty was in the front passenger seat. *Right, of course.* Andi obviously hadn't been thinking clearly. *It's not like Ben would leave a stranger alone in their house—correction—my house. He's moving out.*

They both got out of the Fiat and Ben handed Andi the paperwork. She opened the door and set it on the passenger seat. "Thanks."

Kitty was staring with a look of genuine concern at Andi. Kitty asked, "Are you alright?"

Andi nodded. *No.* She could handle a dead body a whole lot easier than her estranged mother standing next to her looking like she cared about her.

Ben waved off the question and placed an arm over Kitty's shoulders to comfort the woman like they were best friends.

"Honey, she's fine." In an exaggerated southern drawl, Ben asked, "'This isn't Andi's first rodeo, is it darlin'?" Then he looked over at Andi and, returning to his regular voice asked, "How'd you find this one?"

Andi's mouth dropped open. It wasn't like finding a dead guy was an everyday occurrence. It freaked her out each time and guaranteed those faces would be making an appearance in her nightmares for months to come. At least this person hadn't died right in front of her. Witnessing a murder added an entirely new level of terror to her dreams. When Ben winked at her, she realized what he was doing. Sure, it was an odd way to distract her from her mother's unexpected, unwanted concern, but she'd take this diversion.

Looking at Ben, Andi said, "I saw a flash of light in the bushes when I was looking for the hubcap. It turned out to be the dead guy's signet ring. It had some sort of symbol on it, a crest maybe, with Marino printed below the image."

"Whoa Kitty, are you alright?" Ben asked. Kitty began to sway, and Ben held her up.

"Um, yes. Sorry," she said. The woman was clearly lying and was terrible at it. "Is the body over there? I need to see it." Kitty pointed over by the police tape.

Andi said, "Yes. We won't be able to get very close, and he's mostly covered by the bushes, but sure. Follow me."

The three of them walked over to the bright yellow tape that read "POLICE LINE DO NOT CROSS."

"Oh my God!" Kitty whispered.

Andi glanced over at Kitty. Ben still had his arm wrapped around her mother's waist to make sure she didn't faint. Kitty's lips were trembling, and Ben was staring at Andi, his brows raised, with his WTF expression.

"It's easier if you don't look. Seeing a dead body for the first time can be upsetting," Andi said.

Kitty shook her head. "It's not that. I know him."

Chapter Nine

Kendricks pulled his black Tahoe onto the grassy spot next to the patrol car at the homicide scene. His new partner, Ryan Hughes, was riding shotgun. Sighing, Kendricks turned toward the kid who looked like a high school teen dressed up in a tie and jacket. The rookie detective was so damned excited, he'd not stopped talking since they got into the SUV. *Lord give me strength.* Maybe he could still convince the captain to assign Hughes to somebody else. *Anybody else.*

"Listen, I know this is your first homicide as a detective. I want to lay some ground rules. First, I'm not showing you any special treatment just because your grandfather is the police chief. Got it? I might even be a little tougher on you because of it, but that is only for your own safety as well as mine."

The kid grinned. "Yes, sir, but you don't have to worry about that. I haven't gotten treated any differently than anyone else on the force, and I wouldn't want it to start now."

Kendricks raised a brow. *Right. If the kid really believed that bullshit, he was also delusional. Terrific.* "Second, now that you're a detective, your duties are different, but the risks you face out in the field every day are the same. I expect you to always wear your vest and to carry a flashlight, your gun, and handcuffs always. Do you understand?"

Hughes frowned and said, "But can't I just put the vest on as needed?"

"No, because you won't know when you'll need it, and then it could be too late." Kendricks reached into the back and handed Hughes the bulletproof vest. "A vest saved my life last year. This is non-negotiable, understand?"

"Yes," he said reluctantly. He removed his coat, took the vest from Kendricks, and slid it on, securing it before pulling his coat back on. "Better?"

"Good," Kendricks said before continuing. "Now, this is what's going to happen. We'll both get out of the car, and you will remain silent and simply observe me. You will not speak unless I address you directly, and you will only act when I ask for your assistance. Got it?"

"Yes," he said in a slow exaggerated tone.

Hell, the kid even sounded like a whiney teenager.

They got out of the car and Hughes asked, "Are we going to talk to the patrol officer who arrived on the scene first or interview the witness who found the body?"

Kendricks stared at him and sighed. "What part of remain silent was unclear?"

"Oh, sorry. I thought you meant after we do the interviews, you know, before we examine the body."

Kendricks glared at the kid. "*We* aren't interviewing anyone. Remember Hughes, you're not speaking at all."

"Not even to that woman, Andrea Sloan, who reported the body? Oh, unless we're taking her downtown for questioning. Will we transport in your car or ask her to follow us down to the station?"

Andrea Sloan. This was the third day in a row he'd be seeing the woman and two of those days involved a dead body. He shook his head. He could almost laugh about it except that an image of her in his arms last night crying into his shirt flashed through his mind. *How much of last night did she remember?* Kendricks released a sigh. *Doesn't matter.* He needed to simply focus on doing his job while trying not to kill his new partner. That was going to require his full attention.

Kendricks glared at the kid.

"Right. I'll stop talking now and follow your lead."

Kendricks nodded and sighed as they walked toward the crime scene that was protected by a strip of bright yellow tape. He spotted Andi immediately—not difficult since there weren't that many women who were six feet tall and wore black boots with a two-inch heel. She was standing next to a guy who looked like he was comforting another woman that was slightly shorter than Andi.

Andi should be standing next to her car, waiting to be questioned instead of so close to the crime scene. At least she was on the correct side of the police tape this time.

"Sloan!" he hollered, irritation in his voice.

All three bystanders turned around and both women answered "Yes?"

Two Sloans? For the love of God, he could barely handle one.

Andi was on the left, chin lifted in a challenge. She had a grease smudge on her left cheek that made him want to smile. *Focus.* He immediately identified the male—Benjamin Palmer, the roommate—who stood between the two women. The other woman that answered to Sloan was a few inches shorter than Andi, maybe five foot nine or ten. Her hair was the same color as Andi's only straighter. Her face was partially concealed by large, dark sunglasses. Hell, from what he could see of her face, she resembled Andi. Older sister maybe? Cousin?

Kendricks sighed. "Sloan, don't tell me there are two of you."

Andi stiffened. "Detective Kendricks, this is my mother, Kitty Sloan."

Mother? He took a second look at the other woman. Her sunglasses concealed her eyes, so he couldn't get a good estimate of her age. He noticed a tinge of yellow and light purple that peeked around the edges of her dark sunglasses. He'd bet there was a black eye behind those glasses.

Kendricks recalled his conversation from last night with Andi about her mother. She had said her mother abandoned Andi as a baby, and she hadn't heard from her since. *Interesting.* "I thought you told me you hadn't had any contact with your mother."

Andi forced a smile. "That's true," she said, glancing at the woman to her left before turning her attention back to Kendricks. "She just stopped by this morning for a surprise visit."

That had to be a hell of a reunion. Kendricks pulled out his notepad. "Did you all three discover the body?"

Andi bit her lip and glanced at the white Hyundai before looking back at Kendricks. "No, just me. I was repossessing the Hyundai when I got a flat tire. I pulled over there." She pointed to the car. "As I was changing the tire, the hubcap rolled into the bushes, and when I walked over to get it, I spotted the dead guy. I called 911 and then called Ben because I'd forgotten my repo paperwork." She gave a half-smile. "I didn't want to be charged with grand theft auto."

"No. Way!" Hughes said in slow exaggeration. "You're that Repo Girl, aren't you?" Hughes bumped the palm of his hand to his forehead before dropping it back to his side. "Of course! I should have realized this when I heard your name. The ice cream truck drug bust? The elf from the Santa shooting last month? That's you!" Hughes was grinning and reached his hand out to shake Andi's. "It's so nice to meet you. My grandma and I are huge fans. I'm Ryan Hughes, Homicide Detective."

The kid had said that last part so smoothly that Kendricks wondered if he had spent a lot of time practicing introducing himself as a detective to his reflection in the bathroom mirror. Hughes released Andi's hand and pointed a thumb to Kendricks. "Detective Kendricks is my new partner."

Kendricks scowled at the kid. What the hell happened to his direct order for silence?

"Hughes," Kendricks barked out the name like a drill sergeant.

The kid looked at Kendricks, still a little starstruck from his encounter with Andi. "Can you believe it's the Repo Girl?" Then, as realization washed over his face, Hughes said, "Well, of course you know her. What am I thinking?" Ryan pointed to Andi. "Dead bodies," Hughes said, and then pointed to Kendricks. "Homicide Detective." The kid shook his head, returning the megawatt smile to Andi.

Kendricks was never going to get through this interview with Hughes gushing over Andi. Sighing, he said, "Detective

Hughes, why don't you go interview the officer who first arrived on the scene."

Hughes looked back at him, his face lit up like Kendricks had just promised him they'd get ice cream after they finished up here.

"By myself?" he asked, looking unsure, like this was some sort of test.

God give me strength. Kendricks exhaled and then nodded.

"Yes sir," Hughes said and ducked under the tape to join the other patrol officer.

Kendricks turned back to Andi who was now smiling.

He frowned.

Andi's smile broadened. "I like your new partner, Detective."

Before Kendricks could reply, Ben said, "Whoa Kitty, do you need to sit down?"

All eyes turned toward Andi's mother who was clutching onto Ben as she regained her balance. "I'm sorry, I didn't sleep well last night, and I think being here at a crime scene is making me feel slightly lightheaded."

Kendricks looked at Ben. "You two don't need to stay for questioning. I just need phone numbers where I can reach you, in case I need additional information."

Ben rattled off his cellphone number and when Kendricks looked at Kitty, she stared at him blankly.

"I need your number as well," Kendricks said, his pen ready to record the number sequence.

"I lost my purse last night, and it had my phone in it," Kitty said in a soft, fragile voice.

They all three stared at her. By Andi and Ben's reaction, Kendricks realized that this was news to them.

"Okay," he said. "Where are you staying if I need to contact you?"

Another blank look and then Andi and Ben exchanged a long glance filled with unspoken communication.

"She's staying with Andi," Ben said, breaking the awkward silence while staring at Andi, challenging her to disagree. Ben then turned a charming smile directed towards Kendricks. "I've just moved in with my boyfriend Daniel, so Kitty's going to stay in my old room. We'll swing by the store on the way home and get a pre-paid cellphone. I'll call you with that new number as soon as we get it set up."

Kendricks reached inside his pocket and handed them each a business card. "Here's my phone number."

"Now sweetie," Ben said, speaking gently to Kitty, "let's get you home to rest. You look exhausted."

Kendricks and Andi watched as Ben walked Kitty back to his car.

"So, your mother just showed up this morning after years with no contact?" Kendricks asked and turned to study Andi's face for a reaction. She was frowning as she watched them leave. She looked unsettled, staring after them. He'd seen Andi in a wide range of stressful situations, but this was the first time he'd ever seen her look like this. He felt an overwhelming need to comfort her, so he told her the same thing he'd told her last night. "Her leaving you all those years ago had nothing to do with you. You see that, don't you?"

Andi's eyes widened in surprise for a moment and then her brows furrowed as if she was trying to recall some memory. He knew the moment she remembered their conversation from last night, including her crying into his suit, because her cheeks flushed a deep rose color. The tension in his chest eased a bit. Now she was looking more like herself. Despite her embarrassment, she looked directly into his eyes. That was one of the things he admired about her.

She scrunched her nose and said, "Sorry about last night. I wasn't myself."

Kendricks could feel his lips lift in the slightest hint of a smile. "Oh, I don't know about that. As you pointed out, we're friends. I think you were just a little more forthcoming than you usually are." He arched a brow.

She bit her bottom lip. "Maybe. It helped that I wasn't under investigation for murder at the time." She shrugged. "I obviously told you about my mother." She tilted her head and studied him. "And you shared a bit about your ex, as I recall."

Yeah, and he still wasn't quite sure why he'd done that. She'd been loosened up by the champagne and Benadryl. He, on the other hand, had no such excuse. It was time to steer the conversation away from his personal life.

"I noticed Kitty's black eye. She said she lost her purse and phone. Did she say where she's been all these years?" Kitty Sloan was scared, and his gut instinct and her black eye told him that she was running from something or someone.

Andi glanced down at the ground. "I didn't get to ask."

Hm. Breaking eye contact because she just lied or because she's upset?

Lifting her head like she'd read his mind, Andi looked directly into his eyes and said, "To be honest, I sort of freaked out and left her with Ben. I needed time to figure out what I was going to say to her, you know?"

Kendricks frowned. "And you decided that repossessing the Hyundai would help you figure out how to handle your mom? I'm not sure I follow your logic, Sloan."

Andi crossed her arms over chest. "Well, I needed some sense of normalcy." Uncrossing her arms, she began to pace. "It's been twenty-five years!" She stopped and looked up at him. "I never received a single phone call or note from her my entire life, and she just shows up on my porch this morning?" She blew out a breath. "I'm still kind of freaking out about the whole thing." She waved her hand in the direction of where Ben's car had been a few minutes before. "And now Ben's invited her to stay with me. I'm going to kill him."

"It's never a good idea to confess your plans for murder to a homicide detective," Kendricks said.

"What?" she asked, a confused expression on her face.

"I was just saying that relationships can be messy."

"You can say that again," she said with a frown.

"If I had to guess, I'd say Kitty's on the run. You don't know what kind of trouble she could be running from, do you?" Kendricks asked.

Andi glanced over at the body and looked back at the ground, frowning. "No."

That's odd. Was there something she wasn't telling him? *Probably. Nancy Drew here thought she had to solve all the mysteries on her own. Best to approach this from a different angle.*

"As your *friend*," he said, and okay, maybe he felt a little guilty about using their newly defined relationship to get more information, "you know that you can talk to me about this." He shrugged. "I just know that if I were in your situation, I wouldn't trust her."

She nodded and looked back up at him. "Exactly. Thank you. Finally, someone who gets it. Ben is all fascinated that she's lived in New York City and wears designer clothes. Mags thinks I should be ecstatic now that my long, lost mother has finally shown up in my life." Andi sighed. "Meanwhile, I can't help but wonder why is she suddenly here? What does she want? She didn't even know my grandparents were dead." Andi put pointed her index finger to her chest. "I had to tell her."

Kendricks was feeling a combination of anger on her behalf and protectiveness towards her. *Dammit, maybe we are friends after all.* Well, a friend that he thought about kissing. *Focus.* "I'm sorry. People make selfish decisions all the time with no regard to how their actions impact others. You've been through enough. You shouldn't have had to have that conversation with a mother who is a virtual stranger to you."

She looked at him the way she had last night, right before she'd flung herself into his arms. Kendricks swallowed as he rubbed that itch on the back of his neck. *Focus on the job.* He knew in his gut that she wasn't telling him the whole story. Dammit, it bothered him that she looked over at the dead body when he'd asked about her mom. *Wait, did she just say her mom lived in New York City?*

Kendricks gave her his tough interrogation stare. "Your mother lived in New York City? I thought you said you didn't know where she's been all these years. You *said* that you left the house and didn't get a chance to ask her." He arched a brow.

Andi blanched a moment before lifting that stubborn chin of hers. It would be cute if he weren't so irritated with her. "Ben found out after I left. He texted me that little bit of information. I guess I forgot about it what with finding the dead guy and everything." She shook her head. "Anyway, I should let you get back to your investigation."

He glared at her another moment. "Sloan, why are you being evasive?"

She placed a hand on her chest. "Evasive? I'm not being evasive, detective. I've answered all your questions. If you don't mind, I need to get the Hyundai back to the repo lot." She used her thumb to indicate the white car behind her.

He glared at her.

She lifted her chin and glared back like they were in some sort of staring contest.

Fine. She obviously was not willing to share any more information regarding Kitty Sloan, so he asked her for a few details about discovering the victim. He couldn't help that twist in his gut that told him that somehow, Andrea Sloan was even more involved in this investigation than discovering the body. As she answered, he jotted down notes about the approximate time she'd arrived at the scene and how she'd discovered the body. Finally, he asked her if she'd noticed anything else unusual.

"Well, the dead guy was unexpected," she said with a half-smile.

Kendricks grimaced and was about to reply to her cheeky comment when a smiling Hughes stepped toward them.

"Oh hey, you're still here." The kid straightened his shoulders and pulled out his notepad. "Do you mind if I take your number, you know, in case we have any questions later?" The kid gave her a flirty lopsided grin.

Kendricks rolled his eyes. "I've already got her number, *Detective* Hughes." He then turned his attention to Andi and gave her a meaningful look. "You're free to go. If you should remember anything that would be helpful to our investigation, Ms. Sloan, please don't hesitate to call me."

With a grin, she mimicked the tone he'd taken with Hughes. "Will do," she said with a salute. "I've already got your number, *Detective* Kendricks." She turned on her heel and walked back to the white car. Kendricks frowned. *Great.* She was definitely hiding something, and he knew damn well there was some connection between her mother and this dead guy. He felt it in his gut.

"Wow, she's even cooler in person," the kid said.

Kendricks turned to his partner. "She's got a boyfriend, kid." He needed to remind himself of that fact as much as to inform Andi Sloan's latest admirer.

Hughes' red cheeks belied his next words. "Oh, I'm not interested in her like that. No. I mean sure, she's way prettier in person than those photos from the newspaper, but that would be inappropriate since she found the body and everything. Even if I was interested in her, you know, but I'm not. Pfff, no! I just wanted to make sure we had her phone number as a matter of procedure. That's all."

"Right. So, Hughes, tell me what you learned from interviewing the first responder."

The kid, relieved by the change of subject, spent the next five minutes summarizing the information he'd gathered from the patrol officer. When he'd finished, Kendricks nodded, impressed. "Nice job, Hughes."

"Next, we're going to," Kendricks was saying when he was distracted by the black Ford Expedition that pulled in right next to his Chevy Tahoe.

Just great. He recognized that car—Sanchez with his amazing new partner that loved jelly doughnuts. Sanchez stepped out of the driver's side, walked to the back of his SUV, and opened the door. A large German shepherd hopped out. *What the hell?* Sanchez clipped the leash on the dog that wore a bullet proof vest. *What is Sanchez doing with a K9?*

The grinning detective and his dog approached them. Sanchez turned to the dog and said, "Sitz Bleib," or something like that. *What kind of language was that?* The dog sat obediently and watched Sanchez with complete attention as he removed his sunglasses and placed them on the top of his dark wavy hair. His smile left his face as he said, "Kendricks" with a brisk nod and then turned his attention to Hughes and extended his right hand. With a slightly warmer expression, he said, "You must be Detective Hughes. Looks like you drew the short straw, getting stuck in homicide with this guy. I'm surprised the captain didn't assign you to a more experienced detective, like Dixon."

Kendricks sighed and rolled his eyes.

Hughes spoke up. "Oh, I'm excited to get to work in homicide, sir, and Detective Kendricks is one of the best." The kid glanced down excitedly at the dog. "How long have you had the dog?"

Sanchez's grin was back as he looked down at the dog. "We've only been training together the last few weeks. Gentlemen, let me introduce you to my new partner, Officer Lucky."

Kendricks shook his head.

Sanchez lips lifted slightly. "Even though Narcotics is by far the best department, our cases often intersect like today. Don't worry, Ryan. I'll be able to show you how real detectives work on the crime scene."

Kendricks spoke up. "There's no indication that this homicide was drug related. Why don't you take your new puppy and go to the park and play fetch?"

Sanchez tilted his head. "Hm. You just arrived on the scene, so it's a bit early to rule out drugs, yes? Regardless, the captain requested that I bring my new partner in the field."

Sanchez looked at the dog and said, "Gib Laut," and the dog barked and then growled at Kendricks.

"What did you say to her?" Kendricks asked, taking a cautious step back.

"She was trained in German. I simply asked her to speak," Sanchez said with a laugh. "She obviously can sense your animosity towards me. She's a good judge of character. Lucky added the growl on her own."

Sanchez reached into his pocket and gave Lucky a treat.

"I saw that," Kendricks grumbled.

"I was just rewarding her for speaking when I gave the command," Sanchez said, still grinning.

Terrific. It was bad enough he had to deal with Sanchez. Now he had to contend with a happy Sanchez and his ferocious attack dog. He'd never been a fan of dogs. They were related to wolves – wild, unpredictable beasts.

They all walked under the yellow tape, spoke with the patrol officer, and examined the body while they waited for the CSI unit to arrive.

Kendricks asked Hughes, "What do you think the cause of death was?"

Hughes stepped closer to the body, leaned down to see four dark stains in the front of the victim's purple button-down shirt. The kid began to gag, and Kendricks grabbed his shoulders and turned him away from the body to face the woods where he threw up the entire contents of his stomach.

"Welcome to homicide, kid," Kendricks said, with a light pat on Ryan's back.

Kendricks squatted next to the body, put gloves on and searched the man's pockets for identification. He carefully pulled out a wallet from the guy's back pocket and opened it up. "James Marino–New York Driver's License," he said to Sanchez.

"Marino? New York? I've heard rumors about a new drug supplier from up north. This could be related?"

Kendricks took inventory of his wallet. Twenty-three hundred and forty-five dollars in bills, two credit cards, and a business card for the Xanadu Night Club. He glanced over at Lucky who was sniffing the bottom of the victim's shoes. "You know, CSI is going to be pissed if the dog slobbers on those shoes."

"Relax. She's a professional. She's just picking up his scent. By the position of his body, it looks like he was dumped here."

Kendricks had to agree. "He's not a victim of a robbery because whoever shot him didn't bother with the more than two-grand in his wallet." Kendricks observed the quality of his clothes, noticed the signet ring. *What were you doing in Roanoke, James Marino?*

Lucky barked once and began sniffing, wagging her tail, and pulling to go deeper into the woods. Sanchez grinned. "She's picked up a trail. That's it, baby-girl. What did you find?"

Kendricks glanced over at his partner. *Good.* Hughes looked like he'd recovered from tossing his breakfast. He told Sanchez, "We'll follow you, just in case you run into trouble. The vic looks like he's been here for several hours, so I doubt the shooter is still around, but you never know." Kendricks removed his Glock 22 pistol from the holster and unlocked the safety. "Hughes, stay close behind me."

"Yes, sir," the kid said, excitedly.

The three men followed Lucky as she meticulously sniffed the ground through the woods for about 30 yards. The kid was quiet for a change as he followed Kendricks. The forest abruptly ended at a dirt road where there was a blue Maserati Quattroporte with New York plates.

"Nice ride," Sanchez said, "and all the way from New York."

The trunk was open, and Sanchez barely kept up as Lucky raced towards the car, her nose to the ground. She sniffed the tires, the front door, and then went to the rear of the vehicle. She sat and immediately looked at Sanchez, her tail wagging.

"She's detected narcotics. What a good girl!" Sanchez praised his partner as he reached into his pocket to reward her with another treat. He took out his flashlight and a field test kit, and carefully collected the white residue he found in the trunk. "Looks like this might be a drug deal gone bad," Sanchez said to Kendricks as he secured the kit in his pocket. Then he turned toward Lucky and gave his partner a kiss on the top of her furry head. She licked him on the cheek.

Kendricks holstered his gun and placed a latex glove over his right hand as he opened the front driver's side door. Shining his flashlight, he examined the seat and floor. *Nothing.* He looked under the seats and that's when he spotted it – a cellphone. He turned it screen side up and tried to power it on. *Damn.* It was dead.

Hughes was still quiet. Kendricks pulled out another plastic bag from his pocket and dropped the cellphone inside, handing it to Hughes. "We'll take this back with us as evidence. Maybe when it's charged, we can track the victim's navigation to see if he made any other stops when he arrived in Roanoke. There's a pretty good chance that might lead us to his killer, or at least give us an idea who he was involved with for a drug exchange."

Hughes didn't speak. Kendricks put his hand on his partner's shoulder. "Are you okay, detective?"

Hughes swallowed. "Yes, sir. It's just that was the closest I've ever been to a dead body, you know, that wasn't in a funeral home. I'm sorry that I threw up back there, sir. It caught me off guard."

"Hey, you're not the first, and you won't be the last." He turned to Sanchez. "Looks like we found another section of the crime scene. We need to get this area secured as well."

Kendricks looked at the kid. "Our work is just beginning."

Chapter Ten

Andi gripped the steering wheel of the Hyundai and took a slow deep breath as she drove away from the crime scene. *Sweet baby Jesus, that was a close one.* When Kitty dropped the bomb that she knew the dead guy, Andi didn't have time to get any additional details from her before Detective Kendricks showed up.

How the heck did her mother freaking know the dead guy? Was he someone from the Roanoke area that she'd recognized from her childhood? Or was it someone from Kitty's current mess in New York City. Oh, and there was no doubt that her estranged mother was in a mess of trouble. Even Kendricks had suspected Kitty was on the run from something. It didn't take a detective to figure that out, what with her black eye, no luggage, and no cellphone, she must have been in a hurry to leave.

A small, nervous laugh bubbled out from Andi's chest. *My life has just hit a new level of crazy – long, lost mother shows up, I discover a dead body, and Thor brings up my embarrassing ramblings from last night about my mother.* Andi could feel her cheeks heat-up.

But he'd understood why she wasn't ready to welcome her mother with open arms. He'd understood it because he didn't trust people either. Andi shook her head. Was it possible she was becoming friends with Thor? *I mean, Kendricks?* Oh God, then he'd started asking her about her mom and New York and darn it, he knew she was hiding information. Thank goodness that sweet kid detective came back, and she was able to make her escape. It wasn't like she was protecting Kitty. Andi really didn't know much except that somehow Kitty had recognized the corpse. *It's not like I care about her,* she reminded herself.

By the time she'd parked the car in the Repo Lot and walked into the office, she'd calmed down somewhat. She returned the keys to the completed box and grabbed two more folders from a rather high pile of folders, because hey, the mortgage wasn't going to pay itself. Sitting around feeling sorry for herself wasn't going to get her bills paid.

Andi absently rubbed at an itchy spot on her face and plopped in the chair in front of Jerry's desk. He was on the phone talking to a lender, by the sound of it, and ignored her like he usually did. Frowning, he wrote something down on the yellow lined pad of paper in front of him. Jerry was looking a little frazzled, so she decided to keep her feet on the floor rather than propping them on the edge of his desk like she usually did to annoy him. *Wonder where the girlfriend is?* Andi was glad she wasn't here, mismanaging the paperwork.

Jerry hung up the phone, closed his eyes briefly, and rested his head on the back of his chair. After a long exhale, he opened his eyes and looked at her, glanced at the spot where her feet usually rested, and asked, "Oh wonderful. You've got bad news, don't you?" He tilted his neck until it cracked and leaned forward, resting his elbows on his desk and stared at her. "Okay, I'm ready. Just tell me, so I can fix that, too." He waved his hand over his desk and said, "I'm still cleaning up the hellish mess that Madison made. I mean how much could one person screw up in eight hours? We really need someone to do the office work until I have time to train another repo agent." He pointed to the inbox. "That pile gets bigger every day."

Wow, she wasn't the only one having a bad day. She'd better not torture the poor guy. "Relax, for Pete's Sake. I don't have any bad news about a car. I mean, I got a flat tire in the Hyundai while bringing it in, but I changed it, stumbled across a dead body in the bushes, called the police, answered their questions, and brought the car back to the lot. No damage."

Jerry's mouth dropped open. He closed it and shook his head. "What is it with you and dead bodies?" He pointed a finger at her and said, "You've got to stop finding the damn things. It's bad for business."

It was Andi's turn to gape. "Jeez, Jer, it's not like I enjoy it and go out specifically looking for them."

Jerry leaned back in his chair again and sighed. "Well at least the police didn't impound the car this time around."

Andi looked at him expectantly.

"And you didn't get arrested for murder, so there's that," he added. "Happy?"

Andi leaned forward, resting her elbows on Jerry's desk, cradling her chin in her hands. "Finding the dead guy wasn't even the worst part of my day."

A low grumble sound came from him as he turned his attention to an open file folder at the center of his desk. Jerry was no doubt hoping that he could get rid of Andi if he simply ignored her. She'd have thought he would have learned that that never worked with her.

Andi cleared her throat before she continued to speak in her best impersonation of Jerry. "Oh Andi, I'm sorry that you're having a bad day. What could be worse than getting a flat tire and accidentally stumbling onto a crime scene?"

In her normal voice, she said, "Why, thank you for asking, Jerry. The worst part of my day happened this morning when my mother showed up on my front porch."

Jerry stopped pretending to ignore her and looked up. "Your mother?" he asked. When Andi just nodded, he asked again. "*Your* mother?"

"Yes. My mother. The woman who gave birth to me."

He studied her and then asked, "The same woman who skipped town right after you were born, never to be heard from again, breaking your grandma's heart?"

Andi gaped. "Yeah, how do you know all that?"

Jerry shrugged his shoulders. "You know that neighborhood. Everyone knows everyone's business. My grandma used to talk about it. They worried about you." He gave a half smile. "They still do. I hear they dragged you to a self-defense class at the senior center." Jerry shook his head in disgust.

Andi rolled her eyes. "I don't want to talk about it."

"Squirt, when are you going to man-up and stop letting them meddle in your life."

She gaped. "I could give you the same advice. When are you going to stop letting your grandma set you up on blind dates?"

"Touché." Jerry leaned back and sighed. "Right now, I wouldn't mind if she fixed me up with someone who could handle this paperwork or repo cars." Jerry studied her again and titled his head. "Why would your mom show up after all these years?" He narrowed his gaze at her. "What does she want?"

Andi shrugged and stood up. She was feeling too anxious to simply sit. "I have no idea. I didn't stick around long enough to ask her."

"Oh, Jesus, please tell me you didn't leave her alone in your house. She's probably robbing you blind right now–not that you have much to take–but still."

Andi put her fists on her hips and said, "No, Jer. I'm not a complete idiot."

He shrugged and said, "Eh, sometimes maybe just a little."

Ignoring his comment, she said, "I left her with Ben. He found out she's a dancer in New York City. But Jer, her eye is bruised and swollen. Apparently, her ex used it as a punching bag, and she just showed up on my doorstep with nothing—no cellphone, no purse, no luggage. She's obviously in some kind of trouble."

"You want my advice? I assume you do since you're still talking to me about this, and it has nothing to do with business. Cut her loose. You don't owe her anything. She's a stranger to you. There's a good chance that the guy that gave her the busted lip is not far behind. You don't need that kind of trouble showing up at your front door."

"It's a black eye, not a busted lip."

"Doesn't matter. Sounds like she's trouble. The best thing you can do is to send her away."

"I can't. Ben already told her she could stay with us. Well, stay with me. He's officially moving in with Daniel."

Jerry held up his right hand. "Just stop. I don't need to know about your personal life or what's happening with your friends. And last I checked, you own the damn house, so you should be the one deciding who stays and who leaves."

"But Jer, it's not like I have a choice. She's got nowhere else to go."

"Like I've been telling you, Squirt, you've got to toughen up. You can't take in every damn stray you find. The sooner you get rid of her, the better."

***

After an Uber dropped Andi off at Bingley Furniture where she'd left her Jeep, she drove straight to the Grandin Village to meet up with Cooper for their lunch date. She was only a few minutes late. She parked in the back lot and walked through the front door of Farmburguesa.

Oh my God. The restaurant was a warm, welcome haven from the chilly day and everything that she'd been through. The moment she stepped inside, the aroma of burgers and fried potatoes wrapped around her in a comforting way, like her grandma's faded quilt on her bed. Her stomach growled. Andi looked to the dining area to the right and saw Cooper wave over to her. He sat at a small table for two. *Thank God.* She could see he'd already ordered their food.

She walked over to the table where he stood to greet her. He helped her remove her coat and gave her a light kiss on her lips before they both sat down.

"Hope you don't mind. I took the liberty of ordering us each your favorite – The Farmburguesa.

"You've got to be kidding, right? You know the way to my heart, Rockstar." She picked up the double cheeseburger with lettuce, tomatoes, grilled onions, pickles, and the magical special pink sauce and took a bite, closing her eyes as she chewed and savored the party of flavors dancing across her taste buds. "Mmmm," she said and swallowed. When she opened her eyes,

Cooper was looking at her like she was a Farmburguesa burger with special sauce.

Andi smiled at him. She really did love her Rockstar. Cooper returned her smile. "I'm sorry that I missed your call this morning. What's up? Find another dead body or something?" Cooper teased.

Andi's smile fell away, and her eyes widened. "Yes, but that's not why I called you."

His expression mirrored hers and he said, "What the…"

She reached out and grabbed his hand and squeezed it hard. "No Coop. This is much, much worse than the crime scene I just discovered today. Just a little after you left the house this morning, someone knocked on the door. I thought maybe Ben had forgotten his key or something, but no."

Cooper blanched and quickly looked around the restaurant like he was looking for someone before returning a frantic look at Andi. In a quiet voice, just above a whisper, he said, "For the love of God, please don't tell me The Broker came to see you again."

What? The Broker? If only it was that simple. Roanoke's crime boss scared the bejeebies out of her, but she'd at least dealt with him before. Too many times. Facing her mother and all those awful feelings was so much more terrifying.

"No. Worse," Andi answered back in that same quiet voice. "It was my mother."

There. She told him. Andi let out a breath and leaned back in her chair. No matter how many times she said it, she still had a hard time believing it. She reached for her cup of sweet tea and sipped through the straw.

Cooper looked at her slightly confused. "Your mother? Oh, thank God." He let out a breath and leaned back in his chair for just a moment before moving his burger to the side and placing his forearms on the table to lean in to keep their conversation relatively private. "I think you just took ten years off my life. I thought," he looked around the dining area again before saying, "you-know-who had shown back up in your life wanting another favor." He shook his head and shivered at the thought before taking a sip of his tea.

Then he seemed to realize the earlier part of their conversation. "Wait, what about the dead body you mentioned?"

"Oh that," Andi waved that inquiry away with her hand. "I stumbled across a homicide scene when I was changing a flat tire on my repo this morning. Detective Kendricks already questioned me." She shrugged. "At least I'm not their prime suspect this time."

Cooper just shook his head in disbelief.

Poor guy. When was her Rockstar going to finally get tired of the never-ending dark cloud that seemed to hang over her and just walk out of her life? *Just like my mother did.*

"None of that is important. Did you hear the part where I told you my mother showed up at my door this morning?"

"Right. Sorry," he said, and a small smile replaced the worried expression that had been in its place a moment earlier. "That's amazing. I always sort of thought she might be dead." A look of panic crossed his face. "Sorry. God, I'm so sorry. That was such an insensitive thing to say."

"It's okay. For all I knew, she could have been dead. We had never heard from her after she left."

"But she came back home this morning? She just showed up at your door?"

Andi nodded and looked down at the crispy waffle fries. She picked one up and took a bite. She'd always wondered if her mom was still alive. Okay, so maybe she got that her mom was only 17, unmarried, with a baby, and scared, so she ran away. But Andi was 25 years old. In all these years, Kitty had never tried to contact her or Andi's grandparents. Andi knew that Grams missed her. She reached for the ketchup bottle and squirted a glob of it on the red and white checkered paper. She dipped a waffle fry in the ketchup and took a bite.

"Did she say why she came back?"

"She's in some kind of trouble. She's got a nasty black eye that her ex gave her. I would feel sorry for her, if she hadn't royally screwed up my life and broken my grandparents' hearts.

She has nowhere to go, no money, no phone, no luggage. She's going to stay at my place until she can get back on her feet. Coop, she didn't even know my grandparents had died."

"Jesus. Where has she been all this time?"

Andi continued eating her waffle fries. Fried potatoes couldn't solve all of her problems, but they sure tasted delicious. "New York City, apparently, living out her dream of being a dancer."

"Oh my God, Andi. This is unbelievable."

"I know, right? After 25 years, she just shows up at my door."

Cooper smiled. "You must be so excited."

Andi frowned. "What? No! I'm mad. Where was she all those years when I actually needed her? Now that I'm an adult and don't want or need her, she just pops in because she needs a place to stay."

Cooper furrowed his brows and tilted his head to study her. "I get that." He reached out for her hand. "You were hurt by her." He gently caressed his thumb over her hand.

She lifted her chin. "Not just me. She nearly destroyed my grandparents."

"But this is a chance to get to finally know her."

Andi pulled her hand away. "You don't get it. No one gets it." She glared at him. "Jerry and Kendricks understand why I'm angry with my mom. I thought you would, too."

Cooper frowned and looked hurt. "Kendricks? You talked to him about your mom already?"

Andi leaned back and sighed. "Well, he was sort of surprised to see her at the crime scene."

"Wait. What was she doing at the crime scene?"

"I'd forgotten my paperwork, so I asked Ben if he would bring it to the crime scene. He was babysitting Kitty because I was sort of freaking out with her sudden arrival and everything. The thing is," she said as she leaned in closer to Cooper and whispered, "she knew the dead guy from the crime scene."

"What the fu…wait, do you think she killed him?"

Andi shook her head. "I don't think so," she said and then ate her last waffle fry. "She was too surprised to see him to have been the one that killed him."

Cooper ran his hand through his hair. "Jesus."

Andi glanced over at his untouched waffle fries. "Are you going to eat those?'

Cooper pushed the basket towards Andi. "Help yourself." Still frowning, Cooper watched Andi dive into his waffle fries. "Want me to come over tonight after my gig?" he asked.

Andi shook her head. "Probably not a good idea. It's just a little weird with Kitty there."

"Okay. I get it. You might want this time alone to talk with your mom."

"No. God no." Andi made a face. "I definitely can't talk to her now. There's nothing she can tell me that would make me feel any different. Actions speak louder than words. And she's not my mom." She shrugged. "Well, I guess technically she is, but she's a virtual stranger to me." She put the waffle fry down. She'd suddenly lost her appetite.

"It would be a great chance to start over with her. You know, really get to know her."

She snorted. "Yeah, well, no thanks. Not interested."

Cooper looked confused. Like Mags, he wasn't really getting it. They both thought this was some great chance to connect. "It's just too late, Cooper. Too much time has passed for there to be any hope for a happy family reunion." She picked up the half-eaten waffle fry and swirled it around in the ketchup and then began doodling ketchup onto the red and white checkered paper. "Plus, it's not like she came back to see me. She's here because she has nowhere else to go."

Andi dropped her potato pen and stared out the window. *And isn't that really the point - the underlying reason I am so angry. Kitty didn't come back for some desire to finally reconnect with me after all these years. She's only here because she had nowhere else to go.* "She was looking for my grandparents, her parents. I could tell she was surprised to see me there." Andi lifted her chin and replaced that feeling of sadness that was beginning to form in her chest with resentment. Resentment felt so much better than rejection.

Cooper reached across the table, cupped her face with his right hand, and pulled her in for a tender kiss on the lips. "You should definitely talk to her tonight. Get to know her, Andi. I can't imagine that she wouldn't take one look at you and feel anything but love for the amazing woman you've become." He gave her the tender smile. The one that always made her chest fill with warmth. Why did she crave the love from a woman that she didn't even know? She had more than enough love from the man sitting across from her. Andi returned his smile.

His eyes lit up. "Hey, I've got a great idea. Kitty's back and is going to be staying with you for a few days, at least, right? Her return has clearly brought up a bunch repressed feelings you've had about her." He paused and pointed to his chest. "I know better than anyone how challenging it can be to deal with a difficult mother. You should talk with Dr. Martin about it."

Andi gaped. "Oh, that's not necessary."

Cooper grinned. "Right. Except instead of being home dealing with the situation, you ran out of the house at your first chance, and you're stalling by having lunch with me."

"But we already had plans," she said.

He squeezed her hand. "And I'm so glad you're here. Eventually, you're going to have to go home and talk to her, Andi."

Andi rolled her eyes and sighed. Oh, she hated when he was right. "I know."

"Look, you can take my weekly session for tomorrow. My mother hasn't been any more annoying than usual this week, so I'll make do. You, on the other hand are in a code red situation and need to talk to a professional about your mother situation. Dr. Martin is amazing and full of great advice."

"Okay, I'll go," she said. At this point, she'd take any help she could get. With that decision made, she reached for another waffle fry.

***

After lunch, Cooper headed back to the office, and Andi got back into her Jeep and called Ben. He answered on the first ring.

"Where are you? I thought you were coming right back after you dropped off the car." Ben was using that tone he used when he was trying and failing at patience. She could practically see the fake smile that must be plastered on his face. Kitty must be nearby, otherwise he'd be cussing at her like a sailor.

"I know. I'm sorry. It took me a bit longer than I thought, and then I had lunch with Cooper." Andi took a breath. "I still don't know what to say to her, Ben. I'm sort of freaking out. Plus, she recognized the body from the crime scene. What the heck was that about? I managed to leave out that detail when I talked with Detective Kendricks earlier, but he knows I'm hiding something. Did she say anymore to you?"

"Oh, that is so sweet of you, Andi. Kitty, Andi just suggested that I find some clothes for you to wear from her closet since you didn't get to bring any luggage. I'll be right back." Andi heard what she only could imagine was her bedroom door close, and then Ben's voice was just above a whisper. "She's not saying anything. Whenever I bring up the crime scene, she starts to tremble and cry. Could the stiff you found earlier be her ex? Do you think she killed him?"

"I don't think so. She seemed surprised to see him there."

"Well, all I know is the woman is a wreck, and she's obviously in some sort of big trouble. I bought her the new pay-as-you-go phone and called Detective Hottie and gave him her new phone number. Thank God he didn't ask us any more questions."

Andi heard a sound and then Ben swore.

"What's wrong?" Andi asked.

"Why are the fabulous outfits that I put together for you in the back of your closet?"

Andi rolled her eyes. "Jeez, Ben. Don't scare me like that. I thought something horrible had happened."

"This IS something horrible. You need to wear them rather than your uniform of jeans and those god-awful black boots," Ben said.

She loved her best friend, even if he was often a bit dramatic.

"I am not being dramatic. Fashion is my passion," he said.

Andi smiled. It was like they could read each other's minds. God, she was going to miss rooming with him. She hoped their relationship wouldn't change too much.

"I know," she said. She shouldn't give the guy a hard time. He was helping her out, after all. Andi bit her lower lip. "What time is your shift at Star City Bar & Grill? I was hoping I'd have time to run another repo."

"I've got to leave by six-thirty. You know, you are going to have to come home eventually and face her."

Andi sighed. "I know. I just need a little more time."

After she hung up with Ben, Andi pulled out one of the files that she grabbed from the office when she'd dropped off the Hyundai. There was no way she was going back home to get her laptop, so she scanned the file to see if she could simply do the research on her phone. *Hm.* Vanessa Hill, age fifty-three, was three months late on her Audi A6 black sedan. "That's a sweet ride," Andi mumbled as she scanned over the employment section at the time of the loan. *She's an Account Executive at Fischer Insurance, on Salem Avenue in downtown Roanoke.* Andi glanced at her watch – 2:45 pm. There was a good chance Vanessa would still be at the office. Looking up the phone number, Andi called and asked to speak to Vanessa.

"I'm sorry, she's out of the office for the next three days attending a conference in Las Vegas. My name is Cara, her administrative assistant. Can I help you with something?"

Darn. "No, thanks. I guess it will have to wait until she returns." Andi disconnected and bit her lower lip. The problem was, she needed that Audi now. She couldn't wait three to four days for the chance to pick it up. She glanced back down at the repo sheet. *Las Vegas is too far to drive or take a train. Maybe she left her car at home and had a friend drop her at the airport, or she might have taken a taxi.* Andi decided to check home first.

It took her about twenty-five minutes to drive all the way out to Ashley Plantation in Daleville. The houses were gorgeous in this golf course community. Vanessa's home was one of the many humungous, brick homes with a two-car garage. Too bad the doors were closed. *There's no way to know if that Audi is safely tucked there or at an airport.* Andi glanced around the street. It wasn't like she could linger here without being noticed. The beautifully landscaped lawns didn't have a single tree. The only way to know for sure that the car was here would be to take a quick peek inside the garage door window. She'd just have to be fast and casual because there was no time to be arrested for trespassing. Andi preferred to keep her contact with the police to no more than once a day. All she needed was an excuse to be there in case she was stopped by a nosey neighbor. Glancing in the backseat, she spotted the makings of a prop for her cover. She grabbed the brown paper grocery bag and stuffed the soccer ball that Dodger liked to play with at the park, a Virginia Tech hooded sweatshirt that she'd borrowed from Cooper last week and hadn't yet returned, and a half-empty bottle of water that she'd tossed back there. She folded the top of the bag closed so that the contents remained invisible. If anyone stopped to ask her, she'd pretend that she was making a grocery delivery.

Okay, here we go. She pulled into the driveway, parking directly in front of the garage door, got out quickly and jogged with the bag in her hand to the front door. She pretended to ring the doorbell, waited about 30 seconds, and then casually walked back to the garage door. She took a look in the window, because hey, she was just a delivery person making sure no one was home.

No car. Time to go.

Andi hopped in her Jeep, started the engine, and drove out of the neighborhood as she considered her next move.

If the Audi was at an airport, it was most likely to be at the closest one—Roanoke Regional Airport, but it was possible for Vanessa to have left from either of the other two local regional airports in Lynchburg or Greensboro. Heck, she might have even decided to drive all the way up to Washington D.C., if she got a good deal on the flight.

Tricky. Andi needed a plan, and since she was at her most creative genius while consuming chocolate, she stopped at the gas station to get her fix from the convenience store. Once she was back in the driver's seat, she ripped open the share-size bag of plain M&Ms, and poured some of the round, colorful candies directly into her mouth. Andi sighed and closed her eyes, leaning her head against the seat, and chewed. The combination of candy crunch and milk chocolate dissolving in her mouth made her feel instant relief, until an image of Kitty's bruised face danced behind her closed lids. *No, no, no. I don't want to think about her!* Andi opened her eyes. The woman was even ruining her enjoyment of chocolate. *Was nothing sacred anymore?*

Andi reached over to the cupholder and picked up her cocoa. She knew better than to drink it now. She'd burn her mouth. *Why did they make the cocoa hotter than the surface of the sun?* Andi carefully removed the plastic lid and gently blew on the molten liquid. She set the cup back into the holder, picked up her phone, and searched for Vanessa Hill on social media looking for some clue of her itinerary. *Why couldn't she be one of those people that posted a photo of their plane ticket or those handy maps with a dotted line showing their departure location?* There was nothing about the airport – just that she was traveling to Vegas for an insurance conference. *Great.*

There were a few posts from last weekend where Vanessa had enjoyed a fun girl's night out with another woman. Andi saw that her skip had tagged Gloria Berube in the photo. *Hm.* She poured a few more M&Ms into her mouth and chewed thoughtfully as a plan developed in her mind. Starting her Jeep, Andi headed to the City Market to borrow a phone from a friend.

Chapter Eleven

After parking the car, Andi walked up to Simon's truck – The Bull Dog. Mags was just handing some sort of purple drink in a clear plastic cup to a woman when she spotted Andi. When the customer left, Andi stepped up to the counter.

"Hey, I didn't expect to see you back today. Did everything go okay with your mom?"

"I haven't exactly been back home yet. I ended up running a repo, stumbled on a homicide scene, and…" Andi waved her hand and shook her head. "Let's just say it's been a really long day, and I haven't been back home."

"Wait, did you say homicide? As in dead body?" Mags asked with a frown.

"Yes, but I came by to ask if I could borrow your phone to make a quick call."

"Oh no! What happened to yours?" Mags asked, concern in her voice.

Andi lifted the phone out of her coat pocket so Mags could see it. "Nothing. It's right here. I just need to call from a different phone number to try to get information on the location of my next repo. I'll just be a minute. I promise."

Mags shrugged and said, "Take as long as you need." She handed Andi her phone.

Andi typed in the number for Vanessa's desk. *Please answer, Cara.*

"Vanessa Hill's desk. May I help you?"

It was definitely Cara's voice. *Okay. Here it goes.*

Andi changed the pitch of her voice when she began to speak and added a slight, southern draw—nothing too strong. She hoped Cara wouldn't recognize her from her call earlier.

"Hi, Cara? This is Vanessa's friend, Gloria. She tells me all the time how invaluable you are at the office. She doesn't know what she'd do without you."

"Really? Wow, that's nice. Thank you," Cara said.

"Listen, I know Vanessa's out in Vegas this week. I've tried to reach her on her cell just now, but she must not have a signal or maybe she's having luck at the slots. Anyway, I've got a huge problem that I'm hoping you can help me with. We went out for drinks over the weekend, and my wallet must have fallen out of my purse in her car. Do you happen to know where her car is? I absolutely can't do without my wallet another minute."

"Oh, my. I'm so sorry. She was planning to park it at the Roanoke Blacksburg Regional Airport, but you won't be able to get into her car without the keys, and I'm afraid I can't help you with that."

"Oh Cara, sweetie, no need to worry yourself over that. I'm always the designated driver, so I have her extra car key. Thank you. I can see you really are just the lifesaver just like she says. Bye, bye."

Andi disconnected the call, grinned, and returned the phone to her friend who was staring at her with a surprised look on her face.

"I know what you're going to say," Andi said, "and you're right. Lying is terrible, and I do feel bad about it. It's also an occupational hazard that I have to sometimes bend the truth in order to get information for these repo jobs. It's not like I could have called Cara up directly and asked where her boss's car was so that I can repossess it."

Maggy burst out in laughter and then held up her hands in surrender. "Hey, I'm not judging you at all. I'm just thinking you should have gone out for the drama club when we were in high school. If the repo business ever slows down, you could always get a job as a con artist."

Maggy tucked her phone in her apron pocket and then leaned in and asked, "Okay, now tell me about the homicide scene."

***

By the time that Andi had picked up the Audi, paid for a full day of long-term parking, secured the car at the repo lot, taken an Uber back to the airport parking lot to get her Jeep, and then paid for parking again so she could leave the secured airport parking lot, she was tired and more than a little stressed. She glanced at the clock on her dash. It was just about 7pm, which meant that Kitty had been alone in her house for thirty-minutes. Andi pulled into her driveway and turned off the engine. She had intended to get back before Ben left for work, but that just hadn't worked out. Was Kitty at Andi's house right now, stealing her things like her boss had suggested?

Andi sighed. Well, like Jerry had not so subtly pointed out, she didn't have much of anything of value to take, did she? *Okay, and face it, hours have passed, and I still have no idea what to say to my mother.* As she walked up her porch steps, she shrugged. The day hadn't been a total loss. At least she had brought in two repos and earned money.

She stopped at the front door, hesitating to open it as a possible conversation with Kitty played in her mind.

She could start off with something like…*Hey Kitty, so how do you know the homicide victim? Were you the one who killed him, by chance? Is he the reason you came back? Why are you back, anyway? For that matter, why did you leave in the first place? And since we're going there, why didn't you ever try to contact us?*

Andi blew out a breath. Yeah, that conversation wasn't happening. *I'm too tired and hungry to talk.* No small wonder. She hadn't had anything to eat since she'd bought the M&Ms and hot chocolate.

Squaring her shoulders, she unlocked the front door and stepped inside. The first thing she saw was Dodger, there to greet her like usual with his body in a whole tail wag. She smiled. "Who's my best boy?"

His wiggle got faster. She reached into her purse and pulled out a cheese curl. It disappeared in a second. *See. I'm not going to be completely alone with Kitty. I've got Dodger and he's the most wonderful distraction.* She reached in and grabbed a second cheese curl.

She whispered to him. "I'm going to need some extra help from you tonight, big guy. You got my back?" He snatched the cheese curl from her fingers and licked her face. Andi scrunched her nose, patted his head, set her purse on the table by the door, and then hung her coat in the closet.

She heard the laughter of several people coming from the kitchen. *Jesus, Mary, and Joseph.* Had Kitty felt so at home she decided to throw a wild party with a few of her old friends from the area?

Stomping into the kitchen ready to kick everyone out of *her* house, Andi stopped dead in her tracks staring at the cozy scene. The Golden Girls sat around the table with Kitty. Gram's old photo albums were spread across the table, and she heard Mrs. Davis say, "I remember that night. It was your fifteenth birthday and you snuck out of the house and cut through my backyard."

Kitty laughed and said, "Yes, but you caught me and told me if I came inside instead, you'd teach me how you cheat at rummy, promising it would be way more fun than that party I was headed to." She looked lovingly at Mrs. Davis. "And it was! You taught me the card tricks, and we drank Dr. Pepper and devoured an entire large bag of potato chips."

"Gladys Davis, you sneaky, cheating, card shark!" Mrs. Harper exclaimed, mouth dropped open in shock.

"Ethel, we've been hoodwinked all these years," Mrs. Barzetti said shaking her head. "And corrupting our sweet Kitty, too."

Kitty's eyes widened. "I'm so sorry, Mrs. Davis. I thought they all knew."

Mrs. Davis lifted her hands up in surrender and winked over at Kitty. "Well, I guess the gig is up." She began laughing. "I can't complain. It was a good long run."

Everyone around the table burst into laughter.

Kitty shook her head with a big smile. "I never could pull a fast one on any of you." She looked around the table at each of the Golden Girls, stopping at Mrs. Barzetti. "Especially you, Mrs. B. I used to wonder if you had hidden cameras that alerted you whenever I stepped out of the house."

Oh God. Andi felt stomach acid rise to the back of her throat. For a second, she just couldn't move. They all loved her. She could see it in their faces. How could they just sit there and pretend that Kitty hadn't left them all and broken their hearts?

Mrs. Barzetti spotted Andi standing in the doorway to the kitchen. "Andi, I didn't hear you come in. We're looking at old photos from when your mom was just a kid. Here, come sit next to me."

"I can't," she said and darn it, her voice cracked. She ran to her bedroom, slammed the door closed and threw herself face down on her bed. *Don't cry.* What had she been thinking? She wasn't going to be able to do this. How could they all pretend that Kitty hadn't bailed, left them all? Instead, they'd simply welcome her back to the neighborhood like old times. Maybe because they'd watched her grow up. Andi had nothing. No memories just an emptiness whenever she thought of her mom.

I will not cry anymore over that woman. How could there possibly be more tears after a lifetime of tears shed over never knowing her mom? She made a promise to herself when her mother hadn't shown up on her fifteenth birthday and she'd cried for three days straight that she wouldn't cry like that over Kitty ever again. She was done.

There was a knock on her bedroom door.

"Andi, Can I come in?"

Mrs. Barzetti. Andi blinked her eyes rapidly to dry up the tears that had begun to form and sat up on her bed. She glanced around her room. It was fairly straightened, but she hadn't made her bed this morning. She'd been too anxious to get out of the house. Oh well, it would have to do.

"Sure, the door's open."

Mrs. Barzetti opened it, stepped into the room, and closed the door behind her. She walked over to the bed and sat next to Andi.

"I can't even begin to imagine how you're feeling with all this," she said.

Andi shrugged. "I'll be okay. It's just kind of strange to have her here."

"Oh sweetheart," she said and put an arm across Andi's shoulders, gently squeezing her shoulder.

"How can you all just sit out there around Gram's table with her like that? Aren't you mad at her for leaving? Didn't she break your heart when she left? She sure as heck broke my grandparents' hearts."

"Mad? No," she said tenderly. "Relief that she found her way back home, yes. Actually, I always carried a bit of guilt. For years I worried if there was something that I should have done to prevent her leaving. If I'd been able to help her and your grandmother more, maybe Kitty wouldn't have felt so overwhelmed. Maybe she wouldn't have left."

Andi stood up and began pacing. "It's not your fault, Mrs. Barzetti. She did the leaving."

"But she was only 17. She was just a child still and with a sweet baby girl."

"I've had my entire life to think about this. I could forgive her for panicking and running from her responsibilities at 17. But that was 25 years ago. Why didn't she reach out in all those years?" Andi turned and glanced at her door. In a whispered voice she said, "She never called or sent a note or anything. My grandparents died not even knowing if their daughter was dead or alive." Andi crossed her arms and lifted her chin. "I can't forgive her for how she injured them."

Yes. Anger is better. Anger was much more comfortable than the oppressive feeling of hurt that washed over her a little while ago when she'd been talking to Jerry. She'd cling to the anger. There wouldn't be tears with that emotion.

Mrs. Barzetti studied Andi a moment and then said, "You've mentioned my feelings, your grandparents' feelings, but you left out how you feel hurt by Kitty."

"Why would I be hurt? I had the amazing love of Grams and Grandpa and maybe when I was a kid I might have wished for a mom, but I'm a grown adult now, and I don't need one anymore."

Mrs. Barzetti was looking at her with sympathy. She hated when people looked at her that way. Parents used to whisper and give her that look when Grams took her on field trips or volunteered at school. It was a small community, and everyone knew her mom hadn't wanted Andi, so she'd left her to be raised by her grandparents.

She didn't need anyone's pity back then, and she especially didn't want it now. She lifted her chin, not quite meeting Mrs. Barzetti's gaze. "I'm fine. You don't need to worry about me."

"Oh Andrea," Mrs. Barzetti said as she stood up and gave her a hug and then pulled back and looked at Andi. She tucked a wild strand of hair that had danced near Andi's eye behind her ear. "I just want you to know that I'm here for you. Always. Whenever you're ready to talk about any of this my sweet girl, I'm here."

Andi almost lost it then. Instead, she gave Mrs. Barzetti another big hug. "Thank you, but I'm fine." Okay, that was a lie of sorts, but she would be fine. She'd get through this like she got through all the other bad stuff that dropped into her life.

Mrs. Barzetti returned to the kitchen and about 10 minutes later, Andi came out of her room. The Golden Girls were standing in the living room saying their goodnights to Kitty and finalizing plans to pick Kitty up tomorrow morning at nine in the morning to take her to breakfast. They each gave Andi a hug as well and headed out the door. Andi locked the front door behind them and then turned to look at Kitty.

It was just the two of them now. As if on cue, Dodger danced around Kitty until she leaned down and petted him. "Aren't you a sweet boy." He licked her fingers. Kitty patted him on the head and stood to face Andi with a smile. "I think he must have smelled Mrs. Barzetti's cookies on my fingers."

Andi gave her a slight smile and asked, "Did Ben show you the bedroom where you'll be sleeping?"

Kitty was studying Andi closely. When she realized Andi was waiting for her reply, she shook her head and said, "Yes. Thank you so much for letting me stay here tonight. I had to leave New York City in a hurry, and I didn't know where else to go. I had to leave my luggage and phone back in the city."

Andi walked into the kitchen. "Can I get you some coffee or tea?"

Kitty followed her. "I'd love a cup of tea, if you wouldn't mind. I'm not much of a coffee drinker."

Andi put on the kettle, pulled down two teacups, and dropped in the tea bags. She smiled. "Me neither." Well, that was one thing they had in common. *I wonder if there's some sort of coffee gene that gets passed on to your kids.* Andi poured the tea and brought the cups to the table. The photo albums were stacked neatly in the center. She placed Kitty's cup in front of her and sat across the table from her.

Lifting the cup up to her mouth, Andi blew onto the surface of the tea to cool it. "Is that," Andi pointed to her eye, "the reason you had to leave the city in such a hurry?"

Kitty lightly touched her swollen eye and winced. "Partly."

Andi took a sip of her tea. "What about the body of the dead guy from this morning? You said you knew him. Who is he? Is he from around here or from New York City?"

"His name is Jimmy Marino. I know him from New York," she answered, staring into her cup of tea. Andi noticed a slight tremble in Kitty's fingers as she held her cup.

"Is he the one who gave you the black eye?" Andi asked carefully.

Kitty looked up at her. "What? No." She shook her head slowly.

"Did you kill Jimmy Marino?" Kind of an odd coincidence that she had just arrived from New York City and now there was a dead guy she knew from New York City.

"Oh God, no." Kitty stared at Andi like she was just really seeing her for the first time.

Andi just nodded. "I didn't tell the police that you recognized the dead guy."

Kitty blew out a breath. "Thank you."

"Listen, I know the detective handling this investigation. Detective Kendricks is really good at his job, and he's probably going to find your connection with Jimmy. How did you know him?"

"Jimmy is or rather was my boyfriend Nick's brother."

"Sweet baby Jesus," Andi whispered. "Your boyfriend's brother. I'm guessing this boyfriend is the one who used your face as a punching bag?" Andi already knew the answer. She could see it when Kitty said the word boyfriend. No doubt the reason she'd left New York.

"Yes." Kitty said and stood up, picked up her tea and walked to the sink. "I really appreciate you letting me stay. I'm exhausted, so I'm just going to head to bed if you don't mind. I feel like I haven't slept for days." Kitty poured her untouched tea down the sink and washed her teacup. She set it in the dish drain next to the sink.

Kitty wasn't giving out much information tonight. Andi was afraid that if she pushed her, the woman would fall apart. "Look, I know what it's like to be in over your head. You're important to The Golden Girls, so you can stay here a few days until you figure out your next step."

Kitty smiled. "Thank you. I'll repay you once I get back on my feet." Kitty looked away and then said, "The Golden Girls? Is that what you call Mrs. B., Mrs. Harper, and Mrs. Davis?"

"Yes," Andi said. "Actually, Ben came up with the nickname."

"It suits them." Kitty looked around the kitchen "It's so surreal to be back home again after all the years. In many ways it's the same as I remember and yet so different. You've done a great job with the place."

Kitty began walking to the stairs and then turned to look back at Andi. "I'm sorry that I didn't get back before mom and dad passed. I'm glad I got to meet you." She had the saddest expression on her bruised face. It nearly made Andi's heart break.

Kitty said, "You know, there wasn't a single day that I didn't think about you and wonder…" Kitty pressed her lips together tight, and a single tear slipped from her eye. After a moment, she said, "You've grown into a beautiful, young woman. Good night, Andi." Then, Kitty turned and slowly walked up the stairs.

Oh God. She didn't want to like Kitty. It was so much easier to think of her as a cold, callous stranger that had abandoned them all. Dodger rested his head on Andi's lap and made a little whimper as he looked up at her with those sweet brown eyes. She gave him a quick kiss on the top of his head and then reached her hand inside Mrs. Barzetti's tin of cookies. She tossed a peanut butter cookie to Dodger and ate three chocolate chip cookies without even tasting them, trying to erase the image of the sad expression on Kitty's bruised face. After Andi swallowed the last of her tea and let Dodger out one more time before bed, she locked up the house. Her furry pup followed her into her bedroom where she finished getting ready for bed.

Andi climbed into her bed and pulled Gram's quilt up to her chin. It was warm in the house, but she still felt chilled. Dodger hopped up on the bed and curled next to her in his favorite spot. Andi reached over on the nightstand and picked up her cellphone to call Cooper. He answered on the first ring.

"Hey, are you okay?" he asked.

"Yes," she said and reached over and hugged Cooper's pillow. Closing her eyes, she inhaled, smelling his aftershave and expensive Cologne. "It's just weird knowing that the mother that I never knew is here in my house, sleeping upstairs in my old bedroom. Well, I guess it was her bedroom first."

"I can imagine. Did you get to talk to her?"

"Only a little. The guy she recognized from the crime scene is the brother of her boyfriend. She's exhausted and fragile. I was afraid if I asked her anymore questions, she'd shatter into a million pieces. I want to hate her or even feel nothing towards her. Instead, I see how difficult it is for her to be here, and I kind of feel sorry for her."

"Oh, Margarita. I wish there was something that I could do. Are you sure you don't want me to come spend the night?"

"Thanks, but I'll be okay."

She could hear him sigh and then say, "Okay, if you're sure. Guess I'll meet you at Dr. Martin's office tomorrow at 3pm."

"Oh, I forgot about that. Okay. See you tomorrow."

"Love you, Margarita."

"Love you, Rockstar."

Chapter Twelve

Kendricks hated cold weather. Winters were mild in Roanoke, but he dreaded days like this morning when the temperature dipped below freezing and the icy wind brought the low digits down another ten degrees. He had already spent more time outside than he cared, scraping the solid sheet of ice from his windshield before heading to work. With less than a half a cup of coffee in his system, he and his partner were back in the SUV, chasing down a possible lead in the James Marino homicide.

Once he'd started his Tahoe, Kendricks turned the dial to the maximum setting for heat. Cold blasted full force through the vents for about three seconds before he felt a hint of warm air. It was another long seven seconds until he was enjoying the steady flow of heat blowing at his chest and feet.

Ryan sat in the front passenger seat next to him without a damn coat. *Idiot.* He'd taken it off before they got into the car and tossed it in the back seat. *It is twenty-four freaking degrees outside. Only a moron doesn't wear a coat in this weather. Apparently, his partner is a moron.*

Kendricks watched as the kid closed the air vents on the passenger side. The look on his face must have communicated his thoughts because the kid simply grinned and said, "What? I'm warm enough, okay? You're just like my grandfather. I think it must be an age thing. He's always cold, too."

An age thing? "It's more of a commonsense thing," he said with a sigh. Hell, Kendricks wasn't old. He was still months away from hitting 30. It's not like he was in his 60s, like the Chief. Of course, he remembered back to a time when he used to think thirty was ancient. Maybe he was getting old.

"This is like a heatwave compared to a ski trip I took in college with some buddies in Vail, Colorado. Now that was cold. Some nights, the temperatures got down to single digits," Ryan said dramatically.

Ten minutes later, Hughes was still rambling about that ski trip. *Jesus, the kid can talk.* Kendricks made a turn onto Brambleton Avenue. They were almost there, so he interrupted his partner.

"Listen Hughes, I'm going to need you to be a quiet observer while Sanchez and I ask the questions," he said. "That means no speaking."

"Gotcha," he nodded. "So, do you think this is the guy that killed James Marino?"

"Maybe. Champion Auto Glass was the last place plugged into the Marino's GPS on his phone. Jacob Hauser, the owner, was busted three years ago and charged with possession with intent to distribute a Class IV drug."

Ryan thought for a moment. "Class IV drugs include tranquilizer type drugs like Valium and Xanax. But didn't the lab say there were traces of cocaine in the trunk of Marino's car?"

Kendricks pulled into the Champion Auto Glass lot, parking next to Sanchez's Explorer, and said, "Yes."

Ryan nodded. "So, there's a possibility that Jacob Hauser has moved up the drug chain and is selling Class II drugs now like the cocaine that Lucky found."

"It's a possibility," Kendricks said and gave Hughes his intimidating glare. "Once we step out of the vehicle, I don't want to hear another sound from you. Are we clear?"

The kid smiled and said, "You know, my grandfather makes that same face sometimes when he gets frustrated with me." He shook his head. "Must be an age thing."

Kendricks rolled his eyes, but before he could point out that he was not old, the kid was out the door, sliding on his coat, and greeting Sanchez and his new four-legged partner. As Kendricks joined them at the back of the Expedition, he watched a smiling Sanchez clip the leash onto Lucky's harness and give her a scratch behind the ears. As he stood up, he said, "Let's see if we can find some evidence of a crime, gentlemen. Why don't you take lead on this one, Kendricks?"

What? "Who the hell are you, and what have you done with Detective Sanchez?" Kendricks asked, arching his brow.

Sanchez barked out a laugh and patted Kendricks on the back. "Don't worry. It's still me, and I still like to call the shots. That's why while you're distracting Hauser with your questions, I'll be doing the real investigative work with my new partner. We'll take a casual walk around the garage and see if my girl sniffs any drugs."

Kendricks glanced down at the German shepherd. She was sitting, her attention focused on Sanchez, her tail wagging, and tongue hanging out of the side of her mouth. She could easily be mistaken for someone's pet except she had a bulletproof vest strapped to her body with an official police badge clipped on it. He'd heard amazing stories of K9s helping officers find everything from missing persons, corpses, drugs, and even explosives. *So what if she'd led them straight to Marino's car yesterday, how much could a K9 really assist in this murder investigation?* "Well, I guess we're about to see how good of a detective your new partner is, Sanchez." Kendricks shrugged and grinned as he began walking towards the garage with Hughes following close behind. "It won't be hard for her to outperform you."

"Very funny, Kendricks," Sanchez said, a hint of a smile in his voice. "If you really want to see her perform, I'll be happy to demonstrate the bite command on you."

The three men and dog approached the small stone building where the words "Champion Auto Glass" were professionally painted on the large windows across the front of the structure. There was a glass door on the right side that led to the shop's office and a single garage door on the left side. A bell announced their entrance as they all filed in through the shop door to a small reception area that had several chairs, a coffee table, and a television set with a morning talk show playing. There was a counter with a register against the back door. At least this room was heated. A woman in her thirties sat in one of the chairs, looking through a magazine. She looked up as they walked in, studied Lucky, and then gave them all a second look. In Kendricks opinion, that was an immediate mark against Sanchez's new partner. A dog in a police vest was going to attract attention, no doubt about it.

A white male, approximately 5'9" and weighing under 140 pounds entered the room from a door that must have led to the garage bay. His hair was shaved in a buzz cut, and he wore faded jeans and a solid navy-blue long sleeve shirt that had the Champion's Auto Glass logo on the front. He automatically said, "Can I help you?" as he was wiping his hand on a blue microfiber towel. As soon as he saw Lucky, he froze for two seconds and then looked back at the men, setting the blue towel on the counter and immediately putting both hands in the front pockets of his jeans.

Kendricks stepped forward and pulled his badge and ID out of his jacket pocket and held it up for the man to see. "I'm Detective Kendricks. We'd like to ask you a few questions." Kendricks glanced at the woman who was finding this interaction much more interesting than either the magazine or the television program. Kendricks returned his attention to Jacob Hauser. His haircut was shorter than his mugshot on file, but otherwise, he pretty much looked the same. "Do you have somewhere private we can talk?"

Jacob swallowed, let out a slow breath, grabbed the blue towel again and said, "Sure. We can talk back here." He turned and walked back through the door he'd just come through. The detectives and Lucky followed him. Hauser was twisting the towel as he stood by a silver Dodge Caravan minivan that was missing the windshield.

"I appreciate you taking a few minutes to talk with us," Kendricks said and reached inside his coat pocket and pulled out an enlarged photo of James Marino from his driver's license. "Have you seen this man?"

Jacob glanced at the photo, immediately looked away, and compressed his lips. "Um, no. I've never seen this guy."

"Are you sure? Can you take another look at the photo?" Kendricks asked, holding the photo up to Jacob again.

Jacob's eyes darted to the photo for a second before he took a few steps back, twisting the blue towel again. "I'm sorry I can't help you. Like I said, I haven't seen him around."

Kendricks could practically feel the fear rolling off Houser. It could be that police made him nervous, but since he barely looked at James Marino's photo, Kendricks was sure the guy was lying about seeing him, too. Hughes was standing beside him, silent for a change—thank God. Sanchez had murmured something to Lucky, and he and the dog were now walking around the inside perimeter of the garage bay. He needed to stall long enough for Lucky to do a sweep of the garage.

"This is a photo of James Marino, from New York. We discovered his body in the woods not far from here. We have evidence that he was here or at least had intended to come here."

Jacobs eyes went wide, and his mouth dropped open. "He's dead?"

Kendricks nodded. "Murdered."

Jacob raised his hands. "Look man, like I said before, I never saw this guy." He pointed to the minivan and said, "I'm sorry I can't help you, but I've got work to do, so I'll show you out." Hauser looked over at Sanchez and Lucky, seeming to realize that they were wandering around the garage. "Hey, I know my rights. Unless you've got a warrant, you need to leave. Now."

Kendricks nodded at Sanchez, reached into his jacket and pulled out a business card. "Here's my card. Please call me if you suddenly recall seeing him. We'll let you get back to work. Thank you for your time."

They stepped back out into the bitter cold and walked to their vehicles. Sanchez opened the back and Lucky hopped inside. "Damn, I was certain there would be evidence of cocaine in the garage," Sanchez said. He opened a bottle of water, poured a bit of it in a portable dog dish, and watched as Lucky lapped it up.

"Well, at least it wasn't a complete waste of time," Kendricks said. "We learned that he definitely recognized James Marino, even from this terrible driver's license photo. We also can remove his name from our list of murder suspects. He seemed genuinely surprised to learn that our victim was dead."

Sanchez shrugged. "My gut still tells me the drugs tie back to Houser. It's just too much of a coincidence that Marino's GPS brought him here."

Kendricks nodded. "Agreed. Unfortunately, without probable cause, we're not going to be able to get a warrant to do a more thorough search."

Sanchez muttered something in Spanish.

"See you back at the station, Sanchez," Kendricks said, as he walked over to the driver's side of the Tahoe.

"See ya, Lucky," Ryan said as he gave the German shepherd an ear scratch.

When they were back in the front seat of the Tahoe, Ryan said, "But this doesn't bring us any closer to finding the person that killed James Marino. Where do we go from here?"

"Once we uncover the motive, we'll find the killer," Kendricks said as he started the engine. He looked at Hughes. "Nice job silently observing, Hughes. Let's go grab a good, hot cup of coffee. My treat." He glanced over at Ryan and added, "Unless you'd rather get a cold chocolate milk. It's an age thing, right?" Kendricks grinned at the kid as he pulled out onto Brambleton Avenue.

***

Andi hardly slept last night, and when she did manage to drift off to sleep, she had a string of bizarre, terrifying dreams that seemed to include the greatest hits of all the dead people she'd come across since becoming a repo agent. In the final nightmare that woke her this morning, she'd come home, greeted Dodger, and when she opened the closet door to hang up her coat, the dead man from yesterday fell out onto the floor at her feet. She screamed as she jumped back out of the way and turned away from the body only to be staring down the barrel of a gun. She looked up to see Peter's face as he pointed the gun at her, threatening to kill her just like he'd done over and over in her nightmares. She felt her heart pounding as she looked back at the gun and began pleading with him to spare her life. When she looked up at him again, Peter was gone, and in his place, Kitty stood pointing the gun at Andi.

"I'm sorry that I didn't get back before mom and dad passed," Kitty said as a tear ran down her face, just like she'd said last night. "I wouldn't have had to leave my parents at all if it hadn't been for you, Andi. You know, there wasn't a single day that went by that I didn't imagine what my life would have been like if I'd never gotten pregnant with you. You're the one who broke everyone's hearts. I could have had a normal, happy life if it hadn't been for you." Kitty swiped at the tear and smiled. "Even the Golden Girls missed me. Did you see us around the table reminiscing about old times? They all love me, Andi, not you." Kitty shook her head. "Even sweet, talented Ben adores me."

Andi felt her chest constrict and tears raced down her cheeks. "What?"

"What?" Kitty asked, mimicking Andi. "Aw, poor baby girl. You thought they loved you, didn't you? But no one loves you, sweetheart. It's okay, because your mommy is going to make it all better for you. You'll hardly feel a thing."

In her dream, Kitty pulled the trigger, and Andi screamed. She bolted up in bed and wiped her cheeks. Her heart was racing. Dodger hopped up on the bed and began licking her face. She took several deep breaths to calm her nerves. *It's just a dream. It's just a stupid, crazy dream.* Oh, but this one was so much worse than the other nightmares she'd been having. She remembered how Kendricks had suggested she talk to a professional. Maybe if she mentioned the nightmares when she spoke with Cooper's psychologist this afternoon, she'd finally stop having them.

Andi hurried to get dressed, fed Dodger, and was fortunate to be able to sneak out of the house without seeing Kitty. After this morning's nightmare, she was even more reluctant to face the woman.

The morning sky was painted with shades of pink and orange. It wouldn't be long before the sun rose and hopefully added a little warmth to this frigid morning. She started up her Jeep. God, how she hated the cold. Luckily, the brand-new heater warmed up the inside of her used Jeep in no time. Andi was especially grateful for that heat, since she had to spend extra time outside trying to chip the ice off her windshield.

Andi swung by the drive-through at Mill Mountain Coffee and Tea and ordered her favorite herbal tea. It was too hot to drink right away, so she turned up the radio and drove over to The Repo Doctor. If things went well, she'd have time to grab a repo this morning before meeting Cooper's counselor. Memories from her nightmare filled her mind, and she pushed those thoughts away. *Just focus on the job.*

She parked in the front parking space, unlocked the door to the office, and went directly to the pile of new repos. At least business was good. She grabbed three folders and sat down at an empty desk with her cup of tea and five of Mrs. Barzetti's cookies she'd wrapped in a napkin on her way out the door. She opened the lid for her tea, dipped one of Mrs. Barzetti's specialty oatmeal cookies into the hot liquid, and took a bite. *So good.* In Andi's opinion, it was the white chocolate chips that made them irresistible.

Opening a folder, Andi scanned the form. *Hm.* Donald Watson, single, age 65, and three months behind on his Ford Taurus payment. She scanned the employment section and noted that he was retired. It was early in the morning. Heck, if she were retired, she'd be sleeping in. Maybe she could catch Donny at home sleeping soundly while she relieved him of his blue Taurus. Andi popped the rest of the cookie into her mouth, wrapping the remaining four cookies back in the napkin and gently placing them in her purse. She brushed the cookie crumbs from the desk into the small trash can and took the three files with her as she locked up the office again and headed to her Jeep.

In fifteen minutes, she was on Capito Street in Hollins looking for Donald's address. *There it is!* She'd spotted the Taurus parked right in the driveway. It was so close to the house, darn it! Several lights were on which meant there was a good chance that her skip wasn't sleeping. She parked her Jeep on the opposite side of the Taurus, just three houses down from her target. There was lots of activity at several houses on the street where people were scraping their windshields and leaving for work. It would be a risk to make a grab for the car, but she couldn't very well sit here all day. She'd just have to go for it. Andi grabbed the key for the Ford that was clipped onto the folder, took another sip of her tea, and stepped out into the cold.

She was just about to cross the street when she saw an older man that had to be Donald Watson, lock his front door, walk over to the Taurus, and start up the engine. He got back out of the car and began scraping the ice off his windshield. *What the heck! Retired guys are supposed to be sleeping at this ungodly time of day.* Andi hurried back to her car, got in, started the engine, and did a quick u-turn in the street because the Taurus was heading away from her. *Okay. Plan B.* If she was lucky, she may be able to grab the Ford when he arrived at his destination.

Ole Donny-boy was driving about ten miles under the speed limit. Drivers behind them were annoyed at them both as they expressed their discontent with hand gestures and car horns when they passed them. Finally, Donald pulled into a parking lot at a shopping plaza across from the mall. He parked the blue Ford and walked into an IHOP.

Yes! I'm finally getting a break. The poor guy wouldn't have a ride home when he finished breakfast, but at least he'd enjoy a nice, hot meal before he realized his car was gone. Oh, she could sure go for a stack of their delicious buttermilk pancakes with a side of bacon. Her stomach growled. One cookie was not enough for breakfast.

Okay, let's try this again. Andi grabbed the Taurus key, tucked the folder in her purse, so she'd have the proper paperwork this time, locked her Jeep and casually walked over to Donald's car. As she got closer, she realized his car was full of stuff—so full that things were piled high enough that they covered half the windows in the back seats as well as the front passenger seat. There's no way anyone could open any door except for the driver's door without risking things falling out onto the ground. *Maybe he was helping a friend move? Maybe he was dropping things off for recycling?* When Andi stepped up to the car to unlock the front door, she could see there were many different sized binders, folders, old newspapers, used coffee cups and cardboard drink trays. She looked closer in the back window, *Ew.* There were crumpled fast food bags, large plastic trash bags, some old towels, and lots of unopened mail. *Hm.* She would bet his car payment bills for the last three months were probably somewhere in this vehicle. She could only imagine that the plastic draped over the driver's seat was placed there to protect Donald's clothes. *Yuk!*

Just get this over with. She unlocked the car, opened the driver's door, and...*Oh my God.* The smell nearly knocked her over. She turned her head away and placed her hand over her nose and mouth, so she wouldn't gag. *Okay, if I can just breathe through my mouth, the smell won't be as bad.* From here, she estimated it would be no more than fifteen minutes to drive to The Repo Doctor.

With wariness, she sat inside, started the engine, and immediately lowered some of the windows by just a few inches, deciding that she'd deal with the frigid air easier than the putrid smells coming from the trash. Andi realized her mistake as soon as she'd left the parking lot. Driving at 40 miles per hour with the windows cracked open created circulation inside the car and some of the loose trash began to take flight, swirling around the interior. When a sticky napkin landed on the side of her face, she gagged, pulled the paper off her cheek, and immediately closed all the windows. With the vehicle sealed closed, the garbage smell intensified, even though she was breathing through her mouth.

This drive was going to be the longest fifteen minutes of her life. When she was younger, Father Mark had warned of spending an eternity in hell. This must be what he meant. Just when she thought it couldn't get worse, she had to stop at a red light. Andi heard a rustling sound coming from the backseat. That was impossible unless there was something living in the car. *No, no, no, no.* She would die if a mouse ran across her feet. The light changed to green, and she drove through the intersection. *Come on. I'm almost there.* The Repo Doctor was only two blocks away.

She heard the noise again, only this time it was louder and sounded like it was behind her. *Sweet baby Jesus.* "Calm down," she said aloud. "You didn't get much sleep last night, and you're letting your imagination run wild. There's nothing here but trash." Andi pulled up to the keypad, typed in the access number, and drove into the secured Repo lot.

After she'd parked the Taurus and turned off the engine, she heard more rustling sounds coming from the backseat. She turned around and looked behind her. *Oh my God, the pile of trash was moving. A small mouse wouldn't displace that much stuff. Could it be a rat?* Andi swallowed back her fear. Time to get out of the car. Before she could turn around to leave, a large raccoon popped it's head up through the trash, looked at Andi and growled as Andi screamed! She scrambled out of the car, grabbed her purse, and slammed the door closed. Then she ran inside The Repo Doctor through the back door, closed it behind her, leaning against it to catch her breath.

Jerry was sitting at his desk. He looked up at her for a second, and then returned his attention to the paperwork on his desk. Without looking up again, he said, "Please tell me you brought in a car. We're getting so far behind. I'm going to need you to start bringing in a minimum of three to four cars a day if we're ever going to get ahead of that pile."

"I brought in a car, Jer, but you're not going to be happy," Andi said as she slowly walked over and sat in one of the chairs in front of his desk.

He looked up at her, narrowing his eyes. "Did you wreck the car or damage it on your way here?"

"No," she said.

"Did you find another dead body?" he asked.

"No," she said.

He looked relieved and then returned his attention to the paperwork. "Then there's no problem. Turn in your paperwork, key, and bring in any personal items. Then grab a few more new repos while you're over there and get back on the road, Squirt. You've got too much work to do to be sitting around in the office talking to me."

Andi bit her lip, and then said, "You don't want me to bring in the personal items. This guy's car is packed with trash, and I'm not talking about a few fast-food bags. The car is filled with binders, newspapers, old coffee cups, blankets. It's so full that there's no way that you can open any of the doors except the driver's door."

Jerry looked up at her, saw that she was serious, and then rubbed his hands on his face and groaned. He put his hands on his desk and leaned back. "You picked up a hoarder's car?"

Andi nodded, "Yeah. You'd think he was homeless and maybe living in the Taurus, but he lives a nice brick rancher. I saw him leave this morning. I picked up the car when he went inside to have breakfast in IHOP."

"Sorry, Squirt. You're going to have to empty out the car. You can dispose of the trash, but everything else needs to be bagged so that we can return it to the owner. We're required by law."

Andi made a face. "You're kidding, right?"

"Afraid not," he said.

"Well, I haven't even told you the worst part yet. There's a raccoon living in the car."

"Jesus," he said.

"I'm not going back in there until the racoon is gone."

He picked up his phone. "Great. I'll call Wildlife Removal Service. This could take a while. You might as well track down another repo." Jerry frowned and mumbled. "I guess I'll clean out the car for you."

Andi smiled. *Thank God! Finally, some good news.* "Thanks, Jer! You're the best."

Jerry only grunted before speaking to the Wildlife Removal Service department. Andi called for an Uber. While she waited, she grabbed a couple more folders, and sat down at the empty desk. Looking through the collection of repos, she saw a photo of a gorgeous Chevrolet Corvette C8 in Torch Red. After her horrible ride in the trash mobile, this would be a huge improvement. She scanned the details on her form. She needed to track down Jack Silverman, a thirty-six-year-old realtor. His office was located on Electric Road. She pulled out her phone and called his cellphone.

"Hello, Jack Silverman. How can I help you move into your dream home?"

Cheesy. "Hi Jack. Since the market is so good right now, I was thinking about listing my house," Andi said.

"I'd love to help you get the most money for your home, and help you find the next home of your dreams. Let's schedule a time for you to come by and we'll do a quick prequalification to see how much a house you qualify for."

Andi rolled her eyes. *Yeah, that's not happening.* "Um, are you available this morning? I could probably come by," she glanced at her watch and calculated how long it would take her to pick up the Jeep and then get down to his office on Electric Road, "in an hour."

"Oh, sorry. I'm meeting clients here at eleven to show them property. Can we schedule for this afternoon or tomorrow?"

If she could hustle down there before then, she might still be able to get the Corvette. Her Uber ride pulled up in front of the door. "Can I call you back and set up a time? I've got to run."

"Sure. Can I have your name?"

"Oh, of course. I'm Geraldine Harper. Thanks Jack. I'll see you later," Andi said and hung up.

Jerry smirked and looked at her. "Geraldine? Really? And you used my last name."

She got up, tucked all the files in her purse and smiled as she walked towards the door. "Well sure, Jer. You know how it is, covert operations and all. I make this stuff up on the fly."

He pointed a finger at her and turned serious. "Just don't give him my home address. The last thing I need is a realtor showing up trying to sell my house."

Andi placed a hand over her heart and pretended to look offended. "I'm shocked that you would think I'd do anything so diabolical." She grinned and then said, "But thanks for the great idea! I'll take it easy on you today since you're dealing with a raccoon and his nest while I get to drive back in the practically new, sleek, Torch Red Corvette C8." She tossed her hair dramatically over her shoulder.

Jerry sighed. "Yeah, thanks for not rubbing that in my face, Squirt."

***

By the time Andi retrieved her Jeep and drove over to the real estate office, it was just a few minutes before eleven. She parked next door in the Mattress Firm parking lot and spotted that big, bright, red sporty car just waiting for her to steal it away to The Repo Lot. This was going to be so easy. She reached into her purse, detached the key FOB for the Corvette from the folder, stepped out of her Jeep, locked it, and casually walked over the strip of grass separating the two lots. She was about three cars away from her target when the door to the office opened and an attractive man in his thirties wearing an expensive wool coat held the door for a man and woman about his same age. The realtor noticed her right away and gave her a friendly smile.

Please don't be Jack Silverman. The couple split off from the realtor and walked over to their BMW. Now just Andi and the realtor were both walking in the direction of the Corvette. *He is going to talk to me.* She could tell by the way he was sizing her up, like a potential new client. Andi paused and pulled out her phone and held it to her ear, pretending to answer a call.

"Hi, yes. I just arrived. I'm dropping off the paperwork, and then I'll meet you at the property," Andi said walking by him and stepping through the door into the warm office. She turned back to look through the glass door to see the parking lot. *Darn it!* The realtor was getting inside the Corvette.

A woman behind her asked, "Can I help you?"

Andi turned to face a receptionist who was looking at her questioningly.

"Oh, sorry. I forgot something in my car. I'll be back," Andi said. She went out the door as Silverman was backing out of his parking spot. *Okay, maybe there's still time to save this repo.* She hustled back to her Jeep and watched the red Corvette pull out with the BMW close behind. Lucky for her, her repo was easy to spot. Andi followed them in her Jeep as they turned right onto the highway heading south. When Silverman and his clients turned right into a high-end community, Andi slowed up so as not to make it obvious that she was following them. They made a left and then another right before Silverman pulled into the driveway. Andi watched the BMW turn into the driveway as well. She sent up a silent prayer to St. Jude, the patron saint of lost causes, that the BMW wouldn't block the Corvette, and made the sign of the cross.

She breathed a sigh of relief when the BMW pulled up next to the Corvette. She watched from her Jeep as Silverman talked and laughed with the couple, typed in some sort of keycode by the front door and entered the house.

Let's try this again. The house was humongous, so they'd probably be inside a while. She drove by the house, made a left onto Fox Ridge Road, and parked adjacent to a wooded lot. Grabbing her purse and the FOB for the Corvette, she locked her Jeep and started to jog over to the house. *Ouch.* She felt a cramp in her side, so she just walked the rest of the way. She'd parked a bit farther away than she'd intended. Well, she probably still had plenty of time.

Clicking the FOB, Andi unlocked the Corvette, slid into the driver's seat, and closed the door. It still had that new car smell—much nicer than the Taurus she'd just brought back to Jerry. There were like a million buttons on the center console, but it only took her a second to find the start button. *Oh Lord.* The engine was so loud. What did drivers of sports cars find enjoyable about a roaring sound? That volume level was very inconvenient when you were trying to sneak a car away from the skip.

Where the heck is the gear shift? She saw buttons with P, R, D, and N. *Buttons?* She put her foot on the brake and pressed the R button. When she eased up on the brake, the car began moving backwards. She was careful to pull it straight out, so she didn't scrape against the BMW. As Andi eased the Corvette out onto the street, she heard yelling from the house. She switched gears to Drive with a press of a button, glancing over to see a red-faced Silverman pointing at her and yelling, "It's you! Get the fu…" was all she heard before pressing the gas. Wow, this car had nice pickup.

She was able to figure out how to turn on the radio in time to sing along to six songs on the satellite radio before she was back at The Repo Doctor lot. Okay, so maybe she'd taken the long way back, but it was therapeutic, really. After dropping off the key and paperwork for the C8, she'd called an Uber to get back to her Jeep. As they were driving back, she saw Silverman standing in the driveway. The BMW was gone but he was talking to a police officer, no doubt reporting the repo as a grand theft auto. She wondered if the police officer had yet been notified it was a repossession.

Her skip glanced over as the Uber car drove by and saw Andi in the back passenger seat. His jaw dropped and he grabbed the officer's arm pointing to her, saying "That's her. That's the woman that stole my car." *Well, guess the repo hadn't come up in the system yet.*

Crystal, her Uber Driver, saw the exchange and gave Andi a worried look in the rearview mirror. Andi smiled and said, "Don't worry, I'm a Repo Agent, not a car thief."

"Oh hey, I recognize you. You're the Repo Girl." Crystal said.

Andi shrugged. "Yes, I guess so." *Hm.* It was a little disconcerting the way strangers were recognizing her. Was it her imagination or did Crystal's frown deepen?

***

After Crystal dropped her off at the Jeep, Andi drove downtown. She had a little time before she was meeting Cooper at his counselor's office, which was just a couple blocks away from the City Market Building. She needed to talk to Mags. Working had been a good distraction, but now that she was not dealing with racoons or complicated shifting gears in new cars, her mind drifted to thoughts of Kitty and that awful dream she'd had last night.

It was that quiet time of day in between lunch and dinner. Andi was relieved that no one lined up at the Bull Dog food truck. Her plan was to steal Mags away for a quick lunch and conversation. Her stomach ached from a combination of hunger and stress. Mags was such a good friend. What she needed right now was friendship, a margarita, and a pile of nachos.

As Andi approached the truck, she smiled. Mags and Simon were facing off again, Maggy with her hands on her hips looking feisty and saying something that Andi wasn't able to hear from this distance. Simon stood arm's length from her, his hands raised in surrender, his elbows close to his sides. *Poor Simon.* It looked like he was trying to get a word in, but Maggy appeared to be talking with great speed. She tended to do that when she was riled.

In the next moment, Simon closed the distance between them, cradled her friend's face in his hands and kissed her. *Wow.* Andi stopped walking and just stared, shocked. That was not just some quick brush on the lips. It was more like watching Ryan Gosling kiss Rachel McAdams in the rain scene from The Notebook. Andi didn't have time to wonder what Maggy thought about the kiss because her friend wrapped her arms around his torso and pulled him against her.

I knew it! The attraction had been obvious to Andi even though Maggy had tried to deny it. Andi lifted her chin feeling quite satisfied with herself. She completely approved of these two as a couple. In her opinion, Billy just wasn't right for Maggy. He was a nice enough guy, but her fiery friend needed someone to bring out the passion and judging by the kiss that was still going on, Simon was the man for the job.

Andi walked up to the truck counter and said, "That's some kitchen fire you've got going there, guys."

At the sound of her voice, the couple jumped apart, their faces flushed.

"This is a departure from your usual lunchtime show where you banter. I mean, I don't mind, but the city might require that you get a special permit for this kind of entertainment."

Simon recovered first, turning to face Andi. He leaned his forearms on the counter, a little breathless and looking happier than she'd ever seen him. He seemed even more thrilled than when she'd given him the donuts. "Hey, Andi. What can I get you? You name it, my treat."

Poor Maggy looked shell-shocked. Her eyes were wide, her mouth agape, staring at Simon like she was seeing him for the first time.

"Would you mind covering for Maggy so that I can steal her away for about thirty minutes or so? I really need her advice."

Mags looked at Andi, closed her mouth and nodded. "Yes, good idea," she said and then pressed her lips together. She slid the apron over her neck and tucked it under the counter.

Simon turned to look at Maggy. He was looking at her friend with such love and tenderness. "No problem. Take your time, Mary Margaret." *Aw. He's completely adorable and absolutely perfect for her.*

Maggy glanced at him and then away, blushing. "Great. Thanks," she said. She put on her jacket, exited the truck, and grabbed Andi by the arm, dragging her away from the truck.

Andi laughed. "Slow down, Mags. He's not chasing after you."

Maggy looked back at the food truck as if to make sure. "Oh my God," Mags murmured, and picked up her pace.

"Where are we going?" Andi asked, laughter in her voice. She'd never seen Maggy act like this.

"Alejandro's," she said. "I need a drink."

"Day drinking, Mags? On the job, even?" Andi asked. "That must have been some kiss."

"Yeah," she said as she opened the door to the restaurant. The smell of spices wrapped around them, and Andi's stomach rumbled. They grabbed seating for two and a cute waiter came over to them placing two vinyl menus on the table.

"Can I get you anything to drink?" he asked.

"We'd each like a margarita, thanks," Andi said. "Oh, and I'd like the Chicken Fajita Nachos, please. I'm starving." The waiter made a note and then turned to Maggy.

"Spinach burrito with the rice and black beans. No queso, please."

The waiter made a note and smiled. "I'll be right back with your drinks."

As soon as the waiter left for the bar to prepare their margaritas, Andi looked at Maggy and said, "Oh my God, Mags. That kiss. Wow!"

Maggy swallowed, touched her lips with her fingertips and then quickly clasped her hands together on the table in front of her, and looked at Andi. "It wasn't a big deal. He just took me by surprise, that's all. I wasn't expecting it."

Andi burst into laughter. "Wasn't a big deal? How can you even say that with a straight face? You practically jumped the poor guy when he leaned in to kiss you."

"I know," Maggy said quietly and blushed. She turned her attention to the waiter, watching him as he approached their table with their drinks. He placed the beautiful salt rimmed beverages in front of them, each with a slice of lime hugging the rim. "Your food will be out in a minute," he said and winked at Maggy.

When he left, Andi asked, "Are you seriously flirting with the waiter right now?"

Maggy looked horrified. "What? God, no!" She picked up her glass and took two big gulps before setting it back on the table.

Andi took a sip of the margarita. "Then you probably should avoid making eye contact with him until you can get rid of that lusty look that's on your face." Andi smiled. "Speaking of

Simon, what were you guys arguing about before he kissed you so thoroughly?"

Maggy blanched. "I have a lusty look?" She rubbed her hands over her face as if that would somehow magically wipe it away. "Is it gone?" Mags asked.

Silly woman. "Sure," Andi lied.

Her friend was already on edge, so there was no need to tease her about it. She'd never seen Mags behave like this over a guy. Oh, Maggy could act like an insane person when there was an issue with her business, but a man? No, not until today.

Maggy looked relieved. "Well, we were arguing pretty much about everything all day. The space is tight, and he is always in my way. I swear, Andi, we're bumping into each other all the time, and he thinks it's hilarious when I get irritated with him." She pointed a finger at Andi. "And another thing, he's always calling me Mary Margaret, like I'm back in Catholic school, except he says it in an endearing way, so I can't really be mad at him, which only makes me angry, because maybe I want to be irritated with him."

Wow. She said all that without even taking a breath, and it made absolutely no sense.

"We were arguing because he used my special fruit knife to cut an onion for his hot dogs." She made a face.

"He didn't!" Andi said in mock horror and giggled.

Maggy looked insulted and then she smiled. "Okay, so it wasn't that big of a deal by itself, but when you add that on top of every other irritating thing he does, it was all too much. I sort of lost it."

Andi considered her friend. "Hey, not to say I told you so, but I'm not surprised you finally kissed. That tension between the two of you has been building since you moved into the booth next to him."

The waiter brought their hot plates of food to the table and set them before them. "Can I get you anything else?" he asked while looking at Maggy with a charming smile. Maggy was staring at Andi avoiding looking at the poor waiter for fear that she might burn a hole in him like some super villain. Andi looked at him. "No, I think we're all set, thank you."

"Okay. I'll be right over there if you need me," he said, and then left a little slip of paper next to Maggy's spinach burrito before leaving the table. Maggy picked up the paper that simply had the name Carlos and a phone number handwritten on it. She put her head in her hand. "Oh, God." She looked up at Andi. "You were right about the waiter."

Andi tried not to grin but failed. "I'm right about most things, Mags." She lifted a chip with a piece of chicken, a green pepper, queso, and sour cream on it, and popped it in her mouth and chewed. *Yum.*

Maggy stared down at her spinach burrito and frowned. "Why did he have to kiss me?" Maggy asked and looked up at Andi. "It makes everything complicated."

Andi took another drink of her margarita. "Um, I'm pretty sure he had to kiss you because you're a gorgeous, intelligent, passionate, savvy entrepreneur, that he's been crushing on since he met you."

Mags raised her brows. "You think so?"

Andi nodded as she ate a few more loaded corn tortillas and chased it with another drink of her margarita.

Maggy sighed. "It was pretty much the hottest kiss that I've ever experienced." She put her right elbow on the table and rested her chin in her palm. "What if Simon thought it was awful?"

Andi chuckled, "Girl, I think that kiss has short-circuited your brain. Do you even hear yourself speaking this nonsense? Trust me, the guy was practically glowing after he kissed you. The question you need to be asking yourself is what are you going to do about it?"

She sat back in her seat and bit her lower lip. "It can never happen again. I'm still seeing Billy."

"You aren't seeing Billy. Not really, and that's part of the problem. Your schedules aren't meshing. Let's be honest, if he were really important to you, you'd make time to be together."

"Have I mentioned that you're so irritating when you make sense?"

Andi was feeling smug, and it felt good. "So, what's the plan Mags?"

Exhaling, Mags squared her shoulders. "Well, first thing I have to do is have a conversation with Billy, because you're right. The schedule thing has been a problem for a while, now. Neither of us seems to be willing to accommodate the other, so regardless of whether anything happens with Simon, I'm going to end things with Billy."

Andi nodded. "Sounds like a solid plan."

Just then Andi's phone alerted her of an incoming text. She pulled it out of her coat pocket and looked at the screen.

Cooper: Where R U? I'm waiting for you in the parking lot.

"Oh no! How did it get to be so late?" Andi asked Maggy. She texted a quick "On my way" response, and then reached into her wallet and handed Maggy money to cover her share of their lunch and tip. "I'm sorry to rush off. I'm supposed to meet with Cooper's counselor in about ten minutes to talk about my issues with Kitty."

"Of course," Maggy said, taking the money. "I feel bad that we've spent this entire time talking about me, when you've got much bigger issues you're dealing with." She stood up and gave Andi a hug.

"It's actually been great to talk about something other than my problems for a change. And hey, this is such good news. It makes me happy to think of you and Simon as a couple."

"A couple? No, we're not a couple? How can we be a couple? That would be crazy?" Mags shook her head, but then a light blush bloomed over her freckled cheeks. "Well, call me later and let me know how your session goes. Love you."

"Love you, too, Mags."

Chapter Thirteen

Cooper stepped out of his Porsche as Andi pulled in the parking spot next to him. He was wearing a dress black wool coat over his standard day job uniform—an expensive, designer, classic suit and tie. His father was old school and insisted that all the executives wear suits in the office. Cooper wasn't a fan of the dress code, but Andi had always thought there was something extra delicious about her Rockstar in all those fancy layers—sort of like anticipating unwrapping a pretty gift with ribbons and bows. He greeted her with a tender kiss when she stepped out of her Jeep. *Mm.* He smelled like that delicious, expensive cologne he liked to wear and tasted like peppermint.

"I was afraid you were going to stand me up, Margarita," he said.

"What?" she asked, "And miss the fun of talking to a complete stranger about my very personal, most traumatic life experiences?"

He laughed. "Exactly. Why was I worried?" He leaned in and kissed her again on the lips. *Cooper.* She loved how he was always so affectionate with her even in public, giving her light kisses or reaching out to hold her hand. They both seemed to crave a physical connection when they were together. Thank God, the feeling was mutual.

Linking her fingers in his, they walked toward the building. Once they were inside the empty lobby, he turned to face her and walked backwards so he could see her face. "I know it may feel a little awkward first but trust me when I tell you Dr. Martin is the best. She's a great listener and is a huge help in dealing with problem mothers. If she can help me navigate my relationship with mine and prevent me from becoming homicidal, I just know she'll be able to help you, too."

Andi smiled. He was adorable, and it was kind of cute how he seemed a little nervous as he tried to sell her on the advantages of talking to his favorite shrink.

"Don't worry, Rockstar. I trust you," she said to reassure him.

"Good," he said and exhaled. He pressed the elevator button. "How's your day been?"

Andi shrugged. "Okay, I guess. I've been keeping busy with work. I already brought in two cars. My first repo this morning was a Ford Taurus that belonged to a hoarder. Oh, Coop, the smell was revolting, and get this, a raccoon was living in the back seat!"

His expression displayed the appropriate amount of disgust and surprise, which made her grin. She nodded. "But my second repo almost made up for the first one. I got to drive a gorgeous, brand new red Corvette C8 with satellite radio playing through a Bose sound system. That was glorious!"

Cooper smiled and shook his head. He leaned in and kissed her again, and said, "You know I can't resist you when you talk about sports cars."

She gave him a playful shove and yawned. "Sorry. I didn't sleep well last night."

He reached up and caressed her cheek, frowning. "More bad dreams about Peter?"

"Yes," she said. "This one was particularly awful."

The elevator doors opened, and Cooper led her inside and pressed the button for Dr. Martin's floor.

"Instead of the dreams easing up, your nightmares are getting worse," he said gently squeezing her hand. "While you're talking to Dr. Martin about your mother, mention those nightmares, okay?" He was looking at her with so much love and concern, she wanted to push him against the elevator wall and kiss his worry away, making them both forget everything except each other. That thought reminded her of another passionate kiss she'd witnessed today.

"Oh," she smiled, "but I've got some exciting news. I caught Mags and Simon in a steamy kiss inside the food truck this afternoon."

Cooper grinned. "About damn time. I hope this means Maggy has come to her senses and will finally dump the paramedic. I really don't like the guy."

"Hey, Billy is a perfectly nice guy, but I agree he's not right for Maggy. Simon's been crazy for her for a while, but I wish you could have seen how affected Mags was by that kiss." Andi waggled her brows. "They're going to be so good for each other."

The elevator doors opened. "Come on, matchmaker. We're here," he said and led her out of the elevator to a dark walnut door where Dr. Martin's name was engraved on a gold plate. They stepped into a room that could have been someone's upscale living room. There was a man sitting behind an oak library table. He looked up from his computer screen when they walked in. Andi guessed he was in his late twenties. He had wavy blond hair and was wearing a gorgeous deep purple V-neck sweater. His sweater looked so soft—maybe cashmere, though she couldn't be sure without touching it. Now that she was actually here, she was nervous. She gave Cooper's hand a quick squeeze.

Her Rockstar glanced at her with a sweet smile before turning to cashmere guy. "Hi Gavin. This is Andrea Sloan. She's here to take my time slot this afternoon."

Andi swallowed. *This is really a bad idea. Why did I agree to come?* An image of Kitty pointing the gun at her from her dream flashed through her mind. She stood up straighter and lifted her chin. *It's better to just get this over with.*

Gavin nodded and clicked something on his computer. With a slight smile, he said, "Yes, Dr. Martin's ready for you. You can go inside."

Cooper nodded and they walked through the open door to the right of Gavin's desk.

This room was even more cozy than the lobby. There was a sitting area with large comfortable looking sofa next to the wall and an armchair adjacent to it. *Definitely a living room vibe.* On the other end of the room was a table with another computer, similar to Cashmere-guy's set up. *Why don't their desks have drawers?*

A woman in her forties with stylish frosted short hair and designer black frames stood and walk over to greet them.

"Good afternoon, Cooper. You must be Andrea Sloan. I'm Dr. Martin," she said with a genuine smile as she extended her hand to Andi.

Andi shook the woman's hand, and said, "Please call me Andi."

"Of course. Why don't you have a seat on the sofa?"

She followed Dr. Martin as she walked to the sitting area. The good doctor sat in an armchair and motioned to the sofa for Andi. Cooper followed and sat next to Andi.

What is he doing?

Dr. Martin looked at Cooper. "Why don't you wait in the lobby while I talk with Andi?"

After a moment, he said, "Oh, right. Of course. Sorry." He stood up and walked to the door. Before he left, Cooper looked at Andi and said, "I'll just wait for you out here. I'm so glad you both finally get to meet." Then he frowned and looked at Dr. Martin. "Wait, you're not going to talk to Andi about me, right? Haven't you taken some sort of oath that prevents that?"

Dr. Martin looked at him over her glasses. "Relax, Cooper. Andi will be fine, and she'll meet you in the lobby when we're finished."

He grinned. "Right. Okay, then I guess I'll just wait out here and hang out with good ole Gavin," he said and closed the door.

Dr. Martin looked at Andi and gave her another gentle smile that put her a little more at ease. Andi was good at reading people and could spot a fake smile from a mile away. She leaned back against the sofa, ordering herself to relax.

"So, Cooper gave you his time slot today because he said you were going through a difficult time and needed to talk. How can I help you, Andi? What would you like to talk about?"

Just tell her. Andi bit her lower lip and began to bounce her right knee. "Okay, so my mother showed up at my door yesterday morning. She left me twenty-five years ago to be raised by my grandparents—her parents—when I was only a few weeks old." Andi shrugged. "The only explanation my grandparents got was a note with two words—I'm sorry." *What does that even mean? Sorry for dumping my kid on you. Sorry, gotta run and follow my dreams. Sorry I got pregnant. Sorry that I ever had this baby.*

"I get that she was only seventeen years old—no more than a kid herself. I can't even imagine what that must have been like. My father wasn't in the picture. Who knows if he even knew about me? I certainly don't know who he is. Anyway, I'm really angry that she never contacted my grandparents during all that time. My grandmother used to cry over her—a lot. I always sort of figured Kitty was dead. That was an easier thought to consider than the truth that she just didn't want us. Her leaving and staying away broke my grandparents' hearts."

Andi glanced at the door and then back at Dr. Martin. Thank God there was no pity in her eyes, only an intent gaze as she absorbed Andi's words. Andi focused her attention on the floor. "To say I was in shock seeing her when I answered the door yesterday is an understatement. Kitty seemed surprised to see me, too. She was looking for my grandparents." Andi looked up at Dr. Martin to explain. "I still live in the same house. My grandparents were killed in a car accident last year, so lucky me, I got to inform Kitty of their passing. Apparently, she's on the run from an abusive boyfriend and had nowhere else to go, so now she's staying with me."

Dr. Martin's expression didn't change. She just sat there watching Andi, waiting for her to say more. *What more is there to say?*

Andi couldn't take the silence, so she said, "When I was little, I used to pray, wish, hope, and make deals with God that she'd come back in my life. I'd be the best daughter in the world, I'd always eat my vegetables, stop getting into trouble at school, that kind of thing. Don't get me wrong, my grandparents were incredible, but it wasn't the same as having a mom. When she didn't show up by my fifteenth birthday, I finally let go of the idea that she was ever coming back."

Andi leaned forward, resting her forearms on her thighs. "Now she's back, and I don't know what to do with her, say to her. Everyone thinks that I should be so happy. My neighbors are welcoming her back with open arms. My friends are so happy for me that my wish finally came true. My old roommate adores her. Even Cooper thinks this is a great chance to understand why she left and get some closure." Andi shook her head. "All I really want is for her to go away. Heck, if I'm being honest, I wish she'd never come back at all." Andi exhaled and collapsed against the sofa. *God, she was such an awful person.* That was the first time she'd ever said those words out loud.

Dr. Martin continued to watch her, without judgement in her expression, just that same annoying expectant look. What else did she want from Andi? Jeez, she must have been the school champion at staring contests. Andi crossed her arms across her chest. Well, she'd been good at those contests too. She could wait her out.

Maybe.

She wiggled her toes in her boots and checked out the room. It was warm without being cluttered. Not much on her desk, and just three small, framed certificates or degrees on her walls. God, there wasn't anything to distract Andi while she tried to outwait Dr. Martin. She glanced back over at the good doctor to see if she'd looked away or something. Darn it, she was still looking at Andi and waiting. How did Cooper stand this? And how was any of this helping her when she was the one doing all the talking. Lord, Cooper was no doubt wasting big bucks for this useless session.

Fine. She wants me to talk. How about this Dr. Guinness Book of World Records Staring Contest Winner? Andi uncrossed her arms and clasped her hands together in her lap.

"So last night, I had a nightmare. I've been having them a couple times a week, and it's always the same." Andi exhaled, and said, "Cooper probably told you about his client that held me at gunpoint last month, threatening to kill me." Andi shrugged, "I obviously survived. I was able to get hold of the gun and kept him there while Cooper wrapped him in Christmas lights until the police arrived. He's locked away securely in prison for life, so I'm not entirely sure why I'm still dreaming about this. The nightmare usually starts with Peter pointing the gun at me, threatening to kill me except in my dream, I don't get hold of the gun and I die. Well, I assume I'm dead. He's close enough that the shot would be fatal. Anyway, I always wake up at that point, pretty shaken." Andi took a deep breath and tucked her hands under her thighs. "But last night, when I had the nightmare and was pleading with Peter to let me live, I looked back at Peter and instead, Kitty was holding the gun. She was the one who pulled the trigger this time."

Dr. Martin tilted her head and spoke. "Interesting. Did she say anything to you before she fired the gun?"

"Yes," Andi said. The image of Kitty pointing the gun at her instantly appeared in her mind, and Andi suddenly felt nauseous. *Escape.* She looked at the door and back at Dr. Martin and bit her lip. "I hope Cooper isn't driving Gavin too crazy out there. Maybe I should check on him."

"Cooper will be just fine," Dr. Martin said with a kind, knowing smile. Then she said, "Often, recurrent bad dreams or nightmares are revealing some unresolved conflict that keeps replaying during sleep. There's obviously something about that event that you have yet to sort out. It's interesting that in your dream, Kitty is now as big a threat to you as Peter. We'll talk about your mom in a minute. Right now, let's see if we can identify that unresolved conflict and squelch these nightmares. How does that sound?"

"That would be amazing," Andi said.

"Great. Now, I believe you said that your nightmare is different than what really happened because in the actual events, you were able to get hold of the gun, right?"

"Yes."

Dr. Martin tilted her head and studied Andi. "Interesting. So, tell me how you felt when Peter had the gun pointed at you."

"Um, terrified." *Duh.* "He was going to kill me. He had no qualms about it, and he even told me it wasn't personal. I could see it in his eyes."

"How did you get the gun from Peter?"

"I threw a cup of hot coffee in his face and Cooper stormed in a moment later, bumping Peter with the front door, knocking him to the floor. Peter had to break his fall with his hand, and in doing so, dropped the gun. I grabbed it right away. That's the only reason I'm still alive."

"Yes, that must have been terrifying for you. How did you feel when you had the gun?

What? Why is she asking all these crazy questions? "Relieved, of course."

"What else were you feeling?"

"I don't know. Maybe scared that I was going to have to shoot Peter. He kept talking and trying to convince Cooper that I was crazy. I didn't want to shoot anybody, but I didn't want to die, either. I was in survival mode." Andi took a shaky breath. "I'm pretty sure I would have pulled the trigger if he had made a move for me."

Dr. Martin nodded. "Would you say it was just a matter of luck that you were able to get the gun and reverse the situation?"

Andi's chest felt tight, and she realized she'd stopped breathing. She took two quick breaths, but the panic was still there. "So, do you think that I'm dreaming about dying in that moment because at a subconscious level, anyway, I realize it was sheer luck that kept me alive that night?"

Dr. Martin tilted her head and studied Andi. "It doesn't really matter what I think. Do you feel it was only luck that kept you alive?"

Andi felt a wave of nausea wash over her. "Yes," she said.

"Let's imagine your nightmare is a movie, and you are the director. How would you recreate this scene so that you disarm Peter intentionally, without having to rely on the luck?"

She'd thrown the hot coffee, but it hadn't been enough to disarm Peter, just distract him and make him really angry, leaving blisters on his face. Andi thought back to the self-defense class at the senior center.

"If I'd known how to disarm him—to physically remove the gun from his hand—then I wouldn't have had to rely on luck. My neighbors recently took me to a self-defense class. I froze when the instructor used a gun prop to practice disarming. Maybe I should go back to that self-defense class and try again. I'll do anything to stop having this dream over and over again."

"That might work. The odds of you being in this type of life-threatening situation again are slim, but I believe your mind will release this dream when you feel prepared to handle it. Now, let's talk about your mother in this dream."

Andi swallowed and clasped her hands in her lap again.

"How will you disarm your mother?" Dr. Martin asked.

"What do you mean? I'll use the same technique that I learn in the self-defense class."

Dr. Martin continued to look at her. *Not the staring contest again. Great. I guess I got the answer wrong.*

Andi blew out a breath. "I don't know. You're the expert. How do I disarm my mother?"

"Okay, maybe a better question to ask is 'What does the gun represent when your mother holds it? Why do you feel mortally threatened by her?'" Dr. Martin asked.

Andi looked back at the door. *Escape.* How could Cooper possibly put her through this? *No wonder Dr. Martin sent him to the safety of the lobby.* She could throttle him about now. She looked back at the staring Dr. Martin again. Andi blew out a breath. *Fine.*

"Fine. I put all the questions, confusion, and hurt of a mother I never knew in a box and shoved it in the back of my closet, okay? Maybe she broke my heart, leaving me as a newborn and then never even tried to come back or call, for Pete's sake." Andi stood up, needing to move. Andi rubbed her palms on her pants and looked down at Dr. Martin, who simply sat in that darn chair, watching her. "Now she's back and she didn't even come to see me."

Andi dropped back down on the sofa. *That's it.* She would have been able to forgive Kitty if she'd come back to Andi's porch, wrapped her in a hug, and said she was sorry she was unable to be there for her childhood, but she'd love to get to know her now. *God, I am so pathetic.*

But Kitty had come back looking for Andi's grandparents, not her, because even after all these years, Andi was not enough of a reason to return home.

A tear rolled down her cheek, and she brushed it away. She was so tired of crying over this woman. Andi raised her chin and looked at Dr. Martin. *Just get this over with.*

"I'm not enough." She pressed her lips together. "Apparently, I'm not enough of a reason to come back home."

"So, you don't believe your mom left New York City and returned home because of you?" Dr. Martin asked.

"That's right. She was running from her abusive boyfriend."

"Interesting. When she was seventeen, she was running away from parenthood."

"From me," Andi said.

Dr. Martin shook her head. "Not you, specifically. You were just an infant. Newborn babies basically sleep, eat, and poop. There was nothing that you specifically did that caused her to leave home."

Andi sat back on the couch. *Huh.* She'd always thought there was something inherently wrong with her. Something that made her unlovable.

"Did you ever stop to consider that the problem was never you? Your mom, Kitty, runs from her problems, rather than confronting them head on."

"But I always thought it was me?"

"Nope. You were an infant. Your mom, even as a child herself at seventeen, made the decision all on her own. It had nothing to do with you, and everything to do with her."

"Wow," Andi said, staring at the floor. *It's not my fault Kitty left.* That felt weird. She'd been shouldering the guilt for that for her entire life. Her chest felt a bit lighter.

"So, let's try that exercise again. You're the director of your dream. Kitty is pointing the gun at you. How do you disarm her?"

Andi bit her lower lip and shook her head as she looked at Dr. Martin.

"I don't see her holding the gun anymore. It doesn't make sense. If for some reason she is holding it, her hands would be unsteady, and I could easily take it from her. Since she always runs from her problems, it makes more sense that she'd be fleeing the scene."

"Good," Dr. Martin said.

Andi bit her lower lip. "Now, I sort of feel sorry for her."

"Even better," Dr. Martin said and glanced at the clock. "I'm sorry, Andi, but that's all the time we have for today. I hope our session will eliminate those nightmares."

"Me, too," Andi said, and stood up as Dr. Martin rose from the chair. Andi reached out and shook her hand. "Thank you for your help."

"I'm glad you found it helpful," Dr. Martin said and walked Andi to the door. "You know, this new perspective isn't going to wipe away a lifetime of the feelings you have about your mom, but it's a start. Come back and see me if you ever need help looking at a life situation in a new way."

"Thank you. I will," Andi said. She stepped out into the lobby and Cooper was standing behind Gavin, both men looking at the computer screen.

Cooper looked up at her, concern in those beautiful brown eyes. She gave him a smile, and asked, "Ready to go, Rockstar?"

"Yes," he said, and patted Gavin on the shoulder. Cooper reached into his pocket and handed Gavin a business card. "Give me a call, and I'll help you set up a proper investment portfolio."

Gavin took the card, and said, "Thanks, Cooper. I appreciate it."

Cooper walked out from behind the desk, grabbed his coat off the hook, and took Andi's hand.

They walked out into the hallway towards the elevator. Cooper pushed the down button and turned towards Andi. "So, how did it go?"

Andi playfully punched his arm. "Awful. There was a point that I was ready to strangle you for talking me into taking your session. It's a good thing Dr. Martin kicked you out because if you had been sitting next to me..." Andi said, giving him her toughest look with the unspoken threat lingering between them.

The doors to the elevator opened and they got in. Cooper pressed the button for the lobby, and turned to Andi, frowning. "I'm sorry, Margarita. I know she can ask some really tough questions."

Andi shrugged.

"But then she helped me realize that Kitty leaving home at seventeen had more to do with her running away from the responsibilities of being a mother than it had to do with anything that I did."

Cooper frowned as he watched her. "Wait, all this time, you thought that your mom leaving you when you were only a baby was somehow your fault?"

Andi didn't say anything. How could she? It all seemed ridiculous after she'd talked it through with Dr. Martin.

"Oh, Andi," he said in a soft, tender voice, his eyes looking at her with so much love and then he was kissing her. His lips were soft and even though his touch was gentle, her entire body was on fire as if he had dropped a match on gasoline. She returned his kiss with an urgency she didn't try to understand, pressing her body against his until he was backed was up against the elevator wall. His gentle kiss was gone, his hands splayed across her back, pressing her tight against him as he did the most delicious things to her mouth.

Ding.

The elevator doors opened, and Andi stepped back, a little breathless looking at her Rockstar. He was staring at her in that way that always made her feel like a puddle of goo. The corners of her mouth lifted as she backed out of the elevator. He matched her steps, never taking his gaze from hers.

When they were both out of the elevator, he reached for her hand and she grinned, turned and ran through the lobby. She heard him curse, which made her laugh as she pushed through the lobby doors and ran towards her Jeep. Andi screamed, startled when Cooper grabbed her by the waist from behind and swung her so that he was between her and her driver's door.

They were both laughing as she turned in his arms to face him and nipped his chin.

"Hey, Margarita, you're going to pay for that."

"I'd like to see you try, Rockstar."

"Come home with me," he said as he planted a trail of little kisses down her neck.

She closed her eyes, leaning her head to the left giving him better access to her neck, enjoying the feel of his warm kisses. "You have to go back to the office." *And that is a darn shame, because I want to spend the rest of the afternoon with him in his gigantic king-sized bed.*

He lifted his head and looked at her. "Didn't I tell you? I'm suddenly not feeling well, so I'm taking the rest of the afternoon off."

"Really," she said, mock concern in her voice.

"Yes, I just came from the doctor's office," he said pointing at Dr. Martin's building, and then he reached for Andi's hand and held it up to his lips and planted a kiss on her palm. "And I'm fevered, see?" He moved her hand to his smooth cheek, as he grinned. "I think I need bed rest."

"Oh, you do, do you?" She asked, smiling. "Well, I'd better follow you to make sure you make it home alright."

"And you should definitely come up and tuck me in," he said, and kissed her on the lips.

***

It was 7:20 pm when Andi walked into Star City Bar and Grill. She smiled when she realized it was Karaoke night. A trio of women were enthusiastically singing "Love Shack." Huh, they actually sounded pretty good. Andi walked up to the bar, sat at an empty stool, and waved at Ben who was serving a drink to a customer. The bar wasn't crowded. It was still early, so most of the customers were sitting at tables near the stage waiting for their turn at the mic.

Ben grinned and walked right over to her, nodded, and asked, "Margarita?"

Andi slid her coat off and hung it on the back of her stool. She rubbed her hands together, trying to warm them. "Too cold. I'll just take a hot tea."

Ben looked offended. "Oh, please. I'm Roanoke's best bartender. I can do better than a hot tea." He shook his head. "Who comes to a bar for a hot tea, anyway?"

Tilting her head at him, she said, "Since you don't live at my house anymore, I've had to resort to coming to your work in order to see you." She made a pout face.

"Not true. Just yesterday, we met at your work, which happened to be at a homicide crime scene." He winked and left to make her drink.

Speaking of work, she really needed to line up her next repo. Andi retrieved a folder from her purse and opened it on the bar.

Ford 350 XLT – Diesel Engine in Harvest Gold. The skip, twenty-eight-year-old Ronnie Hinson, was three months late on his payment. He was employed at the Valley View movie theater at the time of his loan application.

"Here you go," Ben said as he placed a beautiful glass mug of tawny liquid with a frothy white topping with what looked like cinnamon sprinkled on top. Andi took a sniff. *Mmm.* "What is it?" she asked. Her best friend was a very good bartender, but she still liked to know what she was drinking.

"Amarula Thai Tea," he said, beaming. He leaned forward, looked around to make sure no one was listening, and then said, "Think of this as a spiked tea latte. I used Amarula, which is a cream liqueur, with some Thai tea and added the frothy milk with a sprinkle of cinnamon." He nodded. "Go ahead. Taste it and tell me what you think."

She narrowed her gaze. "Have you made this before or am I your guinea pig?"

"Don't think of yourself as a pig, although you really need to improve your diet. Consider yourself my VIP customer."

"Uh huh," she said and then took a sip of the warm beverage. *Mm.* She licked some of the cream from her lips. "It's very tasty."

He began wiping the top of the bar with his white towel and nodded. "Why, thank you. I thought you'd like it."

He glanced down at her folder and then looked at her. "Why aren't you working from home? Still avoiding your mother?"

"Maybe just a little," she said and took another sip of the tea. It was warming her from the inside out. "I did really want to come by and see how your move went. Are you loving your new roommate and your new place?"

"Yes and no."

"What do you mean?"

"Well, you know I love my drummer boy and his condo downtown is fabulous. The exposed brick walls from the warehouse conversion gives it such an industrial/modern vibe. He said I could use the second bedroom for my studio and there's so much space!" Ben spread his arms out wide and beamed. "It's so much bigger than the tiny bedroom upstairs at your place," he said and added, "No offense. Your house is lovely."

"That all sounds great. What's the problem?" she asked.

He leaned on his forearms and looked at her. "It still feels like Daniel's place rather than ours. I've been sleeping over on and off for the past year. He's being very accommodating, especially moving his office out of the second bedroom so that I can use the space for my fashion studio."

Andi took another sip of the tea. "You could always put out a few photos of the two of you in the living room or maybe you both could pick out a piece of artwork together to hang on the wall?"

"Maybe," he said, resting his chin in his palm.

"You're overthinking this, Benny. You just moved in. Give it a little time," she said and reached over and squeezed his arm. "You guys are so adorable together."

Ben grinned and stood up. "We really are, aren't we? You're probably right," Ben said and rolled his eyes and sighed. "It's just new and strange, that's all. I've never lived with a boyfriend before. We're a deliciously hot couple."

"Oh, speaking of hot," Andi said, closed her file and tucked it away in her bag. She'd drive by Ronnie's house on her way home, just in case she could grab an easy repo. "Guess who I caught kissing in a food truck?"

Ben's eyes widened and he bit his lower lip. "Why Mary Margaret O'Neill, the little vixen." He smiled and shook his head. "And?"

"Simon was all grins, offering to give me free food. Mags was completely discombobulated." Andi leaned in and said, "I kept trying to point out the chemistry between her and Simon that was obvious to the rest of the world, but she refused to believe it." A satisfied grin spread across her face, and she looked quite smug. "She sees it now, though."

"Love it!" Ben said with a smile and then sobered. "Hey, didn't you have that meeting today with Cooper's shrink?"

Andi nodded as she finished off the latte.

"And?" Ben asked.

Andi shrugged. "It was good, I think. There are a million things I'd much rather do for an hour than discuss my private trauma with a stranger but talking to her helped." Andi shook her head. "She did this annoying thing where she'd just sit there and quietly wait for me to speak. It was creepy."

Ben nodded. "I dated a guy once who wasn't a big talker, and I was like, this is my ideal partner because I can talk enough for both of us." He shook his head. "It wasn't as nice as I thought it would be." Ben took Andi's empty mug and put it on the bussing tray under the bar. As he wiped the bar in front of her, he asked, "So what's the plan with Kitty? Are you going to stop avoiding home and talk to her?"

"We talked a bit last night. I guess after talking with Dr. Martin this afternoon, I don't feel quite as angry with her. It's just weird, you know what I mean? This person that I never thought I'd see is now staying in my old bedroom. Well, it was hers first."

"Hey, can we get some service down here or what?" a customer asked from a few seats down.

Ben sighed. "Oh my God, people are so rude the way they expect to be waited on like this. I'd better get back to work," he said as he plastered his fake smile on his face and spoke loudly to the customer. "Of course. I'll be happy to take your order. I'll be right over." He turned to Andi and whispered, "My fashion business better take off soon, so that I can quit this job before I'm responsible for the next homicide in the city."

Andi laughed. "Hang in there, Benny. I'd better get back to work, too." She left money for her drink and a large tip on the bar and slid it towards him. "It was great seeing you. Is it ridiculous that I miss you already?"

She leaned over the bar and gave him a hug. "Not at all. I have that effect on everyone," he said and kissed her on the cheek. "Tell Kitty I said hello."

"See ya, Ben," she said as she slid on her winter coat. She waved to him one last time as she left the bar.

Chapter Fourteen

Nick Marino was exhausted. He and Mason had been on the road since 9 a.m., within an hour after receiving the call. Instead of Frankie barking orders when Nick had answered the phone, there had been silence. His oldest brother simply said, "Jimmy's dead." Nick heard the words, but they hadn't sunk in. Then Frankie was describing how two NYPD officers had shown up at his door first thing this morning and told him that a man matching the photo and in possession of Jimmy's driver's license had been found shot to death in Roanoke, Virginia.

Frankie said, "Take Mason and go to Roanoke, identify Jimmy's body, and make arrangements to bring him home, so we can bury him next to papa." Frankie paused, probably to swallow a shot of whisky, before saying, "Nick, find and kill the son of a bitch that shot Jimmy. We need to send a loud, clear message that nobody messes with the Marino family. While you're taking care of business in Virginia, I've got to go break the news to mama."

Ten hours later, Nick had completed the first three tasks.

Now there was no question that Jimmy was dead. Nick had just identified the body for himself at the Roanoke City coroner's office. His stomach had rolled when the coroner lifted the sheet to reveal the pasty, bloated face that had belonged to his brother. Nick had seen plenty of dead bodies during his lifetime. Hell, he'd even been responsible for the death of many of them. It was one thing to stare down at a dead body of someone he'd just capped because they were in his way. It was entirely different to see the only brother that he liked under a damn sheet in that sterile room. He loved both his brothers, but he actually *liked* Jimmy. Now that Jimmy was gone, there would be no one to smooth the tensions that ran between him and Frankie.

What the hell had gone wrong? Nick was going to find out. Jimmy had been in Roanoke to initiate the first transaction of a small shipment of cocaine. It was supposed to be easy and safe. Frankie had already set up the connections for this new distribution channel in Roanoke. His oldest brother was so damned paranoid about the Feds watching them that he'd left nothing to chance.

Jimmy is dead.

Christ, it felt like Nick's entire world was falling apart. First with Kitty leaving him and now his favorite brother was gone, too. Nick rubbed his hands over his face.

"You okay, boss?" Mason asked as he drove through downtown Roanoke. "It's been a long day. Why don't I find us a room for tonight? We could order room service, get some sleep, and then track down the scumbag in the morning."

It had been a long day, but how could he think about food and rest while Jimmy's killer was still out there alive? Nick lifted his head and looked out the front passenger window. Reaching into his jacket pocket, he pulled out the engraved silver flask Kitty had given him for his birthday five years ago, when things were still good between them. That had been just before his father died, before Nick had taken on a bigger role in his family's business. He twisted the cap off the flask, took a large gulp of the liquid fire and felt the burn of the whiskey as it slid down his throat. He clenched his jaw and said, "No. I need to talk to Jacob Hauser. Now."

Mason nodded. Nick could tell that Mason disagreed with his decision, but one of the things he appreciated about Mason was that he knew how to follow orders. Mason wasn't going to start a damned argument like Kitty with that condescending way she looked at him, chin raised, disapproval in her eyes. Nick clenched his fist. He hated that look. Who was she to judge him? She'd be nothing without him. He'd given her everything. What did he get in return? A bunch of disrespect before leaving him. *Bitch.*

Nick exhaled and unclenched his fist. She hadn't always looked at him that way—not in the beginning. He still remembered the first time he'd seen Kitty in that shit-hole club. God, she was beautiful. She'd been wearing some cheap costume, but he remembered thinking that she was the most beautiful woman he'd ever seen. She danced with such grace and elegance, and Nick had fallen in love with her that night. Dammit, he still loved her, even though she drove him crazy. Sure, he had sex with other women, but they were simply a distraction—a way to release some of the pressure he was always under. Kitty was the one he loved. Dammit, she belonged to him, and he would not let her leave. First, he had to take care of this mess with Jimmy, and then he was going to track her down. It shouldn't be too hard. She had nowhere else to go.

"This is it, boss. Looks like Hauser's probably still here," Mason said, interrupting Nick's thoughts.

"I'm going to handle this personally," Nick said, and Mason nodded once, parking the car in the lot at Champion Auto Glass Shop. He and Mason got out of their vehicle and walked into the lobby as the bell on the door chimed, announcing their arrival.

They heard a man's voice from the open door on the left. "Sorry, we're closed."

Mason turned and locked the glass door that they had entered to ensure that no one would be coming in behind them. Nick unholstered his Sig P320 M17 as he and Mason followed the sound of the voice into a garage. The guy was about twelve feet away, all his attention focused on positioning the new windshield on a blue sedan car frame.

"Jacob Hauser?" Nick asked.

As soon as the glass was secured, the guy wiped his forehead with the back of his left hand and then sized up Mason and Nick.

"Yeah, that's me. I'm sorry, but we're closed. You can call back tomorrow, and I'll get you scheduled."

Nick aimed his Sig at Jacob's chest. "Keep your hands out where I can see them, Jacob. We don't need a new windshield. We're here to discuss your recent meeting with my brother, Jimmy Marino. I just came back from IDing his remains at the morgue."

Jacob blanched and then took a step back, holding his hands up in front of him, palms facing Nick. "Hey, man, that has nothing to do with me." He took another step back. "I'm so sorry for your loss."

Nick stepped forward and said, "What did you do? Meet him here to make the trade, and then decide instead of paying for the product, you would just take the drugs, shoot Jimmy, and leave him in the woods like some kind of fucking dead animal?"

Jacob took another step back until he was back against a red toolbox. "No man, it wasn't like that. Hell, I didn't even know he was dead until the police came by to question me."

The police were here? Nick clenched his left fist and took a slow deep breath to calm his temper. "Why did the police show up to question you? You're a murder suspect?"

Jacob began shaking his head and pointed his right finger to his chest. "No, they had nothing on me because I didn't kill Jimmy. They said they had some kind of evidence that he'd been here. Maybe he plugged my address into his car GPS or something. I don't know."

"Keep your hands out where I can see them," Nick said.

Jacob held both hands out to his side, fingers spread, palms facing Nick. "Look, I didn't kill your brother, man. Why would I do that? This was just the first transaction of many bigger ones. I've got the customers, and you've got the drugs. It's good business. Killing your brother would obviously end any future transactions not to mention put my own life in danger. Think about it. Why in the hell would I want to do that?"

Nick considered that. It didn't make good business sense, but in his line of work, people didn't always act logically.

Nick lowered his M17 thirty degrees and shot Jacob in the left thigh.

Hauser screamed out in pain followed by a string of obscenities. He grabbed a cloth from the top of the toolbox and pressed it against the wound to try to slow the blood.

Tears ran down Jacob's face as he looked up at Nick with a mixture of hate and fear. "Are you fucking crazy?! I swear that I didn't kill your brother. You've got to believe me. I had no reason to kill him. I was going to make a shit-ton of money off this deal with you." He was breathing hard trying to stay calm and no doubt deal with the pain from the gunshot wound.

Nick shrugged. Jacob was going to die tonight because at least one person was going to pay for Jimmy's murder. It might as well be this loser. An image of his brother's face flashed in his mind. He narrowed his eyes and studied Jacob. Nick's instinct was telling him that Jacob hadn't pulled the trigger. He didn't look like he was strung out on drugs, not the way he'd been so precise about installing that windshield when they'd walked in on him. It was true that he did stand to lose a lot of money now that Jimmy was gone.

"Let's say you didn't kill my brother. Who would kill him? Who knew about your arrangement with us?" Nick asked.

"I don't know, man. Honest. I just don't know," Jacob said.

"Aw, come on Jacob. Now you're lying to me." Nick aimed at Jacob's right leg and pulled the trigger. He smiled when he watched Jacob drop to the floor. He needed a name. Nick would find Jimmy's killer much faster with a name.

Closing the distance, he stood over Jacob who was shouting obscenities, trying to use the drenched cloth on both legs now. "I need a name, Jacob."

Jacob was sobbing and shaking his head. "I don't know. I don't know."

Nick held the gun to Jacob's head. "I need a name. I won't ask again."

Jacob yelled, "The Broker. It was probably The Broker, okay?"

Nick bent down so he was looking into Jacob's face. "That's not a name."

"I don't know his name, man. Nobody does."

"Well, how do I get in touch with this Broker?"

"I don't know. He's not someone you ever want to get in touch with. He finds you."

Nick lifted Jacob's chin up with the tip of the barrel of his pistol. "How do I find The Broker? I'm sure somebody knows how to get in touch with him."

"I don't know. I've heard he's done business with the Repo Girl. She probably knows how to reach him."

"The Reaper Girl? Jesus, doesn't anyone in this city have a real name? How the hell am I supposed to find her?"

"No. Repo Girl – you know because she repossesses cars. Her name is Andi Sloan, and she lives in the city."

"You'd better not be lying to me, Jacob."

"Honest man…that's all I know."

Nick stood. "Thanks, Jacob."

Nick joined Mason and just before leaving. Nick turned and shot Jacob in the head and said, "Let's go pay a visit to this Repo Girl."

***

It was almost 10 p.m. by the time Andi finally pulled into her driveway. Finding the Ford 350 XLT had been a bust. She'd driven by Ronnie's house, and when his driveway was empty, she'd tried the movie theater where he worked. The parking lot had been packed, so she drove up and down the aisles to no avail. It was just as well. She was exhausted from her lack of sleep last night and the emotionally draining meeting with Dr. Martin. Andi turned off the Jeep and looked up at the window on the second story. *Dark*. Maybe Kitty was already asleep? Could she be that lucky? *Probably not.*

Andi grabbed her purse and stepped out of her Jeep. As she closed the door, she was jerked backwards as someone grabbed her around her waist and pulled her against a hard body. Before her scream could explode from her mouth, a large hand covered her lips, leaving only a small gap for air to enter her lungs through her nose. She could barely breathe. Dropping her purse, Andi grabbed the arm that was covering her mouth with both hands and tried to pry it away. The arm, which was the size of a small tree trunk, didn't budge.

Don't panic. It was too late. She would have let out a hysterical laugh if she'd been able to make a sound. *Think. This is just like we practiced in the self-defense class.* What was she supposed to do? *Oh yeah, don't fight the energy.* She leaned back into her assailant. *Oh no.* He was taller and wider than her six-foot body.

Terrific.

Leaning back against the wide chest did give her more stability. She moved with him when he stepped back to adjust to the extra force of her weight against him. That's when Andi bit his hand as hard as she could. As he swore, she dropped her left hand back down to her waist, made a fist with her thumb close to her fingers like a hitchhiker, and thrust it up towards his face, making contact with something. She was hoping she'd connected with his eye.

He swore again as he pulled his head back and loosened his grip on Andi. She turned, leaned down to her left side, and using the same fist that had just poked him in the face, thrusted it downward and punched him in his groin. When he gasped and bent forward, she twisted out of his grip and pulled his hand just like they practiced in class, and he fell to his knees. She put her knee into his back to drop him face forward down on her driveway.

Andi's heart was pounding, and she was breathing hard. *Sweet baby Jesus, it actually worked!* She began to smile as relief and adrenaline rushed through her. Now if she could only figure out how to call the police? There was no way she was breaking this magical grip that held the big bruiser helpless, face down on her driveway, to reach her purse that she'd dropped several feet away from where she now stood.

"Pretty impressive. I don't believe I've ever seen anyone drop Mason. You must be the Repo Girl."

Holy Mary Mother of God. Andi jerked her head up in the direction of the voice. A man was standing about a car length away, pointing a gun at her.

Not again.

He took a step toward her. The man looked confused and unsure for just a minute as he continued to stare at Andi. "Kitty? Is that you?"

Kitty? Oh no. New York accent. Andi would bet her next repo check this was the dirt-bag boyfriend.

She narrowed her eyes and lifted her chin. "No buddy, so you might as well move along." What did he want? Did he track Kitty back here? Why did he call her the Repo Girl?

"God, it's like going back in time. You're probably about the same age she was when we first met. You've got to be her kid." He looked her up and down, and a smile spread across his face that made her stomach queasy. "All grown up."

Creep. "I don't know anybody named Kitty or what you're talking about," she said. It wasn't the first time she lied. With the gun pointed at her, the falsehood fell effortlessly from her. She wasn't happy to have Kitty back home, but she sure as heck didn't want to see her back with this loser.

He studied her for a minute and decided to change subjects. "You can let Mason up now," he said.

"Uh, thanks, but I'd rather not," she said. Andi had a feeling Mason might not be too happy with her poking him in the eye and then punching him in the groin. She readjusted her knee to ensure the big guy, Mason, wasn't going anywhere. He grunted. She hesitated, trying to figure out what to do next. They didn't cover this situation in her self-defense class.

The creep with the gun took another step closer. With a sneer, he said, "I would hate to have to shoot your pretty face."

Somehow Andi didn't think he'd lose any sleep over killing her, so maybe she'd take her chances with Mason rather than the psychopath with the gun. She really didn't want to be shot in the face either. She released Mason's hand and quickly stepped to the side, hands in the air. "Look, I don't have much money but go ahead and take my whole purse. It's over there by my car."

"No. I didn't come here to rob you. I heard that you could connect me with someone named The Broker."

She watched Mason get up from the driveway, not quite standing straight and rubbing his arm.

The Broker? Just when she thought this situation couldn't get any worse.

"You seem to know who I am. Who are you?" Andi asked.

He glanced up at the house. "I'm Nick Marino, your mom's boyfriend."

"I don't know what you're talking about," she said smoothly. "My parents were killed in a car accident last year." *Partial truth. Her grandparents were her parents in every way that counted.*

The front porch light came on and everyone turned to watch Kitty storm out the front door. "Let her go Nick. This is between you and me. Leave Andi out of it."

Oh, Kitty. You should have stayed in the house.

"Kitty, my love. I've been so worried about you," Nick said. "Thank God you're okay." His words were nice, but his tone lacked affection.

Kitty must have felt that too, because she stopped frozen at the bottom of the steps looking terrified. "Let her go Nick. She's not involved in this."

"It's alright, love. Andi and I were just becoming acquainted. It's a small world. It turns out she's going to help me connect with a business associate, so you see, she's very much involved. Finding you here just saved me time. I was coming after you as soon as I wrapped up some business." He took a moment to look at Andi in a way that made her skin crawl. She scrunched her face in disgust. *Pig.* "She looks just like you, Kit."

He turned his attention back to Kitty. "She thought she was protecting you by pretending she didn't know you. Kids," he said and shook his head. "She didn't realize you need my protection, not protection from me."

"Let her go, Nicky. Please. I'll come with you peacefully, if you just let her go."

"You'll come with me, regardless, Bitch." Nick said. He tilted his head in Kitty's direction and nodded at Mason. The big guy began walking over to Kitty, grabbed her by the arm and dragged her next to Nick. When he reached out to touch the side of Kitty's face, she flinched. "You should be more careful, Kit. I hate to see your beautiful face bruised like this."

"See look, I'm right here, just like you wanted," Kitty said. "Please let Andi go into the house, and you and I can go back to Manhattan. I promise that I won't try to run away again."

"I can't do that just yet, love. We're all going to go for a little ride first. Jimmy's dead, and Andi's going to take me to meet the guy that killed him. I have to take care of that first before we go back home," Nick said and clenched his fist.

He looked at Kitty, studying her face. "You don't seem surprised by this news. You knew about Jimmy?" He grabbed her by her hair and moved his face within inches of her. "Did you have something to do with it?"

"Get away from her, you creep!" Andi yelled and began moving towards the psychopath threatening Kitty.

Mason pulled his gun out and pointed it at Andi, "Stay where you are, bitch." The big guy sneered, "Or better yet, try something stupid. I would like nothing better than to shoot you right now.

"Don't hurt her!" Kitty screamed at Mason and then turned to Nick. She put her hand on his arm, "Please, don't let him hurt her. Please." Tears began to fall down her cheeks.

"You know I hate it when you cry, Kitty." Nick raised his hand like he was going to slap her, and Kitty flinched and quickly wiped the tears away. Nick smiled a mean smile. "Of course you didn't have anything to do with Jimmy's death. You're afraid of your own damn shadow." Nick turned to Andi.

"We're all going to play nice and get in the car. You're going to take me to The Broker. I would hate for your mother to be injured because you were uncooperative."

Oh, how she was wishing that it had been Nick that she'd knocked to the ground. Andi bit her lower lip while she tried to think of a way out of this. Getting in the car with a psychopath never ended well in the movies.

In the next instant, a loud bang exploded through the air and glass shattered the rear window of the Bentley Continental GT Speed coup that was parked on the street in front of her next-door neighbor's house. At the sound of another round being loaded into the chamber of a rifle, everyone stared across the street at the woman standing on the front porch with her hair in curlers and a pink apron over her green floral housecoat.

"Boys, that's what you call a warning shot. You are going to want to slowly lower your guns and place them on the driveway."

Nick held up his gun and slowly put it on the driveway.

"That means you too, big guy, or my next bullet is going straight in your chest, are we clear? I've got a cherry pie in the oven that is almost ready to come out, so I don't have a lot of time to be messing around with you two."

Mason slowly lowered his gun to the ground, and Mrs. Barzetti nodded.

"Now kick those weapons away from you," Mrs. Barzetti instructed. As soon as Nick had nudged the gun away with his foot, Mrs. Barzetti said, "That's a good boy." Mrs. Barzetti pointed her rifle at Mason, "Are you hard of hearing, son. I was talking to you, too."

Mason kicked his gun away and kept his hands up in the air.

"Now that wasn't so hard, was it? Andi, sweetie, pick up those weapons and you and Kitty come over and stand behind me on my porch. Boys, you need to stay completely still. If you move so much as an inch, I won't hesitate to put a bullet in you. I'm going to be quite upset if you make me shoot you. I really don't want to have to go to confession and explain to Father Mark that I shot someone again."

Andi picked up the guns and then grabbed Kitty's hand and ran with her across the street to stand next to Mrs. Barzetti.

Her rifle-toting neighbor narrowed her eyes at the men. "I suggest you two get in that fancy car of yours and get the hell out of my neighborhood. If you come anywhere near my girls again, I will shoot to kill. Are we clear, boys?"

Both men stared, eyes wide, mouths opened, and nodded.

"Let's go," Nick said to Mason as he climbed in the passenger seat. He yelled out a warning to them. "This isn't over, Kitty."

"Oh, it's over. Don't come back here unless you're tired of breathing," Mrs. Barzetti hollered and then shot out the right taillight as the car tore out of the neighborhood. She lowered her rifle and turned to Andi and Kitty. "If we're lucky, the police will stop them about the taillight. Now, let's get you girls inside and get you something hot to drink before you catch a chill. I wasn't kidding about that pie. It's probably ready to come out now."

After Mrs. Barzetti herded the girls inside the house and locked the front door, she placed her hand over her heart and exhaled a long breath before leaning the rifle against the corner by the door. Then, she took the two pistols from Andi and gingerly placed them in her knitting basket by the recliner and closed the lid. She reached up with her right hand to make sure her curlers were still in place.

"Well," she said a little breathlessly. "That was certainly exciting." She glanced over at Kitty whose face was as pale as whipping cream. The poor girl looked ready to pass out on her living room carpet. In contrast, Andi's face was flushed, her lips formed a straight hard line. Andi looked like she was about to punch her fist through the plaster wall.

This won't do. She needed to calm everyone down, call for backup, and get that pie out of the oven. Then, they could come up with a plan to properly deal with the situation. She pulled her cellphone out of the front pocket of her apron and texted Ethel and Gladys–*911 Meeting @ my house now*—and pressed send. Dropping the phone back in her apron pocket she said, "Come into the kitchen, ladies," and directed Kitty and Andi into the next room.

"I think we could all use a hot drink and a slice of pound cake. I'll put on a pot of tea just as soon as I check on my pie." She made sure they each were sitting before putting on her oven mitts and opening the oven door to look at her beautiful cherry pie. Thank the good Lord the lattice pie crust was a golden brown. She carefully took the pie out of the oven and placed it on the cooling rack before putting the tea kettle on. Then she walked over to the counter, pulled out a couple of plates from her cabinet, some forks from her drawer, and a large knife for cutting the cake.

She set everything on the table. "Kitty dear, would you please cut us each a nice slice of cake." The task might help distract Kitty and settle her trembling hands. She wasn't about to give Andi a sharp knife in her current state.

Mrs. Barzetti turned back to her cabinet to pull down three teacups. She reached in the cupboard above the refrigerator and brought down a bottle of whiskey, filling half of each cup with bourbon. She swallowed the bourbon straight from one of the teacups, closed her eyes briefly as she felt the alcohol heat up her chest, and then refilled the cup before topping all three cups with hot black tea.

"Mrs. Barzetti," Andi said and began to get up, "I'm pretty sure they'll be back. We need to do something. I won't let him take Kitty."

Mrs. Barzetti handed Andi a cup and said, "Nobody is taking Kitty away from us. Now have a seat and sip on this."

Andi sat back down and took a big gulp of the hot tea and began coughing immediately.

"Did you spike our tea?" Andi asked.

Mrs. Barzetti smiled as she handed Kitty a teacup and sat down and took a sip of hers. "Mm. It's called a hot toddy, dear. The warm tea helps the bourbon go down a little easier. I figured we all could use something a little stronger tonight. There's honey in the center of the table if you want to add a little sweetness."

In the next moment, her kitchen door opened, and Gladys and Ethel raced inside and slammed the door.

"What's wrong?" Gladys asked. Both women were slightly winded.

Ethel said, "Did you fire your rifle? At first, I thought it was just Gladys' car backfiring again, but then we got your text."

"Have a seat and we'll fill you in. Help yourself to some hot tea. The kettle is still hot and there's bourbon on the counter. You're going to want some when I tell you what's happened," Mrs. Barzetti said calmly and then she looked at Kitty, reaching over to grasp her hand in hers.

"Now sweetheart, in order for us to protect you, you're going to need to tell us about those men."

Thank heavens Hazel had looked outside her front window to see if Andi was home from work. That's when she'd spotted the fancy car with the New York tags parked in front of her house. Andi had been kneeling on something big in the driveway and a man was pointing a gun at her. By the time she'd grabbed the extra ammo from the kitchen drawer and got her rifle, Hazel saw that Kitty was in the middle of that mess, too. There had been no time to call the police, so she had to take matters into her own hands. She was in charge of the Neighborhood Watch, after all.

Mrs. Barzetti gave Kitty's hand a gentle squeeze for encouragement. She'd known Kitty was running away from something—poor thing. She'd hoped to coax it out of her gently, but after tonight, there was no time. They needed to know what they were up against because she agreed with Andi. Those men would be back, although probably not tonight.

"What's this all about, Hazel?" Gladys asked.

Mrs. Barzetti briefly caught Ethel and Gladys up to date on the excitement before turning her attention back to Kitty. "You're safe, Kitty, darling. We won't let those men hurt you again. Was one of them the man who gave you the black eye?"

Kitty nodded, staring at the untouched cake. Her hand trembled as she held the knife. Mrs. Barzetti reached over and took the knife from her and sliced a nice big piece of cake, placed it on the plate and handed it to Kitty. "Have another sip of that hot toddy and take a big bite of my cake, darling girl. You're not in this mess alone."

She watched Kitty take a sip of the tea and take a bite of the cake before asking the next question. "Tell us what you're running from, Kitty."

Kitty looked into her teacup and said, "Nick Marino. He's my boyfriend. My ex-boyfriend," she clarified. She looked up at Mrs. Barzetti. "I met him about fifteen years ago at a club where I was dancing, and we started dating. He owned an upscale night club and hired me to perform there. Nick was different back then." Kitty looked back into her cup as if she was remembering those times. She bit her lower lip and looked back into Mrs. Barzetti's eyes.

"About five years ago, his dad died from a heart attack. His oldest brother, Frankie, expected Nick to take over more of the business. Up until then, Nick just ran the family's night clubs and managed the illegal gambling that happened in the back rooms."

Kitty glanced at everyone and returned her gaze to Mrs. Barzetti. "Nicky and I fought over this a lot. Illegal gambling was bad enough." Kitty scrunched her face like she'd just sucked on a lemon. "The drug business? That's some dark, scary, sh…stuff, and it's the biggest part of their business."

Kitty swallowed the rest of her hot toddy and set her cup down. "After his father died, Nick changed. He started drinking more, became violent, and very controlling." Kitty looked at Andi. "The night before I showed up at your door, I was running away. My friend Shana was helping me because Nick controlled all the money and watched me constantly. I snuck over to her apartment, and we were just getting ready to head to the bus station when Nick walked in. He was furious that I was trying to leave him. He told me that I had no one and owned nothing. He bragged that my phone led him right to me and that's when he smacked me in the face." Kitty absently touched her cheek. "Shana sprayed him with pepper spray, temporarily blinding him. I ditched my phone, and we ran down the stairs to leave the building. He shot and killed her in the stairwell before we ever made it down to the street level. I kept running, used all the cash that Shana had given me and took a bus here." Kitty's eyes had filled with tears, so she got up and walked over to the counter. She poured the bourbon directly into her teacup and took a big drink. She turned and looked at the women around the table.

"He's not the man that I fell in love with. He just killed Shana like she was nothing. He's a monster." Kitty finished the bourbon that was in the cup and set it in the sink. When she turned around, she looked so tragic. "I never meant to bring this trouble back home." Kitty frowned. "I don't know how he found me."

"Bad luck," Andi said casually as she stood up to join Kitty by the counter. She filled her teacup with bourbon and took a big gulp. "It must be in our genes. Nick said that he came looking for me to help him get in touch with The Broker who is pretty much the scariest criminal in Roanoke." Andi shook her head and frowned. "I don't know how Nick got the idea that I could help him find the guy." She bit her lower lip.

What in the world was Andi doing consorting with a crime boss named The Broker? Such a ridiculous name for a criminal. What, was he five years old playing cops and robbers? Mrs. Barzetti sighed and made the sign of the cross. She'd tried so hard to keep that girl out of trouble, but it seemed to find her anyway.

Andi saw Mrs. Barzetti's reaction, downed the remainder of her hot toddy, and then turned to face Kitty. "Once Nick got a good look at me, I guess he realized that I was your daughter. You should have stayed in the house, Kitty. He didn't know you were here, and I sure wasn't going to tell him."

Kitty placed her hand over her heart and looked at Andi. "I think I aged another ten years when I saw him in the driveway holding a gun to you. As terrified as I am of him, I couldn't let him hurt you. He's dangerous, Andi. I won't let him hurt anyone else that I care about." Kitty reached out and touched Andi's arm.

Aw, my girls are bonding over a homicidal maniac. It made Mrs. Barzetti's heart happy. She sighed. Now, to figure out how to keep them both safe.

Gladys reached over and cut a piece of pound cake, put it on the plate, and took a bite. "What's our next move? Mobsters from New York City is a pretty big deal. Should we call the police?"

Ethel shook her head. "What would we tell them?" She pointed at Mrs. Barzetti. "Hazel's the only one who actually fired a weapon. Twice. We don't want her charged with destruction of property. Plus, didn't you threaten to kill them?"

Mrs. Barzetti shrugged. "I was just trying to scare them off. It was mostly an empty threat."

"How about the FBI? Don't they deal with organized crime? Kitty could tell them about witnessing Nick murdering her friend," Gladys suggested.

Ethel shook her head. "No good. That Nick character probably brought in a cleaner to get rid of the evidence. Sulfuric acid can dissolve a body in thirty minutes. They do that in all the movies. If there's no body, there's no evidence of a murder. Shana simply becomes a missing person."

Gladys said, "Not acid. I read that those claims are grossly exaggerated, and it actually takes several days to dissolve the bones. He probably dumped her body in the river."

"Oh, Shana," Kitty said, and dropped into the nearest seat and rested her head in her hands.

Andi placed a hand on Kitty's shoulder and glared at Gladys and Ethel. "Ladies, this conversation is not helpful." Andi sat down in the chair next to Kitty and looked at Gladys, Ethel, and Hazel. "For some reason, Nick thinks that The Broker is responsible for Jimmy's death."

Ethel leaned forward. "Who's Jimmy?"

Andi waved her hand in the air. "He's the dead guy I found in the woods when I was repossessing the Hyundai." At their blank expressions, Andi said, "Long story. Anyway, it turns out that Jimmy is Nick's brother. Kitty recognized him at the crime scene."

Mrs. Barzetti asked, "Tell me more about this Broker. What's his real name, and for heaven's, how do you know him?"

"I have no idea what The Broker's real name is, and that other part's complicated," Andi said. "Honestly, Mrs. Barzetti, the less you know about him the better. We'll all be a lot safer if we can keep him out of this."

"Andrea Sloan, are you protecting this criminal?" Mrs. Barzetti asked.

Andi gaped. "Heck no. Let me just say that he scares me way more than Kitty's psycho ex-boyfriend." She must have realized what she said, so immediately looked at Kitty and said, "No offense."

Kitty shook her head. "No, you're right. He is crazy and dangerous."

Andi looked at no one in particular as she spoke her thoughts out loud. "It seems like Nick is in Roanoke because Jimmy is dead. Stumbling onto Kitty's location was just an unlucky coincidence. Unfortunately, I have more questions than answers like - why was Jimmy here? Did The Broker really have him killed or was it someone else? Who the heck told Nick that I could lead him to The Broker?"

Mrs. Barzetti sighed. "Looks like we have a lot of unanswered questions. Our number one priority is going to be to keep you both safe. Those men will be back, and we need to be prepared."

Chapter Fifteen

The next morning, back at the precinct, Sanchez wrinkled his nose as he studied the photos spread over the conference room table. "I'll take a good old-fashioned-gang knife bleed-out over the gunshot, execution-style used on this victim. Hauser's brain matter was all over that windshield." Sanchez leaned back in his chair and tilted his head from side to side to ease some of the tension. "That's just so messy."

Hughes leaned forward and took a chocolate glazed donut from the box in the center of the table and asked, "Do you get to see many knife homicides working in Narcotics?"

Before Sanchez could reply, Kendricks, who had been studying the ballistic report, looked up and said, "Looks like Hauser and Marino were killed using different guns based on the bullets found at the scene."

Ryan Hughes raised his brows. "So, you think the murders are unrelated?"

Kendricks shook his head. "No. It's too much of a coincidence that Marino's GPS showed he was at the auto glass shop the night he was murdered. Based on Hauser's reaction to the news that Marino was dead, I don't think he was the one who pulled the trigger. That doesn't mean that he didn't do business with Marino."

Sanchez said, "Given his history with drugs, I would bet he's back in the illegal substance business. Even though Lucky didn't pick up any scents in his shop, that doesn't mean he didn't conduct the transaction off site." He absently broke off a piece of jelly donut and gave it to Lucky.

Kendricks sighed and took a sip of his coffee. "This is all just speculation. What we're missing is evidence or at this point in the investigation, I'd even settle for a solid lead."

There was a knock at the door and then Captain Robert Carlson popped his head in the room without waiting to be invited in. He looked at Kendricks and then Sanchez, and said, "Good, you're both here."

"What's up?" Kendricks asked.

"You're both going to love this. You've been invited to team up with the bureau on a special task force."

"YES!" Hughes said and pumped his fist in the air.

Kendricks sighed. *Terrific.* It was hard enough babysitting the Chief's grandson. Working with this new and improved happy Sanchez and his damn dog was challenging to say the least. Now he was going to have to play nice with the Feds. Dammit, the more people involved in a case, the slower the investigation. His mom used to say that too many cooks in the kitchen spoil the soup. That's exactly what they'd be dealing with now with the FBI and all their policies and protocol. He'd worked with Agents Hill and Roberts from the Roanoke office on other cases. They were okay, but he'd prefer not to deal in multi-agencies if he could avoid it.

"An invitation? How nice. Captain, please send my regrets," Sanchez said, shaking his head. "I'm more of a lone wolf." He leaned over and scratched Lucky behind her ear in what appeared to be her favorite spot. "That's why you partnered me with her, right, captain?"

Kendricks suppressed a smile. "I think this dog was the captain's only choice when he couldn't find another human officer on the force willing to put up with you, Sanchez. The only reason Lucky didn't object to working with you is because she can't talk."

Lucky barked at Kendricks as if to disagree and then licked Sanchez's hand.

"Fine, then," Kendricks said nodding at the dog. "You've obviously gained her loyalty with all those jelly donuts."

The captain gave them both a firm look. "You two are so funny that when I fire your asses for insubordination, you should move out to Vegas and open an act. Let me remind you that even though I used the word invite, what that really means is mandatory cooperation. Apparently, James Marino's death has caught the attention of the FBI. He was involved in a New York crime family that they're looking to take down."

"Who are we stuck with from the Roanoke office? Roberts? Hill?" Kendricks asked. *Please not Burnes.* The guy was a royal pain-in-the-ass.

"Neither," the captain said. "Special Agent Reyna came all the way down here from the New York office. The Chief got the call from their New York office alerting him of the situation about thirty minutes before she showed up at the precinct. The Chief is requesting you in the main conference room now. Play nice - both of you. Are we clear?"

The captain turned and headed back down the hall towards the conference room.

Ryan stood up and clapped his hands in front of him. "I can't believe I'm on a task force with the FBI." He ran a hand over his perfectly neat hair and straightened his tie.

"Not so fast, kid. I need you to stay here and make sure Lucky doesn't eat all the donuts or the files," said Kendricks.

"You're benching me? Wait, you're kidding, right? This is the F. B. I. we're talking about," Hughes whined.

Sanchez looked insulted as he turned to look at Kendricks. "Oh, please. Mi socia won't eat the files. She's a trained police officer." He looked affectionally at the German Shephard and watched her snatch up the remaining jelly donut he'd been giving to her in small bites. "Hm, the donuts on the other hand? Detective Hughes, you'd better guard the donuts."

"Fine," Hughes grumbled, blowing out a breath as he sat back down. "I can't believe I made detective, and now I have to dog-sit."

***

FBI Special Agent Mariela Reyna listened attentively as Police Chief Kevin Bogan talked about the outstanding performance of his organization and past successful collaborations with agents from the FBI's Roanoke satellite office. At least she had support for this joint venture from the highest level of the Roanoke Police Department.

Captain Robert Carlson returned a moment later with a neutral expression on his face. He'd been tasked by the Chief minutes earlier to inform the homicide and narcotics detectives involved in James Marino's case that they'd been invited to join the FBI's Organized Crime Task Force. Captain Carlson's expression was a bit too controlled for it to be natural. That type of announcement usually was received with resistance. In her experience, local police departments were very territorial about their cases and worried that they'd lose control if another outside agency became involved. That was okay. She'd always been an excellent team leader, and she'd had plenty of experience winning over hostiles. Being a Latina woman in a predominately white male work force at the Bureau, she was used to having to prove herself before anyone took her seriously. Hell, in the field, she'd even used that to her advantage. Being able to keep the peace and gain cooperation, as her abuela always said, required a subtle cleverness that many Reyna women were born with. Mariela touched the tiny emerald star that hung from the delicate gold chain of her abuela's necklace.

The Chief turned his attention to Captain Carlson and said, "Well?"

"They'll be here in a moment, sir," the captain said.

He'd barely finished replying when two men walked into the conference room.

"Ah, here are two of my top detectives. Special Agent Reyna, please meet Detective Sanchez from our Narcotics department."

Detective Sanchez stepped forward and offered his right hand. "Special Agent Reyna, I look forward to working with you. It's always a pleasure to partner with the FBI."

He presented her with a bright, wide smile that was surrounded by a dark, heavy-stubble beard. Her oldest brother Austen had a similar beard. It was meant to appear casual/haphazard, but she knew for a fact her brother spent ten minutes each morning trimming his beard to achieve this effect.

Sanchez's jet-black hair was long and wavy at the top and shaved close on the sides and back. He wore a charcoal gray suit with a white button-down shirt, black shoes, and…wait, were his pants legs covered in pet hair? *Interesting. He must have a dog or cat at home.* He earned a point for that. You could tell a lot about a person by their ability to love and care for animals. The entire combination, other than the pet hair, gave him a professional, yet slightly untamed look. His dark brown eyes crinkled at the sides, indicating a genuine smile. In return, Mariela gave him a friendly, professional smile and a firm handshake. "Thank you for agreeing to join the task force. I appreciate your assistance with this case."

"Of course," Sanchez said, releasing her hand. He took a step back and placed a hand on his chest. "Everyone knows that I am a great team player."

Hm. She wasn't buying that for a second. His warm, genuine smile was gone, replaced with a smaller, closed lipped grin that only lifted on one side. Sarcasm with a bit of charm. She had no doubt this man used his charisma to get what he wanted. Her smile widened. *Perfect.* She knew just how to handle men like Detective Sanchez.

Before she had time to further analyze the detective, the Chief was saying, "And this is Detective Kendricks from Homicide."

Detective Kendricks stepped forward and filled the space in front of her. He had short blond hair, broad shoulders and was several inches taller than Sanchez. Mariela had to lift her gaze to make eye contact. *Wow. Did he wear contacts to get that unusual shade of blue?* There was something about him that seemed familiar, although she was certain that they'd never met. She would have remembered him.

He was studying her like she was some sort of puzzle he was trying to solve. That level of concentration would be unnerving if she weren't an experienced agent. Was he trying to intimidate her with that look? He probably used that kind of approach when interrogating a suspect. In contrast to the narcotics detective, there was no friendly, genuine smile to greet her as Detective Kendricks reached out his right hand to shake hers.

Fine. Bring your best detective. I've got nothing to hide. Mariela stood a little straighter, lifted her brow as she watched him take inventory of her navy Sketcher arch-fit ballet flats. They were practical shoes. She never knew when she'd have to chase down an assailant, and she certainly couldn't cover the same distance in her favorite stilettos—well, not as quickly as she could in these Sketchers.

She watched as Kendricks scanned over her conservative navy pants suit, simple white blouse, and stopped a fraction of a second longer to take note of her necklace that rested at the hollow of her neck. His scrutiny was lightning quick. It was so fast, in fact, that most women would have missed it completely because they would be distracted by his handsome face, muscular build, or mesmerized by those shocking blue eyes. Not her, of course.

She gave him a no-nonsense, firm handshake—he was the type to pay attention to that—and then allowed a smile to lift her lips in what she hoped looked natural and friendly without the defensiveness she was feeling in the moment. His expression remained unchanged. Oh, he really did not want to be here and chose not to pretend otherwise, like Sanchez.

"Detective, thank you for coming. I value your time," she said, specifically not thanking him for his cooperation. She'd have to earn his trust and support and that would take a little more time than an initial meet and greet. Mariela always liked a challenge, and she was confident enough to know that she'd create a strong alliance with these Roanoke detectives in no time at all. She'd take the time to do it because shutting down the

Marino crime organization was her number one priority. Too many lives had been lost or were ruined because of Marinos.

Chief Bogan glanced at his watch. "Well, now that everyone's been introduced, the captain and I will leave the three of you to get started." He turned to the detectives. "Special Agent Reyna will get you both up-to-speed on the relevant information about the Marino crime organization, and you can fill her in on the forensic reports and your progress on the investigation of the Marino homicide." He then turned to Mariela and nodded. "You've got our full cooperation. Good luck and let me know if there's anything that I can do to assist with this investigation." He patted the captain on the back. "Robert and I have to head to a luncheon with the mayor." He looked at the detectives and said, "As always, gentlemen, keep the captain apprised on your progress."

As soon as the Chief and Captain left the conference room, the room was silent. Mariela motioned to the chairs and said, "Why don't you have a seat, and I'll brief you on your homicide victim, James Marino."

Mariela took her laptop out of her backpack, turned it on, keyed in her password, and pulled up the Marino file. She connected her computer to the projector and the image of a man in his late sixties appeared on the conference room screen.

"This was Frank Marino, Senior. He was head of one of the fastest-growing organized crime families in downtown Manhattan."

"Was?" Sanchez asked.

"Yes, Frank Senior died from a fatal heart-attack a little more than five years ago. As far as mafias go, they're relatively new. The bureau didn't notice them as a major player in the crime world until about seven years ago. We're not exactly sure how long they've been in operation. Here's what we do know.

"Frank and his wife Angelina had 3 sons. This family photo was taken at Frank Jr.'s wedding a few years ago." The screen showed three brothers standing together wearing tuxedos. "The oldest brother, Frank Jr., is on the left. James, of course, is in the middle, and the youngest son, Nick, is on the right. We believe they are involved in prostitution, illegal gambling, and the sale and distribution of narcotics. We've suspected they're expanding their drug trafficking operation and finding James Marino dead in Roanoke supports that theory."

The sound of a cellphone vibrating came from one of the detectives. Mariela looked in their direction.

Detective Kendricks grabbed his phone from his pocket and sent it to voicemail, frowning as he looked at the name of the caller.

Mariela continued. "The Marino's own a glass manufacturing plant downtown as well as several high-end nightclubs in Manhattan."

She saw the detectives exchange a look. "What is it?"

Kendricks remained quiet, but Sanchez spoke up. "It's just interesting that you mentioned the glass manufacturing plant. We tracked James Marino's GPS. He stopped at an auto glass shop in Roanoke the night he was murdered. We interviewed the owner, and he claimed he'd never met James Marino, but he seemed very surprised to learn Marino had been killed. This morning, the owner of the shop was found dead. He appeared to have been tortured and then shot in the head."

She heard the vibrating cellphone again and she and Sanchez looked at Kendricks. He pulled out his phone, frowning, stood quickly and said, "I'm sorry. This is the witness that found James Marino. I'm going to have to take the call."

"Kendricks," he answered automatically. "I'm in a meeting. Can this wait?"

Mariela watched Kendricks's jaw clench as he listened intently. "Why? What did he want?" In a moment, he nodded and sighed. "Fine. Text me the address. We'll be right over to take your full statement." He disconnected the call and tucked the phone away.

He looked at Mariela and then Sanchez. "We've got to go. There's a new lead on the Marino case"

Sanchez asked, "Andi?"

"Of course," Kendricks sighed.

"Who's Andy?" Mariela asked.

Sanchez grinned as he stood up and put his index finger over his lips. "Don't tell anyone, but she's our secret weapon. She's helped us both bust some of our biggest cases, right Kendricks?" Sanchez said patting the detective's shoulder. "You'll love her, Special Agent Reyna."

Kendricks shook his head and looked directly at Mariela. "She's just an unlucky repo agent who always manages to get tangled in my homicide investigations. Last night, Nick Marino tried to abduct her."

Sanchez frowned and swore under his breath.

Mariela held back the smile of satisfaction that threatened to breakout on her face. *YES! Nick is in Roanoke, or at least he was last night.* She knew she'd made the right decision coming down here to follow up on Jimmy's murder. She felt that familiar feeling in her gut. This could finally be the lead to the evidence that would enable her to take down that family for good.

Kendricks looked at Sanchez and said, "Come on. Let's go get the Kid and your stupid dog."

"She's not stupid," Sanchez said, offended. "She's significantly smarter than you, Kendricks."

Mariela quickly disconnected her laptop and put it in her backpack. She slung it over her shoulder and jogged to catch up with the detectives. "Wait for me. He's not really planning to take a child and dog to the witness interview, is he?" she asked Sanchez.

Sanchez grinned and winked at her before saying, "Come on. You'll see."

***

When Dodger began barking and ran from the kitchen to Mrs. Barzetti's front door, Andi looked out the kitchen window. A black Chevy Tahoe had just pulled into the driveway. She watched Detective Kendricks and his new partner step out of the SUV. "They're here," Andi announced to everyone in the kitchen.

She clasped her hands together and squeezed them gently. *Everything is going to be alright.* She didn't really believe that, but maybe if she thought it enough, things really would be okay. It was one thing for Andi to be angry and resent Kitty for showing up after a lifetime of silence. It was an entirely different matter for Kitty's gangster ex-boyfriend to swoop in and try to take her away from Andi. *Nope. Not on my watch.* Andi crossed her arms. Kitty wasn't leaving unless she wanted to leave or until Andi kicked her out.

After staying up all night considering the best way to handle the threat of Kitty's crazy ex, they had all finally agreed on a plan. It was really the only way they could make sure that Kitty would be safe. They'd tell the police everything except the part about The Broker. Andi had evaded as many of the questions about her involvement with Roanoke's mysterious crime boss because she was certain the less her friends knew about him, the safer they'd all be. Heck, she didn't really know that much about him other than she'd had the misfortune to see him naked briefly on a sex tape he'd asked her to retrieve. Last Christmas he'd impersonated a mall manager, and he'd entered her locked home numerous times, once saving her from a homicidal gang member. They had a complicated association. She didn't want to be connected with the man at all, yet somehow someone had told Nick that she could find The Broker.

"Gladys, would you get two teacups down from the cupboard and set them on the counter by the coffee pot. I want to be able to offer them a hot beverage when they come inside from the cold," Mrs. Barzetti said as she wiped down the table for the hundredth time today. Andi was surprised her neighbor hadn't whipped up a fresh cake or cookies. Mrs. Barzetti usually baked when she was stressed, and heaven only knew they were all feeling anxious and exhausted.

Andi peered out the window again. "Uh oh, you're going to need more teacups. Looks like Detective Kendricks brought more than his rookie partner because a Ford Explorer just pulled in front of the house."

Andi frowned. The vehicle was clearly an unmarked police car. She breathed a sigh of relief when she recognized the detective stepping out of the vehicle. "It's okay. It's just Detective Sanchez. Wait, there's a woman with him that I don't recognize. Maybe he has a new partner, too?"

"Andrea Sloan, stop acting like a nosy neighbor and go greet them properly at the front door and invite them all into the kitchen."

Ha! That was rich coming from Mrs. Barzetti. The woman had perfected being a nosy neighbor since she was always keeping tabs on Andi.

"Listen, I know we're all a little nervous and a bit exhausted, but we've got a plan. Everything will be fine," Mrs. Barzetti said as she removed her apron and hung it on the hook in the pantry.

Andi looked around the room, taking a quick assessment of everyone. Mrs. Barzetti was in hostess mode as she moved to stand by the pot of fresh brewed coffee. Mrs. Harper sat next to Kitty. The older woman was holding on to Kitty's hand in a gesture of support. Mrs. Harper had an excited smile on her face in contrast to Kitty, who nervously chewed on her lower lip. Andi glanced at Mrs. Davis as she was setting a dozen of Mrs. Barzetti's teacups on the counter.

Mrs. Barzetti must have noticed all the cups, too because she said, "Oh for heaven's sake, Gladys, there's no need to empty my entire cupboard. Four cups should be fine. We can get more if we need them."

Dodger barked again as the doorbell rang. Mrs. Barzetti gave Andi a stern look and pointed at her. "Andi, go welcome our guests."

Right. Andi nodded and then jogged into the living room, patted Dodger on the head. "It's okay boy. These are friends."

She didn't know if it was the word friends or her tone of voice that had Dodger's tail wagging and his paws dancing excitedly on Mrs. Barzetti's carpet. She opened the door with a huge smile on her face, trying to overcompensate for the uneasiness she felt. Andi was trying to look relaxed and confident to conceal her nerves. Being interviewed by the police about a crime always put her on edge. Combining that with no sleep and the matter that she had to come clean about withholding information from Detective Kendricks, *ugh*, it felt like her stomach just did a triple axel like those Olympic ice skaters always incorporated in their routines.

Relax, she ordered herself when she was greeted by a scowling Detective Kendricks. He was as mad as she'd expected he would be, with his icy blue eyes boring into her from the porch. Maybe she'd been a bit premature on the "friends" reassurance she'd given to Dodger judging by the look Kendricks was giving her. But she and Kendricks were friends, weren't they? She lifted her chin, squared her shoulders, and took a breath. "Please come in. Everyone is waiting to talk to you in the kitchen."

His gaze turned suspicious, and he asked, "Who is everyone?"

Andi rolled her eyes. "It's not a block party. You already know everyone. It's just me, my mother, and my three neighbors."

"Terrific," he mumbled, "it sounds like the whole neighborhood is here." Kendricks began walking in the direction she'd indicated with her extended arm.

"Hi, Detective Hughes," Andi said, greeting Kendrick's new partner with a smile. At least Ryan was pleasant, giving her a warm grin and nod before moving past her to follow Kendricks into the kitchen.

She was about to turn back towards the door to welcome Detective Sanchez when Dodger growled taking several steps back and sniffing the air.

What in the world? Andi looked at her pup. "It's okay, boy, they're friends."

"Easy girl," Sanchez said.

"He's a boy," Andi was correcting Sanchez and getting ready to introduce him to Dodger when she turned toward the door and saw a beautiful German shepherd wearing a black vest, badge, and a patch that read "K9 – Ask to Pet".

"Oh my," Andi said. "You brought a K9?"

"Yes. She pretty much comes with me everywhere now that she's my new partner," Sanchez said. He bent down to the dog and spoke to her gently. "Lucky, this is Andi. She sometimes helps me find drugs."

Lucky's ears perked up when Sanchez said the word drugs.

She glanced over at Dodger who simply stood back and watched Lucky. "Wow. I've never seen Dodger act this way. Can I pet her?"

Sanchez nodded and must have given Lucky some sort of command with a hand gesture because Lucky walked over to Andi and sniffed and then licked her fingertips.

Andi grinned and gently scratched the top of Lucky's head. "Aren't you just the sweetest girl?" She glanced back at Dodger. "I don't think Dodger knows what to make of her."

Sanchez smiled like a proud parent. "She's an alpha working dog, so it's not uncommon for other dogs to simply stay back and watch."

The woman who was with Detective Sanchez stepped forward and extended her right hand. She stared at Andi for an uncomfortable few seconds before saying, "Hello. You must be Andrea Sloan, the witness who discovered the body. I'm Special Agent Reyna with the FBI – Manhattan Office. I'm working with Detective Kendricks and Detective Sanchez on the James Marino homicide."

Andi extended her hand in a greeting. *FBI – Manhattan Office.* Andi nodded. *That's fast.* The New York City FBI was already involved in the case. Maybe they could snatch up Nick and then she and Kitty would be safe.

"Nice to meet you, Special Agent Reyna. Everyone calls me Andi," she said. "Follow me into the kitchen so you can meet everyone."

Once introductions had been made, Mrs Barzetti invited them to sit down at her kitchen table. The space felt a lot smaller. Mrs. Barzetti smiled warmly at her law enforcement guests, fidgeting with her hair—the only indication she was slightly uneasy.

"Please help yourself to some cookies," she said and then immediately asked, "Would you like coffee or tea?" She looked at Detective Kendricks first.

"None for me, thank you," he answered before pulling his phone out of his pocket and placing it in the center of the table. He set his notepad in front of him and tapped the screen on his phone which opened a recording app. Then, Kendricks looked directly at Andi for his first question.

"Andrea Sloan, do I have your consent to record our conversation?"

Andi nodded.

He stared at her expectantly. "You have to answer the questions verbally."

Oh. She looked at the phone and leaned forward and answered, "Yes."

"You phoned me today at 8:15 a.m. to tell me that you had new information related to my investigation of James Marino's murder. Please repeat what you said over the phone."

Nodding, Andi said, "I told you that James Marino's brother Nick and some guy named Mason tried to abduct me at gun point last night from my driveway."

"What time was that?" Kendricks asked.

Andi bit her lip and tried to remember. It seemed like this all had happened days ago. "I guess it was around 10pm?"

Mrs. Barzetti poured a cup of coffee and set it in front of Detective Kendricks. "I think that's about right. Things were already well underway when I looked out to check to see if you were home. That was at 10:07." She patted Detective Kendricks' shoulder and said, "There's cream and sugar right here, dear, if you'd like to add it to your coffee." Mrs. Barzetti slid a small plate with four cookies next to his notepad.

Mrs. Davis nodded. "Hazel, you sent the 911 text to us at 10:12. I remember because I was right in the middle of watching Matlock." She addressed the three detectives and FBI agent. "It was the one where Matlock has to fly all the way to

England to represent his client that was accused of murdering his father."

Mrs. Harper turned to Mrs. Davis. "Oh, that is a good one."

Detective Kendricks wrote something on his notepad and Mrs. Barzetti leaned over his shoulder trying to read it. He covered his notepad with his hand to block her view before glaring at her. She simply shrugged and then walked back over to the coffee pot and poured another cup.

Special Agent Reyna spoke next. "This is Special Agent Reyna. Andi, how did you know who your attacker was? Did he identify himself?"

Andi bit her lip. "Not exactly." Here was the tricky part. Andi didn't want to bring The Broker into this because that was just going to lead to a whole lot of uncomfortable questions that she wasn't prepared to answer. Detective Kendricks was staring her down, displeased with her vague answer, obviously. He raised his brow in that way he always had of silently waiting her out. It was amazing how that expectant look from Thor always had her rambling. It was an effective technique now that she thought about it.

She'd skip over the part where Nick had called her Repo Girl and asked for her assistance to track down The Broker.

"Nick had mistaken me for Kitty, my mom." Andi glanced at Kitty to see how she was doing. The woman seemed so fragile. It was no wonder after all she'd been through over the last few days.

Kitty cleared her throat. "Nick Marino is my ex-boyfriend."

Special Agent Reyna said, "Yes. I was surprised at the resemblance you share with your daughter when I first met Andi. I can see how Nick Marino might have made that mistake given the darkness of the driveway that late at night."

They all looked at the FBI agent. "We've been investigating the Marino family's criminal activity for some time, so Kitty's been under surveillance as well. I believe you work at one of the night clubs, is that correct?"

Kitty seemed to look even more pale after that comment. She nodded. "I didn't know his family was doing anything illegal other than the gambling in the back rooms at the club. Well, I didn't know about the other stuff for the first couple of years, anyway. By the time I found out what they were doing, I was stuck. Nobody leaves the Marino family, not breathing. When Nicky and I first became serious, he only managed the nightclubs. After his father died five years ago, he got pulled into all aspects of running the family business. That's when I learned that the Marinos were involved in much more than illegal gambling. He promised me he would leave, that we would go away as soon as he'd saved up some money." Kitty shook her head. "Then, he became someone I didn't even recognize." She let out a breath.

Detective Kendricks asked, "Was he responsible for your black eye?"

Kitty nodded. "I was going to leave him. My friend Shana was helping me. I'd saved enough cash for a bus ticket. Nick got to be so controlling. I didn't have my own money, just joint credit cards that he managed. I saved my tips from dancing, so Shana made arrangements for me to go stay with her cousin that lived in D.C." Kitty stared blankly at the tray of cookies in the center of the table. "I met her at her apartment before my evening shift at the club. I'd only packed a small bag of clothes because I didn't want Nick to notice my things were missing until I was safely out of the city." She wiped a tear from her eye as she shook her head and looked at Special Agent Reyna. "But he found us. He came to Shana's apartment. Oh, God, I was so careful. I made certain I wasn't followed, but he stormed into the apartment and said he'd tracked me from my phone. I'm such an idiot."

Mrs. Harper patted Kitty's shoulder and handed her a tissue. "You're not an idiot, sweetheart. That man is a monster. We're just so thankful that you made it back home to us."

Kitty sniffed and leaned her head into Mrs. Harper's shoulder.

Detective Kendricks asked, "So, what happened when Nick discovered you at Shana's?"

"He smacked me across the face, told me that I was a fool to think that I could get away from him because he owned me. He said that I was nothing without him and had nowhere to go." Kitty shook her head. "Poor Shana. I wish I had been as brave as she was. She pulled out a can of pepper spray and sprayed him in the eyes. She took my phone out of my hands and threw it on the floor, grabbed my hand and pulled me out the door. We were running down the stairs when I heard the gunshot." Kitty closed her eyes. When she opened them again, she whispered, "There was so much blood. She was my best friend—my only friend." Kitty shook her head and used the tissues to wipe her eyes. "Oh, Shana. She didn't deserve to die."

"What happened next, Kitty?" Detective Kendricks asked softly, like he was speaking to a small child. Andi's mom looked like a frightened little girl at the moment. Andi could feel her chest tighten.

"I ran." Kitty looked at Detective Kendricks. Her voice was shaky when she spoke, and her face was contorted like she was in physical pain. "I left my only friend, dead in the stairwell of her apartment, and jumped in the first cab." She shook her head again. "I couldn't go to Shana's family in D.C. How could I possibly face them knowing that I was responsible for killing their cousin? I ran to the only place left. Home." Kitty wiped her eyes as she looked first at Andi for a long moment, and then to each of their neighbors. "And now, I've brought trouble to the family that I love."

Andi sat taller and looked at Kitty. "This is not your fault, Kitty. You are not responsible for the psychopath that hurt you, killed your friend, and then tried to abduct us last night." Andi turned to Detective Kendricks and said, "He needs to go to jail for life, Detective. I realize that Shana's murder might not be in your jurisdiction," she said and turned to look at the FBI agent, "but I'm certain you can put him away for life, Special Agent Reyna."

"That would bring me tremendous pleasure, Andi," Special Agent Reyna said. "Kitty, I'll need to get the name and address of your friend, Shana. It would have been ideal if you'd reported this sooner, but I understand you were no doubt in shock and running for your life."

Detective Kendricks glared at Andi as he pointed the phone towards her. "So, your mother must have recognized James Marino at the crime scene the other day, and you failed to disclose this information, Sloan?"

Oh, man. This is the part Andi was dreading.

"Yes," both mother and daughter replied to Kendricks' question at the same time.

Oh, her Thor was very angry, and she was the reason. She felt horrible. Andi reached out and touched his hand that was still holding the phone.

"I'm sorry. Kitty had only just recognized the body just before you came. I didn't know how she knew him, or what kind of trouble she was running from, and we didn't have much time to ask her about it before you showed up." Andi sighed. He was still angry and worse, maybe even a little hurt. She felt awful.

Kitty looked up at Andi. "No, Andi. This is all my fault. We were barely speaking, I was, hell, I'm still a mess what with everything that's happened." Kitty looked at Detective Kendricks. "It's not Andi's fault. She was just protecting me." She glanced at Andi with a hint of a smile. "Which is so much more than I deserve from her." She turned her attention back to Detective Kendricks and then at Special Agent Reyna and Detective Sanchez. "I'll tell you everything that I know about Nick and the Marino Family. I'm afraid I don't know much about criminal activities that happen outside the club where I work. There's some gambling that goes on in some of the back rooms, but other than that, I haven't seen much. I did see Shana killed, and I'll do whatever it takes to make sure Nick spends the rest of his life in prison."

Kendricks frowned. "Let's get back to the abduction attempt. Walk me through exactly what happened, Andi. You arrived home around 10pm, and then what?"

"I stepped out of my Jeep and Mason grabbed me from behind. I used the technique that I learned in the self-defense class to break away from his hold on me and drop him to the ground," Andi said.

Mrs. Davis clapped her hands together and grinned. She addressed Detective Kendricks. "We've been worried about our girl because she always seems to get herself into a jam of some sort or another. It was our idea to take her to the self-defense course at the senior center. Who knew she'd get to use those skills so soon?"

Mrs. Barzetti handed Detective Sanchez a cup of coffee and a small plate of cookies. Mrs. Barzetti told Mrs. Davis, "A lot of good it did the poor girl. Sure, she got the one thug to the ground only to have another one point a gun at her. I told you that all she really needed was for me to take her down to the gun range and show her how to shoot."

Detective Kendricks held a hand up. "Please, ladies. I'd like to just hear from Andi right now."

"Well, I had Mason down on the driveway on his belly, my knee in the center of his back. I couldn't reach my phone because it was in my purse out of reach. I had dropped it when I was grabbed from behind. It didn't matter anyway because that's when Nick pointed his gun at me and told me to release his goon. Then, Kitty came running out of the house," Andi looked at Kitty when she said, "which she shouldn't have done. It would have been safer for her if she'd stayed inside my house. She offered to go peacefully with Nick if he'd let me go. But the psycho decided that he'd just take both of us back to New York City."

Detective Kendricks was studying Andi in a way that made her squirm a little in her chair. She was telling him most of the facts. Why did she get the feeling that he knew she was leaving some of the details out of her statement?

Mrs. Barzetti piped in. "That's about the time that I looked out my kitchen window and saw those men trying to abduct my girls." She shook her head and put both hands on her hips standing in a Wonder Woman pose. Andi's lip lifted in a half smile. "Well, I got my Remington 700 Bolt Action Rifle, stepped out onto my porch and blew out the rear window of the that Yankee's fancy car. Let me tell you, that got everyone's attention."

Mrs. Harper said, "I heard the sound, but I just thought it was Gladys' car. It backfires sometimes."

"Well, I told those boys to place their weapons on the ground. Then, Andi collected the guns, and she and Kitty came over to stand by me on the porch. I told those gangsters to leave and not to even think about coming after my girls again. I shot out the taillight as they were pulling away, hoping that it might get the attention of the police, and they would get pulled over."

Detective Sanchez smiled and said with sarcasm, "Hm. Good idea because the patrol officers might overlook the shattered rear window, but they'd never miss a burned-out taillight."

Detective Kendricks glanced over at him before returning his attention to Andi. "What did you do with the weapons?"

Mrs. Barzetti said, "She gave them to me, and I put them somewhere safe."

Andi said, "Maybe you can tie Nick's gun to Shana's murder?"

"Sanchez, can you go with Mrs. Barzetti to retrieve the weapons?"

Sanchez got up and followed Mrs. Barzetti to the living room. Andi began to get up to go with Mrs. Barzetti when Detective Kendricks said, "Andi, stay here. I'm not quite finished questioning you about last night."

Uh oh. "Once Kitty came outside and Nick had realized his mistake, he was going to take you both back to New York City? Is that correct?" Kendricks asked.

Andi swallowed. "Um, yes?"

"Why?" Detective Kendricks asked. "Why not just leave you and take Kitty? Why not just kill you, since God only knows you're a lot of trouble. You'd already taken out his muscle."

There was that expectant look again. Why was it suddenly so hot in Mrs. Barzetti's kitchen. Andi waved her hands like fans in front of her face. "I don't know." She shrugged and said, "Who can really guess the motives of a mobster, right?" Andi glanced at Special Agent Reyna. "Well, you probably can or a psychologist from your department."

Mrs. Harper chimed in. "They are called profilers, dear. I learned that by watching Criminal Minds. Such a good program."

Detective Kendricks never took his gaze off Andi. "Unless there's a small detail that you might have forgotten to mention, Sloan." He titled his head. "Why would Nick Marino come looking for you?"

Oh, God. "Right?" Andi asked, her voice coming out in a little squeak. "It's not like I was repossessing his car or anything." She coughed a bit. *Pull yourself together, Andi.* She stood up and went to the sink and got a glass of water and drank half of it before returning to the table and sitting across from Detective Kendricks.

"What are you not telling me? I can't help you if you don't give me all the facts."

"There's nothing else to tell you," Andi mumbled, and thought *without putting everyone I love at risk.* She was terrified to even mention The Broker's name to the police. She'd told Cooper about him, but that was only because she had not had a choice. She needed his help to finish the job for The Broker. She was doing her best to keep her neighbors safe.

Mrs. Barzetti came back in the room with Detective Sanchez and said, "Well, I've given you two possible murder weapons. Now Detective Kendricks, what are you going to do to protect my girls?"

***

An hour later, the three detectives and Mariela Reyna watched from Mrs. Barzetti's driveway as a patrol car pulled up in front of Andi's house.

"I wish Kitty would have let us bring her in for her own protection. I'd feel a lot better if she were tucked away in a safe house while we gather evidence on Nick," Reyna said.

Kendricks frowned. "Apparently that stubborn streak must run in the family," he said. "The patrol car monitoring the house will have to do."

Mariela knew he was right, but that didn't mean she had to like it. Kitty Sloan had looked like she was on the verge of a nervous breakdown – understandable given the trauma of having her best friend shot to death right in front of her and an attempted abduction by her ex-boyfriend. The entire situation was frustrating. She had spent less than fifteen minutes questioning Kitty Sloan because Mariela had been afraid to push her any further. Based on Kitty's answers, it appeared that Nick had not shared the other illegal aspects of the business with her. Kitty Sloan was unlikely to be able to provide any new intel about the Marino family. If Mariela could somehow tie Nick to Shana's murder, she could at least get one more criminal off the streets. She might be able to get him to turnover information about the family business for a reduced sentence, although that idea didn't set well in her gut. She wanted to shut down their entire operation and put the two brothers in prison for life. When they got back to the Roanoke precinct, she would follow up with the NYPD to see if anyone reported Shana missing or dead.

Sanchez lifted the evidence bag with one hand while holding Lucky's leash with the other. "I'm going to get these right over to Forensics. It will be interesting if we can tie one of these guns to the Jacob Hauser murder."

Ryan addressed Kendricks. "Sir, can I accompany Detective Sanchez? I'm curious to see the process of submitting weapons."

Kendricks waved him on. "Fine. Just be sure to report to my desk so that you can help me write up the statement."

"Thanks, Detective Kendricks," Detective Hughes said as he beamed and followed Sanchez and Lucky to the car.

"What about you, Special Agent Reyna? Coming with us?" Sanchez asked with a grin.

Reyna smiled. "No. You two have fun. I'll catch a ride back with Detective Kendricks. I want to ask him a few questions about the case."

Perfect. This was a great opportunity to conduct her own informal interview with Kendricks. He was a member of her team, so she needed to know precisely what kind of relationship he had with Andrea Sloan. She'd observed the way they'd looked at each other and the intimate gesture when Andi reached out to reach for his hand. She was going to get to the bottom of this right now, tactfully of course.

Kendricks opened the driver side door and got in as Reyna quickly hopped in the passenger side. He didn't seem particularly happy that she was riding along, but she didn't want him to leave her behind. He'd just started the engine when Reyna spoke.

"So, what's the deal between you and Andi Sloan? Are you involved?"

"What?" Kendricks asked and turned to glare at the FBI Special Agent.

Hm, maybe that was too direct?

"Are you or have you been in a sexual relationship with Andrea Sloan?

"Absolutely not," Kendricks said and then added, "and where the hell did you get that idea?"

"Simple observation. It's just that she seemed very close with you—the way she looked at you, reached out and touched your hand while you asked her questions. Very intimate reactions for a casual acquaintance. I thought that perhaps she's a current or even former lover."

Before he could respond, she held up her hand. "I don't need to know any sexual details of your relationship. I only bring this up because as the team leader, I feel that you may not be objective with the case where Andi Sloan is involved. I'd like to know about any possible obstacles before we go any further."

"Trust me, Special Agent Reyna, Andrea Sloan and I have never had a sexual or even romantic encounter. I'm just not interested in her. For starters, she's in a relationship, and I only date single women. Second, it would be a conflict of interest since she seems to be involved in my homicide cases on a regular basis. Satisfied?" Kendricks scratched an itch at the back of his neck. "She's very much in love with her wealthy, musician, finance-VP, boyfriend."

Reyna shrugged. "Even if there's nothing on your end, she was much too intimate with you during the interview. And please, just because she has a boyfriend doesn't mean she wouldn't be interested in you, too. You're an attractive man and an officer of the law. Have you considered that she's a badge bunny? There are all types of women who are attracted to police officers for the authority and uniform alone."

"Not a chance," Kendricks said and almost smiled at the ridiculousness of that statement.

"Well, your relationship may not be sexual, but clearly you have feelings for her. Even a friendship could bias you in the investigation. You seemed particularly irritated with her this morning."

"Ha, that doesn't mean anything. I find you extremely irritating, and I just met you," Kendricks said, glaring at her with an intimidating look.

Reyna laughed at his directness. She appreciated that in communication because it saved a lot of time. He was looking at her like he wanted to throttle her. "Oh my God, that's it. Ever since I met you, your face has been bothering me."

"Really," Kendricks said and frowned. "Gee, thanks."

Reyna shook her head. "No, no, no," she said and chuckled. She was normally so good with people. Why was everything she said to this man coming out wrong? "You misunderstand me. You seemed familiar to me, but we obviously have never met before this morning." She pointed her finger at him. "But when you got angry with me just now, you reminded me of Thor from those Avenger movies." It was those intense blue eyes and that laser focused expression. She could almost image him holding the hammer in his hand, ready to do battle.

Kendricks raised his brows and blew out a breath. He faced forward, started the engine and backed out of the driveway.

He was still annoyed, but his shoulders didn't appear as tense as they had been a moment ago. She tried to lighten the mood a little more. "Oh, come on. I don't know why I didn't see it earlier. You must get that all the time," Special Agent Reyna said, smiling.

He pulled out onto the highway. "No, not really," he said.

Well, at least he was no longer scowling as he maneuvered the vehicle through the traffic.

She studied him from the front passenger seat. Sure, the guy was attractive. She'd noticed that when she'd met him, but there was an intensity about him that she found kind of hot. She could almost hear her abuela saying "Don't be distracted, Nieta."

Her grandmother used to tell her that when she wanted to play instead of work on her homework. Abuela would tenderly cup Mariela's cheek with her hand and say, "You already have to work twice as hard in this world because you are a woman and Latina." Then, she'd kiss her on her forehead and say, "But we Reyna women are self-reliant, resourceful, majestic, and untouchable, just like this beautiful estrella esmeralda." She would hold out her emerald star necklace for Mariela to touch. She touched the emerald star now that her grandmother had given her when she joined the FBI.

Come on, Mariela, she thought, *get a grip and use those Reyna women resourceful skills abuela talked about so often.*

"Those older women are something else. The rifle toting Mrs. Barzetti reminds me of my grandmother," Reyna said. "The neighbors of Andi's are tough and protective like a family should be, even if they aren't related by blood."

"They're definitely protective," Kendricks agreed.

"They aren't the only ones that are tough. I've seen Mason during our surveillance of Nick Marino. He's a big guy. It's pretty impressive that Andi was able to break free from him and drop him to the ground. That's no small feat."

"I'm glad she didn't hear you say that. She doesn't need any encouragement. The woman is a magnet to trouble."

"You obviously know her pretty well," Mariela said cautiously, trying not to put Kendricks on the defensive. She quickly asked her question. "She seemed a little uneasy when she described Nick threatening to take her and her mom back to New York."

Kendricks glanced at her briefly before returning his attention to the road.

When he didn't respond, she said, "I'm sure the entire event was distressing for both Kitty and Andi, but Andi didn't get fidgety until she talked about Nick taking them back to New York City. What are your thoughts?"

"It could be as simple as PTSD from being held at gunpoint last month," Kendricks said.

"But you don't think that's what we observed this morning, do you?"

Kendricks sighed. "My gut tells me that Andi was leaving out some critical details in her answers to my questions."

"I agree," Special Agent Reyna said. "Lying by omission, but about what?"

"With Sloan? Your guess is as good as mine," Kendricks said.

"Don't you think it's a pretty big coincidence that Nick comes to identify his brother's body and while he's in town, just happens to swing by Kitty's childhood home to pick her up and bring her back to New York." Reyna asked.

"I agree something about that doesn't add up, but for the life of me, I can't think of another reason he would show up at Andi's house," Kendricks said.

"That's bothering me, too."

Chapter Sixteen

Nick and Mason walked into the large foyer of the New York City brownstone that was Nick's childhood home. Frankie now had two men guarding the front door instead of just one. It was no surprise his brother was being extra cautious after Jimmy's murder.

A large burly man that Nick didn't recognize opened the door for them.

"I'm here to see Frankie," Nick said.

The brothers each had their own security teams. Nick had a crew for the night clubs, Frankie had a team for the narcotics business, and of course Jimmy had guys that assisted with distribution. Nick swallowed back the sudden lump that formed in his throat at the thought of Jimmy.

Grief.

Both his father and oldest brother had considered any emotion other than rage a weakness. Well, that was fine because Nick was feeling plenty of both. He pushed the grief down and let the rage race through his blood.

The burly guy stepped forward and said, "Follow me. He's expecting you."

Follow me. Like Nick didn't know the way to his father's office. Well, it had been Frankie's office for years, but it would always belong to his father in Nick's mind. The big guy knocked twice and then cracked the door to say, "Nick and Mason are here, sir."

"Let them in, Gino, and go tell mama Nick's back."

"Yes, sir," Gino said as he fully opened the door.

Nick and Mason stepped inside. The room smelled like cigar smoke. Even though the office was large, being inside had always made Nick feel like he was eleven years old again and being called out by his father for cheating in school. Frankie sat behind the desk and motioned for them to sit in the empty two chairs in front of the desk. Sitting as directed, Nick studied the lines around Frankie's eyes and mouth. He was not only named after their father—being a junior—but of the three boys, he looked the most like him—except for the nose. Frankie had mama's nose. He looked up at Nick as he finished the last of the whisky in his glass in one swallow.

"You fucked up, Nicky like you always do," Frankie said, his cheeks flushed probably from the whiskey and anger.

Nick got defensive, like he always did when Frankie acted like a drunk asshole, which was most of the time.

"I did what you said. I brought Jimmy back. His body is at the funeral home where they're making him presentable, not like the cold, dead corpse of the brother that I had to identify all the way in fucking Virginia. Mason and I then tracked down the idiot dealer that you set up, Frankie. You're usually so careful, but you sent our beloved brother into a bad situation, so if we're going to point out mistakes, let's begin with you. The idiot you used to set up distribution had already been interviewed by the cops. He might not have been the one that pulled the trigger on Jimmy, but he no doubt was going to lead the cops to us. I killed him, so now he's not going to be talking to anybody."

Frankie's rosy cheeks darkened and he shook his head. "So, your solution is always to kill everyone. You're such a fucking moron, Nicky. It's embarrassing."

"Hell, yeah, I killed him." Right now, he'd like to put some lead into Frankie, too. Just like when they were kids, Frankie had always criticized everything that Nick had done. His oldest brother thought he was so much better than Nick. Well, not this time. Frank had screwed up and now Jimmy was gone. Nick shook his head in disgust.

"I'm protecting the family, which is what you should have been doing, rather than put Jimmy into a situation that cost him his life. I brought Jimmy home. I got rid of the only person who could link us to your new drug distribution." Nick spread his arms out wide. "All while you've been sitting here, calling the shots from your safe, comfortable office." Nick felt smug for the first time since he'd gotten Frankie's call about Jimmy's murder.

Frankie raised his brows, surprised by Nick's outburst. That only lasted a moment and then he leaned forward and said, "So, wise guy, you killed our only lead for finding out who murdered our brother. Nice job. You must be so proud. I'll let you tell mama that the murderer of her precious son Jimmy is on the loose and that we'll probably never know who shot him," Frankie said.

Nick squared his shoulders. "That's not true. We got a name before we killed him."

Frankie raised his eyebrows. "So, Jimmy's killer is dead?"

"I'm still working on it. Give me a few more days and it'll be taken care of."

"What do you mean, you got a name?"

Mason said, "It's some guy named The Broker. Apparently, this Repo Girl knows how to find him."

Frankie raised his hands, palms up. "What's with all the nicknames? Is it a southern thing or something?"

Neither man responded.

Frankie asked, "So did you find this Repo Girl?"

Mason glanced at Nick, and then said, "Yes."

"And did you kill her too? Are we looking at a string of murders that are going to have the Feds breathing down my neck? Jesus, Nicky." Frankie said.

"No, of course not. Mason had just grabbed the Repo Girl when things got a little complicated," Nick said.

Frankie studied Mason. "Is that who gave you the new nose job?" he asked.

Mason looked away and gently touched the knot on his nose.

"The Repo Girl did this to you?" Frankie said in disbelief. He turned his attention back to Nick. "Just how complicated are we talking?"

"The girl is Kitty's daughter. Kitty was at the house."

"Your Kitty? The one who disappeared but according to you, she was still in the city because she had nowhere to go? What the hell was she doing in Roanoke? How is she involved in Jimmy's murder?" Frank leaned back in his chair and glared at Nick. "You said you had her under control. What the fuck?!"

Nick spoke up quickly. "It's not like that, Frankie. Kitty couldn't hurt a fly. She's scared, and I do have control over her. I would have had both her and this Repo Girl if it hadn't been for the neighbor."

"The neighbor?"

"Yes," Mason spoke up. "This little old lady blew out the back window of the car and threatened to kill us if we didn't leave."

"The little old lady?" Frankie asked, disbelief in his voice.

"Yeah, man, she was fierce. I would not like to run up against her in a dark alley," Mason said.

"So let me get this straight. My baby brother and his muscle get taken out by your girlfriend's kid and a little old lady?"

Mason said, "She wasn't a kid. She was more like some Amazon warrior."

Nick looked at Mason before turning to Frank and said, "And the old lady was armed and more than a little crazy. We left before she called the cops or shot us."

"Jesus," Frankie said.

Nick looked down to the floor. It was kind of embarrassing the way Frankie had oversimplified everything to make them look bad. His brother had always made him feel inferior his entire life, always treated him like a baby. But he hadn't been the one to ID Jimmy. Someone needed to die. It had felt good to kill someone involved in this fucking mess.

Nick looked up into Frank's eyes and said, "Look, at least I took care of the new distributor. I'm sure he would have eventually talked to the cops."

Frankie said, "But you left loose ends. You left your rogue girlfriend who will no doubt be happy to talk with the Feds, especially after you killed her friend and tried to abduct her daughter. You told me you had Kitty under control. We had to clean up the bloody mess you made at her friend's apartment building and delete the security camera evidence showing you filling her with lead. You're messy, Nicky. Now I've got to go to Roanoke to clean up after you again."

Frankie wouldn't hesitate to kill Kitty, and if anybody was going to kill her, it was going to be Nick. He honestly didn't think it would come down to that. She loved him, after all. She just let that bitch, Shana, poison her mind.

"No, Frankie. Give me another chance. Look, I'll handle everything. Kitty won't be a problem. She's not a threat to us. I kept her clear of the Marino business, so she's got nothing to tell the Feds."

"You killed her friend right in front of her," Frankie said, with an edge of annoyance in his voice like Nick had left the car window down during a rainstorm. "We don't leave witnesses. You know this."

"Witness to what? Where's the body? You took care of that, and I owe you, Frankie, but Kitty won't be a problem. Plus, she was ready to come back with me the other night until the neighbor got involved. I can use Kitty to leverage the daughter to get to Jimmy's killer. Mason and I will take care of everything. I promise."

"Oh, Nicky!" Mama said as she burst into the room.

Nick stood and turned to face his grieving mother. Her face had a blotchy rose complexion, her eyes were puffy, and she held a white cloth handkerchief under her nose. Nick wrapped his mama in a hug as she hung onto him. "You brought my Jimmy home to me?"

"Yes, mama."

"Oh, you're a good boy, Nicky. Now he'll always be with us. Oh, my sweet Jimmy. We'll bury him next to Frank. He was much too young to die."

Mama pulled away to look up at Nick. Holding onto his arms, she said, "You know who took my Jimmy from me?"

Nick nodded.

"You kill that bastard for me," mama said.

"I will mama. I promise," Nick said and hugged her back.

Chapter Seventeen

Andi stepped off the elevator and walked to Cooper's executive assistant's desk.

"Good morning, Karen. I brought you one of Mrs. Barzetti's pies. She just baked it last night."

Karen looked up at Andi and grinned. "Did you know that you are now my favorite person in the whole world?" She reached out and took the pie from Andi and admired the beautiful flaky crust before leaning forward, closing her eyes, and breathing in the aroma of baked, buttered-pastry deliciousness.

Karen opened her eyes and smiled. "Is this cherry?"

Andi nodded.

"Mrs. Barzetti is a baking genius. I should take this home for dessert for my family tonight, but I'm going to have a slice right now." Karen set the pie down on the desk and glanced at the tin of cookies in Andi's other hand. "Looks like the baking fairy is making her deliveries today. That should put a smile on the boss's face. It's no wonder he's crazy about you."

"I'm counting on it. Is he free?"

"For you? Always." Karen glanced at her phone. "Looks like he's on the phone, but you can go in anyway. He won't mind."

"Thanks, Karen."

Andi stepped inside of Cooper's office and quietly closed the door behind her. Her Rockstar was so handsome, sitting behind the desk in a charcoal suit, white shirt, and teal tie, focused on his computer while he was saying some investment gibberish on the phone. She sat on the edge of his clean and organized desk, holding the cookie tin in her lap.

Cooper had been so intent on his conversation that he hadn't heard Andi enter the office. Glancing over at the movement, his eyes widened, and a grin spread across his face when he looked up at her. She couldn't help but smile back at him.

"Bill, something that needs my immediate attention just landed on my desk. I'm going to transfer you to my assistant, and she'll schedule a time for us to go over the numbers in more detail."

He hung up the phone and somehow was standing in front of her in one fluid movement.

"This is a nice surprise. You almost never come to my office." He leaned down and kissed her in that way that made her limbs go weak. It was lucky that she was sitting already.

"I've missed you, Margarita" he whispered before going in for another kiss. As he continued the bone-melting kiss, she moved to get closer to him, but was stopped by the tin box.

Cooper looked down at the hard metal object that was keeping him from pressing Andi against him and grinned. "Aw, did you bring me cookies? You are so amazing," he said as he snatched the tin from her.

"Yes," she said a little breathless. *Focus.* What was about a suit and a tie that made her want to jump Cooper? *Ha.* She felt that way when he wore a t-shirt and jeans. It obviously didn't have anything to do with his clothes.

Coopered opened the tin and took out a cookie, bit into it and groaned in a way that made her think about…

"This is a real treat," he said, looking at her like he thought she was a snickerdoodle. "You and my favorite cookies." He glanced at his watch. "Want to go to lunch? I can maybe take an extra hour, and we can get takeout and eat in at my place. Naked."

Yes. "No, unfortunately, I've got to work. I only stopped in to tell you something that I didn't want to tell you over the phone."

Andi bit her lower lip and crossed her arms. She'd rather go back to kissing and not think about this mess she was in.

Again. Her life always seemed to be flipped upside down. Cooper lived such a normal, nice life in his safe world where his biggest challenges were how much taxes he would have to pay from his gigantic income from his investments and maybe worry over deciding which fun venue he and the guys were going to book for their next show. It still amazed her that he chose to stick around with her. She shrugged. That must be what love is all about. You stand with the people you truly care about, no matter how messy things get.

Cooper frowned and took another bite of the cookie while he studied Andi. "The last time you brought me snickerdoodles, you told me about The Broker."

He set the cookie tin down on the table and swallowed the remaining cookie in his mouth with difficulty. "He didn't contact you again, wanting you to do another job for him, did he?" He studied her face with such worried focus, like he was trying to read her mind.

"No. He didn't contact me," she said. He stepped towards her engulfing her in a warm hug as he held her close to his body. She could feel him release the breath he must have been holding before he stood back to look at her.

"That's a relief. What has put that frown on your beautiful face, Margarita? If it's not The Broker we have to tangle with, everything else shouldn't be that bad."

We. Her chest filled with warmth when he said that. She didn't have to do things alone anymore. Her Golden Girls only had the vaguest information about The Broker. They didn't really have any idea who he was and about Andi's scary involvement with him. She'd confessed all of it to Cooper last month, and he hadn't bailed. Instead, he'd been eager to help her. *Just get this over with and tell him, for Pete's sake.*

She reached out and placed a hand on his arm and gently rubbed it up and down. She knew this was going to upset him. "First, know that everyone's okay."

Cooper's jaw clenched like he was bracing himself for bad news. She hated that she was the cause of that tension.

"Last night, Kitty's ex-boyfriend tried to abduct me from my driveway."

"What the fu…"

"We're all okay, Cooper. A guy named Mason who works for Nick, that's Kitty's ex, grabbed me from behind." Andi smiled. "You know that self-defense course the Golden Girls dragged me to? I used that new move that I learned and dropped a guy who was bigger than me onto the ground." She was feeling quite proud of herself. "I had the situation under control until Nick pulled a gun on me." The smile vanished and Andi wrapped her arms around herself. She looked up at Cooper. "I really hate guns."

Cooper closed the distance between them and wrapped Andi in his arms, kissing her on her forehead. "I know, Margarita."

Andi snuggled into his body. He felt warm, safe, and smelled like that yummy cologne he wore and snickerdoodles. *Perfect.*

"He thought I was Kitty at first, but then recognized me as her kid." Andi looked up at Cooper. "She must have told him about me." *Huh.* Had Kitty thought about Andi? Did she have regrets, too? "Anyway, Kitty saw Nick threatening me and came out offering to go back to New York City with him if he just left me alone."

Cooper held onto her a bit tighter.

"I know her intentions were good, but she should have stayed in my house. Nick might never have known she was here."

Cooper leaned back so he could look at her. "No, Andi. He obviously thought she was there and would have searched inside eventually. Otherwise, why would he be at your house in the first place?"

Andi bit her lip and frowned. "He was looking for me. Finding Kitty was just an unlucky coincidence."

"You? Why in the world would he be looking for you?"

Andi shrugged. "Apparently someone told him the I could help him find The Broker."

Cooper stood back, dropped his arms, and stared at Andi.

"I know, right?!" She said, hands in the air, palms up. "Who the heck is spreading these rumors?"

"He said that you could take him to The Broker? Do you even know how to get in touch with him? I thought you told me he just showed up in some weird, creepy way, like when he came into your living room Christmas Eve like he had a key or something." Cooper said. He looked a little pale. He sort of looked like he could be sick. Andi didn't blame him. She felt sick just thinking about this whole situation.

Andi shrugged. "Exactly. I might have a phone number where I can leave a message for The Broker, but that's it. If the number is even still any good."

"You might have a phone number? Jesus, Andi, there's no might. You either have a phone number or you don't." Cooper took a deep breath and sat down behind his desk. "What happened next?"

"Well, Nick and Mason were getting ready to shove us in the car when Mrs. Barzetti blew out their back window with her rifle."

Cooper lips lifted in a half-smile. "I like her style."

"She threatened to shoot them on the spot if they didn't drop their weapons, so I collected the guns, grabbed Kitty, and we went to Mrs. Barzetti's house while the men drove away."

"Did you call the police? Where's your mother?" Cooper asked.

"Yes. Mrs. Barzetti called Mrs. Davis and Mrs. Harper and the five of us stayed up all night trying to figure out what to do. We called Detective Kendricks this morning. He and Detective Sanchez and an FBI Agent interviewed us, collected the guns, and just left Mrs. Barzetti's house. Apparently, the body that I discovered during my repo and that Kitty recognized was Nick's brother and they're all some sort of New York mafia. The FBI Agent asked her a bunch of questions about Nick's business operations. She doesn't seem to know much about it besides some gambling in the back rooms of the night club. She has no idea what the brothers were involved in, only what she's seen and heard around the night club where she used to dance. But Nick shot and killed her friend who was trying to help her escape from him. We're hoping the police will be able to tie him to the murder with the guns we gave them and lock him up. The FBI Agent wanted to put her in a safe house, but she didn't want to go, so they've got a patrol car watching my house. We're pretty sure that Nick might come back for her."

"And you, Andi, since he thinks you can take him to The Broker," Cooper said.

Andi nibbled on her lower lip again and glanced at the floor. "I might have left that part out of my interview with Detective Kendricks this morning."

"What?!"

Andi looked up at Cooper. "The Golden Girls know about it, but I sort of downplayed the whole thing. If I even mention The Broker to the police, I am concerned that Detective Kendricks will ask me questions that I don't want to answer. You know? The Broker terrifies me, and he made it pretty clear that I wasn't supposed to tell *anyone* about him. He's not the kind of person that I want to make mad."

"I get that, but what about you? What's to stop Nick from snatching you off the street?"

Andi shrugged. "I'll be safe at night while I'm home. Between the patrol officer and Mrs. Barzetti, we should be fine. Meanwhile, I'll just be extra careful while I'm working and avoid any cars with New York plates," Andi said with a small smile.

"Why does that plan not make me feel much better and why is it that I'm just hearing about this now?" He glanced at his watch. "At 11:07 a.m. the next day."

It sounded awful when he said it like that. She tried to explain. "I came right over to your office as soon as the police left so that I could tell you about everything personally. I didn't want to leave this in a text or simply tell you over the phone."

Cooper picked up his pen and began tapping it on his desk like a drumstick in a rhythm she didn't recognize. *Great.* He was probably mentally composing a new breakup song about how he quit drinking margaritas. Her stomach knotted up. This is why she brought the cookies. She knew this wasn't going to go well.

He stopped tapping his pen and stared up at her with a hurt look in his eyes. *Oh no.* "Why didn't you call me, Andi?"

"It was late, and I didn't want to wake you," she said. It sounded lame even to her. Why hadn't she called him? He would have normally been sleeping over at her house, but she'd pushed him away. This whole thing with her mom was making her crazy. She and Cooper's relationship was relatively new, well, the part where they finally said they loved each other. She was scared, okay? Seeing her mom reminded her of how she might still be unlovable, somehow. Logically, she knew she was surrounded by people that genuinely loved her but being confronted with the one person who was supposed to love you unconditionally and abandoned you, well, she obviously still was dealing with some stuff.

"I texted you 'Goodnight, Margarita', like I always do when we're not together." Cooper pointed at her. "You texted me back, 'Good night, Rockstar.'" He stood up abruptly, shook his head in frustration. "You didn't want me to stay at your place while your mom is there. I don't get that, but fine, I was supportive. I know you're dealing with a ton of shit where Kitty is concerned." He walked across the room to the other side of the desk to stand in front of her. "But Andi, I'm wounded." He placed a hand over his heart. "My heart physically aches right here because I'm not the first person that you think to call after you've gone through something awful like last night. I thought we'd moved past this. I thought you trusted me."

"Oh, Coop, I do trust you. You're the only person who knows everything." She looked past his shoulder, too chicken to look him in the eyes, afraid of what she might see. "It's just," she bit her lip and darn it, she could feel her eyes fill up with tears. "It's just that I'm afraid, okay?" *Be brave.* She swallowed and looked him in the eye. "Having Kitty pop back in my life after all this time—because she had nowhere else to go, by the way—is bringing up some lifelong insecurities for me." She tentatively reached out for his hand and laced her fingers in his. "I'm so sorry that I hurt you." She frowned as she looked down at their joined hands. "I do love you, Rockstar. I really, really do."

"Well, that's a relief," Cooper said, his voice was just above a whisper. He cupped her face with his free hand, angling it until she was looking into his eyes which were wet with unshed tears, "because I love you, Andi, and I don't care about all the goddamn dead bodies that you seem to attract like you work in a morgue, or your deadbeat mother, or even the fucking New York mob. Got it? I'm not going anywhere, so don't be afraid to call or text me any time of day when you need me, deal? Even if you only need a hug."

"Okay," she said and nodded. "Can I have a hug?"

Cooper sighed and pulled her to him until she was pressed against him. He held onto her, and she wrapped her arms around him, too. It felt like they were both holding on tight to one another, as if worried that at any moment, they might be forever separated. Right now, their relationship felt so fragile.

"I'm glad you're okay," he said finally, and she could feel him shake his head. "It really shouldn't surprise me that your mother has the New York mafia after her. Like mother like daughter." He pulled back and held her so he could look at her. "You know, I haven't even met the woman yet."

Andi bit her lip. "I know."

He looked at her expectantly, like he was waiting for her to make the next move.

Right. "Want to come over tonight to meet her?" Andi asked.

Cooper continued to look at Andi with his eyebrows raised, waiting. "And stay the night, too." *Might as well go all in.* If the man wasn't scared off by now, he must be as hopelessly in love with her as she was with him.

"Looking forward to it," Cooper said, and kissed her briefly on the lips. "I'll bring dinner."

***

After leaving Cooper's office, Andi headed over to the movie theater at Valley View Mall. She bought a small bucket of popcorn and asked the attendant, "Is Ronnie working today?"

"No. He got someone to work his shift so he could go fishing."

Andi must not have heard him correctly. "Fishing? It's January."

"Right? But he's really into fishing, so he took the boat out on Smith Mountain Lake."

What crazy person would be out on the water in January? The lake was huge. She'd never find him. Luckily, she only needed to find his truck.

Andi tilted her head. "Oh, I love fishing. I bet he's going after bass." Okay, these were all lies. She knew next to nothing about fishing. Goldfish, cod, and salmon were the only types of fish she could think of, but she was pretty sure they weren't in the lake. When she waitressed, she sometimes got customers who were going to the bass tournament, so she figured that should be safe. Now, to locate the truck.

"So, do you know where he launches his boat?" she asked.

The employee laughed and said, "Wow, you really are interested in fishing. I think he said he was going to launch from Hales Ford Public Boat Ramp. He likes that one because it's not too busy this time of year."

Andi bit the inside of her cheek. "I guess not. Well, thanks for your help." Andi turned to leave.

"Hey, aren't you going to watch a movie?"

"Nah. I'm going fishing instead."

She walked out to her Jeep while munching on the buttery popcorn, got into the chilly Jeep, and turned on the engine and heat. *Fishing? In January?* Well, at least her job didn't require her to go out on the water. She typed in the address of the boat ramp into her phone and was on her way.

Forty-five minutes later, Andi pulled into the parking lot of the boat ramp. Her target, the elusive F350 XLT, was the only vehicle in the lot and no sign of the driver, thank goodness. It would have been the perfect retrieval if not for the boat trailer attached to the truck. *Great.* She hadn't realized a trailer would be hooked to the truck. *Duh.* Well, to be fair, it's not like she had much experience with boating.

Andi parked her Jeep and walked over to the tail end of the truck to study the trailer hitch. Darn it, there was an annoying lock to prevent someone like her from simply unhitching the trailer. *Oh well, looks like I'll just have to take the trailer, too.* Jerry would have to make arrangements to return the trailer to Ronnie Hinson.

Heck, she'd repossessed a truck with an attached Christmas Float last month. How hard could it be to take an empty boat trailer? She used the key to open the truck and started the engine. Cold air blasted through the vents for the first few minutes until the hot air began to blow. Andi put her hands in front of the vents to warm them. Then, she put the truck in reverse and turned the steering wheel to the left to back out of the parking space.

Wait a minute?! Why the heck was the boat trailer going the opposite direction? She pulled forward and tried again. The same thing happened. *It must somehow be opposite?* She really should have paid more attention in her physics class. This time, she turned the steering wheel to the right as she backed up the truck and the trailer turned to the left. *Weird.* Thankfully, there were no other cars in the lot. She was pretty much using the entire lot to maneuver the truck and trailer until she eventually was able to pull out of the parking lot. *Phew.* Now, she just needed to drive straight back to the Repo Lot without backing up and she'd be golden.

Thirty minutes later, her phone rang.

"Hello?" she asked. She didn't recognize the phone number.

A woman's voice answered. "Um, hi, this is Vicky Ledford. I'm looking for Andi Sloan."

"Oh, hey, Vicky. This is Andi. What's up?"

"Remember when you offered to help me transport my girls to their dance class?"

Oh yeah. She'd forgotten about that. "Yes."

"I hate to ask you, but could you pick them up from dance class for me? I'm stuck at the dentist office for the next hour with a patient that came in for an emergency root canal. My friend dropped the girls off at their class, but she can't pick them up and I can't leave in the middle of this procedure. Is there any way you could get them and bring them here to the dentist office?"

"Sure, but what about their car seats?"

"Oh, my friend left them with the girls. Oh my God, I can't thank you enough for this Andi. I wasn't sure what I was going to do. They get out of class in fifteen minutes. Are you sure you able to do this?"

"Yes, of course." Andi glanced at her watch. She'd make it in time. "Glad I can help," Andi said and disconnected.

Fifteen minutes later, Andi carefully pulled into the crowded parking lot and stopped the truck with the trailer in front the dance class. There was no way that she was going to try to park this puppy. She put her hazard lights on, stepped out of the truck and walked up to the door.

"Andi!" both girls cheered the minute she stepped inside.

A woman in a black leotard, tights, and ballet slippers stepped up to her and smiled. "Well, I guess I don't need to ask for your name. The twins obviously recognize you. Vicky called to say you'd be picking up the girls. The booster seats are over there against the wall."

Once Andi secured the girls in the backseat of the truck, she hopped in the driver's seat and carefully pulled out.

Tabetha said, "This truck is HUGE! Is this yours?"

"No, I'm just driving it for my job. I get to drive all kinds of cars as a repo agent. Do you like this one?"

Teresa reached into her backpack and pulled out a snack bag of cheddar goldfish. "It's cool!"

Tabetha said, "I like being up this high. We're taller than the other cars."

Teresa asked, "Did you always want to be a repo agent?"

Andi laughed. "No, I just sort fell into it. What do you want to be when you grow up?"

"I'm going to be a princess when I grow up," Teresa said with a mouthful of goldfish.

Tabetha rolled her eyes. "You can't be a princess unless you marry a prince and boys are so dumb. I'm going to be an astronaut. That's way more fun." She reached into her backpack and grabbed a snack bag of oreo cookies.

Teresa said, "Nuh-uh, I don't have to marry a prince if I don't want to. I'll just buy my own kingdom."

Andi smiled. Those girls had spunk and quality snacks. She approved.

Her phone rang again. She glanced at the truck screen. It was Ben, so she answered it.

"Hey, Ben. Keep this rated G, you're on speaker and I have passengers under the age of six."

"Who the fu…fudgesicle is with you?" Ben asked.

"He talks like mommy," Teresa said.

"I'm giving a ride to my new friends. Teresa is a princess and Tabetha is an astronaut."

The girls giggled in the backseat.

"Everything okay, Benny?" Andi asked.

"Yes. No. Oh, I don't know. You think you know someone until you move in with them. I've stayed over countless times, so I didn't think there would be any surprises."

"Like a sleepover?" Tabetha asked.

Andi said, "Yes," and glanced back at her young passengers. "Ben, maybe we could talk about this later?"

Ben continued talking as if he hadn't heard her. "Daniel just reached over and used my toothbrush to brush his teeth this morning."

Andi heard the girls say "Ewwww!" from the back seat.

Ben made a gagging sound and then said, "Just thinking about it makes me want to vomit. I think he just wasn't paying any attention and grabbed my toothbrush without looking."

"Why don't you get different color toothbrushes, so they don't get mixed up?" Tabetha suggested. "I have purple and Teresa has pink."

"And you should each get your own special toothbrush holder and pick one side of the sink that's all yours. That's what Tabetha and I do," Teresa said.

"Great idea," Ben said. "I'm going to get a magenta-colored toothbrush. Thank you, ladies. You've been most helpful."

Andi laughed. "So glad we could help! We've got to hang up. We're at your mom's workplace," Andi said.

"But wait, I've got another Daniel situation."

"Bye, Benny," Andi said and disconnected the call. She pulled next to the curb by the door of the dental office. "Okay, girls, we're here."

"That was fun, Andi," Tabetha said, stuffing another cookie in her mouth.

"Maybe you can give us a ride to dance class next time," Teresa said.

***

After dropping the girls off safely to their mom, Andi drove back to the Repo Lot and pulled into the spot next to the fence. She gathered the loose items from the cab—a crumpled McDonald's bag and empty McFrappe plastic cup, a red and white bobber that was rolling around on the floor mat, and unopened mail that had been tossed on the passenger seat. Andi hopped out of the truck and took the bag with Ronnie's personal items from the glove box and bag of trash into the Repo Doctor office. Jerry was on the phone—always—making notes on a paper on his desk as he held his cellphone to his ear. He glanced up at her for a moment before scribbling something on the form on his desk. Andi dropped the trash off in the large trash can, placed the keys and paperwork in the completed box. There was only one new folder in the inbox. *Now, that's unusual.* They were always swamped with vehicles to bring in. Why was there just this one job? *Strange.*

She called for an Uber to take her back to the boat ramp to pick up her Jeep. When she disconnected the call, Andi dropped into the chair in front of Jerry's desk, waiting impatiently for him to wrap up his call.

"Uh huh. Okay. Got it," Jerry said as he leaned back in his chair. "Yeah, Phil, I understand. You need this one yesterday. I'll give you a call as soon as we pick it up." He disconnected the call and said to Andi, "Funny how every repo is urgent." Jerry shook his head. "Did you finally bring in the Ford 350?"

"Finally? I just got the folder yesterday. You're no better than Phil."

Jerry shrugged. "Hey, we've got to keep our clients happy."

"Speaking of clients," Andi said and held up the folder, "I've never seen the inbox so lean. Where is the pile of paperwork? Are you falling behind or is there some sort of National Car Loan Forgiveness Day that I don't know about?" Andi looked at his neat desk. The only paperwork on Jer's desk was the single folder in front of him that he'd been making notes on during his phone call with Phil.

"No, I'm not behind" Jerry said, looking insulted. "I've hired someone to help us bring in the vehicles."

"Hired someone?" Andi leaned forward. Jerry had been looking for another repo agent because they had been swamped with repos over the last month or two. She'd been working hard to keep up. *Hired someone?* Andi could hardly believe it. Jerry was protective of his business, and he was one of those people that absolutely hated to delegate anything. He'd only hired her because she was practically family and his grandmother had bullied him into it. If he could, Jerry would still prefer to do everything himself. She never really thought he'd follow through on it. *Hired someone.* Andi set the single manilla folder on her lap and frowned. She couldn't afford to split the workload with another repo agent. She worked on commission, getting paid for each vehicle she brought in. She no longer had Ben's rent to help her make her mortgage payment.

"Jer, I'm bringing in the repos as fast as I can. I can't afford to share my paycheck, especially now that Ben's moved out. Remember what happened last time I picked up a side gig to bring in some extra cash." Working as a mall elf during Christmas last month had turned out to be dangerous. Of course, when was her life not hazardous?

"Relax, Andi. I only gave Madison a few jobs as a test run. She was very upset when I told her that she couldn't work in the office anymore."

"Madison? Your girlfriend, Madison? The same person who mixed up the keys?"

Jerry sat up straight and held up his right hand. "Hey, I never said she was my girlfriend. Why did you say girlfriend? Did she say something to you about it?" He scratched the back of his neck with his right hand and looked up at Andi, "Because we're not, okay? Jesus. We just hook up every now and then."

Andi gave him a look.

"Okay, so maybe it's more like every night and maybe a lunch once in a while." A slow smile spread across Jerry's face as if he was remembering something salacious.

Ew. "Okay, please stop. I really don't want to hear anymore."

Jerry turned his attention back to her now all business. "What are you still doing here?" He glanced at the folder in her hand. "Get back out there and bring back the Subaru Outback."

Andi frowned. "This is only one repo, Jer," Andi said while holding up the folder again. "You know I work on at least two at a time." She leaned forward and tried to read the name upside down on the form. "I'll just take the one on your desk since you've given away all of my work to your girlfriend."

"No. I'll get this car, and she's not my girlfriend. I wish you'd stop saying that," Jerry said as he picked up the key FOB and held it tightly in his right hand.

"What's an Alfa Guila Monster Quadrilateral?" Andi reached for the key and Jerry moved his arm out of reach.

"No. It's an Alfa Romeo Guilia Quadrifoglio. That's exactly why you shouldn't get to pick this up. You won't appreciate it like I will."

"You're going to be too busy trying to undo whatever mess your girlfriend is getting herself into right now," Andi said, as she grabbed the folder off Jerry's desk and tucked both folders in her purse. She held her hands out for the keys. "Come on, Jer. You know I'm right. Plus, Phil said he needed this yesterday, right?"

"Keep Phil out of this," Jerry said, frowning at her for a long moment before dropping the key FOB into her palm. "Fine."

"Don't worry, old man. You can take it for a spin when I bring it back." A car pulled into the front lot of the office. "Oh, that's my ride. See you later." Andi stood and began walking towards the door.

"Hey, Squirt, be careful out there, alright? My grandmother told me about your stint last night."

Andi turned to Jerry and put her hands on her hips. *My stint?* "Hey, it's not my fault a New York mobster tried to abduct me from my driveway."

"I'm not so sure about that. Just try to stay alive, okay? I don't want to have to give all your jobs to Madison."

"Aw. I love you too, Jer," Andi said, turned and walked out the door.

Chapter Eighteen

After an hour-and-a-half roundtrip to the boat ramp to retrieve her Jeep, Andi finally pulled into her driveway. She waved to the officer sitting in the patrol car that was parked on the street in front of her house. He nodded as he took a bite of something that looked like a cookie. *Ah, Mrs. Barzetti.* No doubt she had supplied the officer with a few baked goods for his trouble. Andi smiled and walked up the steps to her porch. She paused before opening the door. *Huh.* She didn't have that awful feeling of dread like she usually did when bracing to see Kitty.

Nothing like the shared trauma of barely escaping her mother's psychotic mobster ex-boyfriend to ease a little tension in a difficult relationship. Now, she and Kitty had a common enemy. An enemy that was unlikely to be scared off for long by a rifle toting senior citizen or even a patrol car parked in front of her house. She glanced across the street to Mrs. Barzetti's house and back at the police car. Still, knowing both were there gave Andi some comfort.

She turned back to her door and opened it, expecting to be greeted by Dodger.

Sweet Baby Jesus.

Her living room furniture had been pushed against the walls and in the center of the room, the self-defense instructor from the senior center—Douglas something or other—stood behind Mrs. Davis. His arms were wrapped around her, and his hands clasped around her waist. Kitty, Mrs. Barzetti, and Mrs. Harper sat on her sofa watching the live action entertainment.

Mrs. Davis leaned back into the instructor's chest, turned her head into his neck and asked, "Do I lean back into you like this?" Her voice was almost a whisper.

"Oh, for heaven's sake, Gladys, you're supposed to be trying to break free, not seduce him into marrying you!" Mrs. Barzetti said, crossing her arms in front of her chest.

Douglas Kinser stepped back, eyes wide and hands up in surrender. "Hey, I'm a professional. I'm not looking to get married."

Mrs. Barzetti nodded with a smile. "Now, ladies, that's how you get a confirmed bachelor to release you."

Mrs. Davis put her hands on her hips and glared at Mrs. Barzetti. "I was only trying to demonstrate how to get out of the grab from behind for Kitty." She glanced at Douglas and said, "I'm not looking to get hitched either, but dinner and dancing isn't out of the question." Mrs. Davis finished the sentence with a wink.

Andi dropped her purse on the table by the door. "Can somebody please tell me what's going on?"

Mrs. Barzetti stood up. "Oh good, you're finally home! Doug Kinser was so nice to agree to give us a private lesson here once we explained to him about the attack from last night. He's been working with Kitty on some basic self-defense moves and had been showing Gladys how to use her cane for protection before she started this flirting nonsense. Now that you're finally home, we want you to practice disarming an attacker at gunpoint."

Andi shook her head and said, "That won't be necessary."

"Face it, sweet girl, you attract danger like tailgaters at a Virginia Tech game," Mrs. Barzetti said, shaking her finger at Andi.

"Or seniors on a Tuesday at Hamrick's clothing store for the ten percent discount," Mrs. Harper leaned towards Kitty and said, "It's my favorite place to shop."

"They're right," Mrs. Davis agreed as she stepped towards Andi. "You need to practice so you'll be ready for when those hoodlums return."

"This is all my fault. I just wasn't thinking. I should have never come back. I've put you all in danger," Kitty said.

"Nonsense," Mrs. Barzetti. "Kitty, this is your home, and we will not allow some big-city, Yankee mobsters to come to our beautiful town and terrorize our girls, right ladies?"

When Mrs. Harper and Mrs. Davis enthusiastically agreed, Mrs. Barzetti nodded and asked Doug Kinser to go over the steps to disarm a gun.

This time, practicing with Doug wasn't nearly as intimidating. The bright orange rubber gun was nothing like the real guns that had been pointed at her last night. Guess she could thank Nick and Mason for that breakthrough. When Doug pointed the gun at her near the same spot in her living room that Santa's murderer had intended to kill her just last month, Andi didn't freeze up and wasn't transported back in her mind to that time when she was sure she was going to die.

Heck, she was even able to use the correct move to disarm Doug. Sure, he was older than last night's attacker, and the gun was a ridiculous neon orange color, but she'd done it! Andi was beaming as she stepped back out of reach and pointed the rubber gun at Doug. Everyone was cheering and applauding as the front door opened.

***

"What the fu…" Cooper yelled, stopping himself when he realized the group of women weren't screaming for help, but were excited and happy. It was surprising how similar those sounds were.

He stood in the open doorway, balancing the large brown paper bag of takeout with his left hand while gripping the doorknob. Thank God he hadn't dropped their dinner when his heart had nearly stopped beating. *Jesus.* Walking in on Andi holding some stranger at gunpoint tended to have that effect on him.

He exhaled and a slow smile lifted his lips.

Crazy as it may seem, this wasn't the first time he'd witnessed Andi pointing a gun at a man in her living room. That fact alone should have sent him running in the opposite direction of this woman, gorgeous or not, but he just happened to be head-over-heels in love with her. His grandfather had always told him that you don't get to choose who you fall in love with—not when it's the real deal. It would have been so much easier to be in love with someone from his parent's social circle, but he never did things the easy way, did he?

Lucky for him, he'd noticed a few little details that kept him from going into cardiac arrest. For starters, Andi was smiling that gorgeous, sexy grin that lit up her entire face rather than the pale, terrified expression that she'd worn on Christmas Eve. The gun she held was the color of those traffic cones they used for construction on I-581, so it probably wasn't real.

The people cheering and laughing included her three older neighbors, a woman who bore a striking resemblance to Andi—that must be Kitty—and some old guy he didn't know.

"Wow, Andi, I didn't realize you were throwing a party. I would have brought more food." He stepped inside and closed the door.

"Cooper!" Andi said, her smile growing wider when she saw him. She ran over to him holding the gun out for him to inspect.

"Look at this! I finally did it! I disarmed him!" She wrapped both arms around his waist, snuggling her warm face against his neck, planting a kiss on his jaw, his cheek, and then a quick peck on his lips.

She pulled back and said, "Wait, did you say something about food?" She spotted the bag and took a sniff. "You brought Chicken Tikka Masala?"

Adorable, sexy, and she's mine. Now, he just needed to clear the room, meet and charm her mother over dinner, and then he would finally be free to enjoy Andi all to himself for the entire night.

"Oh, Cooper, how lovely of you to bring dinner for Andi and Kitty," Mrs. Barzetti said and turned to Kitty. "He's such a thoughtful young man, Kitty. You'll enjoy getting to know him."

Mrs. Barzetti turned to everyone else. "While these three get acquainted, why don't you all come over to my house for some supper? I've got a lovely pot roast that's been simmering all afternoon and homemade rolls. Stanley's joining me for dinner, but, honestly, I've made enough food for an entire church congregation. Please come over and help us eat it."

Everyone enthusiastically accepted Mrs. Barzetti's invitation because five minutes later, after moving Andi's furniture back in its place, only Kitty and Andi remained in the living room.

Damn, Mrs. Barzetti is good. She took care of that first task for him.

Cooper approached Kitty and extended his right hand. "You must be Andi's mom. I'm Cooper Barnett. It's lovely to finally meet you."

Kitty smiled and shook Cooper's hand. "I'm glad to meet you, too. I've heard lots of wonderful things about you."

Cooper smiled and looked at Andi. "Wonderful, huh?" He nodded and turned back to Kitty and winked. "Well then, I'm afraid it's all true."

"Ha. Don't you believe him, Kitty. I'd never tell such lies," Andi teased. She reached across Cooper and took the bag of food from him. "Here, I'll take this and set out dinner. I'm starving!" Dodger followed Andi and the food. From the kitchen, he heard her say, "Oh, you brought us samosas, too. I love you, Rockstar!"

"I discovered early on that the secret to winning your daughter's heart is by feeding her," Cooper said as he looked towards the kitchen. He turned back to look at Andi's mom. *Damn.* There was no question these too were related. Kitty looked more like an older sister. Hard to believe there was seventeen years between them.

"So, Andi's been telling you all about me, huh?"

"No. She's been working a lot, and we haven't had much time to talk. I heard a about you from Andi's roommate, Ben," Kitty said to Cooper. "He told me you play in a rock band."

Hm. He studied Kitty for a moment. Would she think that was cool or worry that he was a player? *Don't overthink this.*

"Yes. My good friends and I began the band in college. We loved it so much that we continued to perform part time while working our day jobs. We're doing pretty well, and our audience is growing. I'm still working as a Vice President at an investment firm." Cooper paused for effect. His day job title usually impressed people, and he really wanted to make a good impression on Kitty. Yeah, he knew Andi had a complicated relationship with the woman, but personally, he preferred to be on good terms with his girlfriend's mom—estranged relationship or not.

He just couldn't believe how much she looked like Andi. Their facial features were the same except for the bruising by her eye and a few extra lines around her eyes and lips. Her eyes were a dark brown rather than Andi's beautiful hazel eyes, and her hair was a similar shade of brown, but the texture was different. Kitty's hair hung down straight while Andi always had a mess of curls falling every which way.

Shit. He was staring at her like an idiot. What was he saying? *Oh, yeah.*

"But I'd love to play fulltime. Eventually. Our plan is to create a bunch of albums and go on tour around the world. That's the real dream."

Kitty nodded and before she could say anything, Andi stood in the archway of the kitchen and said, "Come on guys. Let's eat before the food gets cold."

When Kitty and Cooper walked into the kitchen, Dodger was busy eating from his dog dish and Andi was looking into the refrigerator. Without turning, she said, "I've got beer, sweet tea, and Cherry Coke. What can I get you?"

"Just a glass of water for me, please," Kitty answered.

"I'd love a beer, thanks," Cooper said and walked over to the seat at the end and held it for Kitty. *Too much?* She smiled and thanked him. *Guess not.*

Andi placed a glass of ice water in front of Kitty, a bottle of his favorite brew at the place setting next to Kitty, and a can of Cherry Coke at the seat farthest away from her mother. He held the chair for Andi, and she looked at him like he had a just told an inappropriate joke in front of Mrs. Barzetti.

"What?" he asked looking confused.

Kitty grinned. She liked him. Cooper could tell. He'd always had a knack for charming his girlfriends' moms. Their dads—not so much.

"I wasn't sure what you liked, Kitty, so I brought a variety." He pointed to several containers as he said, "There's Andi's favorite, chicken tikka masala. I brought dhal makhani which is black lentils, spices, butter, and cream, just in case you don't eat meat. There's also tandoori chicken, samosa with chutney, and paneer vindaloo, which is a type of cheese in a spicy sauce. Oh, and here's a delicious type of bread called naan."

"This is quite a feast. There were never any Indian restaurants in Roanoke when I was a kid. The first time I ever tried this type of food was when I moved to New York City." Kitty dished a spoon from each container so that her plate was a kaleidoscope of each selection. Cooper watched her lift a spoon of the tikka masala chicken to her nose to sniff it first, just like his Andi always did. He grinned and took a bite of the tandoori chicken.

Kitty looked at them both and said, "It's so strange being back home after all these years. In some ways, it seems like nothing has changed, and yet at the same time, everything is so different. The house, the neighbors, the city. It's surreal."

Andi said, "A lot can change in twenty-five years." She immediately took a bite of food and Cooper could feel her leg begin to bounce. She was nervous. He reached over and gently placed his hand over hers. Andi looked over at him, swallowed, and bit her lower lip. *Oh, Margarita.* Without thinking, he leaned in and gave her the briefest kiss before turning his attention back to Kitty when she spoke.

"I regret missing some things more than you'll ever know," Kitty said in a voice that was just above a whisper. She was looking at Andi with unshed tears as she moved a trembling hand across the table reaching for Andi but stopping midway as if unsure if the gesture would be welcomed.

Cooper's throat suddenly felt so thick, it was difficult to swallow his food. Without thinking, he reached his left hand over to cover Kitty's. He lifted Andi's hand to his lips and gently kissed her knuckles before placing her hand on top of Kitty's.

"The important thing is that you're both here together now. It's really quite amazing isn't it?"

Time to lighten the conversation.

"Kitty, I've got to know," Cooper leaned towards Andi's mom and asked, "Were The Golden Girls as involved in your life as they are in Andi's?"

Kitty laughed. "Yes," she tilted her head and studied Cooper, "although they seem even more feisty than I remember."

Cooper nodded. "I think that must come with age. My grandfather has always been quite the character, and now he seems even more outrageous. He says that at his age, he doesn't have time to be worried about what other people think. He's just going to do as he pleases."

Kitty studied Cooper a moment, glanced nervously at Andi for a split second before turning her full attention back to Cooper.

Andi was taking a drink from her can when Kitty straightened and asked, "So, how did you two meet?"

Andi began coughing like she'd choked on her drink. When he looked at her, she waved her hand and said, "I'm fine. Just swallowed too fast."

Cooper could feel his lips turn up ever so slightly as he turned his attention back to Kitty. *I knew it.* See, it didn't matter that Kitty hadn't been around to raise Andi. She was her mother, and he wasn't surprised at all by her question. "I first spotted her in the crowd one night when our band was playing at Star City Bar and Grill. She stood out,"

"Of course, I stood out. I'm six-feet tall," Andi said as she carefully took another drink.

Cooper shook his head although his smile widened. "It was love at first sight," he said and then turned to Andi when he heard her snort. "Well, it was for me. It took her a little bit longer to warm up to me. I managed to talk her in to letting me ride along on a repo one night. She hit a deer with the repoed car and discovered there'd been a dead body in the backseat. We were arrested and had to spend the night in jail. It was the most unforgettable first date I've ever been on."

Andi elbowed him in the ribs, and he just laughed.

"Oh my God, why do you insist on telling everyone this was our first date? It was a ride along. You know, because you pestered me to take you with me and I felt sorry for you," Andi said this in a tone like she was annoyed, but she had a faint smile on her lips. She reached over, picked up a samosa, sniffed it and took a bite.

He knew he was grinning like some lovesick idiot, but this woman next to him made him ridiculously happy. When he turned to look at Kitty, he realized she wasn't smiling. Instead, Andi's mother was frowning and looking concerned. Perhaps he should have skimmed over some of the details. He'd left out the part about all the blood from the naked, dead guy. Still, no parent wants to learn that her kid spent the night in jail.

"No need to worry, Kitty. Your daughter cleared her name, helped solve the murder, and was part of dissolving a huge drug ring in Roanoke." He leaned over and kissed her on the lips. "She's pretty phenomenal."

Andi elbowed him in the side. "You're embellishing, again, Rockstar."

"Not at all," he said, looking into her beautiful eyes before his gaze dropped to her lips.

Kitty yawned and said, "I'm so sorry. I'm so exhausted, I think I'll save the rest of this for tomorrow." She got up and covered her plate with plastic wrap and put it in the refrigerator. She placed a hand on Cooper's shoulder and said, "It was very nice to meet you. I'm glad Andi's got such good friends. Good night."

As Kitty headed upstairs, Cooper and Andi put away the rest of the food and loaded the dishes in the dishwasher. Then, he grabbed her and held her in his arms in the middle of the kitchen.

"Alone at last," he said and leaned in to give her a kiss. He'd intended it to be light and kind of playful until she made this yummy humming sound and melted against him, wrapping her arms around his waist, holding him tight.

Jesus. She felt so good. He couldn't very well take her in the middle of the kitchen, right? Well, that could be a lot of fun if they had been alone. No, he just needed to get her down the hall and into her bedroom.

He broke the kiss, feeling a bit winded like he'd run a few miles. It made him feel slightly better when he noticed Andi wasn't immune to their kiss. Grinning, Cooper bent forward and lifted Andi over his shoulder. She yelped in surprise as he lifted her off her feet and began carrying her to her bedroom.

"What are you doing? My mother is just upstairs. She'll hear us, you Neanderthal," Andi said laughing.

He dropped her down on the bed and grinned. She was completely adorable. "I'm pretty sure she knows that we're sleeping together, Margarita."

Andi rolled her eyes and sighed. "It's just weird, you know? Finally having her back in my life. Upstairs, right now." She pointed to the ceiling. "It's nothing like I imagined things would be like when she returned home."

Cooper stretched out next to her on the bed. "It's a lot to process." She turned her head to look at him. "Not only just your mom showing up," he leaned forward and kissed the top of her head, "but her crazy, mobster ex-boyfriend came to the family reunion, too." Cooper kissed her on the cheek and stared at her delicious lips for a moment before looking into her eyes. "And we can't forget about the dead bodies. Always dead bodies." He smiled. "I guess you and your mom have that in common, too." Cooper began kissing her lips gently at first, until she slid her hands on the back of his head to pull him closer, deepening the kiss, forgetting about everything but each other.

***

Andi woke up to the smell of bacon. Opening her eyes one at a time as she adjusted to the bright morning light, yawned, and stretched. *Cooper.* Oh, how she loved that man. He was gorgeous, charming, had eased the awkwardness she'd felt at dinner with Kitty, and drove her so completely mad with desire leaving her with no time to worry about everything that was going wrong in her life. The fact that her Rockstar also knew how to make more than a bowl of cereal for breakfast was the icing on the cake. She glanced at her clock as she got out of bed and slid on a robe. It was already nine o'clock. He should be at work, but he must have decided to play hooky. She smiled. Maybe she could go to work a little late today, too.

"Hey gorgeous. Did you save me some of that bacon?" she asked as she walked into the kitchen. Maybe they could bring a plate of bacon back to bed and…

Not Cooper. "Oh, sorry," Andi said, frowning when Kitty turned to smile. "I thought Cooper…" Andi shook her head. "Never mind."

Kitty smiled at Andi. "That's okay. It's been a while since anyone has called me gorgeous. I hope you don't mind that I cooked this bacon for us. I saw it in the refrigerator and mom used to make it for me when I was stressed, so…" Kitty said as she shrugged.

Andi said, "She used to make me bacon for breakfast whenever I had a big exam. She said, 'Breakfast is the…"

Kitty smiled and said along with Andi, "The most important meal of the day." Kitty looked at the photo of Grams that was hanging on the wall. "God how I miss her." She quickly turned back to the stove and wiped her eye. "Do you want an egg? I made you a cup of tea. It's on the table."

"Um, sure. An egg would be great," Andi said and quickly turned away from Kitty to look at the table. *Oh God. Breathe.* Yep. There was her cup of tea. *Relax, it's just a cup of tea, and an egg, and some freaking bacon, for heaven's sake. So, what if your mom is standing in your kitchen making you breakfast for the first time in your life? Stop making a big, hairy deal about it. Chill.*

Andi sat at the table and glanced back at the stove. Dodger sat next to the stove watching Kitty with laser precision. Andi watched with a hint of a smile as Kitty broke off a piece of bacon and pretended to drop it on the floor. Of course, the crispy treat never even touched the linoleum. Dodger snapped it up in one quick motion. "Oh, you're so helpful in the kitchen, aren't you fella? That's a good boy." Dodger wagged his tail at Kitty's praise.

Right. Andi saw straight through her mother. She brought their plates to the table and Kitty sat in the same place she had last night.

"Thanks for the breakfast," Andi said, and quickly took a bite of bacon from her plate. Oh, how she wished Cooper could be here right now to fill the awkward silences with his charming chatter. She'd even share some of her bacon with him. *Probably.*

Her phone rang. Andi reached into her robe pocket and looked at the screen.

Incoming call from THOR

Kitty glanced over at the phone and frowned. "You know someone named Thor?"

She really needed to change the name on her contact list. This was getting embarrassing. It's not like he ever really called her. She was usually the one who called him, and it had seemed kind of funny at the time when she'd entered his number into her phone. She had been on the verge of a nervous breakdown after all.

"Are you going to answer it?" Kitty asked.

"Yes," Andi said, realizing she was just staring at the phone. *Yes. Clearly I'm having another nervous breakdown.* She pressed the answer button and held the phone to her ear. "Hello?"

"Sloan."

Andi glanced at her mother. "Yes. How are you?" she asked in her syrupy waitress voice.

"What's wrong? Are you being held at gunpoint or something?" Kendricks asked.

Sort of. "No, I'm just having breakfast with Kitty."

He chuckled. "Yeah. That's what I said. Gunpoint. Listen, this involves her, too. Can you put me on speaker, and it'll save me a phone call?"

Great. "Sure." Andi placed the phone on the table between the two of them so Kitty could hear and speak into it. She sighed and looked at Kitty. "It's Detective Kendricks. He wants to speak with both of us."

Kitty's frown deepened. "Oh." Then, her eyebrows rose, and she said "Oh, I understand." She smiled at Andi and nodded her head. "Thor. I can see that."

Wonderful. Humiliation complete. Andi put her phone on speaker and then said, "We're both here, Detective Kendricks. Go ahead."

"Special Agent Reyna followed up with the New York City police. No one has filed a missing person's report for your friend Shana Alvarez. The Feds went to her apartment, she wasn't there and there was no evidence of any sort of crime. Unfortunately, the building's security tapes for that evening are missing."

"But I was there. I saw her dead body. There was so much blood. What about her job? Someone must have reported her when she didn't show up for her show," Kitty said.

"An FBI agent spoke to the club manager at The Pink Flamingo. He confirmed that she was a dancer there but figured she must have gotten a better gig when she didn't show up for work this week. They replaced her."

"Oh, God," Kitty said, with a sob. "I should have called the police when it happened."

Andi reached over and squeezed Kitty's hand. "You were running for your life. You didn't even have a phone. You barely had money to get a bus to come here. You're doing something now. We're going to make the FBI keep you safe, and Nick spends the rest of his life in prison."

Andi looked at the phone, "Right, Detective?"

There was a pause. "Unfortunately, the FBI is unable to place Kitty in a Witness Protection Program. There's no evidence that Shana Alvarez is dead, much less murdered by

Nick Marino. He was smart enough to make sure that Kitty wasn't aware of anything illegal happening in his businesses, aside from illegal gambling in the club."

Kitty covered her face with her hands.

"Okay, fine. What about your department, Detective? We provided you with the murder weapon that he must have used to kill the guy from the auto glass place the night he tried to abduct us. You can at least pick him up on local murder charges, right?"

There was a pause. *Oh no.* "What is it?" Andi asked.

"The only prints on the weapon are yours, Andi."

"Not again," Andi said, shaking her head. "You can't believe I killed the glass shop guy!"

"Of course not. I'm sure Nick was wearing gloves the night he came to your house. Do you remember?" Kendricks asked.

"Forgive me if I was a bit more distracted by the barrel of the gun to really notice if he was wearing gloves," Andi said. "I suppose you're going to arrest me again."

Kitty looked up and frowned at Andi. "Again?"

"No," he said with an impatient tone. "Not yet, anyway. The ballistics report shows that the gun you took from Nick fired the same type of bullet that was used to kill Jacob Houser. We just can't specifically tie Nick to the murder. Nothing that will hold up in court."

"Just great, Detective. We're sitting ducks. I guess next thing you're going to tell us is that you're pulling our police protection, too," Andi said.

When Detective Kendricks didn't reply, Andi scooted her chair back and began pacing the kitchen. "Unbelievable!"

He sighed. "I know it's not the news you were hoping for."

Andi shook her head in disgust. "Do you think? Wow, can't pull anything on you, Detective."

"Listen, I know you're upset. Just try to be a little patient. We're going find some shred of evidence to tie the Marinos to both murders. I promise. I can maybe give you another 24 hours of protection, but after that I'm going to have to pull the patrol car. Unfortunately, we just don't have the resources."

Andi glared at the phone, and then closed her eyes and took a deep breath. When she exhaled, she opened her eyes and said, "Fine. I guess we'll just have to handle things on our end. Thank you for your help, Detective."

"Sloan, wait. What do you mean handle things on your end?" he asked.

"Look, you just said you don't have the resources. We'll call you if we come up with the evidence you need." She walked back over to the table.

"No. That's not what I..." Kendricks was saying when Andi disconnected the phone.

Kitty stood then, too. "You just hung up on the Homicide Detective."

Andi shrugged, "It's okay. He's kind of used to it." Her phone began to ring again. She looked at the screen that showed *Thor*. "Yeah, I think I'll turn this off for a while." She pushed a button to shut down her phone.

"I can't believe that Nick can just make people disappear. She was dead, Andi. I saw her just staring up at me. You've got to believe me," Kitty said, and tears began running down her cheeks.

Andi stepped over and gave her a hug. "I do believe you, Kitty." She gave her an extra squeeze. "Listen, Nick Marino is going to spend the rest of his miserable life rotting in jail. We're going to make sure of it. Somehow."

Andi stepped back and held onto Kitty's shoulders. "You're safe here for now while we have the police officer. Why don't you call Mrs. Barzetti and the girls and ask them to come over? You tell them what Kendricks said, and between the five of us, we'll come up with some sort of plan. Meanwhile, I'm going to grab a shower, get dressed, and go chase down a car for work. Still got to pay the bills, whether the New York mob is after me or not." She put on her waitress smile as if what she said was some sort of light-hearted joke. *My life is a joke.* "Plus, I think better while I'm working. I'll be back this afternoon." She stepped into her bedroom, closed her door and leaned against it. *Holy Mary, Mother of God.* She made a sign of the cross with her right hand. She wasn't much for praying, but she figured it wouldn't do any harm this time. *God, if you can hear me, I sure could use some help with this mess. Amen.* They were going to need all the divine assistance they could get.

Chapter Nineteen

An hour later, Andi was showered, dressed, and headed to the Salem Courthouse to track down her skip. She turned on her phone and saw nine missed messages from Thor with 3 voicemail messages. *I'll just check those later.* Dropping her phone in her coat pocket, she grabbed her purse and left the house. Andi had called the law offices of William T. Henning from her car and learned that her skip attorney was unavailable because he was scheduled to be in court all morning at the Salem District Courthouse. Well, based on the photo, his Montreal Green Alfa Romeo Guilia Quadrifoglio shouldn't be too hard to spot. *Now that's a mouthful.* She'd just refer to it as the Romeo job. She'd driven a lot of really nice cars since she'd taken this Repo gig. Why was Jerry so excited about this one?

"Oh, wow," Andi whispered to herself. She'd spotted Romeo in a parking space near the courthouse building. "Now that's green." There was no losing this car in the dark. Andi drove down to the next block and parallel parked her Jeep. She made sure the paperwork was in her purse, unclipped the key FOB, and casually began walking towards the courthouse. Taking this vehicle from an attorney in front of a courthouse next door to the Salem Police Department made her stomach a little jittery.

Act like you're supposed to be here. Come on. Your job is totally legit.

She always liked to remind herself that the skip, in this case, William T. Henning, was in default on his loan payment. If anyone should feel icky, it should be him. She remembered to breathe when the Romeo's lights flashed when she clicked the FOB. *Thank you, Sweet Baby Jesus.* She opened the door, slid inside, and did a quick look for the start engine button. There it was, right on the steering wheel. She pressed it, closed and locked the doors, and checked her rear-view mirror before backing out.

Uh oh. Three suits at 7 o'clock. Relax. Everyone wears a suit to court. They were carrying briefcases and laughing as she put the car in reverse and backed up just about 15 feet from them. *Oh man!* They weren't laughing anymore. She'd bet one-hundred dollars that the guy in the navy-blue suit was William T. Henning because his face was beet red, and he was pointing and running towards Romeo. She couldn't hear him over the robust engine sound, but if she had to guess, he was probably yelling "Help! Someone's stealing my car!" They always said that.

"Show me what you've got, Romeo," she said as she shifted into drive and pressed down on the gas. The car didn't disappoint as it flew out of the parking lot and onto Calhoun Street. Then she took the back roads up to Interstate 81 where she could legally take Romeo up to seventy miles per hour.

Andi drove directly to the repo lot, not wanting to risk getting pulled over on the chance that Mr. Henning reported his Romeo stolen. She checked the interior and didn't find any personal belongings. After phoning for a taxi to take her back to her Jeep, Andi locked up Romeo and walked into the office. She dropped the key and the paperwork into the return box and picked up two more jobs.

Jerry looked up from his desk. Andi smiled and said, "You can stop worrying. I brought Romeo back for you in one piece."

"So, what did you think?" he asked.

"I don't know. It tore out of the courthouse parking lot nicely when the delinquent attorney spotted me." She shrugged. "Other than that, I guess it drove okay." Andi plopped down in the seat in front of his desk. "It made me want Italian food for some reason. I tried to wipe up the marinara sauce from the leather seats the best I could."

"Cute," Jerry said.

"Where's Madison?" Andi asked.

"I had to fire her. Things weren't working out too well. You thought the mix up with the paperwork was bad? I won't even tell you what happened out in the field."

Andi scrunched her face. "How did she take it?"

Jerry smiled and leaned back in his chair, stretching his arms out wide. "Let's just say that I'm single and free again."

Andi shook her head. "I can see this has really torn you up."

"Hey, I'm a sensitive guy, but I do bounce back quickly." Jerry leaned forward and his smile turned serious. "I got a call from my grandma about the trouble with your mother. I can't believe there's nothing the police can do to nail that bastard."

"Right?! We handed the detectives the probable murder weapon and it's not enough evidence. I've got to come up with something. I have no doubt that psycho will be back for us."

Jerry just shook his head. "How do you get into these messes? I almost feel bad about complaining about Madison." He cocked his head to the side. "Almost."

A yellow taxi pulled to the front of the door and beeped.

She laughed as she stood up. "Well, you should feel sorry for me. You could always, I don't know, give me another raise to ease your guilt?"

He laughed. "I don't that feel that bad."

She shrugged. "It was worth a try. That's my ride. See you later."

Andi heard Jerry say, "Stay out of trouble, Squirt!" as she walked out the door.

She climbed into the taxi and said, "Please take me to the Salem District Courthouse."

The driver nodded and started the meter.

Andi sat back and looked out of the window as they drove down Peter's Creek Road. Even though she was able to laugh about it with Jerry, she and Kitty were in big trouble. There had to be something she could do. *Come on, Andi, think your way out of this mess. Maybe I can wear a wire and get Nick to confess to the murders?* Her luck, Nick would kill her before he confessed, or Detective Kendricks would probably say it's "entrapment" and inadmissible in court, or he'd tell her that they don't have the resources for wires or something equally unhelpful.

When the taxi stopped about fifteen minutes later, Andi looked out the window for the first time since she'd gotten in the car. "Excuse me? We're in Salem, but this isn't the courthouse."

"That's correct," the taxi driver said as he hopped out of the car and opened the door for Andi. They were in the parking lot of an upscale restaurant called Morgan's. "If you'll follow me, I'll take you to meet Mr. Brando."

"But I don't know a Mr. Brando. I think you've got me confused with someone else."

He smiled at her and shook his head. "You're Andrea Sloan, the Repo Girl, right? I recognize you from the news although that mug shot photo of you really doesn't do you justice." He laughed. "Get it? Mug shot and justice?" He waved his hand, "Anyways, Mr. Brando contacted me and said he'd pay me five hundred bucks if I brought you here to meet him. I'm supposed to wait for you out here and then take you to where you needed to go. You know, the Salem District Court House, right?"

He looked at her expectantly.

"Yes, but I'm uncomfortable meeting someone I don't know," she said.

He laughed. "Hey, it's a free cab ride and you're meeting in a public place. You got nothing to worry about, kid." He leaned in towards Andi and in a low voice said, "And I kind of got the impression that he's not the sort of guy you say no to, so I'd go ahead in if I were you."

Mr. Brando? Who the heck wanted to meet with her on a Thursday afternoon at Morgan's? The driver did have a point. It was unlikely someone would try to harm her here. "Fine," she said and then pointed at her driver. "But you better still be here when I come back."

He held his hands up defensively, "Absolutely. I don't get paid until I take you where you want to go, so I'll be out here keeping warm in my car."

Andi nodded and turned and walked into the restaurant. It was one of those fancy-schmancy places where you had no idea what time of day it was because the place had no windows. The walls were painted a dark burgundy, the lights were dimmed, and there was a small candle and a tiny vase of fresh flowers in the center of each table. Classical music was playing over the speaker system. She walked up to the host station and an attractive young man, probably close to her age, smiled up at her. "Welcome to Morgan's on Main. Do you have a reservation?"

Yeah, well she had plenty of reservations about being here to meet a stranger, but she was pretty sure that's not what he meant. "I'm here to meet Mr. Brando?"

The man's smile faltered slightly. "I see," he said and then stepped out behind the host station and said, "Please follow me."

Great. Andi followed him past tables where well-dressed customers were talking, laughing, and enjoying their meals. They continued walking by several empty tables until they reached the corner of the room where The Broker was cutting a large, rare steak. Andi suddenly felt nauseous.

"Mr. Brando, you have a guest," the host announced.

"Yes," he said with a smile, "I've been expecting her."

The host slid out a chair and said, "Please be seated." As Andi sat down, he asked, "Can I get you something to drink?"

Vodka. "I'd like a Coke, please?" Maybe that would help settle her stomach. It was never a good thing when Roanoke's Crime Boss requested a meeting. At least this time he didn't abduct her in a parking lot or break into her house. Some might consider that an improvement. Improvement or not, the fact that he could get to her so easily was very disturbing.

"Certainly. I'll be right back with your drink," he said and hurried away. She wished she could go with him. *Might as well get this over with.* She took a deep breath and looked him straight in the eye. "Mr. Brando? Somehow, I don't think that's your real name?"

He shrugged. "Guilty. I like to use aliases from my favorite movies. Marlon Brando made an excellent Vito

Corleone in The Godfather. Did you see it?" He took a bite of his steak, chewed it, and studied her. When Andi shook her head, he said, "You should. It's a classic. Speaking of mafias, I hear you and your mother are having a little problem from New York."

Andi swallowed. *How does he know everything? It's unnerving.*

"Yes, and speaking of New York, Nick Marino is looking for you. Somehow, he got the idea that I could set up a meeting with you." Andi leaned forward and whispered, "Maybe if you stopped abducting me, people wouldn't think I worked for you."

He pointed the steak knife at her and in a stern voice, said "You should be working for me instead of wasting your talents stealing cars for Jerry. Pfft. I can offer you real money. Hell, I even offer my employees healthcare and a 401K. You've got to stay competitive in this market to get and keep good people."

"Oh, for Pete's sake, I don't steal cars. Why does everyone think that? I'm in a legitimate business that won't land me in prison."

He cut his steak. "If that's true, why did I have to post bail for you when you were arrested for murder after only "doing your job?" Anyway, legitimate work is highly overrated." He shook his head and took another bite.

A young woman dressed in all black carrying a tray with a glass of cola approached the table and placed the beverage in front of Andi. The server looked at The Broker and asked, "How's your steak, Mr. Brando?"

"Tell Danette it's perfecto!" he said and planted a kiss on his fingertips before resuming cutting his steak. She smiled with what looked like relief. Andi could only imagine what might result if "Mr. Brando" was unhappy with his meal or service. The server left promptly to share the blessed news with Danette that she would live to serve another meal, while Andi was left alone at the table with The Broker.

"So," he asked, "what's your plan to deal with him."

Andi's eyes widened. "My plan?" She began to speak fast, and her voice rose with each statement. "I don't have a plan.

We're talking about the New York Mob. What am I supposed to do? I turned over their guns to the police already. There are no fingerprints on the weapon to implicate Nick for the murder. My mom saw him kill her friend right in front of her in New York City, and now the body is simply gone. They make people disappear."

"Relax and lower your voice, please," he said, pointing the steak knife at her again. "Drink your Coke." He set his fork and knife down and took a sip of his red wine. "Clearly, you're worried and need my help."

Yes. No.

"You could bring these New Yorkers to me. They're not the only ones capable of making people disappear."

Sweet Baby Jesus.

He shrugged. "This is maybe not the best option since you and your mother would probably be killed in the crossfire."

"Yeah, I don't like that plan at all."

He shook his head. "I don't like this option either. It's messy and draws the attention from the Fed's New York Office, if you know what I mean." He picked up his fork and steak knife and resumed cutting. "Plus, you've already got the attention of the police and that Federal Agent Reyna. I prefer to stay in the shadows on this job."

Andi frowned, and said, "If only the police could catch them in an illegal activity. You know, not murdering me and my mom, but drug or weapon trafficking. Something to put them away for a very long time."

The Broker looked at her and smiled. "Now that's something I can help you with. Maybe I can give you some of those illegal drugs and throw in a few stolen weapons to ensure a lengthy prison sentence for Mr. Marino. You plant them on him and report it to your buddy Kendricks and problem solved.

Andi gaped. "Are you crazy? That's illegal!"

The Broker shrugged. "Take the risk or lose the chance to put him away. Look, you said yourself that he's coming for you and your mom. He's likely to kill you both either way. At least this gives you a fighting chance."

"But everything about this is illegal and dangerous. If I get caught with the drugs and weapons, I'll be joining him in prison."

"Or he'll kill you if he realizes it's a trap. Hey, I admit it's not a perfect plan, but it's better than sitting around waiting to die. Sometimes, that's all any of us really have in this life."

Great. A crime boss who is a philosopher. This is such bad plan.

The Broker reached into his pocket and pulled out a cellphone and slid it across the table until it was next to her Coke.

"I'll call you on this phone to let you know when and where to pick up the merchandise."

Andi stared at the phone like it was a poisonous snake. She couldn't take this phone. She couldn't not take this phone. *Oh, heck.* She grabbed it and dropped it in her purse before she changed her mind.

The Broker grinned. "Good girl. I always knew you were smart."

Andi downed the rest of her Coke. She'd prayed to God for some help and then Satan had answered her prayer instead.

"Of course, you do realize that you'll owe me a pretty big favor since I'm sacrificing some of my valuable inventory."

Jesus, Mary, and Joseph. Andi didn't want to owe The Broker anything.

Andi shook her head. "But I'm really doing you a favor by taking care of Nick Marino, remember? I'm the one taking all the risks to keep your involvement minimal." She let out a nervous laugh. "So, when you think about it, we're even. Right?" she asked nodding her head to encourage him to agreement.

"I forgot about your sense of humor," he said as he chuckled. "I do enjoy doing business with you, Repo Girl. Don't worry. I'll let you know when I'm calling in the favor."

What?! "You know I can't return the favor by doing anything that's illegal, right?"

The Broker smiled. "We leave it to the lawyers to determine what's legal. There are so many gray areas. Was it cold blooded murder or simply self-defense? Gray areas, Andi." His cellphone buzzed, and he glanced down. "Perfect. Looks like my two o'clock is here. Hold on to that phone. Someone will call you to tell you where and when to pick up the merchandise. Be on time and absolutely no police or Fed involvement until you've planted the evidence. Got it?"

Andi had completely lost her ability to speak so she nodded, got up from the table and hustled out the door, keeping her head low. She didn't want to accidentally bump into whoever was unfortunate enough to be the two o'clock appointment. She had enough problems already.

She stepped out of the restaurant into the bright, cold, sunny afternoon. There was her driver, waiting as promised. He hopped out of the car and opened her door for her. "See. I told you everything would be fine. Look at you. No bullet holes or anything. Still want to go to the courthouse?"

Andi nodded and slid in the back seat, and he closed her door. He sat in the driver's seat and looked at her through the rearview mirror.

"I'll have you there in less than five minutes. You're my biggest fare of the year!"

***

Thirty minutes later, Andi found herself standing in front of Simon's food truck. She didn't really remember driving there which was kind of scary because that meant she'd navigated Salem and downtown traffic without paying attention. All she knew was that she needed to see her friend, Mags.

"Holy shit," Maggy said from the food truck window when she saw Andi, and then before Andi could speak, Mags was standing in front of her. "Are you hurt?"

When Andi only shook her head, Maggy pulled her into a big hug and squeezed hard. "What happened? Is it your mom? Cooper? Did something happen to Dodger?" Mags pulled Andi back and asked, "Oh no. Did Dodger get hit by a car? How did he get out?"

"What?" Andi asked. What the heck was Maggy talking about? "No, everyone is fine." Of course, Maggy didn't know anything about The Broker, and there was no time to go into all that now. "I just wanted to see you." *In case it's the last time.*

Maggy frowned and said, "Andi, you're scaring the hell out of me."

"It's just that my mom's psycho ex is most likely coming back to town, and stuff happens, especially to me lately. I just wanted you to know that you've always been my best friend, and I wouldn't have survived my childhood, heck, my adulthood without you. You're the best friend a girl could ever have."

Maggy's eyes filled with tears. "Well, don't think you're leaving me so easy. You need to promise me right now that you're going to stick around and be my bestie until we're at least as old as Mrs. Barzetti." Maggy held out her pinky finger. "Pinky promise, right now."

Andi smiled and linked her pinky with Maggy's pinky. "I promise that I will do everything in my power to survive this, but to be completely honest, I'm sort of freaked out."

"Listen, how many Roanoke City gals have their own god of Thunder looking out for them? You and your mom are going to be perfectly safe. You've got Roanoke's finest protecting your house."

No sense telling Mags that all that was about to change. Instead, she pretended for her friend's sake that she believed she and her mom were going to be fine. "You're right, of course."

"This situation calls for a Triple Dog Dare–one super-sized roll with three all-beef hot dogs loaded with chili, mustard, and onions—on the house," Simon said from inside the truck.

Mags put her hands on her hips and glared at Simon. "My best friend is afraid she's about to be gunned down and you offer to finish her off yourself by giving her three beef hot dogs! What she needs is my Ultimate Chocolate Shake – delicious and healthy." She turned to face Andi. "Give me just a minute to blend one up for you." Mags ran around the side of the truck.

"This is exactly what I needed. I love you both," she said with a genuine smile as she watched them bicker while they shared the tight space of the food truck.

Chapter Twenty

Andi was stuffed. She'd eaten the Triple Dog Dare while chatting with her friends in front of the food truck as if she hadn't just had a conversation with The Broker and was supposed to commit a crime by transporting illegal drugs and weapons to frame a Mafioso. She sipped on the rest of Mag's Ultimate Chocolate Shake as she drove her Jeep home.

Might as well hear what Detective Kendricks had to say on the voicemails. Her day couldn't get any worse. She pressed play and the messages played over her Jeep speakers.

You have 3 new voicemail messages.

Message Marked Urgent from Thor: "Seriously, Sloan? You're going to hang up on me instead of listening to a voice of reason?" BEEP

Message Marked Urgent from Thor: "Oh yeah, that's real mature, Sloan. Turning off your phone to avoid the conversation that we need to have? What, are you five years old? God dammit, answer your phone." BEEP

Message Marked Urgent from Thor: "Obviously, you're upset, and I get that. I really do. I get frustrated when the legal system seems like it's taking longer than I want or when there's no evidence to pin to the bad guys. Trust me, I get it. But the legal system does work and if I didn't believe that whole-heartedly, I would have left

> *this exhausting profession years ago. Lord only knows what crazy, likely-to-get-you-killed plan you've concocted in that beautiful head of yours. As a Roanoke City Homicide Detective AND your friend, I'm going to need you to step back, take a breath, calm down, and sit this one out while I do my job. I'll figure out a way to get more protection at your house, even if I have to keep watch in my own goddamn car when I'm off duty. Okay? I can only keep you safe if you shelve whatever the hell it is you're thinking of doing. Call me. Please." BEEP*

Andi deleted the messages and sighed. It was kind of sweet that he was looking out for her even if it was in a grumpy, yelling kind of way. There's no way she was calling him back to share the details of the deal she'd made with The Broker. She didn't think she could withstand one of his interrogations. He'd break her for sure in her current state. No. She needed to get back home and update Kitty. Oh, how Andi wished that the Golden Girls weren't involved, but there was no way to exclude them now.

Cooper. She'd better call him. He was the only other person she knew who'd ever actually met The Broker. She didn't want to chance talking to him over the phone. God only knew who was listening to her phone calls. The Broker sure seemed to know a lot about everything going on in her life, and that made her wonder who else might be listening. *Paranoid? Maybe just a little.* Cooper would insist on helping her with this, what did Kendricks call it, "a, crazy, likely-to-get-you-killed plan." Andi shook her head. She couldn't ask him to risk his life, too.

Andi autodialed Cooper's cellphone through her Jeep.

"Hey Beautiful. I've been thinking about you all afternoon. How's your day going?" Cooper asked when he answered his cell phone.

"Not my best day," Andi said and thought about it. "Not my worst, either." *Huh, THAT's a scary thought.* "Listen, we need to talk. What are you doing after work?"

"The band's playing at Star City Bar and Grill tonight at 7pm. Why? What's happened?"

"Got some disappointing news from Detective Kendricks this morning and another new development that I really need to tell you face-to-face. Maybe we can grab a bite to eat at The Grill before the show? I'll fill you in then."

"Are you sure it can wait, Margarita?" he asked. "You sound a little stressed. You know, more than usual. I can reschedule my afternoon and meet you now if you want."

Aww. This is one of a million reasons she loved this guy. She was tempted to say yes to his offer if only just to hold him close to her. Instead, she put on her waitress smile and tried to sound lighthearted. "Nah. I'm fine. Well, as good as someone can be with the New York mob after her and her mom. My news can wait. Go make your clients a few extra zillion dollars this afternoon. See you tonight."

She heard him laugh and that made her smile turn genuine. "I love you, Rockstar."

"Love you, Margarita."

Andi disconnected the call as she pulled into her driveway, waving at the patrol officer as she got out of her car. She walked up the steps, opened the front door, greeted Dodger, and hung up her coat before walking into the kitchen. All four women were sitting around her table putting icing on snowflake shaped sugar cookies. Mrs. Barzetti was commenting on everyone's technique and giving pointers. She looked up at Andi and smiled. "Glad you're back home. Now, go to the sink, wash your hands, and join us."

She smiled at her bossy neighbor as she followed Mrs. Barzetti's instructions. That was precisely what her grams would have said. When she joined them at the table, she reached over and grabbed an already frosted cookie and took a bite.

"Andrea Sloan, we're frosting them, not eating them just yet. You'll spoil your appetite for supper," Mrs. Barzetti said.

Andi covered her mouth with her hand as she chewed the cookie and said, "I thought I was the tester."

Mrs. Barzetti rolled her eyes and smiled. "That girl of yours, Kitty. She reminds me so much of you when you were younger."

Kitty looked tenderly at Andi.

Andi swallowed the lump in her throat. It was kind of nice to have her mother back. She sure hoped that they survived this mess, so she might actually get to know her. Andi took a deep breath. *Best get this over with.*

"I assume Kitty told you about the call from Detective Kendricks," Andi said, looking at Kitty who nodded back.

Mrs. Barzetti stood up and put her hands on her hips, shaking her head. "Yes, and I think it's terrible that they can't do more to protect Kitty, and you too, Andi." She pointed her finger at Andi. "I think you should take the next few days off from that job of yours and stay put in this house where we can keep you both safe. I'm sure Ethel can explain things to her grandson, so he won't give you any trouble about it. If the police pull the patrol car, I'll camp out on my porch with my Remington 700 to keep watch over your house. Nobody is going to mess with my girls."

Mrs. Harper said, "I'm sure Jerry will whine about it a bit, but he loves you, Andi, and worries about you in his own way. He'll want what's best for you."

Mrs. Davis said, "We need some way to protect you. As long as Nick is out on the streets, neither of our girls are safe. I saw this movie on Lifetime the other night about a woman trying to escape the mob. She successfully hid for a time, but they eventually found her a few years later and killed her. It was awful."

"If the police have no evidence to convict Kitty's ex, what are we going to do?" Mrs. Harper asked.

"We've got to come up with a plan, of course. We need to find the evidence to get him locked up in the big house for the rest of his life. The question is, where do we start?" Mrs.

Barzetti reached for one of the frosted sugar cookies and took a bite.

"Well, I have a plan. It's a long shot, and it's dangerous and definitely illegal, so if you want to drop out, I completely understand," Andi said looking at each one of them.

Mrs. Barzetti set her cookie down on the table. "What is it?"

Andi bit her lower lip. "Well, I'm thinking that we call Nick and tell him that I've arranged a meeting with The Broker, which I haven't really. When he arrives at the location to meet The Broker, we'll hide a stash of illegal drugs and weapons in his car."

Mrs. Harper nodded, and said, "Yes, then we'll call the police once they have it. That's certainly enough to arrest them for a long while."

Mrs. Barzetti shook her head and said, "That's a grand plan, Andi, except I don't happen to have any illegal drugs stashed in my kitchen cupboards."

"Well, I'm taking care of that part," Andi said.

All four women stared at her in shock. It would be kind of funny if her hands weren't a little shaky.

"Young lady, exactly how do you plan to get your hands on illegal drugs?" Mrs. Barzetti asked, crossing her arms over her chest.

"I met with The Broker this afternoon, and he's going to call me on a burner phone he gave me and let me know when and where I can pick up the stuff." Calling the illegal contraband stuff made it sound less terrifying and illegal.

Mrs. Barzetti threw her hands up in the air and turned away saying something under her breath that Andi couldn't quite hear. She spun around, which was pretty impressive for a woman her age, and put her hands back on her hips. "I don't like that you're consorting with a crime boss."

"Runs in the family," Mrs. Harper muttered under her breath. When Mrs. Davis elbowed her, she turned and said, "Well, it does."

"Criminals can't be trusted, Andi," Mrs. Barzetti said shaking her head. "If this Broker fellow does actually follow through on his promise to deliver the stuff, you'll be taking a terrible risk. What if the police catch you with it?" Mrs. Barzetti began pacing. "Even if your plan works out," she said, stopped to look at Andi, "and that's a big IF," she resumed pacing and shaking her head, "that Broker fellow isn't just going to give you valuable stuff for free." She stopped, looked up at Andi, and asked, "What's the price?"

Andi swallowed. Telling Mrs. Barzetti the entire truth about owing The Broker a favor wasn't going to help anybody. In the best case, Mrs. Barzetti would worry herself over the matter and worse case, she'd try to hunt down The Broker herself and that would be a disaster. Andi decided to just give a half-truth instead.

"It's to The Broker's benefit to stop the New York mob from doing business in Roanoke. With Nick in prison, the threat is gone, only costing him a few drugs and weapons. Not a high cost to pay, in my opinion."

"I still don't like it," Mrs. Barzetti said. "Something feels off about this."

Mrs. Davis raised a brow. "Probably the part where we are committing a felony."

Mrs. Barzetti glared at Mrs. Davis.

Andi shrugged and sat down and sighed. "I don't know what else to do. We either sit here and wait for Nick to come get us, or we try this long shot of a plan. At least this way, we stand a chance of getting the bad guy behind bars and maybe living a bit longer."

"Oh, fine," Mrs. Barzetti said with a sigh. "Well, don't just sit there icing cookies, ladies. If we're going to follow through on Andi's plan, it's about time you girls learned how to handle a gun."

Mrs. Davis grinned. "Now we're talking! I'll drive us to the shooting range."

"I call shotgun!" Mrs. Harper yelled, giggling.

***

This is such a bad idea. Kitty's involvement couldn't be helped since they were dealing with her ex-boyfriend, but Andi should have tried harder to keep her neighbors out of this mess. Her plan was just too dangerous, and it made her stomach knot up at the thought that one of them could get hurt or worse.

As if I could ever keep my determined neighbors from doing anything that they decided to do. They were a force to be reckoned with. Heck, she and Kitty would probably either be dead or sold off in some human trafficking deal in New York City if it hadn't been for Mrs. Barzetti coming to their rescue that night Nick tried to abduct them. *Let's face it, you need their help.*

And Mrs. Barzetti was finally getting her wish. She'd been convinced from the start that everyone needed to learn how to handle a gun, and now here they were, headed to an indoor shooting range to learn from the self-proclaimed best of the best, Mrs. Barzetti. Mrs. Davis was driving her 1995 Buick LeSabre, going ten miles under the speed limit, while Mrs. Harper was riding in the front passenger seat. Andi was sandwiched between Mrs. Barzetti and Kitty in the back seat. At least the Buick was big enough that they all five could ride comfortably. Andi just wished Mrs. Davis would at least drive the speed limit. She glanced in the rear window. They led a parade of eight cars, Andi counted. The driver of the Toyota Camry directly behind them was honking and waving his hands in frustration. Andi couldn't blame him.

Mrs. Davis stopped at a red light and, Jeez-Louise, the LeSabre backfired rattling the entire vehicle. The teen standing at the corner by the crosswalk crouched down low and covered his head with his arms, mistaking the backfire for a gunshot. Andi looked behind her and there was a puff of black smoke blocking the Camry driver from her view.

"Mrs. Davis, you might want to get your fuel system checked out. I can recommend a mostly honest mechanic," Andi said.

Mrs. Davis looked back at Andi in the rearview mirror with smiling eyes. "And ruin my fun? Now, why in heaven's name would I do that, sweet girl?"

Andi shook her head. "Right? What was I thinking?"

In the next moment, the sound of orchestra music began playing from Andi's purse.

"Oh!" Mrs. Harper said as she turned around in her seat to look back at them. "Who's got the ring tone from The Godfather playing on their phone? That movie is such a classic!"

The Godfather? Andi looked through her purse until she found the source. She held up The Broker's burner phone. "It's me, Mrs. Harper. I think this is The Broker's attempt at humor." She answered the call.

"Hello?" Andi spoke into the phone.

"Ms. Sloan? Your order is ready for pickup at the Big Lick Scrap Yard on Orange Avenue. It must be picked up in the next 15 minutes. If you're late, no package. There will be no substitutions, no rain checks, and you will still be charged for the package, so don't be late, and come alone."

"Fifteen minutes? That doesn't give me much time," Andi said.

"Exactly the point, so don't miss your window of opportunity."

"But," Andi said, but the caller had already hung up.

"Mrs. Davis?" Andi began to ask if she would pull over and let Andi drive. They'd never make it in time at this speed.

"No problem, sweetie. I know exactly where it is. If we take the back roads, we should just make it in time. Everyone, hang on to something," Mrs. Davis said as she made a sharp right at the next intersection and floored it.

Holy Mary, Mother of God.

Okay, Andi had changed her mind. She preferred the safer, slow-driving Mrs. Davis to whatever the heck this was. She made the sign of the cross and prayed that they'd arrive safely to the scrap yard on time.

After a harrowing twelve minutes of Mrs. Davis speeding through the residential streets of Roanoke with Andi sliding into

Mrs. Barzetti and Kitty whenever Mrs. Davis made a turn, they arrived at the Big Lick Scrap Yard.

"That was sure fun," said Mrs. Davis. "Reminds me of my younger days, when I used to drag race on the old country roads." She checked the clock on her dashboard, "And we've got three minutes to run into that office and collect the package. I'm afraid I can't do it. This old hip slows me down."

Andi had already popped the door open and was climbing over Kitty. "Thanks, but I've got it from here, Mrs. Davis." She looked at all four ladies and said, "Please stay in the car and lock the doors until I come back. I was supposed to come alone, remember? There's no telling what's going on here." Andi closed the door and ran over to the large metal building with an octagon shaped sign that read STOP—PLEASE WAIT FOR ATTENDANT.

There was no attendant, and no time to wait for one. She didn't want to miss the time frame to pick up her package, so she knocked on the door, opened it, and walked right inside.

"Hello? Anybody there? I'm here to pick up my package, and I've got," she glanced at her phone, "ninety seconds left, so I'm coming inside. Please don't shoot me."

It took a few seconds for Andi's eyes to adjust to the darkness of the room. There were stacks of large wooden crates and cardboard boxes of all different shapes and sizes. Men were emptying boxes and several forklifts were moving stacks of crates to different parts of the building.

"Hey, you can't be in here!" a man holding a clipboard hollered and pointed a finger at Andi as he ran towards her.

Oops! "I'm sorry. I'm here to pick up a package. There wasn't anyone out front, and I didn't want to miss my pickup time. The person on the phone made it very clear that I couldn't be late."

He shoved her into some sort of side office and closed the metal door. *Oh, God.*

"Name?" he said in an impatient tone.

"The caller didn't identify himself, so I'm not sure," Andi said, holding on tight to her purse. She could use it as a weapon if things turned ugly.

"*Your* name," he said, speaking slowly as if she was hard of hearing or something.

"Oh, right. Andrea Sloan," she said.

He ran his finger down the list on the clipboard and looked up at her when he stopped a third of the way down the list. "You're not one of the regulars."

"No. This is a special one-time pickup," she said trying to remember to breathe and act casually confident.

He studied her another moment before nodding and said, "I'll get the guys to load it for you. What are you driving?"

"I drove a 1995 Buick LeSabre. It's just out front."

The guy lifted a hand-held, black radio to his mouth that he had clipped onto his belt and spoke into it. "Mike, go ahead and load number thirty-seven into the LeSabre parked out front."

Oh no. Now is the time to mention I am not alone. "Um, it's kind of funny," Andi said with her waitress smile, "but I was out with my neighbors when I got the call about the package being ready."

Yeah, clipboard guy wasn't finding this the least bit humorous.

"Why do I care?" he asked.

"Because they're in the car right now. See, we were headed to the shooting range when I got the call and there wasn't time to drop them off, so we drove straight here."

He glared at her. "You were supposed to come alone."

"Well, I hadn't planned to bring them, but then I got the call to come here for the pickup, and I was way across town, and there was no time to..."

He shook his head. "Just follow me," he said as he stormed out of the office and led her through the main entrance outside to where the Buick was parked.

"I thought you said you brought people. Where are they?" he asked.

What? Where did they go?! Andi scanned the area for her neighbors and mother.

"Um," Andi ran to the driver's side clicked the button to pop open the trunk. "Let me just open the trunk, and then I'll collect my neighbors and we'll be on our way." She ran back to the trunk and opened it fully. Luckily, Mrs. Davis' trunk was mostly empty except for a cane, a box of tissues, and a can of hairspray? "Here, I'll move these to the front seat, and you'll have plenty of room for the," she said hesitated, "you know, stuff."

The clipboard guy was staring at her like she had three heads. *Just shut up, already.* Andi quickly moved the trunk items to the front seat, closed the door, and said, "I'll just go round up those girls while you load up the car. Be right back."

She passed two men headed for the Buick carrying two long wooden crates and four medium-sized cardboard boxes. *That all should fit in the huge, empty trunk.* Andi was scanning the area when a forklift came flying at her from the corner of a building. Andi jumped out the way just in time. She yelled, "Watch where you're…Mrs. Harper?"

The forklift stopped and the driver, Mrs. Harper, leaned out the window. "I'm so sorry, sweetie. I haven't driven one of these since I used to work the night shift at the train station years ago. I forgot how fast they go."

"Mrs. Harper, what are you doing?! You were supposed to stay in the car. You can't just drive the equipment around without permission," Andi said looking around, worried they'd be discovered. *Too late.* There was a big guy wearing a hard hat running towards them.

Mrs. Harper smiled. "It's alright, dear," Mrs. Harper said. "I got permission from this nice young man right here. Isn't that right, Decker?"

"Yes, ma'am," he said, tipping his hard hat at Andi.

"Decker, this is my darling girl, Andrea Sloan, that I was telling you about. She already has a boyfriend, but she has a lovely friend named Maggy that would be just perfect for you."

"Mrs. Harper!" Andi exclaimed.

"Don't you think he and Maggy would make a cute couple? Anyway, I told him that I used to drive these all the time back in the day, and he let me drive this one." Mrs. Harper began to step out of the forklift, and Decker held out a hand to steady her. "You're such a gentleman. Thanks for giving this old girl another moment back in the saddle. Oh, those were the days."

"It's my pleasure, ma'am," he said with a smile.

Mrs. Harper put her hand over her heart. "Such good manners. It's rare to find that in young men these days."

Oh, Lord. "Mrs. Harper, we've really got to go. Have you seen the others?" Andi asked.

"Hm. I think I passed them earlier. They were on a scrap pile behind the blue building. Where was it? Oh, they're they are. Right over there," Mrs. Harper said and pointed to a spot directly behind Andi.

Decker and Andi looked in the direction Mrs. Harper was pointing. Decker cursed, and Andi felt her stomach drop. *Oh my God!* Mrs. Barzetti stood on a scrap pile of metal about four feet high. Kitty was crouched down on the top of the pile next to her, handing what looked like a baking sheet to Mrs. Davis' outstretched hands. "Mrs. Harper, why don't you head over to the car, and I'll be along in just a minute once I get Mrs. Barzetti down from that mountain of metal."

Andi began jogging over to the scrap pile with Decker running along beside her, apparently so he could reprimand her.

"Are you crazy? Why the hell would you bring a bunch of sweet, old grannies to a dangerous place like this?" Decker asked. "What the fuck were you thinking?"

Well, that wasn't very gentleman-like. What was she thinking?! Wasn't that the million-dollar question. Her life was so completely out of control, and she was having a hard time keeping up with it. Andi would have been happy to explain why her neighbors were with her, but she used all her energy to breathe and move towards Mrs. Barzetti before the older woman fell off the pile of metal and broke a hip or even worse, her neck. There was no extra air left for explaining anything. By the time they reached the scrap pile, Mrs. Barzetti had already begun climbing down. Decker reached up and with little effort grabbed Mrs. Barzetti around the waist, placing her safely on the ground, while Andi bent over and tried to catch her breath. *I've really got to get in shape.*

"Oh! Well, thank you, young man. Getting up was much easier than climbing down. I appreciate the assistance." She opened her large purse and looked through it until she pulled out a small plastic bag of snowflake cookies. "Please take these as a small token of thanks. We just baked them this morning."

"Thank you, Ma'am," Decker said with a smile as he tucked the bag of cookies in his front shirt pocket. "I'm sure I'll enjoy these later." He smiled and was soft spoken to "the grannies" but was not gentle at all when he grabbed Andi by the arm and said, "Excuse me, ladies. I just need a moment with Andrea. Why don't you head to your car? She'll be right with you."

Kitty hesitated, until Andi said, "It's fine, Kitty. Please go with them and make sure they don't make any side stops on the way to the car. I'll be there in just a minute."

Kitty nodded and walked with the neighbors back to the car.

Andi glared at the man's hand where it held onto her arm. "You can let go now, Decker. You may be able to charm Mrs. Harper and Mrs. Barzetti into thinking you're a nice guy but clearly, you're nothing more than a common thug."

Decker released her arm immediately and pointed to his chest. "At least I don't bring innocent grannies to my drug pickup. You're damn lucky Mrs. Harper bumped into me instead of Spike or one of the other guys." He looked over at the Buick and folded his arms across his chest.

"Oh yeah, because letting Mrs. Harper drive around the scrap yard in a forklift is your idea of keeping her safe?" Andi huffed and crossed her arms over her chest imitating Decker. "She could have crashed into a building and gotten herself killed, thanks to you."

He studied her with a frown. "Who are you, Andrea Sloan? You look familiar to me, although I'm sure we haven't met. I would have remembered you." Decker shook his head. "You're definitely not one of the regulars. What's your game? What are you really doing here?"

Uh oh. Andi raised her chin. "That's none of your business, Decker."

"Well, Andrea, I say it is," Decker said, taking a step toward her, no doubt attempting to intimidate her. He was about her height, but all muscle and in way better shape since he could run and talk at the same time and overhead press Mrs. Barzetti. He kind of had that crazy, bad-guy vibe like Bucky from The Avengers—handsome, insane, and extremely dangerous. His intimidation technique was sort of working, too, but she'd learned a long time ago that you never let a bully know you were scared.

He leaned in and quietly asked, "I've got to wonder what a nice girl like you, who travels with a group of senior citizens, is going to do with the twenty kilos of heroin and two boxes of stolen US Army M16s that the guys just stored in the trunk of your Buick?"

Jesus, Mary, and Joseph. She knew The Broker was giving her some of his contraband to frame Nick Marino, but that was a whole lot of illegal, right there. Andi swallowed down the panic that had suddenly filled her throat. How did this Decker-guy know exactly what was in her trunk? *Because he's a bad guy, you idiot. He probably helped pack the boxes.*

"Huh, you didn't know what was in there, did you?" he asked, his frown deepened.

"Of course, I did," which was a half-truth if she was going to split hairs. She just didn't know the specifics. "Because I'm a dealer?" Andi said her voice coming out in a squeak.

Oh, that sounded wimpy. Come on, Andi, imagine he's Lenny Jenkins from third grade trying to take your lunch money. Be tough.

She cleared her throat and pointed a finger on his chest. "Because I'm a dealer, obviously. I've got stuff to deliver and don't have the desire to be wasting anymore of my time talking to you." She turned around and stomped off towards her car breathing a sigh of relief when he didn't follow her or drag her back by her neck for more questioning.

Her day was beginning to look up because Clipboard guy and his men had moved away from the Buick and were busy loading packages into a black van with Florida tags. Andi slid into the back seat of the car, closed the door, and looked back to see Decker still staring at them. Andi said, "Mrs. Davis, please use your fancy drag racing skills and get us the heck out of here."

"My pleasure," Mrs. Davis said as she hit the gas and the Buick peeled out of the scrap yard and back on to Orange Avenue. While Andi was taking deep calming breaths in the back seat to slow her racing heart, Mrs. Barzetti was complaining.

"This is yet another example of how we've become a throw-away society. Someone tossed this perfectly good baking sheet in the recycling bin." She held up her prize—a well-worn, eleven-by-fourteen-inch, stainless steel cookie sheet. "A little bit a scrubbing and this will be as good as new."

Mrs. Davis nodded. "Glad we rescued that pan. You can't get that kind of quality bakeware these days."

Kitty, who was now sitting in the middle backseat next to Andi, placed her hand on Andi's bouncing leg and asked, "What did that guy want to talk to you about back there?"

"Oh, he was just asking me what we were planning to do with twenty kilos of heroin and two stolen US Army M16s," Andi said.

Everyone in the car was silent for a full minute before Mrs. Barzetti said, "Are you telling us that there are two stolen United States Army machine guns in the trunk, because I'm not sure if it's excitement or terror that I'm feeling right now."

"I'm certain that's what we're hauling in the trunk," Andi said, "along with almost 45 pounds of heroin." Andi leaned forward and put her head between her legs. "I think I'm going to be sick."

Mrs. Harper made the sign of the cross, and said, "Dear Lord, we're all going straight to hell."

"Not straight to hell, Ethel. First, we're going to prison for anywhere from five to forty years," Mrs. Davis said.

Mrs. Barzetti whistled to get everyone's attention. "Everyone needs to calm down and stop talking nonsense. We've got a plan. Now that we have secured the stuff, Andrea's going to call Nick. Kitty, you remember his cellphone number, right?"

Kitty nodded.

Mrs. Barzetti tapped her chin with her forefinger. "How long of a drive is it from New York City to Roanoke?"

Kitty said, "It took me almost thirteen hours to get here on the bus."

Andi sat up, sighed, and plugged in New York City in her maps phone app. "Looks like it'll take them just under eight hours if they drive. They're likely to do that again since they drove here last time. We should make the meet up time eight hours from our call, just like The Broker's people only gave us fifteen to pick up the stuff. We don't want to give Nick any extra time to double cross us."

"Good point," Mrs. Barzetti said. "Ladies, synchronize your watches" She smiled. "I've always wanted to say that. It's 4:03pm, so let's make the meet time for midnight at the Big Lick Scrap Yard. It's a perfect meeting place. There's plenty of space and places for us to hide and plant the evidence in Nick's car, and it's already a crime lair, so we won't be disrupting any legitimate business." She leaned over Kitty and looked at Andi. "Remember to be brief, just giving him the time and location for the fake meeting with The Broker."

Mrs. Davis said, "We'll get there ahead of time and set the trap."

Andi handed Kitty her phone so that she could type in Nick's phone number and handed it back to Andi with a shaky hand. Andi reached out and squeezed Kitty's hand reassuringly. "It's going to be okay, Kitty. We're going to make sure Nick gets locked away in a high security prison where he won't be able to hurt anyone ever again. Okay. Are you ready?"

Kitty nodded, and Andi made the call. A man answered on the third ring. "Yes?"

"I need to speak to Nick Marino," Andi said, in a no-nonsense tone.

"You are. Who's this?"

"It's Andi, you know, the Repo Girl. I've managed to set up that meeting you wanted with The Broker on the condition that you leave us alone. Deal?"

"You're hardly in a position to be calling the shots."

"I thought you wanted to meet The Broker, but if you're not interested, I won't waste your time."

"Fine. When's the meeting?"

"It's set up for midnight tonight at The Big Lick Scrap Yard off Orange Avenue. Don't be late because he won't wait. This is a one-time opportunity."

"Can't make it," he said. "Let's do this tomorrow at 3pm."

"Sorry. It's midnight tonight or not at all," Andi said, her tone steady.

"You little bit..," he began to say, and Andi disconnected the call, not giving him anytime for arguing. She immediately blocked his phone number on her cellphone so he wouldn't be able to call her back.

"Nicely done, Andrea," Mrs. Barzetti said. "Okay, let's head home. Gladys, make sure you lock the Buick in your garage tonight. As much as I'd like to check out those guns in your trunk, it's best if no one touches any of it. Ladies, wear all black tonight and make sure you're wearing your winter gloves. We don't want to leave any fingerprints when we hide the stuff in Nick's car. I suggest we go home, get some dinner, and take a little rest. We'll plan to be at the scrap yard by 10pm tonight to get set up for our sting operation."

Chapter Twenty-one

After a long, hot shower, Andi dried her hair, put it in a simple updo, applied light makeup and added a touch of red lipstick to her lips. If she was going to commit a felony and get caught, she might as well look good. Last time she had a mug shot, she looked a wreck. Following Mrs. Barzetti's instructions for their dress code for their sting operation, Andi put on a pair of black leather pants and black turtleneck sweater, the only clean black colored clothes she had in her closet. She studied herself in the full-length mirror. Jeez, with her short black boots, she looked like some sort of cat burglar. *Well, I am about to commit a crime.*

She said goodbye to Dodger, and let Kitty know she'd be back no later than 9pm as she headed out the front door. Apparently, the police hadn't retracted Kitty's protection detail yet since the patrol car was still parked outside her house. Andi waved to the officer, got into her Jeep, and started the engine.

Brrrr, it's cold. It took a full minute with her heat blasting on high for the inside of her car to warm up. Since it was after 5pm in January, it was already dark outside. Oh, how she hated the short days of winter. She backed out of her driveway, headlights on, and drove to Star City Bar and Grill to meet up with Cooper.

Cooper. She was going to tell him everything–she had to–and when she did, he was going to freak out and insist on going with them. Well, she would just have to figure out a way to keep him from joining them tonight. It was too risky. What if the police caught them with "the stuff" before they got a chance to plant it in Nick's car? It would ruin his career. What if Nick found them and killed them all? Andi bit her lip. This was such an insane plan. What was she thinking?

I was thinking that I have no other options.

After pulling into the parking lot of Star City Bar and Grill, Andi turned off the engine and locked her Jeep. She was crossing the parking lot walking towards the restaurant door when a black BMW M7 Series came racing into the lot, nearly running her over.

Jeez! What an idiot!

The black sedan abruptly stopped in front of her, the front and back passenger doors opened, and two men jumped out. It all happened in an instant and before she realized what was going on, the larger man grabbed her from behind, pinning her arms to her sides.

Oh no!

This was familiar. As she screamed, "Help!", Andi leaned back into her attacker, using the same move she had used on Nick's thug, Mason. Unfortunately, a second man was bending in front of her, grabbing her legs, and duct taping her ankles together.

What the heck?

Andi began losing her balance, falling forward and as she did, the duct tape guy gripped her wrists together and wrapped them tight with more tape. Then he jerked her face forward and slapped a piece of duct tape across her lips mid-scream. The guy behind spun her around so she was facing him for a moment. *Mason.* In the next instant, he pushed her into the back seat and closed the door.

No, no, no!!

"I told you midnight tonight wasn't going to work for me. Tsk. Tsk. You shouldn't have hung up on me like that. It was very rude."

Andi turned her head and saw Nick Marino sitting on the other side of the back seat watching her as he lit a cigarette, brought it to his lips, inhaled deeply, held his breath for a moment, and then blew smoke from the smallest opening in his thin lips. The smoke filled the tiny space in the car.

Ugh. Andi coughed.

Nick looked at her and grinned, enjoying her discomfort. He held the cigarette between his two fingers and studied the glowing end of it. "I've been trying to quit for years. Kitty always hated that I smoked, so I cut back but never could give it up entirely. Smoking relaxes me in a way that few things do anymore."

He brought the cigarette back to his lips and inhaled, closing his eyes briefly as if savoring it before releasing more of the disgusting, toxic, pollutants into their shared space.

I'm going to need another shower. Yuck. Andi turned her head away and tried not to breathe the smoke.

"If you would have only cooperated when I asked for your help the first night we met, I wouldn't have to be so rough with you now. Your neighbor and her shot gun caused me considerable expense. Repairs on a Bentley don't come cheap."

Asked for my help–HA! More like tried to abduct me.

"Forgive me for not trusting you, but I couldn't help but think our meeting tonight is a set up. Especially with that police car conveniently parked outside your home. Do you think I'm an idiot?"

Yeah, pretty much. Andi shrugged.

He grabbed her face below her chin and held the glowing end of the cigarette butt close to her cheek. "It shouldn't be a surprise you are an ignorant, rude, hellcat since you grew up without your mother. It would be my pleasure to begin your lessons in etiquette now, even if it means leaving a scar on your beautiful face."

Andi could feel the heat from the cigarette as he moved it within an inch of her cheek. She flinched as she braced herself for the burning sensation and then in one quick movement, he was putting the cigarette out in an ashtray. "Lucky for you, I'm more interested in meeting your broker. We've got some unfinished business to discuss. Plus, we need to pick up your mom on the way. What's Kitty's new phone number?"

Andi stared at him with a look that she hoped conveyed *You are an idiot if you think I can answer you with this tape on my mouth.*

He leaned close to Andi and said, "If you're anything like your mother, I think I'm going to regret this."

Oh, you're going to regret this, buddy! Andi had no idea how, yet, but she'd figure out some way to get out of this mess.

Nick ripped the duct tape off Andi's mouth in one quick painful motion.

"Owwwww!" Andi screamed and closed her eyes. *Don't let him see weakness.*

"Oh, I'm sorry. Did that hurt?" Nick asked and smirked.

"How did you find me?" Andi asked.

"Easy enough, little girl. Mason put a GPS tracker on your car the night your neighbor so rudely shot up my Bentley. I told you we'd back for you, and I'm a man of my word. Now, Kitty's new phone number?"

Andi shrugged. "I don't know it."

Nick sighed and grabbed her purse and began rummaging through it. He pulled out Gram's binoculars. "Christ, what kind of useless shit do you have in here? Two phones? What do you use this one for?" he asked, holding the burner phone in one hand.

"It's how I communicate with The Broker."

Nick nodded. "Untraceable. That's what I would do. Call him."

"Um, I don't have the number to reach him. The phone only works one way. He calls me."

"You better hope he shows up tonight. Otherwise, nobody is going to be finding you anywhere. Capisce?"

He looked at the contacts list on the other phone until he found Kitty's name. "Look at that." He shakes his head. "You'll learn that there are consequences for lying to me."

He pressed the call button on Andi's phone.

Kitty answered after the first ring. "Andi? Is everything alright?"

Andi managed to shout, "Kitty, I'm fine. Don't listen to the…" and then Nick silenced her with a smack across the face. The force of the blow pushed her head into the passenger window where it made a loud thump, and everything went blurry for a few seconds. Nick put the tape back over her stinging lips.

"Andi?" Kitty asked.

Nick spoke into the phone. "Well, Andi's tied up and can't come to the phone right now, Kit-cat, but she's mostly fine, although I'm pretty sure she's going to have one hell of a headache. Whether she remains healthy is entirely up to you, sweetheart. You're going to need to leave the house without the cop out front seeing you. I've got a car waiting to pick you up at the other end of the block. I know you're resourceful when you want to be. Oh, and Kitty, if you alert the police or decide not to leave the house, your daughter is as good as dead. You'd better hurry. You know how I hate it when you make me wait."

He disconnected the call and dropped both phones back in Andi's purse and looked up at her. "Now, let's head over to the scrap yard and wait for your Broker and mother, shall we?"

***

Cooper let out a stream of curses. He had pulled into the parking lot of Star City Bar and Grill in time to see Andi shoved into the back of a BMW with New York plates. In the next instant, the car was on the move, pulling out of the parking lot. He cursed again and backed up, turned his Porsche around, and exited the other side of the parking lot where he'd just entered. He watched to see which direction Andi's abductor was turning, so he could follow them at a discreet distance.

If he'd been a few minutes later, he would have missed Andi completely. He would have had no idea that she'd even been abducted. Dammit, if he'd arrived a couple minutes sooner, he might have been able to help her fight them off. Or, they might have just shot him and left him for dead in the parking lot.

Cooper cursed again. No doubt this had something to do with what she was going to tell him tonight. He could tell something had really upset her when he spoke with her on the phone. Cooper should have insisted on meeting with her when she called, but he didn't want to push her. Now, he was following her on the highway as the BMW took the exit for Orange Avenue.

What should I do? Call the police? That might get her killed and thrown out of the car if the assholes that took her felt threatened. Cooper shook his head. He'd just have to follow them and see where they were taking her.

He watched as the BMW pulled into the gravel driveway entrance for Big Lick Scrap Yard. *What the hell?* He drove past the turn because he didn't want them to know he was following them. Cooper turned around at the next parking lot, a Dairy Queen, and got back onto Orange Avenue, turning immediately into Big Lick Scrap Yard drive. He shut off his headlights and slowly drove up the gravel path. Up ahead, about 100 yards, he could see the BMW parked near some metal building. He pulled his car behind a scrap pile and turned off his engine. Then, he called 911.

After stating his name and verifying his phone number, the responder asked, "Where are you?"

"I'm at Big Lick Scrap Yard off Orange Avenue. Listen, I need you to get in touch with Detective Kendricks from homicide. This is related to a case he's working."

"What's happened?" the 911 responder asked.

"My girlfriend, Andrea Sloan, was grabbed from the parking lot at Star City Bar and Grill and shoved into a black BMW with New York plates. I was too distracted to notice any other details about the license plate number. I just saw they were from New York. Pretty sure it's the same New York mobster that attacked her the other night."

"What time did you witness her abduction?" the responder asked.

"I don't know. About ten minutes ago? Look, I just followed the car here and am calling you so that you…oh shit! They're getting out of the car and going into the building. Fuck! Some guy is carrying Andi over his shoulder." *Why are they carrying her? Is she hurt? Must not be hurt too bad, because she's squirming around a lot. The guy's having a hard time holding onto her.* "Alright, I'm going to go see if I can help her. Just let Detective Kendricks know, okay?"

"Sir, please stay in your car or, if possible, leave the scene without drawing attention to yourself."

"Yeah, sorry. I'm not going to be able to do that. Inform Detective Kendricks," Cooper said as he disconnected the call and dropped the phone in his pocket.

I'm going to need a weapon. What can I use? He looked at the clean interior of his Porsche. *Nothing.* He opened his glove box...registration, owner's manual, a few guitar picks, an old guitar strap, and a plastic bag with extra electric guitar strings. He grabbed the strap and the strings and slid them in his jacket pocket. He shut the glove box, popped the trunk, and got out of the car and walked around to the back. Looking at the trunk, he lifted the carpeted trunk floor where his spare tire was located. He'd never changed a tire in his life. He'd always used a service for any car problems, but there had to be something in here that he could use! *Yes!* Cooper reached down and pulled out a lug wrench and held it in both of his hands. *Nice weight, solid steel. This will work.* Quietly closing the trunk, Cooper walked towards the building to rescue his Margarita.

***

Hazel Barzetti was stretched out on the sofa in her living room with her eyes closed as she tried to sleep. An episode of *Murder She Wrote* that she'd seen more times than she could count was playing on the television providing a soothing background sound. Still, sleep evaded her. She knew she needed to rest up for tonight, but how could she relax enough to take a nap? Normally, she'd get in the kitchen and bake until her nerves settled, but this evening, she'd already used all her eggs to bake six dozen cookies, two pies, and a crumb cake, and she still felt anxious.

She sighed. Who could blame her when her sweet girls were in a mess of trouble? Every time she thought about that awful Nick Marino threatening her family it made her mad enough to chew nails and spit out a barbed wire fence. Kitty and Andi might not be related to her by blood, but they were her family just the same. For goodness' sake, she'd practically raised both. She and her dear Henry hadn't been blessed with children of their own. Oh, they would have made wonderful parents, but for some reason the dear Lord had other plans. Maybe He knew that these two Sloan angels would require the bulk of her attention. Hazel smiled. She was more than happy to give it.

When her cellphone rang, Hazel sat up and reached over to the coffee table, picked it up and looked at the screen. *Kitty.* Poor thing. She was probably feeling anxious, too. Hazel answered the phone.

"Hello Kitty, dear. Are you having trouble resting, too?" Hazel asked.

"Nick's taken Andi! I know he's not bluffing because he called from her phone, and I heard her voice. I don't know how or when he grabbed her, but he told me that he's got a car waiting for me at the end of the block. I'm supposed to get to his car without the police seeing me. He said if I call the police or if I don't go to his car, he'll kill her. Oh, God, Mrs. B. I've got to go to the car. I won't let him hurt her."

Oh, heavens. Hazel leaned back against the sofa cushion. *Think, Hazel. There is no time for panicking.* She sat forward and cleared her throat and in her calmest voice said, "Everything is going to be fine. I want you to wait fifteen minutes and then sneak out the back door like you used to do when you were a teenager. Cut across the neighbor's backyards until you get to the end of the block. We'll meet you there with Mrs. Davis' car. Looks like we'll just have to bump our plans up a bit and improvise, I suppose. It can't be helped."

Kitty said, "But what about Nick's men and the car?"

"We'll handle the men and the car. You take Dodger with you. He'll make sure no one messes with you. I'll call the girls."

"Oh, Mrs. B, what if he hurts Andi?" Kitty asked.

"Now, none of that, Kitty. We're not letting that evil man hurt you or our girl. I need you to dig deep and be brave. We've got to go rescue your baby. You can do this, and we'll be right there with you."

"Okay," Kitty said a little shaky before taking a deep breath. "Okay. We're going to do this, and Andi's going to be okay. I'll meet you there. Be careful, Mrs. B."

"Oh, don't worry about me, child," Hazel said and smiled. "I already warned those boys not to mess with my girls. They don't have the good sense God gave a rock, so they deserve what's coming to them. Now, remember, wait fifteen minutes before heading out."

"Thanks, Mrs. B. I love you," Kitty said.

"I love you, too, darling girl," Hazel said and then disconnected the call.

She took a deep breath and sent a text to Gladys and Ethel.

Ten minutes later, Gladys, Ethel, and Hazel were dressed in their black attire, winter coats and gloves, sitting in Gladys' car.

"Ready for Operation Granny, ladies?" Hazel asked.

"Ready," said Ethel holding up her cane.

"Gladys?" Mrs. Barzetti asked.

"I don't know why I have to sit this one out. I want to be in on the action," Gladys complained.

"You are in on the action. You're the getaway driver. That's an important job," Hazel said.

"Fine," Gladys said. "It's just that I wanted to practice some of my new self-defense moves."

Hazel rolled her eyes. "The night is young, Gladys. I'm afraid you'll have plenty of opportunity to put those new skills to the test."

Gladys pressed the button on her garage opener, and once the door raised, she pulled out onto the driveway and made a left onto their street. She stopped at the end of the block.

Hazel said, "Look, there's the car parked right next to the curb. That must be the one. It's got New York plates. Go ahead and pull right up behind him."

Gladys nodded, turned on her left blinker and pulled behind a Chrysler 300.

Ethel got out of the car and dawdled up to the driver's door, back hunched over leaning heavily on a hooked metal cane. She knocked on the window, "Excuse me," she said in a loud voice to be overheard by the Chrysler's engine.

The window lowered and a man with a crew cut and close-trimmed beard stared at her. "Is there a problem?"

"Well, young man, I just wanted you to know that you have a flat tire. Looks like you must have run over a paring knife," Ethel said, stepping back and pointing at the tire.

"What?" he said as he opened the door and got out of the car. He turned away from her to look at the tire and said, "Lady, there's nothing wrong with my tire."

Before he turned back to face her, Ethel used both hands to grip her cane and thrust it up between his legs hitting his groin with such a force that he yelped and dropped to his knees onto the sidewalk. She then wacked him on the neck and then across his back until he was on the ground, groaning and cursing. He placed one hand on his groin and the other to cover his head.

"What the fu," the man in the passenger side was saying as Hazel opened his door and pointed the Remington 700 Bolt Action Rifle to his chest.

"Now, there's no need for language," Hazel said. "My doctor said I've got trigger finger which makes it unpredictable. I'm going to need you to slowly step out of the car and keep your hands up where I can see them. I don't want this thing to accidentally go off and shoot you in the chest, especially at this close range. I'll get blood stains all over my favorite wool coat and it will be ruined."

"Who the hell are you?" he asked.

"Hazel Barzetti, president of the Neighborhood Watch program. We received a tip that you boys were thinking about committing a crime in our quiet, peaceful neighborhood." Hazel shook her head. "We can't allow that to happen, can we? Now walk to the back of the car."

"You're a fucking crazy woman. Do you know that?" the man asked as he slowly stepped out of vehicle and walked to the back of the car.

At the front of the Chrysler, Ethel looked in satisfaction at the criminal curled on the sidewalk groaning. She reached inside the vehicle and pressed the button to pop the trunk open, turned off the engine, and dropped the car keys in her purse. Ethel reached into her coat pocket and removed the rooster printed dish towel that was wrapped around her kitchen paring knife. She stabbed the small knife that she'd used to peel potatoes just this morning into the front tire of the Chrysler. *Paring knives are quite versatile.*

"See, look at this. I told you there was a paring knife stuck in your tire." She smiled in satisfaction when she heard the hissing sound as the tire deflated. Ethel pulled her knife out, carefully wrapped it back in the dish towel, and returned it to her coat pocket.

When the trunk popped open, Hazel pointed her rifle at the punk and said, "Go on and climb in the trunk of the car."

"I am not getting in no fucking trunk," he said, hands still in the air.

"Young man, your mouth is as filthy as a garbage can after a church fish fry." Hazel lifted the rifle so that it was pointed at his chest, and said, "I'm beginning to feel a twitch in my finger, son. You'd best hurry and get yourself into that trunk."

Mrs. Davis revved the engine of her Buick and a loud firecracker popping sound exploded from the car's tailpipe.

The man cursed and grabbed his chest, looking down for signs of blood. He said, "Don't shoot! I'm going!" and then dove into the trunk. "Just please stop pointing that rifle at me."

At the front of the Chrysler, Kitty and Dodger came running up to the car. "Oh my God, Mrs. Harper, we heard a gunshot. Are you alright?"

Ethel smiled at Kitty. "Of course, I'm fine. I'll be feeling better once this hoodlum gets in the trunk with his buddy. Now get up so I don't have to hit you again with my cane."

One moment, the driver was curled on the sidewalk groaning in pain and the next he'd rolled over onto his back and was pointing a handgun at Ethel.

"I'm not going anywhere, lady. You need to drop that cane or I'm going to drop you right on this sidewalk."

"Oh dear," Ethel said. "We didn't cover this particular situation in class."

Dodger growled and clamped his jaws on the man's wrist that held the gun.

The hoodlum let out a string of curses and dropped the weapon. Ethel bent over and picked up the gun and pointed it at the man while Dodger gripped the man's wrist with his teeth. He whimpered and said, "Lady, for the love of God, please get your dog to release my wrist."

"That's a good boy, Dodger. I'm going to give you extra bacon next time you come over." Ethel handed her purse to Kitty while continuing to point the pistol at the man on the ground. "Now tell us where you were going to take Kitty, and I'll consider calling Dodger off of you."

"Jesus, lady. You're crazy!"

"I prefer the term resolute."

Dodger growled and tightened his grip.

"Okay, okay! We were taking her to meet the boss at the Big Lick Scrapyard."

"See, that wasn't so hard. Kitty, dear, can you check my purse. I know I've got a dog biscuit in there. Go ahead and give it to Dodger, and he'll probably let go of his wrist."

"Probably? What do you mean probably?" the man asked, panic in his voice.

"Oh, don't be such a baby. Now, I'm no expert, but you'll most likely be able to use that hand after a few stitches and maybe a little physical therapy," Ethel said.

Kitty took Mrs. Harper's purse and looked through it until she found a small milk bone. She held it out to Dodger. "Here boy. I have a treat for you for being such a brave hero rescuing us from this mean man."

Dodger released the man's wrist and turned so that Dodger's nose was only two inches from the man's face. The dog let out a low, deep sounding growl before turning back to Kitty, wagging his tail, and sitting for the treat.

Ethel took a step back so that there was plenty of space between her and the man on the ground. She didn't want him close enough that he could snatch his gun back.

"Get up nice and slow and walk to the back of this car," Ethel said. "My arms are a bit shaky after performing Cane-Fu. If you make any more sudden moves, I'll shoot you."

The man slowly stood up holding onto his injured wrist and walked to the back of the car where Hazel was holding a rifle. He stared into the trunk observing that his partner appeared terrified. "Move over Leo," he said. "Looks like I'm supposed to join you in the trunk."

"Man, what the hell did they do to you?" Leo asked.

"No talking. You boys will have plenty of time to catch up once we lock you in the trunk," Hazel said.

"You can't just leave us out here like this. We could freeze to death," the driver said as he climbed in next to Leo.

Gladys walked up to the trunk with one of the bags of heroin from her trunk. "It's no fair that you girls got to have all the fun without me." She tossed the plastic bag in the trunk and said, "There better be more bad guys when we meet up with Andi." Gladys turned and stomped back to her car.

"Do you think we're savages?" Ethel asked as she closed the trunk with the men inside. "We wouldn't dream of letting you freeze. We'll call the police and notify them of your location and your intent to distribute narcotics in our neighborhood."

"Come on, Ladies. We've spent long enough with these two. Let's go rescue our girl," Hazel said as she patted Dodger on the head.

Chapter Twenty-two

Cooper hid behind a pile of scrap metal as he surveyed the large warehouse where the men had taken Andi. There was an armed man guarding the building on the other end of a huge, gravel parking lot. It's not like he could sneak up on the guy. No. Cooper needed to somehow distract the guard and get him to move away from the entrance if he was going to get inside that building. That was going to be a challenge considering that guard had a gun and Cooper only had a lug wrench. *Wait. I also have my Porsche.*

Reaching into his pocket, Cooper pulled out his smartphone and opened his Porsche Connect App. He tapped the phone screen and the Porsche started with a loud roar of the engine. The car's headlights illuminated the area. Cooper looked back at the warehouse. The guard must have heard it too because he was headed this way.

Yes, that's right. Come see what the noise is all about. Cooper would have to do something about those bright headlights before the man got much closer, or there was a good chance he'd be spotted crouching by the pile of scrap. He'd be a sitting duck. Using the app, Cooper turned off the engine and headlights. The guard paused, pulled out a flashlight and a beam of light shone on the Porsche. The man continued moving forward, his right arm extended straight out holding a pistol, his left hand holding the flashlight. The guard had almost reached the car and was shining his flashlight inside the windows looking for the driver when Cooper snuck up behind him and hit him with the lug wrench.

When the guard collapsed to the ground, Cooper took the gun and tucked it in the back waistband of his jeans. He reached in his jacket pocket and pulled out one of the replacement guitar strings. This one was made of copper, so he used the cord to tie the man's hands behind his back. He used another string to tie his feet together. *There. That should hold him when he regains consciousness. Wait. What if the blow from the lug wrench killed him?* Cooper felt nauseous and immediately put two fingers on the man's neck searching for a pulse. *Thank God* – he felt a steady rhythm. Of course, Cooper didn't want this guy yelling for help when he came to, so he reached into his pocket and pulled out the leather guitar strap, layering it until it was three-inches thick. Then, Cooper opened the guard's mouth and shoved it inside, effectively making a gag. He made sure the man's nose was clear, so he'd be able to breathe, just not speak. Now that he felt the guard was adequately secured, Cooper stood up and ran towards the door of the large warehouse, quietly stepping inside, hiding behind bales of crushed aluminum cans stacked more than seven feet high.

He could hear voices, so he moved towards the sound, keeping hidden behind the bales of recycled metal. One of the voices must have belonged to Kitty's mobster boyfriend, and it sounded like he was talking to Andi. Poking his head around the corner, Cooper surveyed the situation.

Andi was sitting on the floor, tape wrapped around her ankles and wrists, and duct tape over her mouth. There was a bit of blood on her temple, but otherwise she seemed okay. Actually, she looked mad as hell, which made Cooper feel a bit relieved.

"We'll just sit here and wait for my boys to bring Kitty. She's clever enough to sneak out of the house without being noticed by the patrol car." Nick squatted down and held the tip of the gun to Andi's chin and lifted it until she was looking at him. "And she's protective of you for some reason. When I first saw you, I had planned to bring you back to the city with me, but now I think maybe you're too much trouble."

She made some sort of sound that was probably along the lines of "bite me" knowing Andi. Her chin was lifted in that defiant way she had, and Cooper suspected she would have spit at the guy if not for the duct tape that had sealed her mouth. He only saw two other armed, large men.

Hold on, Tiger. Just wait for the police. They should be here soon, right? It seemed like an hour had passed since he'd called 911, although it was probably less than five minutes.

"Someone needs to teach you manners," Nick said, "but that will have to wait until after I deal with your boss, The Broker. After I take care of him, I'll deal with you."

The Broker?! Fuck. Could this night get any worse?

As a matter of fact, yes because just then a big-ass rat, the size of an overweight Beagle, ran across Cooper's foot. He yelped and jumped back, knocking down a stack of recycling that was hiding him from view.

Now he had everyone's attention and three firearms pointed at him. *Wonderful.* He spread his arms to his side, palms open in his best, casual, non-threatening pose and said the first thing that came to his mind.

"Ah, gentlemen. I believe you're expecting me. I'm The Broker."

Andi was shaking her head no and making more unrecognizable sounds.

Nick said, "You expect me to believe that you're The Broker? You don't look like you've killed anything bigger than a fly. You look more like some kind of rockstar."

Cooper smiled. "A rockstar? You really think so?" He glanced at Andi who was shaking her head no. He nodded at her and said to her, "Don't worry, I've got this."

She rolled her eyes.

"Well, I'm not a rockstar, of course. No. I'm a businessman like you." He could do this. He just needed to buy some time for them. He'd called the police. Detective Kendricks was probably on his way right now with a SWAT team. They'd be surrounding the building in no time at all. This was no different than bluffing during a poker game. That thought made him feel a bit more comfortable as he tried to ignore the guns pointed at him.

"Let's get down to business, shall we?" Cooper, asked in a serious tone, his smile gone. He was a Vice President and handled million-dollar transactions on a weekly basis. He could negotiate a deal, or at least fake it. "I'll start. How about this? You let go of Andi, and I'll let you walk out of here unharmed."

Nick smiled. "You're hardly in a position to negotiate those terms. I only see one of you and you appear to be unarmed. There are four of us."

It was Cooper's turn to smile. "You're not very good with math, are you Nicky? That's too bad. Not to brag or anything, but numbers are my specialty. You're actually down to three. You can't really count the guard that is incapacitated out front. Anyway, do you really think that I would be stupid enough to come down here alone? My guys have this place surrounded." *My guys as in the Roanoke City Police Department. Any time now would be just about perfect.*

Cooper tried to maintain his cool facade as Nick considered him. "I think you're bluffing. You don't look like a crime boss, and you come in here unarmed? I don't think so. Secure him and put him over with the girl."

"You don't want to do that," Cooper warned, his voice low and intimidating.

Nick smiled. "I'll take my chances."

Shit! He was out of ideas. Two men approached Cooper with their guns pointed at him. Hell, they looked like they might enjoy shooting a couple holes into him. One of the men frisked him, easily locating the pistol tucked in his jeans, removed his cellphone, guitar string and picks, and of course, the lug wrench. *Damn.* This was hardly the rescue he'd imagined. They duct taped his wrists and walked him over to stand by Andi before securing his ankles with the tape and shoving him on his ass.

He turned to look at his Margarita, who looked worried. He gave her a slight smile and said, "Are you okay?" She nodded once, and then he said, "Don't worry about a thing. I've got this. I lov…" was all he managed before the big guy stuck tape over his mouth.

Then he gave Cooper another shove and said, "For the love of God, will you just shut the fuck up."

Nick turned to a big guy. "Go see what happened to Rocco. His weapon looks like one of ours."

***

Gladys cautiously drove her Buick up the gravel driveway to the scrapyard.

"Anybody else feeling a little DÉJÀ VU?" Ethel asked, "Except this time, it's dark and Gladys isn't barreling down this bumpy road to get us here on time."

"Hey, isn't that Cooper's fancy car over there?" Gladys asked. Dodger barked once when he spotted the Porsche and Kitty gave him a soft pat on the head. "It's okay, boy."

Hazel sighed. "What is that young man doing here? This was not the plan. Nick wasn't supposed to abduct Andi or send men to pick up Kitty. Cooper was not supposed to be here. Heaven only knows what that boy is up to, not to mention we haven't even had time to prepare for Nick's arrival. Nothing is going right tonight."

Ethel said, "This isn't a snickerdoodle cookie recipe, Hazel. Things in life rarely go according to plan. I don't know why you're so surprised."

Gladys added, "It's going to be alright. We're not doing so bad adjusting. Ask the hoodlums we locked in their trunk back in the neighborhood."

Ethel said, "Well, I'm sure they're in handcuffs headed to the station by now. We practically gift wrapped them for the police. That hunky narcotics detective will be pleased."

Gladys pulled next to an unoccupied BMW and whistled. "That's a nice set of wheels."

"They won't be after I slash my paring knife into those tires," Ethel said.

Hazel said, "Okay. This is it, ladies. Everyone clear on our mission? Gladys and Ethel will take care of things outside while Kitty, Dodger, and I go in to get Andi. It looks like we'll be rescuing Cooper, too. Kitty, darling, make sure you've got that leash on Dodger. We don't want him running off into trouble. That's the last thing we need right now."

Kitty nodded.

Hazel stepped outside the LeSabre, holding her rifle with both hands, surveying the area for trouble. She looked at Gladys and Ethel. "You girls be careful out here, okay? It's been a night full of surprises and my gut tells me we're in for some more."

Gladys winked. "I'm ready for some action." She held up her purse and her cane.

Hazel rolled her eyes and said a silent prayer. They were going to need all the help they could get tonight. "Come on, Kitty. Let's go get our girl."

***

Ethel went to work on the tires, while Gladys popped the trunk of the BMW.

"Don't look now, Ethel, but I believe we've got some serious firearms in here before we even add our illegal stash. I wonder if they have a permit for these?" Gladys asked, and made a tsk, tsk sound as she walked over to her trunk, bending over to lift one of the wooden crates.

"What are you doing here?" a deep male voice asked from behind her.

Gladys grabbed her cane and turned around ready to attack.

The man was faster than she was and quickly disarmed her, tossing the cane behind him out of her reach. She looked up and said, "Decker? Oh, thank goodness. You shouldn't sneak up on people my age. I could have had a heart attack."

He lifted his brow. "I think I was the one in danger the way you were wielding that cane. Nice move, by the way. Lucky for me, I recently took a Cane Fu class at my dojo."

"Thanks. I've been itching to try it out. Sorry. I didn't know it was you."

"Why are you back here?" he asked.

Gladys leaned forward and whispered, "We're on a top-secret rescue mission. Since you're here, can you help me move these boxes into that trunk? They're heavier than I thought."

"Not until you tell me what you're doing here," Decker said, folding his arms across his chest.

Ethel approached them holding her paring knife out in front of her with both hands. "Freeze, big guy, and put your hands in the air. I've just taken out three, like-new, Bridgestone tires with this sharp knife, and I'm just getting warmed up."

Decker chuckled and put his hands in the air. "I'm sure glad that I'm on your side. You two are scary."

"Oh, Decker! I didn't recognize you in the darkness. What are you doing out here?" Ethel asked.

"You, first," Decker said. "I didn't expect to see you ladies back here. Where's that young troublemaker you were with earlier?"

"Oh, you mean Andi?" Ethel asked. "She's the reason we're here tonight."

"I figured as much," Decker said.

"She's been abducted by the New York City mob. Nick Marino wants her to take him to Roanoke's crime boss, The Broker," Ethel said.

"The Broker?" Decker asked. "Andi works for The Broker?"

"Ethel Harper, we're on a top-secret rescue mission. You're not supposed to go blabbing about it to the first tall, chiseled man you bump into at night. For heaven's sake!"

Ethel waved away her friend's reprimand. "Of course she doesn't work for The Broker. She's a repo agent that works for my grandson, Jerry Harper, at the Repo Doctor. She's had a few run-ins with the Broker and for some reason, some bad people think she knows how to get in touch with him."

"Ethel!" Gladys said.

"Are you selling the heroin and stolen guns to the New York Mob?" Decker asked.

"Oh, goodness, gracious, no!" Ethel said and smiled. "We're planting it on them. As soon as we load it in their trunk, we'll call the police. They'll come here, find the drugs and guns in Nick Marino's car. They'll go to jail, the drugs and guns stay off the streets, everyone wins." Ethel frowned. "Well, not the mobsters, but that's okay." Ethel's grin returned.

"Hm. I'm beginning to get the picture," Decker said, a slight smile forming on his lips. "That's a pretty dangerous game you ladies are playing."

"Ethel Harper, you are impossible! Great! You've told him everything," Gladys said, stomping her foot.

"Decker won't tell anyone. Will you?" Ethel asked.

"Of course not. We forklift drivers have a code of honor," he said and winked at Ethel.

"Oh, you are such a polite, clever, handsome young man!" Ethel said.

"Let's get this loaded in the trunk, you can call the police, and then let's go get those forklifts and see if we can lend your friend a hand," Decker said, and bent down and lifted the wooden crate like it was a loaf of bread while both women watched, admiring his strength and good looks.

"If I were fifty years younger," Ethel whispered to Gladys, and they both giggled like schoolgirls.

***

Mrs. Barzetti, Kitty, and a leashed Dodger quietly entered the building in time to hear Nick order Mason to look for someone name Rocco outside. She motioned for Kitty to take Dodger and hide in the dark room on the left. It looked like some sort of office where she could hide safely out of sight. Then, she positioned herself so that she was standing next to a large stack of recyclable metals, bound together by wire. With her rifle at the ready, she quietly waited for Mason to walk past her. It only took a moment for the large man to pass by her, unnoticed, holding his pistol in front of him. She aimed her rifle at his back and loaded a round of ammunition.

Click-click

Click-click

Mason stopped and stood completely still, obviously recognizing the sound, just as Mrs. Barzetti had hoped. "I thought I warned you to stay away from my girls. What part of that was unclear?"

She hadn't expected an answer, so she said, "I want you to move as slow as a 90-year-old needing a hip replacement and set your pistol on the ground." When he complied, she said, "That's better. Now kick it over to that door over there and slowly clasp your hands together behind your back."

Once the gun slid across the floor near the office door and Mason was holding his hands behind his back, Mrs. Barzetti said, "Okay, Kitty, come out and pick up that gun. I need you to bring Dodger over here and reach in my purse for the butcher's twine and some plastic wrap." They approached and Dodger sat in front of Mason and growled. "Good boy," Mrs. Barzetti said. "I wouldn't move if I were you. Dodger is very protective."

***

Andi looked over at her gorgeous, courageous, insane Rockstar who was now bound with tape sitting a few feet away from her. He must have seen her getting tossed in Nick's car at Star City Bar and Grill and followed them here. That's the only explanation for why he was here now. She hoped he had the sense to call the police before attempting this sweet and foolish rescue.

She'd felt nauseous when he'd been discovered hiding behind the pile of scrap metal. When he'd claimed he was The Broker, she'd been sure Nick was simply going to pull the trigger and end his life in that moment. By some miracle, Cooper was still alive, breathing, and unharmed, at least for now. Her abductor was a short-tempered psychopath so there was no telling what he'd do with them. She had to figure out a way to get them out of here, and it looked like now was their best shot at escaping. Cooper had apparently really taken out the guard out front, Mason was still gone, so that left Nick and one other bad guy. Those odds weren't too terrible. She'd have to act quickly before Mason returned or those other men came back with Kitty.

Oh poor Kitty!

Andi didn't have time to worry about Kitty now. She would have to figure out that rescue plan once she and Cooper made it out of this mess safely and called Detective Kendricks. She was pretty sure she could break free from the duct tape using the same technique she'd used in the past to get out of zip ties. It should work in theory. All she needed was some sort of distraction. She was looking around the large room for inspiration when she heard the unmistakable sound of Mrs. Barzetti's voice.

"Nicholas Sebastian Marino. Your parents gave you the name of not one but two blessed saints and look how you've wasted your life."

Sweet Baby Jesus.

Nope. She hadn't imagined it. Standing about thirty feet away was Mrs. Barzetti pointing her trusty rifle in the general direction of Nick and his goon. Mason stood about three feet to her right with his hands tied behind his back with something that looked like Mrs. Barzetti's butcher's twine, and plastic wrap over his mouth and tied behind his head creating a make-shift gag.

Holy Mary Mother of God. Looks like I won't have to rescue Kitty after all.

Kitty was standing near Mrs. Barzetti, holding Dodger on a leash with one hand while pointing a pistol at Nick with her other very shaky hand. When Dodger spotted Andi, he pulled away from Kitty and came bounding towards her, licking her on the face.

Nick only spared Andi a cursory glance before returning his attention back to the armed and dangerous Mrs. Barzetti.

THIS was the distraction Andi had been hoping for. From her sitting position on the floor, Andi raised her arms above her head and thrust them down and out to the sides. The force ripped the duct tape, and she quickly unwrapped the tape that was holding her ankles. She glanced over at Cooper and saw that he was copying her moves to break free. *Good.* She ripped the duct tape from her mouth and held in the yelp of pain that wanted to break free as the skin around her mouth pulled away from the tape.

"So, I hear you've gone to all this trouble to abduct my girls because you are looking for some hoodlum called The Broker," Mrs. Barzetti said.

Nick laughed and said, "Wait, don't tell me, you're The Broker? That's about as likely as this pretty boy claiming he was The Broker."

"Oh, please! I don't hide behind some silly name intended to intimidate people and conceal my identity. I'm perfectly proud of my name and who I am—Hazel Barzetti, President of the Neighborhood Watch."

"Then, I guess I'm lucky that we're not in your neighborhood," Nick said sarcastically.

"While that's true, you and your gagged and bound friend ignored my warning about keeping away from my girls, so now you have a bigger problem," Mrs. Barzetti said.

While Mrs. Barzetti was talking, Andi, Cooper, and Dodger snuck unnoticed behind one of the stacks of scrap metal.

Andi turned to face Cooper just in time for him to place a hand on each side of her face. He gave her a fast, fierce, kiss on the lips, looking at her in that way that turned her to goo. "I was afraid I was never going to be able to do that again. Do you have a plan?" he whispered.

"We've got to somehow get a hold of one of our cellphones, call the police, and then help Mrs. Barzetti and Kitty before Nick kills them," Andi said in a voice just as quiet.

"The police should be here any minute. I called 911 when I followed the car here and asked for Detective Kendricks."

"How did you take out the guard outside? He's a big guy."

"Lug wrench," Cooper whispered.

"Hm, great idea," Andi said and looked around the piles of scrap. "Maybe we can use something like this?" She carefully pulled out a rusty cast iron fireplace poker.

Cooper grinned. "I like the way you think, Margarita. Remind me to never make you angry." He reached up and grabbed a three-foot long piece of rebar.

Armed with their weapons, they walked to the other end of the scrap pile with Dodger on their heels. Andi peeked around the corner. Nick and his goon were having a face-off with Mrs. Barzetti and Kitty.

Nick took a step towards Kitty. "Aw, Kit-cat, why don't you put that gun down. Look at your hand shaking. You know you won't hurt anyone. Let me have the gun, and I'll forgive you. We can go back to New York, and we'll just pretend you never tried to leave me. Things can go back to the way they were before."

"No, Nick. I'm never going back to you. You killed Shana. You abducted Andi and threatened to hurt her. You're not the same man I fell in love with all those years ago. You've become a monster."

Mrs. Barzetti said, "I blew out your fancy car taillight from more than fifty feet away. If you take one more step in the direction of my girl, I won't miss the even bigger target of your body at this closer range."

Ignoring her warning, Nick took another step towards Kitty and in a tone that was impatient, he said, "Kitty, you don't mean that. Now put that gun down and come over to me or I won't be so forgiving."

A shot painfully cracked the air and Andi's ears began ringing.

NO! Without thinking, Andi ran towards Nick who was still standing, so he must not have been the one shot. *Oh God, please let Kitty be okay.* Andi swung the poker like it was a gulf club at Nick's legs, sweeping his feet right out from under him and knocking him to the ground. Then, she slammed her knee into the center of his back, and grabbed Nick's hand, holding it in the way she'd held Mason in her driveway that kept Nick immobile and on the floor.

She frantically looked around the room. Behind her, Cooper sat on top of Nick's guy who was flat on his back pinned to the floor as Cooper held him in place in a chokehold with the rebar. Mrs. Barzetti and Mason were staring at Kitty, who stood wide-eyed and in shock, holding the gun pointed at Nick and Andi.

Mrs. Barzetti was saying something that no one in the room could hear. They must have all been suffering from temporary hearing loss from the sound of the indoor gunshot. Andi knew the moment Kitty realized she was pointing the gun at Andi and Nick. Kitty threw the gun to the floor, running over to Andi, wrapping her in a huge hug. That was sweet and all, but Andi was still a bit preoccupied with keeping the psychopath on the ground.

Mrs. Barzetti and Kitty had made quick work of tying Nick and his goon with the butcher twine and plastic wrap while Andi and Cooper held them in place. No one would be busting out of that strong twine while they waited for the police, and Andi was relieved not to have to listen to the psychopath ramble on anymore. After a few minutes, the ringing stopped, and everyone's hearing returned.

"Let me text the girls and let them know that we've got the situation under control," Mrs. Barzetti said as she pulled out her phone.

"Slowly set the weapons on the floor and put your hands in the air," a man's voice called out from the entrance.

Oh, thank goodness, the police had finally arrived!

Andi set the poker down on the ground next to her and put her hands in the air. Smiling, she turned around expecting to see Detective Kendricks and half of the Roanoke City police force, but instead saw a man that looked a little older and rounder than Nick Marino. Instead of the S.W.A.T. team, there were half-a-dozen men with guns pointed at them.

"Oh, no. More Marinos," she mumbled under her breath.

Cooper groaned. "Seriously? What the fu…"

"Nicky, Nicky, Nicky," Frank Marino said in disgust. "You continue to be an embarrassment to the family. I ask you do one simple job and look at you. You're tied up like mama's

Sunday roast." He squinted his eyes to get a second look. "Are you gagged with plastic wrap? Jesus. What kind of people do that?"

Mrs. Barzetti typed something on her phone and tucked it in her bosom before saying, "The kind of people who don't appreciate the New York City Mob coming in and messing with their family."

***

Gladys and Ethel were in the other building with Decker, starting the forklifts, when the text from Hazel buzzed on their phones. Gladys checked her phone and said, "It's Hazel. She says that stage one is complete. Big Trouble—7 more Yankees."

"I'm afraid to ask. What's stage one?" Decker asked.

"It means Hazel has successfully rescued Andi and tied up Nick and his cohorts," Gladys said. "That was the plan, anyway."

"Until seven more mobsters from New York showed up," Ethel said. "She's out gunned and needs our help."

"The police should be here soon," Decker said. "If we just sit tight…"

"Sit tight? Not a chance," Gladys said. "We need to create a distraction in order to draw some of those mobsters outside to make it an even fight."

Decker gaped while Ethel said, "I've got an idea how we can make some noise with these forklifts."

***

Frank looked at Mrs. Barzetti, his eyebrows raised in surprise that she didn't seem intimidated by the firearms directed at her. "I recognize Kitty and what must be her daughter and boyfriend. Who the hell are you?"

"I'm Hazel Barzetti, President of the Neighborhood Watch and head of this family that your brother has been messing with. You boys need to take your guns and your drugs and leave my city and my family alone. Capice?"

Nick rolled his eyes. Frank chuckled and looked at Nick. "I'm guessing this is the little old lady that blew out your rear windshield. Mama pampered you too much, Nicky. You're too weak to even deal with a bunch of women. Pathetic." He sighed and shook his head, turned to his men, and said, "Untie Nick, Mason, and Joey and then collect the weapons on the floor."

"We won't stand by quietly while the Marino family distributes drugs in our neighborhood or tries to abduct our daughters and granddaughters from their own driveway," Mrs. Barzetti said. She was speaking kind of loud considering Frank was standing so close to her.

Oh my God. Either Mrs. Barzetti had a death wish or she was trying to get Frank to admit to criminal activity. Could she be recording them on her phone? *Dang,* did Mrs. Barzetti even know how to do that?

Implicating Frank Marino using her phone would have been a great plan except that Andi could see that Frank was losing patience with Mrs. Barzetti if that bulging vein on his forehead was any indication. She needed to redirect his attention and try to buy them all a little more time. The police had to be arriving any minute.

Andi asked Nick, "Why do you think this guy you call The Broker killed your brother? Is it because he was setting up a new drug distribution in Roanoke and the local crime boss didn't like it?" Frank turned to glare at her. *Hm…getting warmer.* Of course, now that she had Frank's attention, maybe this wasn't such a good plan after all.

Nick looked at Frank and said, "Frankie, The Broker is on his way here tonight. We can take care of him together. For Jimmy."

Pieces to the puzzle were beginning to form a picture that Andi didn't like. Did The Broker give her the same illegal goods that Jimmy had tried to distribute as some sort of message to the Marino Family?

Holy Mary, Mother of God.

Well, there was one way to find out. If she could get Nick to confirm this and Mrs. Barzetti was recording their whole conversation on her phone, it just might be worth the risk. *That's a lot of ifs.*

"Jimmy was trying to sell the 20 Kilos of heroin and two stolen US Army M16s in Roanoke when he was killed, wasn't he?" Andi asked.

She froze when she saw the expression on Nick's face. *Sweet Baby Jesus.* Andi had seen a lot of angry people, especially since she began working as a repo agent, but she'd never seen anyone as furious as Nick Marino. She swallowed back the fear and overwhelming need to run.

Nick walked over to Andi, shouting, "Bitch!" The slap cracked hard across her face. "How did you know exactly what Jimmy was selling? You have something to do with his death?"

Ouch. Her head jerked to the side from the force of Nick's slap, her cheek and temple stung. *That's going to leave a mark.* Andi gingerly touched the side of her eye. She was going to have a shiner just like her mother, and what was icy fear turned to red, hot, rage.

Kitty began pleading with the psychopath. "No, Nicky. Please. Andi didn't mean it. She doesn't know what she's saying."

Cooper lunged toward Nick but was restrained by Frank's men. Dodger began barking, growling, and pulling on his leash that had been secured to one of the metal beams supporting the roof of the building.

Frank told his men, "Shut them up."

Duct tape was applied to Kitty, Cooper, and Mrs. Barzetti's mouths, and one of Frank's awful men hit Dodger on the head with the butt of his rifle. *No!* Her pup whimpered and dropped to the ground.

Lifting her chin, Andi glared at her attacker. "I can see why you're an embarrassment to your family, Nicky," she said, mimicking Frank. "What kind of gangster throws punches like a two-year old? Does hitting defenseless women make you feel like a tough guy? You really are pathetic."

In a blur of motion, Nick pulled a gun and pressed the cold metal barrel against Andi's forehead. "How about this? Is this gangster enough for you?" Nick asked.

Jesus, Mary, and Joseph. Andi felt paralyzed, forgetting to breathe as she stared into the psychopath's eyes. He was going to kill her right here and now. She could see it in his hard, wild, gaze. *Oh, God, I'm not ready to die. Cooper*—she wanted more time. This was so unfair. They were just at the beginning of their incredible relationship. *Kitty—I'll never get to know her.* Her mother finally showed up in her life, and it was too late. *This is it. It's over.*

A loud crashing sound came from outside the building, causing Andi to jump, reviving her from the despair that had threatened to suffocate her. *Have the police finally arrived?*

"What the hell was that?" Frank asked. He sent three of his men outside to investigate.

Oh, the Golden Girls! Please let them be alright.

Frank turned his attention to Nick. "For Christ's sake, put the gun away, Nicky. You can kill her after we find out what she knows."

***

Gladys watched in delight as Decker flipped one of the BMWs with the forklift. He had not been happy about Ethel's idea to make some noise, but he'd gone along with their plan when he realized they were doing it with or without him.

Hot diggity dog—that was some loud crunching noise when the car flipped onto its roof. The mobsters had to have heard it from inside the building. Gladys hid in the shadows just outside of the structure where Hazel and the girls were being held captive. Her part in the plan was coming up. Back in the day, she used to be a pretty good softball player. She held her cane like she was up at bat.

Right on schedule, two men came barreling out of the building, guns raised in front of them. With the outside light smashed thanks to her good pitching skills, they didn't see the tripwire that Gladys and Ethel had set up. As soon as their shins hit the wire, they faceplanted on that uncomfortable gravel parking lot, their guns falling on the ground in front of them just out of reach.

A third gunman came behind the other men and carefully stepped over the wire and began shooting at Decker on the forklift. With his attention on Decker, Gladys snuck up behind him and wacked him behind his knees with her cane, dropping him to the ground like those other two hoodlums. She then collected the guns and placed them in her handbag.

Ethel flipped the second BMW onto the driver's side with her forklift and began pushing it towards the men as they scrambled to their feet

Red, white, and blue lights flashed as a parade of police vehicles sped up the driveway. *Oh, thank heavens!!* She wasn't sure what they would do if more of those Yankees came out of the building.

Car doors few open, and Gladys heard a man shouting, "Police. Remain where you are and place your hands on your head."

Relief washed over her. She felt as giddy as an evening spent drinking a few glasses of champagne with the girls on New Year's Eve. Gladys grinned at Ethel as she placed her hands on the top of her warm knit hat. They'd successfully completed stage two of their mission. Decker's forklift was vacant, and she heard an engine in the distance. *Motorcycle?* Decker must have split when the cops showed up. His employment was questionable at best, but he was a man with a good heart and had been a huge help to them tonight. The police might not see it quite the same way she did, so she just wouldn't mention his involvement when she gave her statement.

Oh, please let Hazel and the girls be alright.

The detectives and Special Agent Reyna jogged up to them. Detective Hughes helped Ethel step down from the forklift.

Detective Kendricks spoke first. "We received two 911 calls with this address. One from Cooper Barnett and one from Gladys Davis."

"Yes, that was me. You came just in time. We're headed inside to rescue Hazel, Kitty, Andi, and Cooper. Hazel had everything under control until more of Nick Marino's guys from New York showed up. We haven't had communication from her in a while. We'd better head inside to make sure she's okay."

Kendricks shook his head. "No, you're going to stay outside with Detective Hughes." He looked around the yard at the flipped cars and injured men. "Looks like you've done enough for tonight. Detective Sanchez, would you and your partner search those vehicles? Special Agent Reyna and I will take several officers and investigate the building."

"But that's not fair," Gladys and Detective Hughes said at the same time.

"That's an order, Detective Hughes. I need you to take their statements while we wait for the paramedics to make sure everyone is okay."

Gladys smiled at the kid and winked at Ethel. "This kid has spunk. I appreciate that in law enforcement. Tell me, Detective Hughes, have you ever watched Matlock?"

Chapter Twenty-three

Breathe. She could do this. Andi just needed to pretend that the psychopath was Douglas Kinser and that gun pressed to her forehead was the non-lethal, orange, rubber pistol from the self-defense class.

"I'm not waiting, Frankie. I'll just kill her now. We have no more use for her. Plus, it will give me great pleasure to be done with this annoying bitch."

St. Jude, patron saint of desperate cases and lost causes, I could use a little help. With that final thought, she put her palms together forming a v and thrust her arms upward while dropping down low so that the pistol was now pointing at the ceiling. She kneed Nick in the groin, and he doubled over. Grabbing his gun, Andi held his hand in a way that had him dropping to the ground.

In the next moment, there was a burst of movement as police officers raced into the room, weapons raised.

"Police. Nobody move," Detective Kendricks yelled.

Andi looked up. *Thank heavens!* Detective Kendricks, Special Agent Reyna, and about a dozen uniformed police officers were spread throughout the building, guns pointed at Frank and his men, and her? Oh, probably because she was holding Nick's gun.

"Well, what a surprise to find Frank and Nick Marino threatening the nice citizens of Roanoke, Virginia. It looks like you've taken hostages, and I believe I heard Nick threaten to murder this young lady here," Special Agent Reyna said as she disarmed Frank.

"Once again, you've got nothing on us, FBI Special Agent Reyna," Frank said. "The way you've been following me around, I should charge you with harassment, really. I'm an innocent businessman. This doesn't prove anything, and I'm not saying another word until I get to talk to my lawyer."

"Well, it gives me great pleasure to inform you that you do have the right to remain silent," she said as she placed handcuffs on him.

Detective Kendricks began walking towards Andi, his gun pointed at Nick. She exhaled the tension she'd been holding tight in her chest. *Thank God this nightmare was finally over.* Before she even realized what was happening, the psychopath twisted the gun from Andi's hand, held the barrel against her temple, and placed her body in front of his as a shield.

"Don't come any closer or I'll kill her," Nick said dragging Andi with him as he backed away from Detective Kendricks.

Kendricks continued pointing his gun at Nick's head. "You don't want to do that, Nick. Set your gun down, let Andi go, and I'm sure your brother will hire an expensive attorney that will take care of this whole situation. If you pull that trigger, there's no attorney that can keep you from doing twenty years to life in prison. That's a long time to be locked in a small cell. I can guarantee it's nothing like your nice place in New York City."

"Nicky, don't be stupid. Put the gun down," Frank said.

Nick turned to Frank while pressing the gun barrel into Andi's head. "Shut up, Frankie. I'm so fucking tired of taking orders from you. You think you're always right and constantly criticizing me. Well, not this time. I'm going to walk out this door with Andi and get in my car. If anyone tries to stop me, I'll put a bullet in her pretty head, and this becomes a bloody homicide scene. Got it?"

Jesus, Joseph, and Mary. What could she do? He had an iron grip on her, trapping both of her arms with his left arm wrapped across her chest and holding that gun to her temple with his right hand. He began walking backwards, steering them so that they were edging their way to the exit when from out of nowhere, Dodger came bounding towards them. His chewed off leash dragged behind him as he barked and lunged at them, baring his teeth. Nick redirected the gun from Andi's temple to her sweet pup.

No!

With all her strength, Andi pushed back into Nick, causing him to stumble backwards. He was still holding onto her with his left arm, taking her with him as they began falling to the floor. At the same time, she saw FBI Special Agent Reyna shove Detective Kendricks to the floor.

Andi heard the deafening sound of Nick's pistol firing.

"Dodger!" She screamed his name but could only hear the loud ringing in her ears. *No, no, no!*

As if in slow motion, she felt herself fall to the floor landing on her back on top of Nick. He must have released her at the last moment to break the impact of the fall, so she quickly rolled from him.

Dodger locked his jaws onto Nick's right wrist forcing him to immediately release the pistol. Andi pushed the gun out of reach with her boot. Her hero's body was stiff, his furry ears flat, and his unblinking eyes were directed at Nick.

Kendricks was there in the next minute, placing handcuffs on Nick and talking to Andi, but her ears were ringing again and all she heard was muffled, indistinguishable sounds. He was looking at her with those icy blue eyes, a concerned expression on his face.

Andi pointed to her ears and spoke loudly, saying, "I am fine. I just can't hear anything yet."

He let out a breath and the tension around his eyes relaxed as he smiled at her, nodding before dragging Nick off with Frank and Special Agent Reyna.

Andi squatted next to Dodger who gave her a couple big, sloppy kisses on her face before knocking her down the rest of the way and plopping in her lap. She wrapped her arms around her sweet pup and gave him a big hug.

Chapter Twenty-four

Twenty minutes later, Andi's hearing had returned. She'd been seen by the paramedics and refused their offer to be taken to the hospital to be checked out more thoroughly. Instead, she'd gratefully accepted an ice compress and held it gently to her temple.

She was leaning against one of the forklifts in the scrapyard. Dodger was sitting at her feet, standing guard—sweet boy. Cooper was glued to her side, his arm resting comfortably across her lower back, hand on her hip. Kitty flanked her other side, her hand resting on Andi's arm. It was kind of nice.

Her neighbors were standing nearby, huddled together, involved in some deep conversation that Andi couldn't hear from where she was standing.

Detective Sanchez and his partner Lucky approached. He squatted down to Dodger's level and scratched him behind his ears. "I heard about this guy's act of bravery tonight," Sanchez said, reaching into his pocket to give Dodger a treat. "Nicely done for a civilian." After tossing the dog treat and watching Dodger snatch it from the air, the Narcotics Detective stood and studied Andi for a minute. "Looks like I owe you another thank you, Andi Sloan."

Her neighbors spotted Detective Sanchez and walked over to join the conversation.

He said, "We found heroin and stolen weapons in a car registered to Nick Marino as well as other stolen weapons in the two BMWs that didn't have the slashed tires." He glanced over at the older women. "That was quite a rescue attempt. Slashed tires, totaled vehicles so the kidnappers couldn't escape. It's amazing to me that you both can drive a forklift so effectively."

Andi noticed Gladys pressing her lips together and glancing down to the ground. "I also appreciate how your Neighborhood Watch program called in to report two suspicious men attempting to distribute narcotics in your neighborhood." He gave them a stern look. "In the future, please call the police rather than acting on your own. You were very lucky that you weren't harmed or killed. The people that deal in illegal drugs and weapons trafficking are ruthless."

Her neighbors just beamed, and Detective Sanchez shook his head. He turned to Andi. "I can see where you get your tenacity."

Detective Kendricks, Detective Hughes, and Special FBI Agent Reyna joined them.

"We're headed back to the precinct. I know we've taken your statements, but please don't leave the area. We may have additional questions and need to get in touch with you," Kendricks said.

"Do you think you have enough information to convict Nick and Frank Marino?" Andi asked.

"We're going to be keeping their attorney busy. After tonight's attempted murder, possession of illegal substances and weapons, and kidnapping – just to name a few of the charges they've racked up tonight- they're unlikely to be allowed bail no matter how good of an attorney they have."

Mrs. Barzetti reached inside her coat and pulled out her phone. "I was able to record some of the conversation after Frank Marino arrived. Some of it fades in and out, but hopefully you can use it."

Detective Hughes grinned, "That was quick thinking, Mrs. Barzetti."

Oh no! That would be great, but how would she explain how she knew the amount of illegal merchandise the Marinos were trying to sell? How would she answer questions about The Broker.

FBI Special Agent Reyna transferred the file to her phone and played it. Everything was loud and clear. Mrs. Barzetti had recorded everything from the time Andi saw her drop the phone under her sweater. Then, they came to the part she'd been dreading. Andi heard her own voice saying,

> ***Why do you think this guy you call The Broker killed your brother? Is it because he was setting up a new drug distribution in Roanoke and the local crime boss didn't like it?***

Then Nick was saying,

> ***Frankie, The Broker is on his way here tonight. We can take care of him together. For Jimmy.***

The recording abruptly ended. Mrs. Barzetti shrugged her shoulders. "That's it. Obviously, there was more, but I must have bumped a button or something when those awful mobsters were manhandling me." Her eyes were wide and innocent. A little too innocent. Andi recognized that expression. Mrs. Barzetti was fibbing!

Special Agent Reyna looked at Andi. "Who's this Broker they were referring to?"

"I don't know," Andi said—a half truth. She'd had the misfortune of running into him, but she didn't know his real name or how to get in touch with him. Andi nibbled on her lower lip.

Special Agent Reyna looked at a frowning Detective Kendricks who was studying Andi, before turning back to Andi and asking, "You said he's a local crime boss that may have killed Jimmy Marino?"

"I was just guessing," Andi said, which was also true. "I figured that if the New York City mob were setting up a drug distribution network, any kind of local drug dealers wouldn't be happy about it if they weren't getting a cut of the money."

Special Agent Reyna looked over at Kendricks. "Looks like we might have uncovered another criminal organization." She turned to Mrs. Barzetti. "Thank you for this recording. We'll see what we can use. Kitty, I'll keep you apprised of any new information we have on your friend's murder."

Kitty nodded, and quietly said, "Thank you."

Reyna turned to Kendricks and Sanchez. "I'm going to go with transport to ensure we get the Marinos safely to the precinct. Looks like you gentlemen are stuck with me for the foreseeable future. I'm going to stay in Virginia to ensure we cross every t and dot every i. I want to make sure the Marinos receive the justice and sentencing that they deserve. See you back at the precinct."

Detective Hughes turned to Detective Kendricks. "May I ride along, sir? It would be a great experience."

Sighing, Detective Kendricks said, "Sure. I'll meet you at the precinct."

Sanchez said, "We'll give you a ride, Special Agent Reyna." The narcotics detective and Lucky jogged to keep up with the FBI agent.

Kendricks lifted a brow and said, "A word, Sloan?"

Uh oh. When Andi and Kitty both took a step, Kendricks said, "Just your daughter, this time."

Andi followed Kendricks a few steps away from the group where their conversation wouldn't be overheard.

"The Broker? Who is he?" Kendricks asked.

When Andi didn't answer, he rubbed the knot of tension on the back of his neck. "You've been telling me half-truths since you found Jimmy Marino's body," Kendricks said. "It's just you and me. Off the record. Who's The Broker?"

Andi bit her lip. "Honestly, all I know is I don't want to have anything to do with him. I don't know his name, where he lives, what he does. He just sometimes shows up. Frankly, it gives me the heebie-jeebies."

Kendricks cursed and sighed. "Why? What does he want from you?"

"Usually he wants my help finding something that he's lost," Andi said.

Kendricks raised a brow, and said, "Explain."

"You know, because I'm good at finding cars that I have to repossess," Andi said.

"Yeah, I get why. What stuff have you found for him?" Kendricks asked.

"Um, let's see. I found a personal digital video file that someone had stolen from him." Andi could see Kendricks looking like the god of thunder, so she quickly added. "I saw the video. There wasn't anything illegal on it."

"I don't like it, Sloan. You're playing a very dangerous game," Kendricks said.

Andi pointed to her chest and said, "I don't like it either. He's offered to hire me, and I've turned him down. I feel guilty enough doing my legitimate job of repossessing cars. I don't want to work for a crime boss."

Detective Kendricks stared at her in frustration. Hey, it wasn't her fault that The Broker contacted her. She strongly discouraged it.

Andi blew out a breath. "Thanks for trying to talk Nick out of putting a bullet in my head."

"Yeah, well, your mutt is the one that saved the day," Kendricks said and looked over at Dodger. "Thank God because I didn't have a clear shot when he used your body as a shield."

"So, FBI Special Agent Reyna is going to stick around Roanoke. That should be fun," Andi teased.

"What are you talking about now, Sloan?"

"I see a bit of chemistry there," Andi said. "Oh, and she did knock you off your feet tonight." Andi grinned. "I told you that you would find someone."

"Great. What, now you're a matchmaker?" Kendricks said and he looked annoyed, but not really. Andi was beginning to see he was mostly bark and no bite.

"I think I might have a knack for it. I am good at finding things, after all," she said and grinned.

"Yeah, try not to be quite so good at finding dead bodies, alright? I'd better head back to the precinct. Try to stay out of trouble, Sloan."

"I'll do my best," Andi said smiling as she walked back to her family.

"I didn't think he'd ever leave," Cooper said as he embraced Andi in a big hug and dipped her and planted a kiss on her lips.

Aw, Coop. It felt so good to be in his arms once again.

"Who's hungry?" Mrs. Davis asked.

Kitty looked confused. "But it's midnight."

"Who can sleep after a night like this? Let's all go back to my place and celebrate. I'll heat up a pan of lasagna and some homemade bread. All this crime fighting has made me hungry," Mrs. Davis said.

"I'm in," Mrs. Harper said.

"I'll bring dessert," Mrs. Barzetti said.

Andi grinned and looked at Kitty and Cooper. "Who can say no to that? Plus, I'm starving. I was kidnapped before I had a chance to eat dinner." Andi reached out a hand to Kitty and squeezed it tight. *Here's my second chance to get to know my mom.* She'd thought for sure that Nick was going to pull the trigger and take everything from Andi. Maybe having Kitty around wouldn't be so bad after all. Andi smiled tenderly at Kitty and said, "Welcome home."

Thanks for reading Repo Girl Homecoming!

If you enjoyed this book and would like to read more adventures with Andi and her friends, the next book Repo Girl Vegas Vacation will be available 2023!

Find out about my latest books, favorite story recipes and giveaways by signing up for my e-mail list at www.JaneFenton.org.

If you enjoyed this series, check out the first book in the Mystique Books Series.

Kate would feel silly for having a crush on a fictional pirate—if he wasn't standing right in front of her.

After discovering that her long-term boyfriend has been cheating on her, psychologist Dr. Kate Barnes decides she's still going on their romantic Bahamas getaway—alone. Her vacation takes a turn for the weird when an eccentric bookstore owner insists Kate purchase *Pirate's Treasure*, claiming it's the perfect book for her. The more she reads, the harder it is to separate fiction from reality, especially when the devastatingly handsome Captain Blackjack swoops into her life to save her from ruffians at a bar.

As they grow closer, the similarities between the book and Kate's real life become more pronounced. When the arrival of a puzzle-box from one of Kate's patients launches her into a mystery that seems like it was pulled straight from the pages of *Pirate's Treasure*, Kate starts to wonder if her sanity is leaving her, too.

But when bullets start flying, the book may be Kate's only clue to solving the puzzle box—and saving her life.

Join My Facebook Group "The Repo Girl Book Club" where we discuss the fun books we're currently reading, share our favorite bookish memes, and post adorable pet pictures.

The first book in the Repo Girl Series:

Debt, Dating, and a Dead body...What's a girl to do?

Twenty-five-year-old rookie Repo Agent, Andrea Sloan, doesn't like accepting help from anyone – especially not arrogant musicians who are too charming for their own good. Even though she swore off men years ago, Andi finds herself drawn to handsome rockstar, Cooper Barnett, as he continually pops up in her life when she least expects it.

Their budding relationship becomes even more complicated when Cooper talks Andi into letting him ride-along on one of her repos, and they come across a very naked, very dead body. Being charged with murder and spending a night in jail is bad enough, but when the police don't seem to be making any headway on finding the real killer, Andi begins to do her own investigation – much to the frustration of the homicide detective in charge.

The closer she gets to discovering the killer, the more her own life is in danger. Time is running out. Andi must figure out who the killer is before she goes to prison for a crime she didn't commit or, worse, becomes the next dead body.

2020 Next Generation Indie Book Award - Finalist - Chick Lit Winner! If you enjoy reading Janet Evanovich's Stephanie Plum series, you'll love this fast-paced mystery with lots of laughs and a little romance.

The second book in the Repo Girl Series:

She never imagined her part-time job would be so dangerous!

Life was going well for twenty-five-year-old Repo Agent Andrea Sloan. She hadn't stumbled across any more naked dead guys at work, and her love life was pretty much wonderful. Her biggest problems were keeping warm in a car with a heater that's on the fritz and figuring out what to get her boyfriend for Christmas.

When she picked up a part-time job working at the mall for some extra cash as an elf, she never imagined she'd witness Santa gunned down in the parking lot. Just like that, Andi became tangled with friends and foes from her past in a race to find Santa's stolen bag of cash before Christmas. Her life depended on it.

Join Andi and her hilarious friends as they maneuver through this dangerous holiday season.

Acknowledgements

First, a huge thank you to all my readers! Your enthusiasm for my characters has inspired me to push through to the end of this story—finally!! Thanks for your patience, your encouraging comments, and wonderful book reviews. Congratulations to Amy Miller for winning the contest to have her favorite car model (Alfa Romeo Giulia) repossessed by Andi, and for Mary Simons and Jeanne Glass Troisi for suggesting the name of Sanchez's new partner. I want to give a special shout out to those playing with me in the Repo Girl Book Club Facebook Group. You are absolutely wonderful!

Big love goes to my amazing editing team (Emma Fenton, Candy Andrzejewski, Sue Quaintance, Debbie Teeple, and Julie Vice). They made time for editing around the holidays and other obligations, bravely read my final draft, and made suggestions to ensure that the story makes sense AND is grammatically correct! Thank you, ladies! Your feedback is priceless!

Ah, Emma Fenton. You had no idea when I asked you to be the Creative Director of our publishing company that I'd drop into your office like a crazy woman because a new character showed up in my scene unexpected! This was not in your job description, I know. Thanks for all your help with brainstorming, outlining, goal sessions, genius developmental editing, help with publication deadlines, and generating the most beautiful covers for all our books—this is actually in your job description—ha ha!

Thanks to everyone in my family—you help me in so many ways. My niece and nephew (Addy & Dennis Rider) help with story ideas as we walk my dogs. Thanks mom, Amy, Andy, Emma, and Peyton—my loving husband and best friend—for encouraging (a.k.a. nagging) me to write and helping me make time and space for it. Love you all so much!

About the Author

Jane Fenton is an avid reader and writer of books that combine romance, mystery, and laughter because they're as satisfying as a triple fudge sundae—without the calories. Although she shares her heroine's love of Roanoke City, good friends, junk food, stray dogs, and Jeep Wranglers, she's quite happy to create these fun misadventures from the comfort of her quiet farmhouse in the foothills of the Blue Ridge Mountains in Virginia where she lives with her family.

Made in United States
North Haven, CT
24 July 2024

55393842R00192